The Staircase of Dragon Jerico

Other Titles by Nathan Everett

Jackie the Beanstalk

TALL SKINNY JACKIE is a fresh 18-year-old high school graduate, still in her cap and gown when she is given the keys to her grandfather's 1968 Ford Fairlane 500 Fastback. Jackie, her 25-year-old Aunt Misty, and her dog Roadkill jump in the car and take off following an old fashioned TripTik map into an alternate dimension. In this alternate dimension, Jackie is a Warrior Wizard encountering robbers, mountain monsters, ogres, rival clans, obstreperous customs officials, a stowaway princess, an adopted bobcat kitten, werewolves, ghosts, giants, and dragons—all on her way to rescuing the Sovereign's kidnapped son. As she travels, she discovers her magic powers, and the powers of all the weapons she carries—her cap and gown, honor cords, stole, basketball, and things she picks up along the way—including a pocketful of magic beans.

A Place at the Table

THOUGH THE AMERICA Liam Cyning lives in is quite similar to the America of half a century or more ago, it is also fundamentally different. Ten clearly defined classes are the underpinning of American Society, determined by the educational system. As a newly assigned member of the Leader class, Liam is still uncertain what his role and responsibilities are. This story is a Bildungsroman, a literary genre that focuses on the psychological and moral growth of Liam Cyning from youth to adulthood. With his grandmother as an example and Meredith by his side, Liam earns a place at the table as he exposes the fundamental weaknesses of the very system that made him who he is.

City Limits

WHO AM I, really? It's a common question. It's part of being self-aware. But is it important? Are we really nothing more than our accumulated lifetime of memories? Or is there something inside that makes us inherently who we are? Stripped of his memories and identity, Gee Evars must come to grips with who he is as he attempts to make a home among strangers by simply doing the right thing. *City Limits* is the story of Gee's loss of memory and the life and love he gains.

Wild Woods

WHEN GEE EVARS wandered into town, he lost his memory in a daring rescue of a toddler in the raging Rose River. Now the man without a memory has become a force that even the Families need to reckon with. When the city votes to annex South Rosebud, Gee accompanies a small army of high school students to tear down the fence that has separated the cultivated hickory Forest from the Wild Woods. This is where the sequel to the popular novel *City Limits* begins. Gee and his crew must find a way to tame the Wild Woods, uncover its secrets, and live to tell the story. Gee's real work in Rosebud Falls has just begun.

The Gutenberg Rubric

TWO RARE-BOOK LIBRARIANS race across three continents to find and preserve a legendary book printed by Johannes Gutenberg. Behind them, a trail of bombed libraries draws Homeland Security to launch a worldwide search for biblio-terrorists. Keith and Maddie find love along the way, but will they survive to enjoy it?

For Money or Mayhem

COMPUTER FORENSICS DETECTIVE Dag Hamar has been hired to help a credit card company beef up network security, but are his new co-workers helping him or attacking him? Security video doesn't lie, does it? Dag is about to get dragged from behind his computer screen—away from the comparative safety of cyber-space—into the dirty streets of Seattle where an online predator has become a real-life serial kidnapper. But will he be in time to save his new romance and the daughter who is a victim.

For Mayhem or Madness

COMPUTER FORENSICS DETECTIVE Dag Hamar is on the case again! In this sequel to *For Money or Mayhem*, Dag is commissioned by the Financial Crimes Enforcement Network (FinCEN) to find and stop a dangerous hacker who appears to be a credible threat to national security. Follow Dag as he erases his own digital identity and goes on the trail around the world to track down and neurtralize Hacker X before he does something really dangerous like erase all the nuclear launch codes in the world. Or maybe, Dag should help him.

For Blood or Money

DAG HAMAR IS a hard-boiled computer forensics detective with all the trimmings: the Seattle Waterfront office, the sexy young assistant who adores him, and an attitude to match the constant gray drizzle outside his window. And a new missing person case. The only problem is he's a middle-aged computer geek who doesn't do missing persons. And the only clue he has is the missing man's laptop. Dag Hamar and Deb Riley discover hidden files and computer code can be as dangerous as dark alleys and flying bullets as they enter the high-stakes game of of tracing a missing friend and the billion-dollar fortune that disappeared with him.

Municipal Blondes

COMPUTER FORENSICS DETECTIVE Deb Riley has been cut loose to continue the work of her partner, Dag Hamar. He sent her to get the code from a dead man's tattoo. He told her she needed to crack the encryption on Simon's thumb drive. He told her he loved her. And then he died. Now Deb finds she is in possession of something everyone wants and will do anything to get. Including kill her. Enter the world of Deb Riley, code breaker, detective, and master of disguise, as she races into the heart of the mystery and risks discovery or worse in Seattle, Belize, and Croatia. She has Dag's reputation to live up to.

Stocks & Blondes

COMPUTER FORENSICS DETECTIVE Deb Riley is on the case again, this time with a dead woman named Georgia and a house full of computers. Georgia's father doesn't believe the police finding that she committed suicide. He's sure there was foul play involved. He had no idea how foul it was. Hacking into the computers starts a deadly game as neighbors, friends, and even Georgia, prove not to be what they appear to be. Infiltrating the cabal throws Deb into her deepest disguise ever while trying to balance her real life with a new boyfriend, who might also be different than he appears. Worse, it puts her in danger of ending up just like Georgia.

Steven George & The Dragon

STEVEN HAS ALWAYS known he was a dragonslayer, but on the day his village sends him to slay the fearsome beast he realizes he doesn't know what a dragon looks like, where it lives, or how to kill it. His quest is facilitated by the exchange of "once-upon-a-times" with the people he meets on the endless road. Think Grimm. For young adults, not children.

The Volunteer

JOURNEY INSIDE THE head of a chronically homeless man--a man that in a less politically correct age we might have called a hobo. Gerald Good, known now only as G2, volunteered to take the place of a homeless man, believing he would work his way back quickly. Ten years later, twenty... thirty years, find G2 alone in his head, his memories, and his boxcar.

ISBN 978-1-955874-86-1
Designed by Nathan Everett
Cover photo by Terence Toh Chin Eng ID 1313924522 licensed from Shutterstock.com
https:www.nathaneverett.com

A special thank you to my editors and advisers
who stuck with me through this entire project.
Your help was immeasurable.
Michele Palmer
Lyndsy Fernandes
Denny Wheeler
Jim Ness
Jim Burt
Les Bagley

The Staircase of Dragon Jerico

Nathan Everett

ELDER ROAD BOOKS
LYNNWOOD WA

Chapter One

"BE MY WIFE and I will give you anything your heart desires," Prince Drake said on bended knee.

"Anything?" Princess Isolde asked, teasing him.

"I would bring down the moon and hang it about your neck if that was what you desired," the prince affirmed.

"You know, I've always wanted a dragon!"

The princess smiled innocently. But the prince stood, drew his sword, and swore that he would call for her when he could give her a dragon.

It seemed hopeless, but the prince had an idea; he got a large piece of paper and a pencil. On it he began to draw the perfect dragon. He summoned a woodcarver, and together they brought a great log into the castle and began carving a dragon.

When it was finished, the prince called for the princess and showed her the dragon and asked her again to be his wife.

"Yes!" she declared. "What other man would honor his wife's most frivolous wish? I give my heart to you forever."

The prince and princess were married on the third step of the Staircase of Dragon Jerico, and they lived happily ever after.

THIRTY-TWO-YEAR-OLD PRESTON CARVER, Chairman of the Board and CEO of JeriCorp, closed the storybook and showed the cover to the gathered children as he stood on the third step of the great dragon staircase. The third-graders applauded, though the story was a little simple for them. Preston had written and illustrated it himself when he was about their age.

Lawrence Jerico, Preston's grandfather, stood nearby and beamed with pride. His grandson had made it through the reading of the entire book without a stutter or tremor. Little victories in his battle against severe anxiety were always welcome.

"Did it breathe fire?" asked one of the children.

That was off script and Lawrence could see Preston freeze up. He turned to his grandfather with panic written on his face.

"Mr. J-j-j- G-Pop!" Preston spit out.

Lawrence laid a hand on his grandson's shoulder and pointed him off toward the kitchen where Preston fled. He explained to the children that this dragon had dropped walnuts.

Preston sat at the kitchen table gasping for breath as if he'd run a marathon. Matilda, the family cook and housekeeper, gave him a glass of water that he gulped down. She rubbed his shoulders.

"I've always loved that story," she said soothingly. "You read it so well. Here. I have a nice sandwich made up for you with bread I baked this morning. You'll need your energy to go out to the lake with Mr. Lawrence."

"Th-thank you, Tilly. I'll be okay. I just couldn't a-answer the question. It's a piece of wood. How could it breathe fire?"

"They're children. They imagine all kinds of things—just like you did. Now eat up. I'll go rescue Mr. Lawrence before the children have *him* too flustered to speak." Matilda placed a Rubik's Cube on the table next to Preston's plate and left while Preston focused on the calming effect of the toy.

EVERYONE PRIVILEGED TO tour Jerico House stopped to stare at the massive staircase carved in the shape of a dragon. It had been the sentinel of the Jerico family for nearly two hundred years and had been a significant part of the reason Jerico House was listed on the National Register of Historic Places, even though the family still owned it and mostly lived in it.

Part of the agreement in having it listed was permitting tours of the grand old mansion at least twice a year. That's how Timmy Blake happened to be in the house with eyes as big as those of his third-grade classmates as Lawrence Jerico attempted to tell a bit about its history. And Timmy had questions.

"Where did the dragon come from?" Timmy asked.

"Well, it was carved from a huge old walnut tree. My great-great-grandfather was the artist who drew the picture of the dragon," Lawrence said. "A wood carver executed the design here and was the sculptor of the city's dragon gate in Waterfront Park."

Lawrence kept telling himself that he loved kids and this was a way the family could give to the community, as four generations before him had done—though each in a different way. He had only one child himself and she in turn had only one, so the Jerico name was at a dead end.

"The picture of the dragon is hanging here on the wall. You can see how detailed it is. Not to minimize the great artistry that the woodcarver had, but the whole concept was my ancestor's."

"But did the prince go fight the dragon in the woods to bring it back here?" Timmy asked.

"No, no. That's a fairy tale. Mr. Carver wrote it when he was your age and has signed this copy to give to your class. An interesting thing, though, is that many artists say that carving a statue like this is a process of revealing the subject inside by cutting away everything that wasn't a dragon."

"Is there a dragon in you, too?" Timmy seemed convinced the dragon was more than the walnut stair railing.

"People said old Drake Jerico, Senior could be a dragon at times, but I think they were just referring to his temperament. The stories say he could become very angry," Lawrence said. "Of course, I never met him myself. He passed away before I was born."

Lawrence was thinking he should definitely have had another cup of coffee this morning in order to keep up with these kids. He wished he had a script like Preston had.

"Did anything exciting ever happen here?" Lily Thomas, another of the children in the class asked. Lawrence wondered what third graders thought was exciting.

"There have been many weddings on this staircase, of course. The first was back in 1838 when the dragon was first completed. Drake Jerico married Isolde LeClerc right here where I'm standing. It's been a family tradition to marry where the dragon can bless us," Lawrence said. "Oh, and Princess Bea of Moldavia visited a number of years ago, and had her portrait painted while standing on this stair right here."

The princess had also continued up the stairs to Lawrence's bedroom where things progressed to the point of Lawrence's wife departing from the house and moving to Florida, where she lived comfortably until her death some fourteen years prior. Sadly, Beatrice had stayed with Lawrence only a few months before she traveled to her country for the first time in her life, attempting to reestablish the throne there. Unsuccessfully.

"My own father was awakened in the middle of the night from where he slept in the study. He grabbed his shotgun to shoot a burglar on the stairs as the intruder ascended toward the master bedroom."

There had always been questions about that. The seventeen-year-old Peter Jerico was quite drunk and the burglar in question was also a drunk seventeen-year-old, perhaps making his way up to the bedroom of Peter's sister. Neither Lawrence nor the law had discovered any reason to believe it was a setup. They'd all assumed it was legitimately a home invasion and Peter was just protecting his home and sister. She never forgave him, and died a spinster some thirty years later.

"Did your great grandpa turn into a dragon on the stairs or is he still alive in the forest?" Timmy pressed, still not satisfied with the dragon.

"My goodness, boy. Drake Jerico Senior died many years ago and is interred in the city cemetery in the Jerico family mausoleum. His son, Drake Jerico Junior is there, as is Drake Junior's son, Emmet Jerico. My father, Peter Jerico, is out there, and I expect one day I will be laid to rest there."

"Don't the girls get buried there, too?" Lily asked.

"Well, yes, of course. Isolde LeClerc Jerico, my aunt, my own wife, all the wives and those female children who stayed around here. They are all interred in the family mausoleum."

Children were so different these days than when he was that age. Some days, he couldn't remember ever being that age and other days, he was certain it was just yesterday. So much for sharp wits and eternal youth in his seventies.

THE STAIRCASE HAD not been quite finished in 1838, when Isolde LeClerc was sent from the finishing school in Massachusetts to become Drake Jerico's bride. Drake gave her the mansion and lots of money with which to furnish it, while he resided at the hotel in town a mile away. It would not have been proper for them to live together before the wedding, and Drake felt the hotel was better suited to a man. There was plenty of domestic help to keep Isolde company, and Drake visited twice a week to court his bride-to-be.

Isolde was utterly fascinated with the carving of the dragon—and the sculptor, Joseph Carver. As talented as Drake was with pencil and paper, he was hopeless when it came to cutting wood and making the dragon take shape. That task had fallen to Joseph, who had selected the tree trunk and hired the men to move it into place so he could begin cutting and carving and sanding and polishing. The log—an old growth walnut tree from the Jerico estate—was over twenty feet long, and bent in such a way that Joseph could fashion the sculpture along the arc of the curved staircase.

The head of the dragon was at the second-floor landing, over-looking the main foyer. The tail curved over the back, forming the newel post at the bottom of the stairs. Wings spread to support the rest of the railing. The burl grain of the wood made the dragon look as if it were a living being, just taking flight.

Joseph worked on the sculpture nearly every day for over a year. For much of the last month, before Isolde and Drake were married, she sat at the foot of the stairs enrapt, watching the mighty beast take shape.

Drake, on the other hand, properly staying in the hotel so as not to cast a shadow on the honor of his bride-to-be, was occupied as the architect and planner who turned the riverfront into a city. The other eleven men, who had each been given a land grant of some 1,200 acres to found the town, depended on Drake's planning and design. They willingly named their fledgling settlement Jerico City.

The precise service the twelve had rendered to the government, entitling them to such extensive land grants, was still unclear, even closing in on two hundred years later. Some said the land, at the confluence of two navigable rivers, was part of Thomas Jefferson's dream for westward expansion. It was no accident that among the founders were men skilled in iron and woodworks, steam engines, mining, river navigation, fabrication, and various industrial practices.

Within a decade of the founding of the city, barges and paddle-wheelers had made the city a regular stop for repair and maintenance. Twenty years later, the rail line broached the river with an iron bridge, carefully planned to be sure not to obstruct the river traffic.

Jerico City was a thriving metropolis before Isolde arrived. Already, the two-story frame businesses along Main Street and branching onto Water Street along the river were being expanded and rebuilt of brick to reach higher and spread wider. Nearly two thousand souls occupied the settlement.

Of course, Drake had reserved a block fronting both Main and Water Street for his own business. This included his architectural and planning firm, and the headquarters of the construction companies in which he was a partner. Drake was a very busy and prosperous man.

"CAN WE SEE it fly?" Timmy asked a perplexed Lawrence. He merely shook his head.

"Do the steps go all the way to heaven?" Lily asked.

"No. That's a different stairway," Lawrence chuckled, thinking of an old rock and roll song.

"How many steps are there?" asked a different child. It was a question Lawrence was actually prepared to answer.

"There are twenty-three steps from the main floor to the sec-ond-floor landing," he said. "From the second floor to the third, there are nineteen more. Another seventeen steps lead from the third floor to the rooftop terrace. You will notice that all the flights are prime numbers: twenty-three, nineteen, and seventeen. The sum of the three is fifty-nine, also a prime number. That was part of the genius of the architect, old Drake Jerico Senior," Lawrence said.

"Can you turn into a dragon now?" Timmy asked excitedly, refusing to be derailed from his assertion that the dragon was more than carved wood.

"Boy, what makes you think the dragon is anything more than an old walnut tree a man carved almost two hundred years ago? There is no such thing as a real dragon. Just this old carved tree!"

Lawrence was ready for the tour to be over and the little brats to get out of his house. Allowing the educational tours had been part of having the house declared a national historic site, but he didn't think the agreement required him personally to be confronted by children who had more questions than he had answers. Besides, he had a meeting soon and needed to get out to the new site to monitor the surveyors with his grandson, Preston.

"My nan said Old Man Jerico is more dragon than man," Timmy sulked.

"Your nan?" Lawrence would need to find out more about the kid's family so he could decide what he'd done to offend the old woman. But he was done for now. "Matilda will take you on the remainder of the tour," he said shortly. "Don't touch anything!"

WHILE DRAKE JERICO was in town being the newly elected mayor, Isolde continued to spend much of her time watching and talking to Joseph Carver, and becoming quite infatuated with the woodworker. He was more than a craftsman. He was as much an artist as her hus-band-to-be was. They simply worked in different media.

She appreciated the skill and artistry of Drake. He had sent her many drawings during their courtship, while she still lived back East. She had chosen this one to realize as the great stairs. Joseph was also working on a monument sign that would welcome people to the city at the waterfront. It was another of Drake's designs and Isolde was convinced the town would one day be known as the City of Dragons. After all, it was the meaning of Drake's name.

"How do you make this creature so lifelike?" she asked Carver.

"The secret is in hiding the action of the knife," he said as he worked on a fine detail near the eyes. He stood on the ladder to reach the bit. "No part of the dragon can give away its true nature as a walnut tree. The grain, the colors—the carving must all become the dragon."

"What do you mean by hiding the knife?" Isolde asked. She found Joseph's words to be almost as mesmerizing as his actions in carving.

"Well, Miss, if you touch the eyes, here, I believe you will be able to tell," Joseph said.

"What? Am I supposed to lean over the unfinished railing and feel for the eyes, while all the time being perched at my peril?" she teased.

Joseph Carver was a simple man when it came down to it. He embodied the very essence of innocence and artistic awareness that was required by the delicate work he was doing. Isolde could not help but think of him in the same breath as the dragon, the two being so closely linked to each other.

"My lady, if you would climb my ladder, you would be in less peril," Joseph said.

"I foresee that my peril would be different, but at least equal," Isolde sighed. "Yet it seems the only way I will ever see the image closely. Is the ladder sturdy?"

"I will steady it to be sure you are secure," he answered.

Joseph stepped off the ladder and held it as Isolde began her ascent. She was scarcely aware that Joseph stayed just a rung below her as she climbed. Yet when she reached out her hand to touch the dragon's eye, she was fully encased in Joseph's arms. Her heart beat wildly.

"If you stroke across the area I have been focused on, you will find it as smooth as the finest silk," the craftsman said. Indeed, he was proud of the work he had done. Polishing the cut wood with sandpaper and wool cloths had left no mark of the chisel. In fact, this was the part of the job he liked most, for he could feel the living wood beneath his fingers.

Joseph guided her hand to the dragon's eye and as she stroked the wood, he caressed her hand.

"Oh, my!" Isolde said. "It is so smooth; it almost feels soft. It is so sensuous."

She let her fingers explore further and Joseph, emboldened, also explored further with his fingers. Both found all the features they could reach were silky beneath their fingers. Her heart beat more rapidly as she turned on the ladder and found herself face-to-face with Joseph.

"As soft and sensuous as you, fair lady," he whispered.

She was not sure who moved to let their lips come together, but the kiss at the top of the ladder, as her hand felt across the dragon's nose, was full and sensual and led to much more than was permissible. Isolde fell into Joseph's arms.

TWO HUNDRED YEARS later, Lawrence did not mention to the children—nor did he know—a child was conceived of their passion right there on the staircase of Dragon Jerico. Isolde fled from Joseph's presence and swore herself only to her husband's arms. Drake and Isolde were married just days after the final polish was applied to the dragon. She took her wedding vows on the very step on which she had only recently been sullied.

Lawrence watched the children disappear up the stairs after Matilda, who was gleefully filling their little heads with more impossible stories about people who had seen the dragon fly. She also pointed out the little indentations on the back of the dragon where some of the shot from Peter's gun had struck when he killed the burglar.

Lawrence went to the study where he sat to go over the most recent progress in the purchase of land for Preston's planned community. The concept was good. It harkened back to the family roots, two hundred years previously. Acquire a sufficient amount of land to develop an entire community—just as Drake had done with his eleven partners and Jerico City.

Of course, Royce Duval, the public face of the company, would be responsible for funding the development, but Lawrence had committed himself to the land acquisition nearly twenty years earlier. The property was sufficiently remote that his purchases of acreage surrounding the lake had gone unnoticed. All except the one hold-out. He assumed the consortium owning the last parcel of land would sell it, once a premium was set on its value.

The concept itself had all been Preston's idea. The boy was a genius when it came to envisioning a community. Boy. Lawrence's grandson was thirty-two years old. His mind was as sharp as any Lawrence had ever encountered. It was too bad Preston was seized with such anxiety that he couldn't face so much as a board meeting to talk to the directors. He sat as the chairman of the board and CEO at his grandfather's insistence. But the talking was all done by the President and Chief Operating Officer, Royce Duval. Most people just assumed Preston was a figurehead and Royce was the brains of the company.

One-on-one with people he knew, Preston had learned to communicate without difficulty. There were few people, however, who managed to get close enough to him to see the real brilliance of the chairman.

"Grandfather," Preston had said, "our ancestor made his mark by planning and designing this entire city. There are plat maps still in the files for the expansion of Jerico City, which could be pulled and executed as needed, nearly two hundred years after the initial platting. It was built around transportation—the shipping lanes and the railroad right of way. Times have changed. Now we are the center of other kinds of commerce. We have furniture manufacturing, woolen mills, a printing company, electronics, chemicals, food processing... We have all these. But we don't have tourism! Tourism and recreation are the bywords of the future. That is what we need to build."

Lawrence was less certain, but Preston's enthusiasm was contagious. Then they were struck with the damn plague. It looked like it would kill all tourism forever. But Preston had rolled with the punch to see a wider expansion for the resort as a 'working retreat' where people could connect remotely to their offices.

Even while he was designing the Jerico City Community Center Complex at the peak of isolation, Preston continued to make plans for his resort community. His anxiety and his stammer made it difficult for some people to work with him, but his life was controlled by his vision. Preston was surely made from the same mold as his ancestor, Drake Jerico.

Lawrence packed up his notes, his briefcase, binoculars, and heavy boots. He stepped into the kitchen to grab his sandwich and join Preston, going to the site to observe the surveyors as they began to stake out the perimeter of Cloudhaven, about seventy miles upriver from Jerico City.

THE CHILDREN FINALLY left to return to school with their teacher. Lawrence and Preston were already on the road, and by this time, the inexhaustible housekeeper Matilda was ready to go back to bed. She would have if not for needing to get lunch ready for Jacqueline Carver, Lawrence Jerico's daughter and Preston Carver's mother. Jacqueline had divorced Lyle Carver only months after Preston was born and the hapless teen boyfriend had gladly taken the share of her wealth he was entitled to in his prenup, and left town. Jacqueline considered it to have been a fair price to pay for the son she bore.

Lawrence had been the only father figure Preston had ever really known. Maybe that was why he was such a social recluse.

Jacqueline descended the dragon staircase more regally than the children had, and headed to the dinette where Matilda was setting out lunch.

"Miss Jacqueline, your meal is ready," Matilda said, setting a simple salad and tea before her.

"Did my father and son get lunch?"

"They asked that it be packed and it is gone, so I assume they took it before they left."

"How did the tour with the halflings go this morning?" Jacqueline asked as she sampled the baby arugula and spring greens salad.

"Oh, they are energetic young ones, they are. I don't remember Mr. Preston being half so lively as a child."

"It's just been so long ago that we've forgotten how much livelier we were ourselves," Jacqueline laughed. "I wish he'd get busy and marry so I could have grandchildren around."

She enjoyed lunches with her long-time housekeeper and friend—not what one might assume of a privileged woman. When she finished her salad and tea, she cleaned up her own dishes and prepared for a meeting of the arts council in town. Jacqueline was quite active in the community and even tried to keep a hand in what happened on the JeriCorp Board.

On her way to her car, she stopped and looked at the giant dragon staircase again. On that step... the step where generations of Jericos had spoken their wedding vows... One day she would see her son stand there, if only she could find the right match for him.

THE STAIRCASE WAS the silent witness to all that had occurred in the past two hundred years. Isolde's infidelity before her wedding vows. The birth of Drake Junior. And the knowledge that all the generations of Jericos who came after were not related to Drake Jerico Senior at all.

Chapter Two

"I KNOW YOU'LL just love this cozy little bungalow. It's the perfect starter home for a young couple. With that all-important room for expansion," Livy Olson gushed. She'd introduced young couples to their first homes frequently over her twenty years as an agent for Family Real Estate in Jerico City. When the Silvers had entered the office, she was immediately called to talk to them and she loved it.

She unlocked the little house and held the door open for Bruce and Erin.

"It smells new," Erin said, sniffing at the air.

"The entire home has been refreshed," Livy said. "New floors, new kitchen, new bathroom. I have an inspection certificate for the electrical and plumbing. And, of course, with your exclusive Family Home Buyers' Warranty, if you discover a problem with any appliance or mechanical system in the house in the first year you own it, we fix it or replace it!"

Livy was astute. In her interview with the couple, she'd found that Bruce was newly employed by JeriCorp as an architect, but she detected that unemployed Erin was really the decision-maker. She'd seen women who elected to give up a career in order to start a family, but she didn't doubt that in a year, Erin would be employed and earning far more than her husband while the baby was in the care of a nanny.

"Look, honey," Bruce said. "This would be the perfect baby's room. It's like they planned it for that."

"Let's not put the cart before the horse," Erin laughed. "You know all those stress factors they talk about. Marriage, pregnancy, new job, and moving are right up there at the top. We've already got three out of four. I've no intention of doing the family thing by myself."

Just as Livy thought. Erin was managing the process. They'd been married three months and even though she'd quit her job to move to Jerico City with her husband, she hadn't dived headfirst into pregnancy—if that was the way one dived into pregnancy.

But Erin was thirty and her biological clock was ticking. She'd said in their interview that she didn't want her children to have 'old' parents. As it was, she and Bruce would be in their late forties before any child they had would graduate from high school.

"There's lots of space in the back for various stages of a child's life and play cycle," Livy said.

It was a good thing the back yard was the last thing they saw and not the first. The 12 x 12 deck outside the patio doors sat flat on the bare ground. It had a few damaged boards and looked like it would need to be replaced. The yard itself had no grass. A single oak tree dominated the center of the yard and threatened the dilapidated swing set with falling branches.

"The previous owners had three children, if you can imagine that in this little house. And they were enthusiastic pet owners," Livy said.

It was apparent the yard had been dominated by large dogs. It had to be dogs, plural, because no one could imagine any one dog so completely tearing a yard down to bare dirt.

Still, if that was all they found wrong with the property, fixing the landscaping was probably low on the difficulty scale. Bruce was waving from the garden shed/garage at the back of the property. Erin stayed on the deck with Livy.

"If we ever get lucky enough to have grass out here, we have space to store a lawn mower," he laughed. Somehow, Bruce seemed much younger and less mature than Erin.

"Which of us gets to have *her* car in the garage?" she asked.

Bruce ignored the broad hint.

"I suppose I'll have to be sure my car is protected and ready to get me to work in the mornings. We might even discover you don't need a car at all. This is hardly Cleveland," Bruce said.

"The elementary school is only three blocks from here," Livy said unhelpfully. "You'll join dozens of others walking your child to school."

Livy knew the right lines to use when selling the house, but she fully expected it to be back on the market before any child of Erin and Bruce was old enough to walk to school. This would be the fourth time she'd sold the property.

Bruce was on a management track at JeriCorp Architecture and Development. Livy was sure they would want to trade up their home in three or four years. This was a starter home, not a stayer home.

"I guess I'm sold," Erin finally said. "What do you think, Bruce?"

"How soon can we move in?"

SINCE THE HOUSE was unoccupied, they were able to close in two weeks. Bruce's new company was paying for relocation, but he had to stay in Jerico City to start his job while Erin returned to Cleveland to pack their belongings and supervise the moving company getting things to Jerico City. Even though she'd already quit her job, she at least had friends in Cleveland who would help.

"Is it everything you dreamed of?" her best friend, Dee Bonner, asked. She was helping Erin pack things in boxes that would either go to the new house or to storage in Jerico City. Not everything would fit in the little house.

"It's a start," Erin said. "It's not how I plan to be living in five years. I honestly thought Bruce had a little more put aside for a down payment and we'd be able to afford something more upscale. With just what I could borrow against my 401k for a down payment, we're not getting as nice a place as we imagined. But it's in good condition with a new bathroom and kitchen and floors."

"Are you regretting things?" Dee asked, concern for her friend showing clearly.

"Oh, no! I realize I won't be in a high-powered corporate job anymore, but I'll have children to occupy my time. Eventually. Of course, I'll miss everything here a little. You. And everyone at work," Erin said. "It's just a big change."

"It must be a drag being separated from your husband while you're getting ready to move," Dee said.

"It's only a couple of weeks. I wouldn't survive the packing without friends like you to help me."

"I'm ready to pack up your awards."

"Make sure the box is clearly marked. It's one that's going to storage. I don't have room to display a bunch of corporate awards in the baby's room," Erin laughed. "I anticipate pulling them out when I'm rocking a grandbaby and spinning tales of my glory days."

"Ten years at Allard Holding Company," Dee said, looking at a crystal pillar before she carefully wrapped it in bubble-wrap.

"I started as an intern when I was still in college," Erin laughed.

"And shocked everyone when you announced your departure as a regional vice president," Dee nodded. Erin had a lot of awards, certificates, and commendations, most of which were already off the walls of her apartment. She and Bruce had lived together in the apartment for the past six months and it was really too small. And the house in Jerico City wasn't much bigger.

"Going south to where everyone talks with an accent," Erin laughed.

"At least you won't get cold like here," Dee said, looking on the bright side.

"It does snow, but the winter is a bit shorter. I wonder if the city has a decent bus service. We aren't all that far from Bruce's office, but it's too far to walk. I haven't had a chance to look for a job yet," Erin said.

"You're going back to work?"

"I have no intention of sitting home alone all day, even after we start a family. I'm thinking of something that gets me in touch with people. I can't exactly take a job on with as good a career track as I had here, but I'd go crazy if I didn't have something."

"Just remember, I'm only a phone call away. If you need me, I'll be there."

LANDING A PLUM job at JeriCorp was a dream for Bruce Silver. Life was really coming together for him at thirty. He had a nice car, a great job, and had landed a strong and sexy wife. He was afraid he'd lose her when he suggested they move to Jerico City for a new job opportunity. It was a long way from everything they knew.

But Erin had surprised him, talking about how she'd like to have children and they weren't getting any younger. They'd married in the spring and by the end of summer, Bruce was working for the huge architecture and development company.

Erin had turned down multiple offers to stay, resigned from her job, and was getting their little nest put together in Jerico City.

"Bruce, the Mackenzie Building drawings should be reviewed," the director of design said to him. "I'd like you to head the team to do a full review of the designs and the plans. That includes taking over as our point man with Mackenzie. You might need to put some miles on, getting into St. Louis, but we have generous travel allowances. Pull together your team and let's get this project handed off to construction."

"Yes, sir. I'm on it."

This was exactly what he was hoping for when he came to JeriCorp: real responsibility and authority. It's what he'd trained for, served his apprenticeship for, and moved five hundred miles for. He immediately called up the drawings on his computer and then sent a meeting request to all the people who had worked on the project so far. This would be a full-day review before he drove to St. Louis to meet with the client. He wanted to know everything was perfect.

Everyone accepted the meeting request in short order, except the initial architect, Preston Carver. When Bruce checked with his director, he was told that Carver wasn't important to the project and he had all the team he needed.

Weird.

"IT'S WONDERFUL!" ERIN said at dinner that night. "I'm so proud of you. You've worked hard for this and it shows that moving here to Jerico City was the right thing to do."

"I'm not pretending my job is anything near what you could have had in Cleveland," he said, holding his wife tenderly. "But I promise I'm going to make the best of this and be as successful as I can be. You won't ever regret coming with me."

"I'm enjoying nesting and getting our home settled. If things continue the way they are, maybe we won't need to wait until spring to get things started. What would you like for Christmas, lover?"

"You'll be such a great mother!"

"Well, I'm not going to just sit around eating bonbons. I need to get out and find a job now that we're settled in the house."

"Will we still have time...?"

"I guarantee it. I'm just going to get a job, not a career."

Erin knew from her experience exactly what it was like to lead a team, even though they'd been in different industries back in Cleveland. She managed the region and was on track for executive management in the parent company. Bruce's leadership position spurred her to get moving and find a job as well. If Bruce was going to be working long hours and traveling, Erin wanted to be someplace where she could meet people and talk to other adults.

JERICO CITY HAD a thriving economy with businesses focused on electronics, real estate development, furniture manufacturing, textiles and clothing, steel works, transportation, and fine arts. It was tempting for Erin to walk in with her credentials and try to get a job in one of these large corporations, but that wouldn't be fair when she was intending to work only part time. Besides, she'd become a bit burned out in her corporate position. She really wanted to simplify her life. She chose food service.

"We do a brisk breakfast business. People on their way to work are only here because they don't want to waste time cooking and cleaning up their own breakfast. You'll find a lot of people who just look in the door, decide it's too crowded, and turn to leave. They grab a cup of coffee and a sandwich up the street at the coffee shop,"

Dolores said as she gave Erin a tour of the Top Knot Diner. "We have more customers at lunch, but they are more relaxed. Usually, they sit with two to four at a table, unlike the solo breakfast crowd."

"I love the kind of old-fashioned atmosphere," Erin said.

"Not much has changed here since the sixties. Biggest difference is the clientele. Used to be a big after-school crowd, but when they built the new high school east of town, that made it too far for the kids to drop in after class. Of course, I wasn't here in the sixties. Well, not working here, at least," Dolores laughed. "We still try to keep the same atmosphere. Some of the lunch crowd are business execs who were here as teens in the sixties. Of course, most have aged into retirement, but those are the ones who come in for an early dinner. If it weren't for those who still carry the good memories of what the place was like back when, we'd close up at two instead of seven."

"I like people," Erin said. "All ages. Being new in town, I haven't met many yet."

"Let's have a seat and a cup of coffee," Dolores said.

She grabbed two mugs from behind the counter and poured coffee. They sat in a corner booth to talk over Erin's application to be a waitress.

"I have to ask why you want to be a waitress. Your resume is stellar. Surely there are a dozen places in town that would hire you at a level you're qualified for," Dolores said.

"I followed my husband to Jerico City," Erin said. "Quit my job and moved five hundred miles. We just bought a little place on the near east side of town. We plan to start a family, maybe this winter or early spring. I know what I look for in an employee at the level you say I'm qualified for. Part of it is longevity. A prospective mother would be low on my list to employ and I won't lie to an employer about that."

"And you think I don't want long-term employees?" Dolores asked.

"I think I could continue doing this type of job through most of pregnancy and into motherhood. It's not like my need for human contact is going to lessen after I have a baby," Erin explained.

In fact, she felt she might need the job more desperately after a baby was born than before. She had no friends in Jerico City yet.

Of course, she was sure she'd meet other new mothers in things like birth classes and daycare, but she couldn't fathom a life where that was the entire depth of her relationships.

"Honey, you might find differently when you've been walking the floor all night with a colicky baby and then come to work with a temperamental customer," Dolores laughed. "But I like you. You're friendly and outgoing. I'll put you on the lunch shift so you don't lose time with your hubby at breakfast or dinner. If you plan to make a baby, you'll need some of that time. So, show up at ten on Monday morning. Let's get you fitted for a uniform. A lot of our girls still wear masks while they're working. I encourage it, but don't require it. There are customers who really appreciate it."

"I have no difficulty with that. I consider myself to have been very lucky so far. Part of that luck is avoiding risky situations," Erin said.

"Smart cookie. I'll be surprised if you don't have my job by the time you have a baby."

SMART COOKIE OR not, there was still training to be done before she could be set loose to wait tables by herself. She showed up for work on Monday, changed into the uniform the diner provided, and attached her nametag: Maizie.

"No one uses her real name here. We just choose from the tags available. They're all popular nicknames from a bygone generation. You didn't think my real name was Dolores, did you?"

Erin wore her hair up in a knot and under a net with a little cap over it. The uniform was a pink pinafore with a white blouse and apron. It was about mid-thigh length and worn with bobby socks and tennis shoes. Erin thought it was rather cute. Once completed with the mask, however, she doubted even her own husband would recognize her if he came to the diner for lunch. She imagined herself on the *Newlyweds* game show to see if the husbands recognized their wives in different settings.

Of course, he was supposed to be saving money and eating the lunches she carefully prepared for him each morning. She was sure he'd have some occasions to eat out with co-workers, though. She certainly would if her job didn't automatically include lunch.

It was a new experience for Erin to reach in her apron pocket and find cash there. Even her first day's tips were more than she normally carried in cash. Who carried cash? Apparently, many of the diner's customers. Many paid with a credit card, but left a cash tip. If the tip was included with the credit card payment, it was added to the tip pool and divided among the waitresses and kitchen staff according to their hours. They received their portion with their paycheck and proper taxes were deducted. Cash tips went into the server's pocket.

Erin worked only a four-hour shift, from ten until two, but she felt like she'd walked miles. Doing this every day would surely have her in good shape by the time she was ready to carry a baby.

She stopped at the supermarket on the way home from work and bought chicken breasts, asparagus, and rice for dinner. Then she bought an apple pie as a treat for dessert. She was glad she hadn't given up her car.

BRUCE WAS EXCITED as he described the project he was working on at dinner.

"The president stopped by my desk to congratulate me on taking the leadership of this project," he said as they ate.

"Of the United States?" Erin asked with tongue in cheek.

"Of what? Oh! No. The president of the company. What a guy! I tell you, he's brilliant. Knew absolutely everything about the Mackenzie Building and everyone involved in the project."

"Wouldn't a company president normally know what projects people are involved in and who they are?" Erin was teasing a little. Her own company president back in Cleveland had been a very smart woman who consciously mentored new employees and always got the best out of them. That Bruce was finally experiencing something like that was a good sign.

"There are two hundred people in our building in five corporate divisions," Bruce explained. "Most of the divisions only have the executives in the building and work with a scattered workforce.

Architecture is the largest division in the building. But Royce—he told me to call him Royce instead of Mr. Duval—even asked how my move had gone and if my wife had managed to get settled. He asked if we needed anything. The whole company has a real family atmosphere."

"I'm so glad you have such a good job and management," Erin said. "We made the right move to come to Jerico City. I'm even going to enjoy my job. Not nearly as glamorous as yours, though."

"It's hard to believe you work in a restaurant all day and then come home to make dinner and do housework. Let's make sure that Friday, we go out to eat. I feel guilty about you working and taking care of the house, too."

"It's shorter hours than I was working in Cleveland. And you still come home to help after work. It will change after we have a baby, you know. I really don't have an idea how much work that will be!"

"You can count on me. Let's get the dishes done and go out for a walk before it gets completely dark. I've hardly had a chance to explore our neighborhood."

Walking another mile after being on her feet at the diner was not high on Erin's priority list, but it was good exercise and an opportunity to be with her husband.

Chapter Three

"TWENTY-ONE!" PRESTON CALLED** out as he sank another basket. That felt good.

"Are you practicing all the time, bro? You were never that good when we were playing back in school," his friend Gene panted.

They'd managed to get together for hoops at Jerico House every Sunday morning all summer long. It was their way of breaking out after the pandemic. They played without masks.

"Just hyped about our new project. It makes everything easier," Preston said enthusiastically. He'd hinted at the new project several times, but Gene was on the board of directors and Preston didn't want to tip his hand until he was sure everything was lined up. "It takes all my time. I even passed the Mackenzie project on. I don't have time for it."

"I hope you're not isolating yourself in your ivory tower too much. The economy has been a little unpredictable when it comes to building and development."

"Nothing is recession-proof," Preston said. "But we learned things from the pandemic. We didn't shut down. Jobs were retained and a new business model emerged."

"So, you're getting the company back on its feet. Bravo. Of course, everyone believes that's Duval's doing. What are you doing to get back in the world now that the pandemic is supposed to be over?" Gene asked.

"I've never been very good at facing the world, Gene. You know that. I can talk to you. I can talk to Mom and G-Pop. It's all I can do to rap the gavel in a board meeting. I got along better with the world when I could stay isolated and not talk to anyone. I'm not eager to get out in it again."

"I think you slipped backward during the pandemic. Have you continued seeing your therapist?"

"Yeah, yeah. We go through hours of talking about my childhood and nothing changes. Hell, I had a great childhood. I don't understand where the anxiety comes from."

"Is that all your therapist does?" Gene asked in disbelief.

"No, of course not. That's me talking about things I can't control. She's big into cognitive behavior therapy and I've learned some ways to deal with it. Then, I enter a room full of people and I can't even breathe."

"It's not healthy to stay isolated all the time. You might even find some things that would help you with your new project if you got out once in a while."

"It would be fine if I could stay safe while interacted and watched people. I use my binocs from the rooftop to watch people sometimes. But to get out there and interact? That's torture."

He'd tried to overcome his social anxiety. He had counseling, speech therapy, and even got involved in sports. At six-two, he'd been good at basketball, but that hadn't translated to social circumstances. His family was well-known as city founders with one of the oldest homes in Jerico City. He still carried the Jerico name as his middle name, though the Carver clan had been around the city almost as long. They simply hadn't been as influential.

Taking the prescribed drugs, going to counseling, and practicing speeches he never managed to give. The last time he'd called a woman his mother wanted to set him up with, he'd hyperventilated while on the phone with her until he passed out. The woman had called 911 and refused to speak with him again.

"How about a limited interaction environment? Here's an idea: Slip out to a different restaurant once a week for lunch. You might find some new dishes you want to try. See some interesting people.

All you'd have to do is point at what you want on the menu and nod when they ask you how it was. Make it a study, my friend. Watch people from a little closer than your rooftop. Listen."

"I'd end up with people watching me. 'What's Preston Carver up to, eating by himself? We should say hi,'" Preston said. "You know, I went out to a play a while ago and by intermission, there was a reporter waiting in the lobby to interview me. I don't even know why they know who I am."

"You're Preston Carver, Chairman of the Board and CEO of JeriCorp. There's a page dedicated to watching you on social media."

"They all want to know why I'm chairman and CEO. I quit following them when they started talking about how Royce Duval is the brains keeping JeriCorp alive."

"You know, it doesn't take that much to disguise yourself these days. Masks are still a thing. Put on dark glasses and wear a baseball hat or something."

"I don't know, Gene. You and I can talk. We've learned over the years. My own assistant at the office is always trying to finish my sentences for me. She walks all over me."

"I'm thinking of you, my friend. I know it's hard, but try it. See if you can manage just a little anonymous interaction. If it doesn't work, we'll figure something else out. Really, man. It's got to be better than another blind date your mother arranges."

"No kidding. I'll try it."

"LET'S SUPPOSE A woman you meet was only interested in your money," Jacqueline said at Sunday dinner.

It was a family tradition and Preston endured it after his morning basketball game with Gene nearly every week. Preston's mother was a would-be matchmaker, and he simply tuned out her well-intentioned interference in his life. He appreciated her intent. Really. He had just been burned often enough to not be enthusiastic about dating.

It started with Beverly, back in high school. Preston had fallen hopelessly in love and she'd been his first lover. But she'd shown her

 Nathan Everett

true colors when she got pregnant by another classmate and tried to convince Preston it was his.

"They are only interested in money," Preston sighed. He supposed, as his therapist had told him, that was a terribly unfair declaration. There were days he wished he had no money. But that scared him, too.

"Well, what's the downside? Just make sure any relationship is locked into an ironclad prenup and enjoy yourself. Someplace along the line I'm sure to end up with a grandchild."

"I think that's called prostitution."

"It's what I did. Lyle looked at the agreement, then looked at me. He signed it. I assume my standing in front of him naked until he signed might have had something to do with it, but he signed. He married me so everything was legitimate. He got me pregnant, exactly as I planned, and then I kissed his ass goodbye. He took what was owed him in the prenup, and your father was never seen nor heard from again."

"I'm supposed to be happy I never knew my father, Mother?"

"Believe me, son, you'd have been bored to death with him," Lawrence said. "I wasn't sure what Jackie saw in the boy until I met you. Getting her pregnant was probably the greatest accomplishment of his life. The second greatest was leaving."

"What I'm saying is that you don't have to be alone," Jacqueline said. "It's not healthy. Find someone who is poor, pretty, and desperate. Take her out. Show her the agreement. Marry her and enjoy her for as long as it pleases you, making sure you get an heir out of her. Then divorce her and pay her what she's owed in the prenup."

"It's what Royce has done," Lawrence nodded. "After his first wife took half of everything he'd worked for and the children, he presented Shannon with the prenup, so she knows exactly how long she has to put up with him and what she'll get for it when it ends. He gets a beautiful young wife and she gets pretty much whatever she wants."

Preston laughed at the thought of his chief operating officer and his young wife.

"Neither one of them can keep their pants on," Preston said. "No thanks. I honestly think they work together to seduce whoever one or the other wants to bed. They grin at each other like conspirators."

"Royce is a good and effective public face for the company," Lawrence said. "Believe me, I locked him into as tight an employment agreement as his prenup with Shannon."

"In return for which, he gets to take credit for every success the company has. Everyone believes the City Community Center was his idea. They actually believe he designed the Mackenzie project himself," Preston snorted. "He never had an original idea in his life. You even designed his prenup with Shannon."

"But the man can sell," Lawrence said. "I know you spent hours with him to make sure he understood what the Community Center concept was and the reasons for it. He can be a little dense sometimes, but then he took the concept and sold it to the city, to the board of directors, and to the rest of the company. And let me remind you that you did not have to make a single presentation."

"I... I... know, Grandfather. I'm a g-great disappointment," Preston stuttered. As soon as he was on the spot, he froze up. Detecting his grandfather's criticism, it was like his tongue swelled in his mouth. He couldn't get a sentence out that made sense. If he could, he wouldn't need Royce as a front man for the company.

"Preston," Lawrence said gently, "you have never disappointed me. You have vision. You have talent. And you understand the market trends better than anyone I know. Having a puppet who can present those ideas and sell the concepts is no disgrace. It's what I hired Royce for in the first place. And he knows he's a puppet. He takes your words, your ideas, and packages them together with his natural charisma and glib presentation style. It's a winning combination. You just need to pull on his strings once in a while to make sure he's dancing to your tune."

Maybe that was what Preston needed in his social life, too—a puppet who could sell him to a good woman without him having to actually talk to her.

It had always been that way. It was why Beverly thought she could control him by pretending he got her pregnant in high school. It had been a satisfying first sexual experience, but he'd fallen in love with her. When he found out she just wanted his family fortune, it was devastating.

Since taking over from his grandfather as Chairman of the Board and CEO, Preston had remained isolated in his penthouse office at JeriCorp. He had a private elevator that rose to the apartment, so very few people saw him enter or leave the building. He met with Royce each week to go over plans and coach him on the details of any project needing to be sold.

He had a personal assistant he worked to the bone, just carrying messages to the executives on the staff and reviewing projects. He never had a personal assistant who worked for him more than a few months. His people skills were so poor that he drove his assistants away.

GENE HATHAWAY, PRESTON'S high school friend and staunchest non-family ally on the board of directors, had encouraged him to get out of his office for lunch once a week. It took Preston until Thursday before he got up the energy to leave his office and explore a little.

Lawrence had designed the penthouse office and apartment when Preston first graduated from college. The two shared the office for several years before Preston took over the company. The space was comfortable and Preston didn't really like leaving it. His grandfather had insisted on a few rules, however. During business hours, the space was the office. Both men wore suits and ties to the office. A secretary had her space next to the elevator and reported to work each day in proper business attire.

Royce was considerably less formal in running the rest of the office on the lower floors. Architects and engineers often wore jeans and casual shirts unless they were meeting in the penthouse. It was understood that anyone who came into the penthouse during business hours was to wear proper business attire and use formal terms of address for Mr. Jerico and Mr. Carver and Ms. whoever happened to be their assistant.

At Preston and Lawrence's end of the office were floor-to-ceiling windows with sliding doors that opened to the rooftop terrace.

Of course, Lawrence's desk was now empty most of the time, but the old man still came in regularly to consult with his grandson and advise him on the business. Between the two spaces was a comfortable meeting area for when a table was not needed. The sofa and chairs were formed in a U-shape facing the windows.

A loft was Preston's private sleeping and lounging area with his bath and closet. Beneath it, next to the central office space, was his kitchen and dining area.

The assistant's space was as large as any office in the building. It was fully networked with printers, projectors, file cabinets, and computer system with multiple screens. Beside the assistant's area was a restroom and a large storage area.

When his assistant left for lunch Thursday, Preston quickly removed his jacket and pulled on a hoodie sweatshirt from his alma mater. He put on dark glasses and a mask, took a deep breath, and left by way of the elevator directly to the ground floor exit.

He was going to do it. He was going out to lunch.

THE TOP KNOT Diner had a good reputation, according to online ratings. It was only three blocks from the office, so Preston made it his destination for his first adventure. Of course, he couldn't expect the diner to serve food as good as what he would make for himself. If he hadn't been born into the Jerico family of architects and designers, he could imagine himself owning a restaurant and cooking up his own special dishes. He'd have gone to culinary school and become a great chef. These days he only cooked for himself and occasional family meals at Jerico House.

The first thing he noticed at the diner was that it was clean. That was an important issue for Preston. Restaurants often kept the lighting low so dirty floors and seats went unnoticed. The bright lights in the diner would have exposed any mess or spill that went untended. As he waited for a seat, he saw a waitress grab a clean towel, wet it in hot water and go to the last booth in the corner of the restaurant to scrub it down. She even washed and dried the plastic menus at the table. Preston was sold.

When she turned away from the booth, he startled her, standing just behind her.

"Okay?" he asked, pointing at the booth.

"Sure. Sorry, you startled me."

"Th-thank you for... using cl-clean cloth. To... you know..."

"Oh, sure. It doesn't help to wipe a table down with a dirty cloth and old dishwater," she laughed. "Can I get you a drink? Coffee? Water?"

"Y-yes."

The waitress, named Maizie according to her nametag, hurried off to get his drinks while he looked at the menu. Maizie had nice legs and arms, though that was really the only description he could manage. The pinafore uniform looked exactly like all the others in the diner, the hat covered her hair, and she wore a mask, like he did. He supposed it was suspicious for him to keep his sunglasses, mask, and hoodie on, but he'd seen half a dozen employees in the diner when he arrived and wasn't going to risk being recognized.

When Maizie returned to the table with his drinks, she asked what he'd like.

"J-just... th-th-the...," Preston just pointed to the note on the menu for the Blue Plate Special. Maizie nodded.

"Have it for you in a jiff." She was gone again.

That was refreshing. She didn't try to finish his sentences for him. She just took the direction from his gesture and went about getting his food. When she brought the meatloaf, mashed potatoes, and green beans, she set it down so Preston would get the best pre-sentation of the old-fashioned comfort food.

"I'm Maizie," she said. "If I'm not near or not paying attention, give me a shout if you need something."

"Yeah. Oh. I-I-I'm Jerry."

"Nice to meet you, Jerry. Enjoy your meal."

He bent his head over the food and lowered his mask just enough so he could eat. The bright lights of the diner meant he could see fine with his dark glasses. And the food was good. Maizie stopped by to refill his coffee cup and then was off to wait on her other customers. He was impressed with how cheerful she was, even in the demanding atmosphere of the diner.

"I'll be happy to be your cashier when you're ready," she said when she delivered the check for $13.45.

"Oh. Um... I-I have it here," he said, digging in his pocket. He handed her a $20-bill. "Keep... the... uh... change. Enough?"

"That's very generous of you, Jerry. Take your time with your coffee. Thank you for choosing the Top Knot for lunch."

He saw her run the twenty through the bill reader at the cash register and then count out her change. He left before she returned to her station.

He was back at the office before Mrs. Armstrong returned.

Chapter Four

"A SIX-AND-A-HALF-DOLLAR TIP!" Erin exclaimed to Bruce at dinner. "I mean when four guys sit at the table and all order lunch, it's a miracle if they tip five."

"That's disgusting," Bruce said. "Um... How much should they tip?"

"Don't tell me you don't know how to tip a waitress! Standard is between eighteen and twenty percent. If you have a ten-dollar meal, it's nice to tip two dollars," Erin said. "So, if the total bill is forty for four guys, they should tip eight dollars."

"It seems like that adds a lot to the bill," Bruce said.

"Well, if wait people were subject to minimum wage, tipping wouldn't be so critical. It dates back to the days when people were just hired off the street to do an errand and the boss gave them a little something for their effort. It was never supposed to be a job title. I make eight dollars an hour. So, even with my six-and-a-half-dollar tip, I'd come up short of the fifteen-dollar minimum wage."

"Well, if they paid food servers minimum wage, hamburgers would cost twenty dollars."

"Bruce, I can't believe you can spout that nonsense. I talked to Dolores about this and she's working the numbers for what the real difference would be if she raised everyone to minimum wage. There's this chain of drive-ins up in Washington that gives all its employees a minimum of $19 per hour. They get free health care, three weeks paid vacation, 50% 401k match and $9,000 for tuition and child-care. There isn't anything on their menu that's more than $5. Their basic burger costs $1.80."

"Well, they have to make up the wages somehow," Bruce insisted.

"Yeah. They raised their prices this year to afford the pay increase and supply chain increases. Their deluxe burger went up by twenty-five cents."

"I bet people still complained."

"Here's a riddle for you. Three guys go to a restaurant and their check comes out to $25. They each toss in a $10-bill for a $5 tip. The owner realizes the check was miscalculated and should only be $20. So, he gives the waitress $5 to return to the customers. The waitress is greedy, though, and only gives each of the men $1. She keeps the other $2 for herself. Now each of the customers has contributed $9 and the waitress kept $2. Nine times three is twenty-seven, plus two is twenty-nine. Where did the other dollar go?"

"That doesn't sound…" Bruce shook his head and went back to the previous subject. "Why do we constantly hear about how much prices will increase if minimum wage increases?"

"Because if the lowest paid worker gets a doubled salary, from $7.50 to $15.00 an hour, the president of the company gets a triple increase from $250,000 to $750,000 a year. It's not the workers who drive prices up!"

"Um… Weren't you on a fast track to become one of those high-paid executives?"

"Am I still there?" Erin asked. "Allard paid everyone in the company a fair wage, and that included executives. They set a limit on how much more an executive could be paid than an hourly employee. I was on track to earning a great wage, but I wasn't going to be an obscenely paid president who earns a hundred times what a regular employee does. There is no business brain that is worth that much. They're criminal brains. For every high-paid executive in the United States, there is another person who could do just as good a job for less than half the price."

"Well, please don't start capping wages at my company before I get mine up to where it will support our family."

"As if I would go to work for your company," Erin sighed. "As soon as we're stable, I'll have all I want at home with the children and cooking for my husband."

"Your husband wishes he was home for more meals," Bruce said. "I didn't realize how much more than just full time it was going to be to manage a project like this. I'm going to be in St. Louis most of the week next week. I have meetings with the client and with the construction teams."

"Just remember, no matter what kind of meals you get on your per diem, they won't compare to what you could have waiting right here at home."

"Not to mention all the side benefits," Bruce said, reaching for his wife. She gladly came into his arms.

ERIN ENJOYED WORKING at the diner. It was a completely different kind of stress than what she'd been used to in corporate management. It was especially nice during those weeks when Bruce was out of town managing his project. She got together with other employees occasionally. She met new people. She explored her town. Still, she missed her husband. They spoke every night before bed and she envied the excitement of his job just a little.

But she was counting the days until she felt she could go off birth control and be ready to start their family. She finally decided that if she went off at Thanksgiving, she and Bruce could spend the Christmas holiday playing 'Let's make a baby.'

She'd acquired her own small contingent of customers at the diner who wanted to sit at one of her tables, just as many of the other waitresses had. One of them was her Thursday regular, Jerry. He was a very low-key guy who always kept his head and face covered. As they'd gotten to know each other, he'd become more comfortable talking to her, though. She seldom noticed his hesitation.

Maizie always greeted him when he came in and had 'his' table ready for him. She checked to be sure the menu was wiped clean with a disinfectant wipe before handing it to him. She didn't mind providing a little extra care for him since he was always so generous with her.

The Thursday Blue Plate Special changed every week. She could pretty much bet that Jerry would order it, no matter what was on the menu. Each was priced at $9.95. With coffee and taxes, that came to $13.45. And Jerry always left her a twenty to cover the meal and tip.

She greeted him by name and tried to be pleasant, no matter what was happening that day. She'd even started giving other customers the extra service of a freshly disinfected menu, handled their plates and flatware with a clean cloth rather than her hands, and tried to be bright and friendly with her conversation.

"Tell me about the special today," Jerry said when he was seated.

"I haven't eaten yet, but I sampled what the cook has back there. A lot of people don't eat pork because they think it's too fatty, but the cook's pork loin is lean and flavorful. He could have gone all traditional and just served mashed potatoes, but he put together a mushroom risotto that is unbelievable. He's suggesting the green salad with the meal today because he says cooked vegetables just won't stand up to the rich flavors of the pork and risotto."

"Wow! Your chef is a real gourmet! I'll have that special."

As far as Erin was concerned, the cook was very good, but she made up the descriptions. Her fellow waitresses would listen to her tell about the special and use the exact same words for their customers. As a result, sales of the Blue Plate Special were going up.

"Jerry, the cook made an apple crisp dessert today. I confess, I tried it and it's really scrumptious," Erin said at the end of his meal. "Can I bring you a piece? On the house."

"That would be lovely, Maizie. I think I'll need another cup of coffee to go with it," he answered. She smiled at him and hurried to get his dessert. She wrote herself a bill for three-fifty for the crisp. It was just a little extra she could do for her favorite customer.

She wasn't terribly surprised to find an extra five tucked beneath the twenty he usually left.

"MY FINANCIAL CONTROLLER gave me a nice compliment today," Bruce said at dinner. "We're working closely on managing the expenses on this project. She reminds me a lot of you as far as her business sense goes."

"Oh? Is she reminding you of me in other ways?" Erin teased.

"Don't be silly! She's... Well, I guess she's about our age. Redhead. And most importantly, married to the president of the company. I treat her nicely and he comes around to compliment my work occasionally."

"So, what was her compliment today?" Erin asked.

"Just that she appreciated the work I'd done to get the numbers ready for our trip to St. Louis Monday. She's suspicious that the client is not being up front about their financial condition. They're thirty days late on their payments."

"I hope that doesn't negatively affect your project," Erin said with a trace of concern. She knew all too well how the supply chain worked.

"No, we'll get it worked out. I'm flattered that she wants me beside her when she meets with Mackenzie. It looks like we'll be working more closely together over the next few weeks."

"Just don't work too closely together, okay?"

BY THANKSGIVING, MAIZIE'S friendly attitude and attentive service had built her a following of loyal customers at the diner. More and more regulars wanted to sit in her section, but she made sure to reserve the corner booth on Thursday for Jerry.

Of course, the diner was closed on Thanksgiving and Erin fixed a full Thanksgiving dinner for her and Bruce. She tried to control the portions that she cooked, but even a small turkey is a lot for two people. She and Bruce ate turkey all weekend and she still had enough remaining to make a big kettle of soup that would supplement their meals until Christmas.

For the first time in a long time, they had a long weekend to just be together without running to the office or the diner. Erin felt they were renewing their relationship all weekend and was happy to have her husband paying attention to her and not to his project in St. Louis. Or to his financial controller.

She admitted to being a little jealous of the redhead she'd never met. She'd love to travel to St. Louis every other week with her husband. The Thanksgiving weekend put those thoughts to rest, though, as they went shopping for a Christmas tree and decorated their little home for the holiday. They even got lights that Bruce hung on the eaves, while Erin held his ladder steady.

Monday, of course, things were back to the same hectic schedule. If Bruce wasn't traveling, it seemed he was working late night after night.

MAIZIE WAS JUST preparing Jerry's booth on Thursday after Thanksgiving when two guys in business suits came into the diner and headed straight to the corner booth.

"I'm sorry, gentlemen. I already have a customer for this booth," she said pleasantly.

"There's no one here," one of the guys said.

"There will be as soon as I finish wiping it down."

"We'll take it."

Erin was not normally hard to get along with. She was flexible in most things, but she was loyal to her loyal customers. Something about the attitude of these guys just put her off. It was an attitude she'd learned to hate during her ten years in corporate politics that indicated these men felt they were entitled to whatever they wanted and no one could stand in their way. They were about to find out differently.

"I said no," she responded. "I have a customer for this booth."

"We're here first."

"That doesn't really make a difference. I serve this table and if you insist on sitting here, you won't have any service. I have a customer."

"Where?"

"He's waiting politely by the register."

The men turned to see a fellow in a hoodie sweatshirt, sunglasses, and a mask.

"You're saving a place for a homeless guy who shouldn't be seen in public?"

"He's my regular."

"Where's your manager, girl? We'll see about this. Call your manager."

"Certainly, Karen," Erin said.

"Bitch!"

"Dolores? Could you re-seat these gentlemen, please?" she called.

"Sure. I'm sorry, you arrived at the wrong time to have this booth."

"You need to fire this bitch," the man said. "You're losing paying customers because she's a woke bleeding heart with a homeless guy."

"To my knowledge, that man has never failed to pay for his meal, nor has he stiffed a waitress. I seem to recall the last time you gentlemen were here that you left a quarter tip for a thirty-dollar tab. No one in the diner wants to wait on you."

"She was a lousy waitress. I had to ask twice for coffee. She's lucky she got two bits without spreading her legs."

"Get out of my restaurant and don't come back," Dolores snarled, pointing toward the door. All the waitresses and the kitchen help moved to Dolores's side. Faced with the wall of disapproval, the men moved toward the door.

"Who needs this greasy spoon? Once people read our reviews on Good Eats, you'll be lucky if even the homeless come to beg for scraps."

They left and the diner returned to its normal bustle. Jerry made his way to the table as Erin wiped his menu with a disinfectant wipe.

"You... um... didn't need to... uh... do that," he said as Erin motioned him to his seat.

"Jerry, I don't believe you are either homeless or particularly poor. But even if you were, I'd still save this table for you and treat you with the same respect. Those men were disgusting and if they proved to be the Jerico himself, I'd have treated them the same way. For all I know, one of them was!" Erin giggled. "Now, we have a magnificent country fried steak for the special today that I know you'll like. Want that?"

"Yes, thank you, Maizie. Thank you."

"I'm not usually such a demanding bitch," Erin confided in a whisper. "My system's all crazy at the moment. I miss my husband."

Jerry stared at Erin and both snorted a laugh.

PRESTON WAS A bit distracted when he met with his Grandfather Friday afternoon. They sat in the meeting area between their desks, drinking coffee and going over the plans for the new development. But Preston's mind was on the waitress at the Top Knot Diner.

Of course, just because Maizie was nice to him and was easy to talk to didn't make her a possible date. For one thing, she wore a wedding ring and Preston would never consider going out with a married woman.

What he needed was a woman like that who was actually available to suddenly drop into his life and take it over.

As he talked with his grandfather, he absently worked a Rubik's Cube, turning the colors this way and that as they gradually fell into place. It was one of the things he did to control his anxiety and focus his thoughts. There were cubes lying all over the penthouse in every size from 3x3x3 to 7x7x7. No one spoke to Preston if he was working a 7x7x7 puzzle. It was a sure sign he didn't want to be disturbed.

"We have just the one holdout," Lawrence said. "I know you wanted the whole piece before we announce the project, but I think you should prepare to launch the plan anyway."

"Who owns it?"

"A consortium out of St. Louis. I believe word of the project leaked somehow. It was purchased after we started putting offers out on the big blocks of land. We'll get the property, but it will be at a premium once development of the other parcels has begun," Lawrence said.

"How could word get out?" Preston puzzled. "Do we know who is in this consortium?"

"A couple of smaller developers and a recreational property developer. Probably some wealthy individuals backing them."

"We certainly don't want them to start developing something before we put our stamp on the area. Can you imagine what a glass and steel monstrosity would look like compared to our planned community?"

"We've kept the nature of our interest well-concealed. Our Interlake Holding Company is listed as an agricultural development company. But we've had to make inquiries with the county regarding development in order to make sure it was a sound investment. Those records are open to the public."

The two men got up from the sofa and moved to the central conference table. It was seldom used for conferences. For the past few months, it was the staging area for Preston's planned community. He'd downloaded the topo maps from the USGS and fed them into a 3-D rendering program. He'd used this to send each portion to his 3-D printer and assemble a scale model of the entire development site. It was almost like being on site.

They walked around the 3D map on the table and Mrs. Armstrong jumped up with a notepad. She was used to having them simply ignore her until they needed something and then she had better be ready.

The problem of developing without the holdout parcel was that it was where he'd intended the entrance to Cloudhaven to be. The bite out of that section would move the entrance nearly half a mile toward the lake and make the property more U-shaped than consolidated.

He wanted that piece of property, but he would have to trust his grandfather to force the sale. He'd go ahead and plan the development as if it were a fait accompli.

It was curious that word of the project had leaked far enough that a competitor could jump on it. The property acquisition was not done through JeriCorp. They had leveraged nearly every penny of the family fortune to acquire the property themselves as Interlake Holding Company. Three sections of lakefront, missing a single bite of 160 acres. Lawrence and Jacqueline had put their trust in him when he planned the project. He owed it to them and to the Jerico name to make it successful.

Not that he was a Jerico. His mother had married Lyle Carver, his father. Why she didn't revert to her maiden name when she divorced was a mystery to Preston, but he bore the Carver surname with Jerico as his middle name. It was the name he used at the diner, though no one knew that Jerry was short for Jerico.

Regardless, it was time Preston started platting the new community and designing the buildings that would make it a destination resort.

Chapter Five

"**T**HE COMPANY ISN'T** hosting a general holiday party for all employees," Bruce explained. "Instead, we're just doing individual group parties. With Christmas on Monday, we figured Friday night after work would be the best. No big venues, and it's employees only, without a plus one. Since we see each other almost every day, it's not likely to be a late night. I'm going to take a cab from work, though, because I'll probably have a few drinks."

"I suppose that's the way it is," Erin sighed. "Do try to get home early if you can. I have a special party planned for just the two of us."

"You know I love your special parties," he said, kissing Erin. "Don't wait up, though. I'll wake you when I get in."

"Better wake me before you try to get in. I want to be an active participant."

"You bet!"

ERIN WORKED HER four-hour shift Friday and then stopped with her fellow waitresses in the back of the kitchen to exchange modest gifts. Everyone was in a happy holiday mood and it was beginning to look like they might have snow for Christmas.

"Big plans for your first holiday in Jerico City?" one of the waitresses asked her.

"Oh, I guess it will be pretty quiet. Might even spend the whole weekend in bed," Erin giggled.

"Now that sounds nasty. Cheaper than buying the guy a present, though," Penny said. Erin didn't know any of their real names. They all went by their diner name badges.

"You know that's all guys want anyway," Debbie said. "I mean, unless you're giving them a choice of sex or a 50-inch TV. I think most guys would take the TV."

"Not my guy," Erin laughed. "I'm not sure there's anything I could offer him that he'd prefer. We've only been married seven months."

"Newlyweds! Give it another five months. If he wouldn't trade sex for a 50-inch TV by then, he's a keeper," Penny laughed.

The women hugged each other and Dolores gave each a $50 gift card with her wishes for a happy holiday. Erin decided to walk around downtown and look at the decorations. Downtown didn't have all that much in the way of retail. It was mostly offices and support businesses. The real decorations would be found at the mall. She thought about it a while and decided to drive out and do some shopping with her $50 gift card. Maybe even have dinner.

BRUCE KNEW HE wouldn't get home too early. Shannon had promised lots of slow dancing and plenty of booze. She'd even asked him for his favorite and said she'd have it there.

Most of the work groups at JeriCorp weren't having a holiday party at all. Shannon had taken care of discreet invitations and no one on his team mentioned the party at all. Bruce had tallied up the ten people who were eligible to attend and saw they were evenly divided between men and women. At least the slow dancing wouldn't be with another dude. His last trip to St. Louis had been rewarding with Shannon cuddling up to him for the night. What a fiery redhead!

He knocked at the door of the hotel suite where the party was to be held and Shannon opened it for him.

"Come on in, sugar," she said. "Let's party!"

It was only eight o'clock, but Shannon acted like she'd been partying for quite a while. She met him with a very sloppy kiss just inside the door. Bruce was surprised and was afraid the other people on the team would react, but as he looked over Shannon's shoulder, he saw the room was empty—none of his team was there.

"Am I early?" he asked.

"Any later and I'd have finished without you," she laughed.

"Um... Shannon?"

"Oh, come on, Bruce. I didn't invite anyone but you. Have a drink. I got your favorite scotch," Shannon said.

She poured him several shots over ice and handed it to him. He quickly took a sip before Shannon was pressed against him again, probing his mouth with her tongue.

"I shouldn't really..."

"Bruce, remember St. Louis? We can pick up right where we left off. Don't tell me you don't want to have sex with me. I can feel that you do."

"I'm married."

"Me too. Lucky girl. Does that mean we can only make it when we're out of town?"

"I... uh... Oh wow!"

"If you take any longer, my clothes are going to start removing themselves. Show me what you give the little missus when she wants big bad Brucey."

"Geez, Shannon. I didn't expect this was how we'd spend the night."

"Eat, drink, and be merry. Who knows what the New Year will bring?"

"Right. Oh, Shan!"

Bruce knew he'd been set up. If he was any kind of husband at all, he'd have turned around and walked away. It was hard enough keeping his slip-up in St. Louis a secret. Shannon could be so damned persuasive—especially when she started removing her clothes. Facing the prospect of a night of unbridled sex with the stacked redhead, all the things he 'knew better than' flew from his head. He filled his hands and his mouth with her breasts.

They'd been flirting ever since Bruce joined JeriCorp and they were assigned to the same team. On their last trip to St. Louis, the two had bad news. Mackenzie couldn't meet their next payment. It was likely the company would pull the plug on the project before they sank any more time and energy into it. He and Shannon had sat on the sofa in his room commiserating with each other. That mutual comfort had taken the form of kissing and then petting and then stretched out right there on the sofa screwing.

He'd fantasized about her before then, but never imagined she would be available. 'Available' seemed an understatement now. He liked it when a woman took control and he could give up all initiative and responsibility. This whole encounter wasn't his fault. He was a victim here. *Yeah.*

BRUCE WOKE UP, drunk from the night of debauchery and sex. His hand was still on one of the redhead's big breasts. She was pretty, but with her carefully applied makeup and hairdo in a mess, he could see how much of that was artificial. What had he been thinking?

It was two in the morning. He needed to get out of the hotel room and get home. He'd make a plan on the way. Erin had said she had a surprise for him. It was probably too late for that.

He started to push himself up when Shannon looked at him through heavily lidded eyes.

"Oh, good. Ready for another round? Come here, big guy. Make this girl happy."

He didn't leave until after three.

ERIN HADN'T WAITED up for Bruce. She knew how office parties went. She'd certainly been to enough of them in her days of working. Once people got into an unsupervised environment where human resources couldn't see them, there was bound to be some flirting, close dancing, and maybe even a few shared kisses. She wouldn't hold it against Bruce.

After all, he had no idea what she had planned. She'd been off the pill for thirty days. She'd had a period, even though it was light. Maybe they wouldn't be successful at making a baby the first time they tried, but trying was half the fun.

After scrubbing the house thoroughly so there wasn't a speck of dust to distract them, she went to bed, looking forward to the return of her husband.

Was she sure this was right?

She'd asked herself that question a hundred times and always arrived at the same answer. Bruce was a good man, even with his faults. He treated her well and was looking forward to having a family. He was kind and exhibited all the traits Erin considered herself to have. She only planned to be married once and this was it.

She was sound asleep when Bruce stumbled in and took a shower.

WHEN ERIN AWOKE in the morning, Bruce was snoring next to her. She slipped out of bed and made coffee the way he liked it. This was sure to bring him to life. She opened the blinds and the late morning sunlight streamed in through the window. She held the fresh cup of coffee to the side while she kissed him slowly awake.

"Mmm. Smells good," he said. "Um... I'm a little hung over."

"What kind of party would it be if you weren't hung over the next morning? But it's almost afternoon now. Here, have a cup of life."

"Oh, that's good," he sighed, sipping at the coffee.

"Now just relax and let me do all the work. I'm ready for my party now."

She began working her way down his body and found the arousal she knew she could inspire.

"We shouldn't until..."

"Shh. It's time. I might not be fertile this morning, but it's time to start planting the seeds for Baby Silvers. You want it, too, don't you?"

"God, yes. I'm so sorry."

"Maybe, but it seems like you're still functional."

Bruce set the coffee aside and Erin mounted her husband. She sighed as they became one.

"Things changed in the past year," she said. "I didn't think I'd ever slow down and have children. Then I met you and I realized the perfect father had stumbled into my life and I'd be stupid to let this opportunity slip by. All of a sudden, my career didn't mean as much as I thought it did. Since we moved here, I discovered I could be just as happy waiting tables as running a division. We'll have such beautiful children."

"Oh, Erin. I want to be the father your children deserve. I'm so afraid I'm not what you think I am. It's a lot to live up to."

"You're handsome, loving, intelligent, and a good provider. What else do you need to be?"

Erin sped up her motions and before long Bruce moaned and did his part.

ERIN HAPPILY GOT up while Bruce continued to lounge in bed. She made breakfast and fresh coffee and served them on a tray.

"Technically, I suppose you should be serving me. After all, I'm the one you're trying to get pregnant," Erin laughed. "Now tell me about your party last night. A suitable start to the holiday season?"

"It... um... I... uh... It was... you know."

"Bruce? You went to your team's holiday party last night, didn't you?"

"Um... Yeah. I thought it was going to be different."

"How different?"

Bruce inhaled deeply. Erin saw tears forming in his eyes.

"I thought the whole team was coming to the party. It turned out Shannon didn't invite anyone else."

"It was just you and that finance woman?"

Erin couldn't believe what she was hearing. How could he go out and cheat on her the night they were going to try to get pregnant?

"Did you...?"

"She got me drunk pretty quickly and then I found out no one else was coming and then we were kind of dancing and there was a bed in the hotel room..."

"You went to a hotel with a woman, got drunk, and fucked her?" Erin cried out. "How could you?"

"I didn't mean to!"

"You didn't mean to stick your dick in your co-worker and keep it there most of the night? I know you didn't get home until after three. I'm not that sound a sleeper."

"It was just a thing. It didn't mean anything."

"It meant something to me!" Erin screamed. "Oh, my God. Then you came home and came in me. I could catch a disease! I could be pregnant! Pregnant from a cheater! I believed in you. I loved you!"

"I love you, Erin."

"Right. You love me so much you fucked someone else before me. On the same night!"

"Erin, it will never happen again. I promise."

"Oh, I promise it will never happen again. Get out! Get out! Never mind! I'm leaving."

She jumped out of bed, dumping the breakfast all over him. She dressed and threw some clothes in a bag while Bruce pled with her. All her dreams, up in smoke. How could she have been so deceived?

"WHAT AM I going to do, Dolores?" Erin moaned. "He cheated on me! He spent the night in the arms of another woman and then came home to *my* bed. I had sex with him! Unprotected! Oh, God! I could be pregnant. I have to... I have to do something."

"Let's go to the pharmacy, honey," Dolores said. "You can get a morning after pill on demand. Our pharmacist isn't one of the religious nut cases. He understands reality and will give you what you need."

"Yes. Yes. I need to do that. I can't have a child with a man who cheats on me. I can't even live with him."

Dolores and Erin left the diner to walk the block to the drugstore on the corner. Through her tears, Erin explained what she needed and the pharmacist got the package and carefully explained the instructions. Erin thanked her and they went back to the diner where Dolores got her a glass of water. Erin looked at the pill in her hand a long time before she put it in her mouth and swallowed it with the water.

"God damn that fucking bastard!"

Dolores turned the restaurant over to her senior waitress and escorted Erin back out of the diner to her car. They drove to Dolores's house and went inside to have a quiet chat. She made tea. Perhaps she'd overstepped her bounds when she suggested the morning after pill, but pregnancy should be a joyous situation. She was genuinely concerned that Erin might hurt herself if she found out she was, indeed, pregnant. This way, no one would ever know. If they reconciled, they could begin the process again.

"It wasn't supposed to be like this," Erin moaned. "We were supposed to spend the day talking about our plans. Guessing if we'd have a boy or girl. Thinking about our happily ever after. How could he do this? How could he take away our dreams?"

"What did you tell him, honey?"

"I told him to get out and that I never wanted to see him again," Erin sobbed. "And I don't! Dolores, I'm terrible. He made a mistake. One little mistake and I threw him away. What if I'm wrong? What if I threw away my one great chance at happiness? What if *I'm* the terrible person?"

"Well, you'll stay here tonight. In the morning, things will look clearer to you. You aren't in any condition to re-evaluate things when you are so hurt," Dolores said.

"What... um... What about your husband?" Erin asked.

"Henry's harmless. We made it through our rough patches years ago and reached détente. Come on. I've fixed Dennis's room up as a guest room. He didn't like it much when he came home for Christmas, but he left for school again yesterday. I already washed the sheets."

Erin went with Dolores and the two women talked well into the night, with the help of a bottle of Chardonnay.

"I DON'T KNOW. Maybe I'm not as ready as I thought I was. Maybe I'm not even as mature as I thought I was. Dolores, when I was working, I could handle a meeting with a couple hundred people in it. I could make decisions that affected people's lives and bank accounts. I approved quarter-million-dollar purchases. I thought I was a good judge of character. Maybe I'm not any of those things."

"You made a huge adjustment when you decided to marry, quit your job, and move five hundred miles away," Dolores said. She hadn't known the extent of Erin's experience and authority, but she couldn't say it surprised her. Even in the restaurant, there was no employee Dolores trusted more. "Maybe it was just too soon to try to make all the dreams happen at once."

"Would it have made a difference? Would it just mean that it would have been longer before I found out what kind of guy I married? I feel like such a dunce!" Erin declared.

"How long did you study to manage a business like you did?" Dolores asked.

"Four years of college and two for an MBA. I started as an intern with Allard when I was a senior and worked there ten years. They paid for my master's."

"And you think you could know everything about a man in a year? Married people keep finding out about each other for years and years. What does Bruce dream of? What does a happy life look like to him?"

"A fresh vagina for his dick every few months," Erin growled.

"Well, you can't really make that assessment based on one night."

"I'm not," Erin sighed. "He confessed that last night wasn't his first night with that woman. They've been going to St. Louis on business together for the past several weeks. And there was a woman at a company outing in Cleveland. I made up my mind that I wouldn't say anything about it because Sue could be very insistent and Bruce and I weren't married yet. I blamed her. She knew I saw. She even winked at me when they got back. I don't feel like I need to make another exception every six months."

"Oh, honey. I wish there was anything I could say or do that would make this easier. I'm afraid you are in for a rough few months. Just remember, you have friends. We'll still be here. We might not have solutions to your problems, but we have shoulders to cry on and arms to hug you. We're here."

Chapter Six

PRESTON STOOD ON a hill, looking down toward the lake. It was almost like being transferred into the terrain map in his office. He knew where every land feature was and how to navigate among them. He couldn't talk to people, but he could talk to the land—and it answered.

His grandfather said Preston had a gift for spatial analysis. He could call it whatever he wanted. The way Preston's mind worked, he could visualize a completed project before the first shovel of dirt was turned. He'd come to this piece of land on a fishing trip when he was barely in his teens. From his boat on the water, he looked up at the gently rising slopes and saw the entire Cloudhaven community in his mind's eye. He'd talked his grandfather into acquiring a little cabin on the lake and Preston had spent many hours in the seclusion it offered, sketching and drawing his vision. Over the years, he'd maneuvered to have the family acquire more than a thousand acres of shoreland in the name of Interlake Holding Company.

He'd had soil tests done, environmental studies, and surveys. He held his plat map in hand as he looked out over the terrain. He would have the surveyors out first thing after the New Year to lay out the streets. He was not happy about the holdout on a single parcel of land, but he could work around it if he had to.

Preston had done several fly-overs of the property with his

grandfather, taking hundreds of photographs, from which they'd created the terrain map. But the next steps would require the board of directors to approve the project. Of late, the board had been tightening the belt on speculative projects—partly as a result of the pandemic. People were slow to get back on board with development. Preston's research, however, showed people with money were much more interested in developing unique community concepts than in office buildings like the Mackenzie project. That project had definitely gone sideways this week.

Preston would depend on Royce's ability to sell the Cloudhaven concept to the board. He wished he could do it himself, but it would be bad enough to attend the board meeting. He'd rap the gavel and call the meeting to order, then turn it over to Royce. He would sit at the head of the table in a suit and tie and his mask, listening to everything that was said, and would dismiss the meeting. The week before a board meeting, he would meet with Royce for hours every day, making sure he understood exactly what needed to be sold. Royce would take care of convincing people. That's what the chief operating officer was there for.

Preston stepped up on a stump.

"This is where the front desk of the hotel will be," he said. His grandfather looked up at him.

"I want to get a GPS reading on that location," the spry old man laughed. "I'll check it against the actual location when the hotel is built."

"I'm going to have a house just down the street—not as massive as Jerico House, but it will still be impressive. Right up behind the cabin. Cathedral ceiling and floor to ceiling windows looking down over the lake. I'll see the sunrise over the water every morning."

"It's a seventy-mile commute to the office in Jerico City," Lawrence said.

"We won't need to worry about it," Preston said. "I don't see anyone at the office anyway. I can just as well telecommute."

"I've been thinking about that. You should be seen more often in the office. I believe people are beginning to think you are a ghost. I don't mean you need to stop and talk to people, but come down floor by floor and just walk through the office like you own it. You do.

You might find out some interesting things about your employees," Lawrence said.

"I suppose."

"You said 'we won't need to worry about it,' a minute ago. Who is the 'we?'"

"Oh, me and my mythical wife and children. I'm thinking I'll just have to wait in a duck blind out here until I see a woman I like and rush out to capture her. I'll show her the house and invite her to stay. That will be all the conversation we'll have."

"You know you'll never be happy with that. Take a look around the office. I know there are single women there."

"I don't think I should date in the office pool. They're going to hate me when the pink slips come out anyway," Preston sighed. "Mackenzie is defaulting. I'll have to let fifty people go. The first thing Royce needs to get done in January is complete our investor portfolio. We need $100 million in guaranteed funding in order to break ground in April. It's going to be tight."

"Take care of your housekeeping. We've been planning this community for fifteen years. If we need to plan another year, it won't hurt a thing."

"It's getting cold. We should head back. I don't want my G-Pop to get too cold."

"Let's get a cup of coffee in Willington on the way."

"THE HUMANE THING is to execute the layoffs immediately," Royce said. "We know who is going to be cut. We should give them a nice Christmas gift this afternoon and their pink slips. They'll be ready to start their job searches on New Year's Day."

"No. No layoffs before the holiday. It's bad enough to do it at this time of year at all. Are you sure we need to lay off so many?" Preston insisted.

"You've already cut it from fifty, which was the recommendation from finance, to thirty. With Mackenzie defaulting, we need to act as soon as possible. Two more weeks on the payroll means five more people cut."

"We can handle this with the severance package I've put together. We'll have some volunteers. None of our workers deserve this," Preston insisted. "I'll finalize it and have it back to you this weekend. We'll make the cuts on January second."

"You're soft, Preston. It isn't about what people deserve."

PRESTON WENT THROUGH the list again, trying to decide if there were any exceptions he should make to the staff cuts proposed by HR. In general, they followed standard rules. Most were simply listed by department, position, and last name. There were no notations concerning age, salary, seniority, or other characteristics. It was supposed to be fairer that way. Of course, Preston knew how to look each of his employees up on the network and had access to their employment records.

As he looked through the five hundred employees and contractors in their database, he finally paused when he saw a familiar face. Not far down the list of that department's employees was another image he recognized. He looked through the cuts designated for that department and gave two borderline employees a reprieve. In their stead, he entered the names of the two men who had given his waitress such a hard time in the diner a few weeks ago. His company didn't need people like that.

There were many things Preston didn't like about controlling his family's company. Decisions like letting thirty people go were among them. But there was also the sham of trying to keep the appearance of corporate health, when he himself couldn't stand in front of the employees and wish them a Merry Christmas without hyperventilating. Royce handled that.

Royce had already made the presentation to the board of directors, justifying the cutbacks, and describing the severance package that would be granted to the laid off employees. The board congratulated him on the humane treatment of the severed workers.

As if Royce had anything to do with it. Preston had met with his HR director and CFO and worked out the details in an hours-long meeting. He didn't want to dismiss anyone and did so with great care for their well-being. Royce would have simply scattered pink slips randomly through the office on Christmas Eve.

The thing was, with Royce's flair and charisma, he probably could have done it without offending anyone. They wouldn't know they'd been screwed until sometime next year. All the contractors working on the Mackenzie project had already been notified that the project was halted.

Soft-hearted and overwhelmed by anxiety in the presence of others, Preston had to content himself with sitting alone in his penthouse office and let others carry out the mission he set before them.

PRESTON HAD AN obligation to his mother. Personally, he thought a date on Christmas weekend was a disaster to start. His mother had assured him that a suitable venue was available. The Jerico Madrigal Singers put on a production before Christmas. That was fine by Preston. He enjoyed music and going to a performance freed him from most interaction with the woman he was accompanying.

He pulled his six-year-old sedan out of the office parking ramp. This had been his mother's idea, too. Left to Preston, he'd only drive the pickup truck, but his mother insisted it wasn't appropriate to take on a date. He drove to the address his mother had given him. It was an older home on the northwest side of town. He parked, took a deep breath, and went to the door.

"Who's here?" a deep voice sounded. The door opened and a small mountain of a man filled the frame. "Yes?"

At six-two, Preston wasn't a small man, but this guy had him by at least two inches and seventy pounds. Intimidating.

"Uh… uh… I… I'm Preston. I'm… I'm here to pick up J-J-Janice," he managed to get out. The mountain looked him up and down.

"Kind of old, aren't you?" he demanded.

"I-I-I'm thirty-two."

"That's what I mean."

"Daddy! Stop intimidating my date," a woman behind him said. He stepped aside and Preston saw a young woman in her early twenties. He wanted to ask the man to pardon him, and admit he was definitely too old. Janice took over the interaction, though. "Hi! I'm Janice. You must be Preston. Your mom told me all about you, so don't worry about a thing. I'm harmless. And so's Daddy most of the time. I'll be home by one, Daddy. If I'm late, don't worry. I'm a big girl and can take care of myself. And Preston's a nice guy. Help me with my coat, Preston?"

She handed Preston a winter coat and he held it while she slipped her arms into the sleeves.

"Have… uh… fun," the mountain of a man said. He closed the door behind them.

"Don't let Daddy bother you. He's really a big teddy bear. He always puts on a gruff act the first time a boy picks me up for a date. This is a nice car. Is it new? It looks so clean and shiny."

Preston held the door open for her and she slid into the seat. He took another deep breath as he walked around the car, wishing he was eating leftovers in his apartment. He'd yet to say anything since admitting his age to the girl's father. He got into the car and she was off again.

"I know your Mom said you don't talk much. I think that's cool. I guess I talk enough for two people anyway. You look nice," Janice said.

"Um… Six years," Preston said.

"Huh?"

"The car. Not new."

"Oh! Yeah! I kind of figured that out. I didn't think you looked like the kind of guy who went out to buy a new car every year. Bet you drive them until they don't go any farther and then get another one. That's what I'd do with a car like this. You keep it really clean and shiny. It feels so warm and comfy. Oh! It's got seat warmers! That's why. Thank you for warming it up for me. They say it's going to get down to twenty or something tonight. Of course, not right now. But it's still nice to have the seat warmer."

Preston pulled away from the curb and headed into town. He didn't know why he let his mother talk him into a blind date like this. First, there would be an interminable dinner. At least the food would be good. Janice was nice to look at, but he wasn't sure he'd still have ears by the time the evening ended.

"I know your mom from the beauty salon where she gets her hair done. I'm not like just a typical haircutter, though, you know? I mean, I could certainly cut your hair and it would look great, but I like to find the essence of the person and bring that out in the hair style. I went to the Paul Davis Atelier School of Beauty all the way up in Minneapolis, so I feel like I was really well trained, you know?"

Preston pulled into the valet parking at La Boheme, a restaurant he felt was far too fancy for a first date, but his mother had made reservations. In his experience, that just set the expectation of him being a big spender. And often it said he expected something in return from the date. He didn't. He wasn't into meeting a woman and going to bed with her. He just wanted to survive the evening. In fact, it had been a long time since he'd been to bed with a woman.

"So, this is nice," Janice said as they were seated. "You know, you don't have to spend a lot on me. I mean, I'm impressed and everything, but it doesn't change anything about the evening. I want to have fun, like you do. I'm excited about going to the madrigal performance. Christmas is like my favorite time of year. I feel like a little kid during this season. Like, I'm going to look up the chimney for Santa on Christmas Eve."

"Um… uh… H-How old… are you?"

"Oh, wow. I don't like to talk about that because then people don't take me seriously, you know? I'm twenty-three, but everyone says I'm really mature for my age. Like, I'm not going to talk about boy bands or try to get you to go to a rave or anything. I'm really kind of a homebody, you know?"

Preston didn't know what she meant by that. Unless pushed, he didn't leave his apartment. That was a homebody. Janice seemed much more social. And he couldn't imagine being trapped in his apartment with her non-stop narrative.

Occasionally, however, Janice tossed something quite unexpected into the conversation.

"Did you see the article in *Social Style* on the resurgence of Art Nouveau decorating in public buildings? I mean, really, it doesn't surprise me. Style is a cyclical thing and old styles will resurface periodically. But with the new conservatism in society, I didn't expect such a turn toward decorative vines and flowers. Not that I think that's all Art Nouveau is. Like the dragon staircase in your mother's home definitely shows the sinuous curves of the style, but preceded the introduction of the Art Nouveau style by fifty years or more. There were many things in the early Victorian style that paved the way for the later style."

"Nature um... is often... an inspiration," Preston managed.

"Yes. You see that all the way back in ancient Greek architecture. What was it? The Corinthian capitals that were all leaves and flowers? I try to take all that into consideration when I'm designing a hair style. People should reflect the style of their surroundings. Don't you think?"

It was a great intro to a topic Preston could feasibly discuss. He certainly knew enough about it, having studied architecture, urban planning, and history for most of his life. Unfortunately, however, by the time he had collected a thought to contribute to the conversation, Janice had moved on to places in the world she had traveled and her preference for air travel over rail, even for short hops in Europe, because you never know what you're going to get on a railroad, you know.

Preston escorted Janice out of the restaurant after he had settled the bill with his signature and called for his car. In the theatre, Janice was finally quiet, though Preston could sense that not talking was a strain on her. She took his hand and frequently squeezed during a piece of music she liked.

The madrigal was mostly secular Christmas music from the sixteenth and seventeenth centuries. The theatre at the School of Arts included more than just singing the carols. There were also some spoken recitations, Morris dancers, and mini dramas. And naturally, there were a few of the more traditional religious songs that had everyone in the audience singing along.

Preston led the way from the theatre to where he'd parked, nodding to people who greeted him, but not really saying anything. No one expected him to say anything. Janice kept hold of his hand and continued to hum some of the songs they'd heard. It was a very 'feel good' performance, and even Preston left a little lighthearted.

"You know, Preston, you wouldn't need to take me home right

away. We could go someplace… more private. You're such a nice guy and a great listener. We could continue the night as long as you'd like," she said.

There it was! She'd tolerated an entire evening with him and now she was laying the trap! If the evening went beyond a goodnight kiss, it would imply an obligation. Preston was on guard at once.

"Um… Not um… proper, you know?" he managed. "I would n-n-not presume on you um… for more than… you know… a first date."

"You are so sweet and respectful. A 'first' date implies there will be more. I do hope you've had as much fun as I have."

"N-n-nice. Thank you."

He walked her to the door as she clutched his arm tightly. Once on the porch, she did not let go, but pressed herself to him and lifted her lips to his. As soon as they touched, she wrapped a hand around the back of his neck and kissed him insistently. It was breathtaking.

Preston had to actively extract himself from her embrace and step back.

"Th-th-thank you. Nice evening," he said. "Goodnight."

He stepped backward off the porch and nearly tripped down the steps on his way to the car.

"Goodnight until next time, Preston," she sighed.

She went into the house and Preston could see the shadow of her father through the open door. He got directly in his car and pulled away.

PRESTON RETURNED TO his parking spot at the office and stumbled to the elevator. Once in the apartment, he hung his coat and hat, and kicked off his shoes. He was exhausted and wondered if he had ever listened to more words in such a short period of time before.

He plopped down in his sitting area with a glass of scotch and idly flipped through the television stations until he came upon an old black and white Christmas movie. Outside his window, it began to snow.

Hmm. He could have had company watching his old movie, but he was absolutely certain it would have come with obligations. And she probably would have talked instead of watching the movie.

A good listener? There was no chance to say anything. Not that he would have been eloquent, but he might have done more than nod his head. He set the drink aside and grabbed the 4x4x4 Rubik's Cube from the side table.

Before it was solved, he was asleep on the sofa with the movie still playing.

Chapter Seven

"WITH AN EMPLOYEE?"** Royce bellowed. "You know better than to get it on with an employee!"

"He was convenient, good looking, and well hung. You can't expect me to do without all the time."

Shannon didn't feel bad about sleeping with Bruce. It had been fun. She was pretty sure Royce had spent at least one night this week with that classless beautician. If she was anything with him like she was in the beauty parlor, he'd have had to gag her to get her to stop talking. At least Bruce was an intelligent guy, and not looking to wreck her home.

"I've never complained about little affairs—and you haven't either. But there has always been one rock-solid restriction. Not with anyone in the company! What does it look like when the president's wife is getting boned by one of his employees? Do you think people won't find out and talk? Your lover would be passed over even for legitimate promotions, just because it might look like favoritism. It's that Bruce guy in architecture and planning, isn't it? The one on the Mackenzie project. I should have known with all the trips to St. Louis. I expected so much better of you!"

"Like me sleeping with a guy you're trying to cut a deal with? What was getting a commitment from our little consortium in St. Louis worth? Certainly, it was worth sharing your wife," she fumed.

Not that Royce had to pressure her to sleep with the developer they'd met in St. Louis. But the guy was at least fifty. Gross. If it hadn't been for her having pulled the deal together in the first place, they wouldn't be sitting pretty now. Royce could sell anything, but it was Shannon who identified the opportunity that Interlake Land Holding was going to provide. They'd almost been too late to acquire the piece that would be big enough for a golf course.

"I'd be better off without you," Royce shot at her.

"Don't even think about it. If you try to divorce me for infidelity, I have enough evidence against you for the same to get the entire pre-nup thrown out. You'll become the penniless president of JeriCorp."

"Ha!"

Royce poured himself a glass of bourbon, then put two ice cubes in a second glass and poured for his wife. He handed her the glass. Anyone looking in on their bizarre relationship would believe they hated each other. Divorcing Shannon was unthinkable. He'd broken his own rule when he started dating the young finance person in his company. And it had been worth it. They were a team.

"We're quite a pair, aren't we?" he chuckled.

"A marriage made in hell." They clinked their glasses together.

"Mostly hell for others," he said. "It isn't all that bad."

"We have our moments," Shannon laughed, glad to put aside the shouting at each other. Royce could be so dominating, it turned her on. "By the way, you know that bit you were out with this week is only after one thing."

"That was obvious. Did you know she was out with Preston last weekend? Didn't take long for that to fizzle."

"I was a little preoccupied that night. Preston's smart enough to keep a girl from taking half his empire. Are you?"

"Yes, but I'm also smart enough to use a condom. Preston dropped her off and never called her back."

"Well, at least you know I'm not sleeping with anyone who wants to replace you."

"That girl could never take your place. She had some talents, though."

"Do tell." Shannon put her glass down and put her arms around her husband's neck. "Better yet, show me."

They'd start celebrating New Year's Eve a couple of nights early. Shannon could feel fireworks coming on.

"I'VE GOT TO tell you, Preston, it will be hard to sell Cloudhaven in the wake of the upcoming layoffs," Royce said as they met in Preston's sitting area. They spoke quietly so Mrs. Armstrong couldn't hear them at the other end of the room.

"It's the way of our future. It's not dependent on... on someone else's profits. Not like Mackenzie. I never much liked that partnership."

"You designed it," Royce said.

"The design was good. Mackenzie wasn't. I think we could foreclose on the property and continue construction under our own name. It's speculative, but we could have it near completion before we can get anything constructed at the lake."

"I like that idea. The bank there was friendly until Mackenzie defaulted. We could buy it out for pennies on the dollar. And then get them to fund the completion."

"That's thinking. It's why you sit in the big chair."

"You sit in the big chair, Preston. Don't ever think I don't remember that. I wish you could make these presentations to the board."

"Don't worry. I'll provide the slide deck and narrative for you. You just need to sell it—like always," Preston said.

"We need to let it rest a while and take the jobs in order. First, the personnel. Second, Mackenzie. Third, Cloudhaven. It's the only way they'll understand it."

"I can be patient."

Royce took the folder of papers on Cloudhaven with him. He'd need to study this carefully for the next month. He'd run it by Shannon, as well.

He went to his office. It wasn't as large as Preston's, but he didn't live in it, either. Still, it was an opulent corner office overlooking Main Street. He had maximum visibility to employees. His secretary carefully guarded access to his inner sanctum, but he emerged several times a day to walk around the company, stopping to greet employees and ask about their projects, their families, and even the latest sports scores.

That was what Preston didn't understand. Glad-handing the employees made them think they were important. He looked out over the open office on the fourth floor and contemplated how many people would be gone on Tuesday.

He opened the folder of employment cuts that Preston had given him. There was one adjustment he needed to make and no one needed to know he'd changed it.

THE DAY AFTER New Year's was turning out to be a very bad day for Bruce. He'd tried to talk to Erin over the weekend, but she told him she never wanted to see or hear from him again. He didn't blame her. Erin was more loyal than anyone he'd ever met. It was one of the things that attracted him to her, even though he wasn't in her league when it came to love and loyalty.

He guessed he'd need to be the one to file for divorce. Mostly because he didn't want to be the one served papers.

When he got to the office Tuesday morning, he was conscious of people looking at him. He couldn't be imagining the hushed tones in the office or furtive glances as he walked by. How could anyone even know? He didn't think Shannon was the kind of woman who spread word of her conquests around the office. It would harm her ability to do her job, just like it would hurt him. He sat at his desk, expecting to get started on a normal day. He'd been told to start putting together a plan to recover the Mackenzie project without Mackenzie involved.

First, email. There was a new meeting request, sent out that morning by his boss for a one-on-one. Bruce wasn't worried about his performance and figured this would be about how to approach continuing the project. He'd managed the design reviews and meetings with Mackenzie perfectly. It wasn't his fault that the company defaulted. He got his notes and files together and went to meet his boss in the downstairs conference room.

Ellen Barrett was with his boss. He hadn't seen her since his initial interviews with HR months ago.

"Bruce, have a seat," his boss said. "There's no easy way to put this, so I'll get right to the point. The Mackenzie project put a big hole in our finances when it was canceled. They announced they were filing bankruptcy and closing their doors. We have no choice but to eliminate our expenses for the project as quickly as possible. I'm afraid that means you and your team have been terminated."

"Terminated? You mean fired?" Bruce asked in disbelief. "But what about taking over the project independently from Mackenzie? I have the folder here with all the numbers in it."

"I'm afraid so, Bruce," Ellen said. "We have people with longer service. Last in, first out. The entire company is being affected, not just your team. We've cut five percent of our employees, plus several contractors. I know you relocated to Jerico City recently and I want you to know the company is still committed to covering your relo costs, a portion of your housing, and we're giving you a three-month severance package that includes your health benefits for that period. You should probably be sure you and your wife get doctor, dentist, and optometry appointments taken care of in that period of time."

"Doctors," Bruce mumbled. *What if Erin was pregnant? This could be even more disastrous than getting divorced.*

There was more. He had to sign a letter accepting the benefits. Ellen said something about an employment agency and assistance preparing his resume. And then a security person accompanied him to his desk and watched as he packed the few personal items he had there, collected his ID badge, and escorted him out.

ON WEDNESDAY, BRUCE waited at the diner until Erin got off work and met her outside. She agreed to sit down and talk at the house when he told her he had important news he needed to share with her. Erin assumed it was about getting a divorce.

Instead, he told her he'd been fired and they had just three months of income to live on. It was shocking news.

"If I had any faith in you, I'd consider it just another rough spot we needed to get control of," she said. "But what are you going to do now? Is there anything left here in Jerico City for you? We were supposed to have a good life so we could build together for our family. You threw us away before your company threw you away. I gave you everything. I borrowed against my 401k to make a down payment on this house and turned it into a livable home. I made you meals. I gave you sex whenever you wanted. I got a job so I could be a contributor. All for what?"

"I admit it all. I failed, Erin, not you. I'm not asking you to reconsider. I'll get the papers drawn up. You need to know I got three months' severance. There's no way we can keep the house past that."

Erin heaved a big sigh. She didn't really want to come back to the house again anyway, though she was afraid she'd need to before her welcome wore out at Dolores's house.

"I'll call Livy Olson and get it on the market," she said. Bruce nodded.

BRUCE ALWAYS THOUGHT Erin had a fiery temperament, but the reality was she had high expectations for people and didn't easily tolerate disappointment. Bruce would 'do the right thing' by her and file for divorce. It would be easier for both of them if they just started over. Erin had been a rising exec in a national company when they met. Bruce had been an architect with a small firm in Cleveland. He'd promised Erin they would build the life they dreamed of. And he destroyed it.

"Mr. Sample will see you now," the secretary at the law office said.

Bruce was conducted into a neat, but not elaborate office. This lawyer specialized in domestic issues, including divorce. Bruce just hoped he didn't try to take too big a cut as his fee.

"Mr. Silvers, how can I help you today?" the lawyer asked.

"How quickly can I get a divorce?" Bruce asked bluntly.

"Thirty days from filing. Is that what you want? No chance of reconciliation?"

"No," Bruce said, not committing to what question he was answering. "It shouldn't be too messy. Equal division of assets. No children. The only major drawback is the house we just bought. She can have it. She owns most of it anyway."

"Hmm. Your wife is able to afford the house?"

"Probably not. It will go on the market. I can't afford it now, either. I lost my job. I'll sign my share over to her."

"O-kay. Let's go over the process, the costs, and start the wheels in motion. If after our meeting today, you decide this isn't the right thing to do, I'll waive the fees. If we go beyond today, the standard fees will be due. Here's my rate card."

Bruce drew a deep breath and nodded. Of course, maybe it would be easier if he drove off a cliff somewhere, but he wasn't that depressed. Maybe he'd pick up some cute girl on his drive back to Cleveland.

THURSDAY, ROYCE WALKED all five floors of the office, comforting and reassuring employees as he'd done the past two days. He assured them there were no additional layoffs planned and this had been a direct result of their largest client defaulting and declaring bankruptcy. It was vital the employees have faith in his leadership. None of them knew he was just a mouthpiece for Preston. They didn't know Preston. By the time Royce had added his spin to the layoffs, people were believing the company was on the verge of a new era of profitability.

He walked into Shannon's office and his wife smiled at him.

"What's the temperature of the company today?" he asked.

"It spiked late yesterday. Things are settling in to normal today. We already have employees raiding the spaces of those terminated for everything from staplers to more comfortable desk chairs to abandoned plants," she said.

Shannon was a vital link for Royce in the office. In her role as a financial controller, she had plenty of opportunity to talk to others and assess weaknesses. She'd shown that ability soon after coming to JeriCorp after college. And she applied the same principles to leveraging human capital as she applied to leveraging money. She'd exercised that ability when she decided Royce would be the right one to attach herself to.

She was probably smarter than Royce was, but Royce had the ability to put a good face on anything. Whatever scheme Preston came up with, he could sell. And Shannon was valuable to him for providing the insights and information from lower in the company.

"I'm still a little pissed that you cut Bruce. Was that necessary?" she asked.

"Not my call, you know. Preston signed off on all the cuts," Royce said. Actually, it *had* been his call when he came into the office the previous Friday and edited the list before handing it off to HR. "It's for the better, though. No word of your dalliance escaped. No one's the wiser."

"It wasn't that big a deal, honey," Shannon said. "When do you think Preston will be ready to move on that resort project? I need to talk to our consortium and reassure them it's happening. We've been holding that piece of property for two years."

"He'll move on it this spring. He wants to lay out the street grid as soon as the snow clears."

"I sure hope it pays."

"It will, honey. Sweet talk those St. Louis boys and keep them in line. We'll be set for life."

Yes, Royce could overlook Shannon's infidelities, just as she overlooked his. Hers were often more profitable. Together they were unstoppable.

"THE SPECIAL TODAY is a hot roast beef sandwich with gravy and mashed potatoes," Erin said when she'd seated Preston that day. "May I assume you'd like to try it?"

"Yes, thank you," Preston said. Something was off. "Are you okay, Maizie?"

"I thought we were set for life," she sniffed. "But my husband proved he couldn't be trusted. He cheated on me and we're getting a divorce. Happy New Year."

"I-I am so s-s-sorry, Maizie," he said. He didn't usually stutter in the diner, but emotion turned him into a wreck.

"Oh, Jerry, I don't mean to burden you with my problems. You look kind of down yourself."

"I had to make some difficult business decisions this week. I'm sure some people were hurt by them."

"You're so sensitive. You need to take care of yourself. People recover from our kind of problems all the time. We will, too."

"Are you going to stay in Jerico City?" Preston asked. It would be terrible if her divorce caused her to move away.

"I think so. I'm meeting with the real estate agent this weekend to list the house because I can't afford it on what I make here. I've got an appointment Monday with an employment agency and plan to start papering the town with my resume. When I moved here, I didn't think I'd need a higher paying job, but the idea of children is off the table now. I'll be a working girl again."

"A working girl?" Preston had little social interaction, but the term brought a very specific image to mind. He hoped he misunderstood.

"A girl who goes to work at 8:00 and goes home at 5:00," she laughed. "Let me get your order in, or you'll be late getting back from lunch."

Erin busied herself getting his lunch and waiting on her other tables. Preston focused on his food. He wondered if there was any way he could help her without revealing who he was. He could scarcely offer her a job after having just fired thirty people.

"I DIDN'T EXPECT to see this house on the market again so soon," Livy said Saturday morning when she met with Erin.

"I didn't expect to be single again," Erin said as she sat at the table with the real estate agent.

"Oh, dear! Will we have difficulty getting a clear title?"

"My husband filed the divorce Wednesday and left town on Friday. He gave me a quit-claim deed for the house."

"You know the quit-claim deed doesn't excuse him from his liability to the bank for the mortgage," Livy said.

"I have three months of mortgage payments guaranteed before I have to go into default. It was part of his severance package."

"Oh dear. Lost his job, too? I guess that pretty clearly defines our timeframe for getting this sold. Will you be looking for work?"

"I'm getting ready to paper the town with my resume. It seems there are quite a few people suddenly out of work after the holidays. The agency told me it could be a long process, though they thought my resume was good if they can find a position commensurate with my experience."

"Yes, everyone has heard about the cutbacks at JeriCorp and seem to believe they signal a downturn to the economy. Other businesses are following their lead. Let's start the listing at ten percent above what you paid for the house. That might be too much to ask, but we can adjust downward if necessary."

"I'll keep it ready to show at any time," Erin said. When Bruce left town on Friday, Erin decided she needed to move back into the house and out of Dolores's home. It was hard to be in the house alone, but she disciplined herself to accept what happened and get on with her life.

"Good. You will be living here, then. We should take down the holiday decorations and make the house as market ready as possible. Let me give you a hand."

Erin signed the contract and Livy stayed to help her put away the Christmas decorations. Erin was thankful for the help, but even more for the company, as she was near tears with every ornament she packed.

Chapter Eight

PRESTON SAT IN his office listening to Mrs. Armstrong berate him for the cutbacks in the company. He'd about had it with her. She'd wasted no opportunity in the past week to tell him how cruel he was.

She'd started her employment with him the previous summer, demure and efficient. She became more caustic and aggravating the longer she worked for him. When she'd found out about the layoffs, she instantly started defending people.

"Surely, firing Georgia in the development group isn't going to save enough to make a difference to the company. But it will make all the difference in the world to Georgia. She has three children and her husband is on disability. What kind of heartless monster would fire her?"

"I don't know. I approved the cut list; I didn't create it," Preston growled.

"As if you don't know everything that happens in this company. Other people might be fooled by you sitting in this private office and never appearing in public, but you can't hide from me. Mr. Carver, this isn't like you."

"No, it isn't like me. I hated every second of it. And I hate hearing you talk about it. I'm responsible for the company, not an individual employee in development. If we can get Cloudhaven off the ground this spring, maybe we can start hiring people back again. But every-one is at risk if we don't make the cuts necessary now," Preston said slamming a Rubik's Cube down on his desk.

"Well, like usual, Mr. Duval blamed you for the cutbacks and went around the office encouraging employees with his smile. You need to address the company so they know you are not a heartless villain."

"I can't do that."

"You do fine in this office. Why not in the auditorium?"

"This office is safe. Even you, when you are being intolerable, are safe. I can't speak to everyone. It's bad enough that I have to go to the board meeting and listen to Royce explain things to them. I doubt that I'll even go to the meeting this week."

"Of course you will," Mrs. Armstrong said, softening. "I know you are smarter and more creative than anyone in the company. Having a little speech impediment doesn't change that."

"It's not a sp-speech imp-ediment!" he said getting frustrated. "I'm going to go take a nap. Don't disturb me."

"Of course, Mr. Carver. You go get some sleep. It's safer up in your bed."

Preston glared at her and stomped upstairs.

INGRID ARMSTRONG WATCHED Preston go up to his nest on the next floor. She'd had about all she could take of his temperamental outbursts. So, he stuttered a little. She'd scarcely heard it in his voice in the past two months. They'd worked out initial rough spots after she went to work for him.

But when there was real pressure on him, he went to bed like a three-year-old, covering his head to hide from the monsters. Or he worked one of the damned Rubik's Cubes. She went around the office apartment spotting the cubes wherever he left them, and scrambling them again. It seemed they were the only things he ever left out of place in the office.

Mrs. Armstrong did not appreciate being delegated the domestic jobs Preston wanted done. When she started, it had been explained to her as if he were handicapped and needed assistance. She would be his personal assistant, given as many domestic tasks as professional tasks. She picked up his laundry and cleaning to send out and made sure it was properly put away. She supervised the cleaners who came in twice a week. She ordered his groceries, which were delivered to the elevator where she took charge of putting them away.

It had been fine when she started, but she soon discovered his only handicap was his stuttering and ridiculous panic attacks. He kept the apartment office fairly clean on his own and it was only his obsession with cleanliness that required cleaners to come in at all. He made his own bed and did his own dishes. Immediately. When a dish was used, it was washed and put away. There were no dishes in the kitchen sink or drying on a rack. He was quite capable of all these tasks.

As a result, she complained or did a slipshod job on some of them. Preston responded with a raised voice and she retreated to her desk where she handled his business relations. For as much as a week she would speak to him only by way of email. She knew what she needed to do and could not understand why Mr. Carver didn't understand what he needed to do. It was like having an adversary in the office rather than a boss.

He'd never even invited her to share one of his gourmet dinner creations. She was sure that if he hadn't been born into the Jerico family, he'd have become a chef. She went over his grocery lists each week and was amazed at the things he ordered.

It wasn't as if he expected sex from his assistant. Well, Mrs. Armstrong was older than his mother. But in some ways, he expected all the other duties of a nice domestic housewife.

Not that he would ever attract a wife. If he expected her to act like his personal assistant, she would be gone before she arrived.

Mrs. Armstrong sat at her desk and composed an email message to the full company, explaining the necessary cutbacks from the office of the chairman. It would be on Preston's computer when he had hidden long enough and he could sign and send it.

Then she looked at the map of the resort development and picked up the pieces of a building, thinking she could put them together.

They didn't fit the way she thought, though, and she quickly gave up on it. She went back to her desk to run the numbers on what would be saved through the layoffs.

IT WAS TWO weeks later that the lid blew off the pressure cooker and Mrs. Armstrong threw her hands in the air in frustration.

"That does it! Mr. Carver, I don't need to put up with your abuse any longer!" Mrs. Armstrong said.

"What abuse?" Preston asked. "I simply want you to do your job the way I want it done! Is that too much to ask?"

"I am not your mother. Playing with your Rubik's Cubes is bad enough, but listening to you complain about your underwear not being folded correctly is just too much," she said. "I don't know what you will do without me taking care of actual important things, like your memo to the company or the board minutes, but I'm not a domestic servant. You have no right to ask me to shop for your groceries and do your laundry. Now, complaining there are scraps of your model under the table is beyond the pale. You dropped them there! You have house cleaners for cleaning. If they still come to clean for you after the last temper tantrum you threw."

"I didn't throw a t-temper t-tantrum!" Preston objected. "I explained h-h-how I want it done."

"Well, explain it to your next assistant!" Mrs. Armstrong yelled. "If you can find one! I quit!"

"Please, Mrs. Armstrong…"

"No, Mr. Carver. I've had enough. I don't need you adding to my gray hair. I'll stop at HR and turn in my keycard."

Mrs. Armstrong snatched up her purse and headed to the elevator. Her purse was all the personal possessions she had in the office. Preston had objected to her bringing personal things into his home. It would be too much like living together.

He flopped in a chair next to the window and gazed out at the snow on his rooftop patio. It would be melted soon. The plat map for Cloudhaven was finished. He'd sent the plans to the engineering department for specifications of the needed utilities and streets.

They would divide it into proper phases and get it ready for survey and construction. This was all work he could direct to be done without board approval. It required no additional investment and was fully within the scope of the department's responsibilities.

Next was preparing building plans for spring. Before they could break ground, though, he needed board approval to create the partnership for the community and get financing. The time was coming quickly.

He solved a Rubik's Cube and set it aside. He really needed an assistant.

"I THOUGHT YOU were getting on well with Mrs. Armstrong," Jacqueline said at Sunday dinner. Preston sat with his mother and grandfather the first Sunday of February, as he did on most Sundays.

"She turned into a real bitch," Preston said. "She actually complained to me about the staff cuts and demanded that I reinstate a friend of hers. She blew up when I pointed out there were modeling scraps under the table that hadn't been swept up. And taking care of my laundry was not a new responsibility. She's been in charge of that and the groceries since day one. There was no reason for her to start simply shoving things helter-skelter into my drawers. The socks weren't even mated. I just want the jobs done right. I require that of all employees; it isn't new for my assistant."

"Well, she's right. You need a wife," Lawrence said. "Once you pay a woman to do those things, you realize how wives who do them are vastly undercompensated."

"I'm willing to pay that price," Preston said. "The thing is that she handled the phones. I've had to talk to three people this week on calls that should never have come to me in the first place. How am I supposed to concentrate on my work when I keep getting interrupted?"

"Speaking of which, we're going to need the board approval for Cloudhaven soon. We need a solid partnership agreement so we can finance the infrastructure," Lawrence said.

"Royce will present the entire proposal at the next board meeting," Preston answered. "I just wish he were as good a person as he is a salesman. I need him out there in front making the sales, but I really don't want to deal with him."

Jacqueline laid down her silverware.

"Okay, I'll do it temporarily," she said.

"What?"

"I'll be your assistant while we search for a new one for you. There's too much going on right now to have you so distracted by help you don't have. I did the work when you first took over the company. I know what you need. I'll make sure the next assistant understands the rules and rewards. Mrs. Armstrong was what? Your eighth assistant since you took over?"

"Ninth," Preston muttered. He understood that he was hard to work for.

Few companies had a position for a person who functioned in all aspects of both professional assistant and personal assistant. He should have been born in an era when he could employ a gentleman's gentleman. Except he'd tried working with a male in the position—his fourth assistant, he thought—and it was disastrous.

Not at first. At first, the guy seemed like a perfect fit. He made sure Preston's accounts were balanced, that his laundry and groceries were taken care of, and that his correspondence went out without any errors in it. But the guy had ultimately confused the position with the person. He adopted Preston's mannerisms and personality to such an extent that people thought he *was* Preston. When Preston discovered 'extra payments' made from his personal accounts, he stopped his assistant short.

He did not file charges against him. His assistant knew far more than Preston wanted exposed about him. He just quietly paid him to go away. He'd learned from that experience that men could be gold diggers, too.

"Okay. But I don't want you to be my assistant any longer than necessary. Your job number one will be to find your replacement. And please don't confuse finding me an assistant with finding me a wife. That last one was a disaster," Preston said.

"Janice was devastated when you didn't want to see her again. You can't blame her for taking up with Royce when you declined. She said she knew all about Royce and that it was a one-time fling with him, but that she'd had higher hopes for you."

"Let me remind you that *you* had higher hopes. I couldn't shove enough food in her mouth to keep her quiet. She actually tried to talk to me *during* the madrigal performance. I'm better off the way I am," Preston said. "Besides, I read and watch television. I know women are rejecting the traditional roles of being housekeeper, cook, and mother. I'd never ask a wife to do all that. Even after I get married—should such a thing ever happen—I would continue to hire an assistant to take care of all the menial tasks."

"Be careful you don't take away too many of her perceived responsibilities. You'll end up like Royce and Shannon. You'll have a full-time prostitute instead of a wife," Lawrence said.

"Isn't that what Mother was suggesting? Wed and bed with an ironclad pre-nup and then pay her to get lost after she provides an heir. Like my father."

"You are in a difficult position," Jacqueline said. "You are wealthy. Anyone who finds out about that will be interested in it. The pre-nup is simply supposed to protect you from predators, not stop you from having fun."

"It's too bad they don't have those kind of finishing schools out east anymore," Preston said. "You know, like ever-so-great-grandmother Isolde came from. Drake went, interviewed the potential matches and signed a contract with her. As soon as he had a place for her, he sent for her and they lived happily ever after—guaranteed by the school."

"Well, we can assume there was a happily ever after," Lawrence said. "I'm afraid the family doesn't have that great a track record when it comes to marital bliss."

There were no immediate solutions to any of Preston's problems. Jacqueline promised to start work Monday morning and immediately start searching for a replacement, whom she would train to be exactly what Preston needed.

A wife? Or a mother?

PERHAPS... JUST MAYBE... she had contributed to Preston's dependency on an assistant. Jacqueline pondered the situation as she dressed for work Monday morning. It felt good to put on a business suit and prepare for the corporate world she'd spent so little time in as her father's assistant. It wasn't that Preston was helpless when it came to his home. If anything, the extra help was needed because he was so obsessive about having everything perfect.

His kitchen, for example. There was not a dirty dish to be found anywhere in Preston's apartment. And not only did Preston wash his dishes as soon as they were used, he dried and put them away. Preston loved to cook, and washed each item he used in preparing his meal immediately after using it. If anything, this led to a lot of extra water being run down the drain.

Jacqueline had, herself, lectured him on washing his clothes before there was a full load of laundry to be done. Now, he carefully placed his dirty underwear, socks, and shirts in the laundry chute where it fell into a bag and was sent out once a week to be laundered, pressed, and folded. His assistant should have been happy that she only had to send the laundry out and put it away when it was returned. If he had a washer and dryer in the apartment, she'd have to actually wash, dry, fold, and iron before putting it away.

The problem was that Preston got distracted easily. Obsessive. When he was working on the plan for a $100 million project, he couldn't be expected to think about scraps dropped on the floor beneath the table where he was working on the model. So, of course, when he noticed them, he got upset that they hadn't been cleaned up. Jacqueline had suggested a robotic vacuum for the apartment, but they were built too low to grab some of the scraps.

She was in his apartment before eight Monday morning, and had the offending scraps swept up before Preston came downstairs for breakfast. She had the coffee brewed and waiting, but she would not infringe on his private breakfast routine. It was part of his morning ritual.

While he took care of his breakfast, she went upstairs, wiped down his bathroom, and made sure everything was neat. She twisted his solved Rubik's Cubes into new patterns, hoping she set them in as difficult a pattern as possible.

They'd discovered the Rubik's Cubes when Preston was in middle school. They'd tried various devices to help him concentrate, including stress balls, worry stones, and fidget spinners. It was not until presented with the challenge of a puzzle that Preston had been able to calm his mind enough to listen in school. He'd become quite competitive with the cubes and had won a state championship.

Jacqueline checked through email and his schedule for the day. He planned to work Phase One of the development plan at the same time the infrastructure was being reviewed. People would question his idea of building any housing before there were jobs or services available in the community. His notes showed an answer for that as well. When the first grading was completed, delivery and convenience vans would be dispatched to the community. They would start with food for the laborers and expand to grocery delivery and laundry services as residents arrived.

She forwarded half a dozen questions to Preston's inbox and handled everything else herself. She was no stranger to the company. She was a part owner. Even when she'd been a new mother, she'd worked as her father's assistant in the company and knew the business like the back of her hand.

"DID YOU CONSIDER applying for the job yourself, Ellen?" Jacqueline asked the HR person who was searching for a new assistant for Preston.

"Don't try to trap me into that situation," Ellen said. "I hate to say it, but your son is impossible to work for."

"I'm doing it."

"He wouldn't dare complain about his mother's performance," Ellen laughed.

"Well, do we have any resumes?"

"Yes. Everyone knows we just went through cutbacks, so applications have fallen off. However, there are a few people out papering all the businesses. I have a couple of interesting ones. This is from Mrs. Armstrong's niece. She insists she can follow directions, even though she has no experience."

"Janice Holmes? Absolutely not. I'll save you the agony of having her fired her first day on the job."

"That bad?"

"History. Preston dated her. Once. I've been told in no uncertain terms they are not compatible," Jacqueline chuckled. "Who's this?"

"Erin Scott? Great resume. Way overqualified. She was on an exec track at Allard Holding when she quit to marry and move to Jerico City. I did check her references, because as soon as we lift the hiring freeze, I think John Olivetti in Marketing has the ideal place for her. Her references were quite forthcoming with more information than needed."

"Currently working as a waitress?"

"Hard times. Shows she's willing to do anything if it will give her a leg up," Ellen said. "Current manager also speaks highly of her."

"I like her. Let's talk about what kind of strategy we could put together that would entice her to take a job for which she is vastly overqualified."

Chapter Nine

"**H**OW GOES THE job search?" Dolores asked. They had just enough time to wipe down the restaurant thoroughly between the breakfast and lunch rushes. She made it a point to work beside Erin.

"I've had a couple of informational interviews, but so far, no real job interviews. I spoke to the president of Vaughn Furniture Manufacturing; it was nice that he took time to talk to me. And an HR person at GenCo Electronics said she'd like to find something for me but didn't have an active opening," Erin said. "I'm still waiting to be called to interview for an actual job."

"Shelly wants to cut her hours to only Tuesday and Thursday mornings. Interested in taking her Monday, Wednesday Friday shifts? It would put you here from six a.m. until two p.m. three days a week. Nobody else works both breakfast and lunch," Dolores said.

"For three days a week, I could stand it," Erin answered. "If you'll try me, I'd be happy to take it on. I only have one more mortgage payment guaranteed and I'm trying to put away enough to make another month before I have to talk to the bank. I can defer pay-ments on my 401k loan until the end of the year if I need to, but the mortgage will be a problem. Home sales are going slow at the moment, too."

"How are you holding up?"

"I've got time. If I pick up the three breakfast shifts, I'll still have most afternoons to interview if someone calls me. The divorce is final. I have my maiden name back. I've got to believe there's something out there. My next option is to start looking at the national market and see if there's a job available in the city. I really don't want to leave Jerico, though."

"We'd definitely miss you here. Not thinking of going back to Cleveland?"

"No. I like the climate here better, even if I'm a lone fan of the Browns. I left my friends that I had in Cleveland. I don't want to leave the friends I've made here. And Bruce went back to Cleveland. I don't see any reason to risk running into him," Erin said. "You and the other girls. Livy, the real estate agent. She's even suggested I study for a real estate license. I don't want to leave."

"We want you here. Which reminds me... Some of us have decided to try forming a bowling team. Are you interested?"

"I haven't bowled since I was in college and got a PE credit for it. Sounds like fun!"

Erin prepared her tables, content to know she had a little extra income expected, even though it was far less than needed to be truly independent in Jerico City.

"GOOD MORNING, JERRY," Erin said when she seated him on Thursday. She handed him a freshly disinfected menu. "Special today is fried chicken with mashed potatoes and caramelized carrots."

"Good. How is the job search, Maizie?"

"Oh, I just got called for an interview after work today. I just hope I'm not too nervous. I haven't *really* interviewed in a long time."

"I'm sure you'll do great. Just relax and be yourself. I don't see how anyone could help but hire you."

"You're sweet, Jerry. Let me get your coffee and get your order in."

Jerry looked around the room and out the windows. He still wore his hoodie, sunglasses, and mask. He was afraid his mother might be spying on him.

It had been easy to just have Mrs. Armstrong take a long lunch on Thursdays. She'd felt that was a well-deserved bonus for putting up with him. His mother was a different matter altogether. She wanted to know why he needed a long lunch and where he was going. She wanted to know if he was 'seeing' anyone. He finally grabbed his things and left. He dressed in his lunch clothes in the elevator and left by way of the garage to hurry the three blocks to the diner.

He still had the uncomfortable feeling that his mother could spot him at any time, and didn't know why that should concern him so much. He felt like he was sneaking out of his room again at sixteen to go out on the river with Gene.

The fried chicken was perfect, and he managed a little broken conversation with Erin as she hustled to her other tables.

"Any news on selling your house?"

"The good news is I have an offer. Livy called last night. It isn't quite what I was hoping for, but I'm out of time and I can cut my expenses significantly by moving. I'll probably spend the weekend cleaning out the house and getting ready to move," Maizie said.

"That's great news, Maizie. Um... Anything I can do to help?" he asked.

"Oh, that's sweet of you, Jerry. I think I have everything set. My bowling team is coming to help. I wouldn't want you to feel uncomfortable around so many strange women. They don't come any stranger than us," she said lightly.

She'd noticed his discomfort around people and it didn't seem to offend her. She was concerned for him! Wow!

Preston imagined himself casually going for a walk downtown and bumping into her. He'd smile and ask her out. She'd wonder who the heck this guy was if he wasn't wearing his sweatshirt, mask, and sunglasses. Yeah. For that matter, he wasn't sure he'd recognize her if she wasn't wearing her pinafore uniform and name tag. Was Maizie even her real name?

He left the diner after lunch and wandered through the nearest residential area where there were apartments. Next week. Next week when he came to lunch, he'd definitely ask her out. If necessary, he'd write a note. He could continue to be just Jerry. He stepped into his private elevator and removed his makeshift disguise on the way up to his office.

"HOW WELL DO you get along with difficult people?" Ellen asked the interviewee.

"Hmm. That's not as simple a question as you present it to be. There are different kinds of difficulty. In general, I'm pretty tolerant. There are people who have a difficult trait that makes any kind of relationship hard. Those people merit an extra step in trying to understand and get along with them," Erin said. "At the other extreme, there are people who are simply disdainful of the existence of others and nothing is of importance but themselves. Those people need to be cuffed alongside the head and told to sit down and shut up. Figuratively, I mean. In a practical sense, it is not usually worth the effort to try to change them."

"Is that what you would say happened with your marriage?" Ellen persisted.

"I don't think that's an appropriate subject for an employment interview," Erin said.

"You are right about the question, but the overall topic is very important. In an employment situation, would you say a manager might act in a difficult manner, but if it is according to expectation... If the manager could be trusted within those bounds, you could work things out?"

"Let me preface this by saying, *I'm* not that kind of manager," Erin laughed. "I make expectations clear and get agreement for them. When there's a failure to meet expectations, we can meet, address it, and go back to doing our jobs."

"But in your manager?"

"The idea of being difficult is not the same as being abusive. An abusive manager needs to be disciplined, and an employee needs to report that behavior. However, a manager who expects no more from an employee than from herself may be difficult because she holds herself accountable and expects the same from her employees. In my book, frankly, that is an ideal manager."

Ellen shuffled some papers around, apparently thinking about ending the interview.

"Erin, I don't have a job for you in marketing," Ellen said. Erin heaved a sigh and prepared to leave. "I do have a job, however, and you might be suited for it. If you could take the time for a second interview, I'd like the incumbent to talk to you and explain the situation."

"Why is the incumbent leaving?"

"She's temporary, but has a deep understanding of the situation."

"Okay."

Erin waited in the HR conference room for ten minutes before the incumbent showed up. She was a middle-aged woman—Erin guessed in her fifties—fashionably dressed, with hair and makeup impeccably done. She wore sensible heels, not the tall spikes Erin had seen on some of the younger women she'd seen in the office.

"Erin Scott? I'm Jacqueline Carver."

"I'm pleased to meet you, Ms. Carver," Erin said, standing to offer her hand. Jacqueline took it in a firm but non-aggressive shake.

"Ms. Barrett tells me we might have a match in our search for a special position on our staff. Let me say that I reviewed your resume and called your references before you were called for an interview. I sincerely hope you are everything I imagine."

"Ms. Barrett said this position is not in my major area of marketing," Erin said. "May I ask what kind of position it is?"

"It is a job as the personal assistant to a top executive," Jacqueline said. "But let's not be too hasty in declaring that it is not a marketing job. As a marketing executive, you had responsibility for various projects, managed teams, watched budgets, and had responsibility for the client relationship. The position of a personal assistant is much the same. The responsibility is to enable the executive to do his job, efficiently and without upset. If we said the executive needed to be a strategist, his assistant needs to be a tactician."

"I see. And if I may infer from Ms. Barrett's questions, this executive is deemed to be difficult to work with."

"He has had nine personal assistants in the past seven years."

"Ouch."

"The job has simply been both more and less than the assistants expected. I propose to make sure you are fully disclosed on the expectations and the difficulties before we hire you."

"That would undoubtedly help," Erin said. Ms. Carver hadn't stood to leave, so either she was really desperate or Erin truly had the necessary skills.

"After I've described the job and we talk, I will be willing to make a proposition that will ultimately get you where you want to be. If you last six months in this position with a favorable review by the executive, we will find you an appropriate marketing position, truly making use of all your skills. I have noted the career path you were on at Allard Holding before you got married and moved to Jerico City. JeriCorp would be a good place for you to realize your dreams."

"Begging your pardon, Ms. Carver. Ms. Barrett indicated that you are a temporary employee. May I ask how you have the authority to make such an offer?"

"Oh, you're good. I happen to also be a major shareholder in the family business. The position we are discussing is personal assistant to my son, the CEO and Chairman of the Board. And, frankly, the brains of this organization."

Erin caught her breath. Personal assistant to the person at the top of the organization? She needed to listen very carefully.

"I GOT IT! I got the job!" Erin cried when she reported to the diner on Friday.

"Congratulations! I knew you'd succeed," Dolores said. "Now, I suppose I need to cover your shifts."

"I'm sorry, Dolores. I really am. They want me to start Monday morning. I had to talk them out of starting today."

"They must be really desperate. Not that you aren't completely qualified and all, but to want you the next day?"

"Actually, they say I'm way over-qualified, but I have my foot in the door. If I last six months at this job, they'll find me a position that matches my qualifications," Erin said.

"Six months and a promotion? That's pretty aggressive."

"I don't completely trust them on that. I'm going to work for the same company that hired Bruce and then fired him in a cutback. You know: Acts of nature, acts of God, the economy, whatever. There's always a way out. But at least I'll have a decent paycheck for now and I can pay my rent and buy groceries."

"You could probably have saved your house," Dolores said.

"I didn't really want to," Erin answered. "It was supposed to be a place for Bruce and me to raise our children. Living there alone... It was just a lot of work I didn't need. And I got most of my down payment back. You know we borrowed against my 401k for the down payment. When we close, the money goes right back in it. I'll have the rest paid off in a few months."

"Good for you, girl. And I know you'll be successful. Better hustle your buns, though. Friday breakfast is incoming. Go collect those tips."

"Thanks, Dolores."

OVER THE WEEKEND, Erin carefully went through her closet. She had professional clothes, though she'd recycled several outfits through a secondhand store when she moved to Jerico City. She thought she'd never need business suits again.

"Well, that was foolish of me. That blue Ann Taylor suit cost $200. It will be a while before I have money to spend on clothes again," she said to herself. "But it was a pants suit, too. Not good on the first day working for a new male boss. Don't want him to think I'm challenging his position. Men can be so fragile about those things."

She tried on her charcoal suit with a simple white silk blouse. The skirt came just to her knees. "Besides, I've got nice legs and this doesn't show too much. His mother was wearing a skirt this length." But there were other problems. "You've lost weight, girl," she said critically to the mirror. She gathered a fold of material at her waist. "Nothing to do but fix it. I can't afford to go out and buy new clothes."

She dug out her sewing machine from the closet and set it up on the kitchen table. Her mother's sewing machine. It had been three years since she inherited it. The traffic accident claiming the lives of her parents had severed the last bonds of family she had.

"*I only wanted you to be able to take care of yourself,*" she could hear her mother say. "*I'd have taught a son to sew just as I did you.*"

"He'd probably have complained less," Erin laughed. If she was going to talk to herself, she might as well have her mother for company. "I'm so sorry I didn't give you a grandchild while you were alive, Mom. Now, who knows if I'll ever give you one."

"*Do you think I care? You rushed into marriage with Bruce with the single-minded desire to have a child because your parents were gone. That's not the right reason to have children.*"

"Was that the only reason I wanted children? I saw you and Dad every day. You had a real partnership. I wanted the same kind of life."

"*And I was envious of you getting your degrees and climbing the corporate ladder. That's the kind of success the women of my generation aspired to. I surely didn't want you to be stuck checking groceries like I was.*"

"You taught me that all work was good work. Why didn't you pursue a career? What motivated you to marry and have a child thirty-two years ago? Gram was still around until I was out of college. You didn't feel the pressure to have a grandbaby."

"*It was a different kind of pressure. Dad wanted me to somehow carry on the family name. He felt betrayed when I married Andrew and took the name of Scott. That's why I promised I'd give you the middle name of Jericho. Silly name to give a baby girl.*"

"And now I live in Jerico City. Suppose my ancestors are from here?"

"*Not even spelled the same. I think every family name in the world either has a town named after it or was named after a town. Yours was a town in the Bible.*"

"Hmm. When I filed to regain my maiden name after the divorce, did I ask for my middle name back? Oh! I couldn't even see the form clearly through my tears. I was so angry that day—I just wanted to erase Bruce Silvers from my life."

Erin focused on taking in the seams of her skirt and trying it on. She hadn't had an imaginary conversation with her mother since she split with Bruce. She didn't want to hear her in her mind saying '*I told you so.*'

She should have known better than to fall in love and get married so quickly. If she looked at her relationship with Bruce objectively, there were all kinds of warning signs. She just wouldn't listen to her own head when her heart was involved.

Satisfied that she had adjusted her suit and was ready to work, Erin greeted the members of her bowling team and got busy packing up the remaining items in her house. She would be ready to move into her new apartment on Sunday.

Chapter Ten

MONDAY MORNING, ELLEN met Erin in the lobby and took her to have an ID badge made.

"This is the only way you can get to your office," Ellen explained. "The badge is keyed to areas where you have access, and very few people have access to the penthouse suite. Part of your job will be calling the elevator when there are authorized visitors. You press the badge against the reader in the elevator and then tap your floor number."

"I take it my boss doesn't have many visitors."

"I guess we accept it because the penthouse is his apartment as well as his office. But don't worry about that. The areas are separate. And he doesn't like close contact with people. He's out of the office today, surveying a land acquisition. As soon as we get the paperwork taken care of and go through the new employee orientation, Mrs. Carver will take you up to the office and give you the specific job instructions. She'll work with you all day tomorrow to be sure you've got the systems down, and then you'll be on your own."

"I can do this."

"I'm sure you can."

ERIN FILLED OUT tax forms, signed for the employee handbook, got set up for health insurance and a new 401k, and listened to the benefits person go through her payroll deductions and corporate policies. The company had a liberal vacation and time off policy. In general, the people she saw around the office seemed happy and productive.

Just before lunch, Royce Duval stepped into the room and introduced himself as the president of the company. Erin didn't really know the organization of the company. Mr. Duval did not look like the kind of person with the social interaction problems Jacqueline had told her about the previous day.

She looked at Ellen with a question on her lips, but Ellen shook her head, so Erin held her piece until Royce left.

"Do I work for him?" she asked.

"No. I mean no more than everyone works for the president of the company, but by that token, we all work for your boss, the chairman and CEO. I have to tell you that Royce is the real engine that powers this business. He comes up with ideas that make us all a fortune. And he can stand in front of a thousand people and have them eating from the palm of his hand in five minutes."

"Impressive."

"You know we've done some belt-tightening in the past couple of months and you're the only new hire that's been allowed. We've heard Royce is about ready to present a business-reviving idea to the board next month. He's been behind closed doors most of last week with just a few engineers and architects with him. No one ever sees your boss. He's the chairman because his mother and grandfather own the company. Royce is the real brains."

"Oh. That's interesting," Erin said noncommittally.

Maybe Mr. Duval was everything Ellen said, but Erin had worked in marketing and management for ten years. She'd seen people like Royce in other companies. They could sell anything, but they were nothing without a product. Ellen called a stop to the training when Jacqueline came into the room.

"Are we ready for lunch?" Jacqueline asked.

"Just waiting for you, Mrs. Carver," Ellen said. "Why don't you take Erin to lunch and continue the training at your pace. Good luck, Erin. I'm sure I'll see you around."

"Thank you, Ms. Barrett," Erin said. She gathered her jacket and followed Jacqueline out of the office.

"I'M SURE ELLEN filled your head with nonsense, but that's her job," Jacqueline said as soon as they were out of the building.

"I... uh... Ms. Barrett was very informative," Erin said.

"You've mastered lesson one," Jacqueline said. "Our company is generally informal. People refer to their coworkers by their first names. They dress in what is usually described as business casual—though sometimes that becomes a little too casual for a business environment, if you ask me. That applies to all employees except you. You represent the Chairman of the Board. He is also the Chief Executive Officer. It might seem pretentious, but you will always address your boss as Mr. Carver and he will return the respect by calling you Ms. Scott. Unless you prefer to be 'Miss?' No, I didn't think so. You'll address every employee as Mr., Mrs., Miss, or Ms. If there is a question about which to use, fall back on Ms. There is probably only one employee in the company you could go wrong with and he used to be a she. Don't ask. We just use the preferred mode of address."

"I see, Mrs. Carver. Using honorifics is an established way of maintaining professional distance. Mr. Carver is a man who is not comfortable with familiarity. Maintaining the formal address keeps him from uncomfortable situations."

"Yes, Ms. Scott. You *do* understand. You may also assume that anyone attempting to address you by your first name, or your boss by his first name, is attempting to insinuate himself into a closer relationship where none exists. If Preston decided to have a first name relationship with anyone, it would be his choice, not that person's."

The two women ate Caesar salads at a pleasant restaurant a block from the office. They took time to enjoy the meal while Mrs. Carver found out more about Erin and Erin learned more about her new boss.

"If you will pardon me, ma'am, Mr. Carver sounds like... let us say, an *older* gentleman. A man much older than would be possible as your son."

"Yes, you are right. He sounds that way. It's his grandfather's fault—the former chairman of JeriCorp. My father, Mr. Jerico, established the rules during a time in which that form of address was the standard. It's the way Mr. Carver was trained to take over the duties. Formality is a protection against his social... awkwardness. It works well and you will never misunderstand him."

Jacqueline paid for the meal and they walked back to the office. The streets were wet, but most of the snow had melted.

"It is unnecessary for you to walk through the common areas to get to your office. Come directly to this entrance and go to the top in the elevator. You do not need to announce your presence when you step off. Greetings are not required."

Jacqueline watched as Erin used her keycard to operate the elevator for the first time.

"Your office is here, immediately next to the elevator. You'll find you have a top-of-the-line setup. If you need any hardware or software, let the tech people know and they'll get it for you. This office has all the supplies you'll need without having to go to the lower level supply cabinets. You just need to be on top of reordering as needed."

"This is impressive. I can hardly wait to get into my work."

"While Mr. Carver is on his site visit, let's tour the entire office. First, masks. Mr. Carver insists on masks in his office. He had a bout with the pandemic a year ago and has been overly conscious of it since."

Erin snapped a mask over her face. It was convenient to have masks available in the elevator so she needn't worry about carrying them around or forgetting one.

She was impressed with the open room in front of her. Her office area next to the elevator was well-defined. It was completely open to the rest of the large room, in the middle of which was a table with a three-dimensional terrain map. Beyond the map table, Mr. Carver's desk was on an elevated platform. A second work station was in the other corner.

"Don't be put off by the dais," Jacqueline said. "It isn't a power trip. It's very difficult to get a good perspective on his project if he's on the same level. Sometimes you'll see him go upstairs and look down over the loft railing. He isn't spying on you. He just needs a bird's eye view. He has no boundaries in this office. If he wants to see what you are doing, he will walk directly up to you and look over your shoulder."

"That's not too spooky."

"It's actually quite refreshing. You may have worked in places where you get the feeling someone is looking at you but can't see it. Mr. Carver leaves you in no doubt," Jacqueline laughed. "Let's start at the top and work our way down. Are you familiar with Rubik's Cubes?"

"Oh, yes. I competed in speed competitions when I was a teen," Erin said.

"Don't mention that to Mr. Carver. He'd want to test you and compete. But whenever you see a Rubik's Cube around the office or apartment that has been solved, scramble it. I've bookmarked a web page on your computer that will provide instructions for randomizing a cube without following a pattern. Mr. Carver works them as he is contemplating problems in his project or in the business. You'll find upward of twenty of them of varying degrees of difficulty scattered around. For example, this one by his bed he uses to put himself to sleep at night."

"A 7x7x7? Wow! He must have trouble sleeping if it takes that much."

"His mind is working at a speed you can't comprehend. His record for solving the 5x5x5 Professor's Cube is fifty-one seconds. The world record for the 7x7x7 cube is 1:36. Mr. Carver is significantly slower than that, which is comforting."

"Why?"

"It tells me that no matter how brilliant he is, he is not an idiot savant. He has many things in that mind of his," Jacqueline said. "Now, you will notice his bed is made and there are no clothes out of place. He is obsessively clean and tidy. When he awakens in the morning, he showers and dresses. Everything he has worn or used is deposited in the laundry chute that drops into the bathroom on the lower level. He makes his bed and dresses in clean clothes. You're responsible for tying the laundry bag and sending it down in the elevator when the service comes to pick it up on Friday. Monday morning, you will receive the clean laundry and put it away. Learn the order of his drawers carefully."

"I get the feeling I'm a sort of domestic servant," Erin said.

"It's a part of the job, but isn't the extent of it. Check the sitting room, bedroom, and bathroom for anything that looks out of place or may have been dropped. The kitchen is his special domain. Mr. Carver fixes nearly all his own meals, but if you make a great cup of coffee in the morning, you'll endear yourself to him. Picking up, straightening, and generally making sure the space is tidy is a very important part of your job as his *personal* assistant. Now, let's talk about your business responsibilities."

Erin was thankful for the detailed instructions Jacqueline gave her on routine procedures and how to make decisions on non-routine things. It was an entire business education in an afternoon—customized to the way JeriCorp did business.

"Ms. Scott, you have one job above all others. You will keep anything that prevents Mr. Carver from focusing on his job out of his way, and that includes making sure he has everything he needs in order to do his job. Everything else is your responsibility. It has proven to be too much responsibility for many who have come before you. That is one of the reasons I felt your management and executive experience were good qualifications for becoming Mr. Carver's personal assistant."

"I assure you, Mrs. Carver, I will strive to be the best assistant Mr. Carver has ever had."

"I believe you will succeed. Meet me at the elevator downstairs at 7:45 tomorrow morning. I'll work with you for the day tomorrow. Now, let's call it quits for today."

Jacqueline took her jacket from the coat rack and put it on while Erin went behind her desk and picked up the instruction sheets she had been following. She put them in the desk drawer and arranged her desktop in an orderly fashion. Nothing was on her desk except the tools she would use every day. Jacqueline watched with a hidden smile as Erin went to Preston's desk and went through the same general steps, making sure everything was in its proper place. She wiped down his desk and chair with a disinfectant wipe and then grabbed her own jacket. She joined Jacqueline at the elevator.

"Yes. I believe you will succeed."

"IT TURNS OUT, I'm still pretty much a waitress," Erin laughed on the phone with Dolores. "Or a maid. But there are some interesting projects, too."

"So, who are you working for that was shrouded in such mystery?"

"The head honcho of JeriCorp. What's ironic is that it's the same company that Bruce worked for," Erin said.

"The head? Be careful. I've heard he's quite the ladies' man. Goes through them like water," Dolores said.

"Really? I haven't actually met him yet. They've prepared me for as many faults as they can, but no one mentioned being his private call girl. I don't think it jibes with what I've found so far."

"Just be careful, honey. You're still emotionally vulnerable. Don't let him take advantage of you," Dolores cautioned her.

"Thanks, Dolores. You're such a good friend. Did the new girl work out okay at the diner?"

"She's a little scattered but I have hopes for her. It will take some time to get her proficient, though. Seems like you had the job down in a day. I'm going to need to watch this girl every step of the way for a while."

"Well, if it turns out my boss wants sex in the morning, I'll be right back there busing tables. As long as all he wants is for me to make reservations for his date, I'm good with it."

"You don't sound very morally outraged by that kind of thing."

Erin really didn't have any qualms about making personal reservations for her boss. It was all part of the job. She really didn't care who he slept with, as long as it wasn't her.

"When Bruce cheated on me, it was a personal affront to the trust we had in each other. I wasn't offended by his morals. It was the breach of our contract with each other. One of the classes I took during my MBA was on how to *use* a personal assistant, assuming we'd all be on the executive end. It included a professional who talked about her role. She said a personal assistant can't afford morals. If she is offended by her boss's behavior, she's in the wrong job and needs to quit. Otherwise, as long as he isn't engaged in something illegal, *moral* judgments don't have a place in the office. The job is to facilitate my boss's performance."

"Wow! I never thought about it like that."

"She also made a distinction between morals and ethics and said she demanded ethical behavior from her employer. I guess tomorrow morning, I'm going to meet him for the first time. I'll find out then if I can cast my lot with him or if I've made a big mistake."

ERIN WAS AT the elevator at 7:40 in the morning, determined to go to her job at 7:45, whether Jacqueline was there or not. Jacqueline showed up just as Erin was stepping into the elevator.

"Good morning," she said, taking a mask from the box in the elevator. She held her key card to the reader and pushed the button for the top floor.

"Are you an overachiever, Ms. Scott?" Jacqueline asked.

"I don't think so, Mrs. Carver. However, I am very conscious of my responsibilities."

"Excellent. Start with the coffee and then scan for cubes that need to be reset. Don't go upstairs until Mr. Carver has come down to the kitchen."

"Yes, ma'am."

Jacqueline sat at Erin's desk and started up the computer to check the morning mail. That was the obvious reason for sitting there, but she was also watching Erin as she went about her work. The smell of coffee was soon in the air. Erin worked her way through the lower level of the penthouse, resetting cubes and wiping off surfaces with a disinfectant wipe. Jacqueline noticed Erin had also pulled on a pair of latex gloves.

At Preston's desk, Erin paused and looked puzzled, as if she were memorizing the position of everything on the desk. Then she went about the process of wiping down the surfaces. She went to the sitting area next to his desk, and was resetting a cube when Preston came down the stairs. He wore a suit and tie, and a mask. His dark brown eyes were a perfect match for his thick dark hair.

"Ah... M-Ms. Scott, I assume," he said, pausing at the kitchen door.

"Yes, Mr. Carver. Good morning."

"R-right. Carry on. I'll... have... things to go over... after breakfast."

"Yes, sir."

Erin returned to her task without looking again at Preston. Preston hesitated a moment as he watched her, shrugged, and went into the kitchen. Before long, the aroma of bacon cooking filled the apartment.

"Uh... Mrs. Carver," she said quietly, "who sits at the other desk?"

"Oh, that's Mr. Jerico's desk. He seldom comes in unless he and Mr. Carver are working together on a project. Please do make sure it is tidy and ready for him at all times."

"Yes, ma'am."

Erin went upstairs and found the bed freshly made. She checked for cubes and spent nearly five minutes resetting the 7x7x7 according to the instructions on her tablet. She wiped down the bathroom surfaces and made sure his toiletries were organized. She noted his bottle of moisturizer was nearly empty. She would order a replacement.

When she got to her desk, Jacqueline was on the phone instructing someone to put the delivery in the elevator.

"I delayed the delivery of Mr. Carver's laundry, since we were not in the office yesterday morning. That will be it arriving now," she said.

Erin called the elevator and took the laundry bag. It was smaller than she thought it would be, but then, it was only laundry for one person. Erin had been doing her own laundry only once every two weeks because her loads were so small. She took the bag directly upstairs and opened it on the bed, sorting out the piles of underwear, socks, handkerchiefs, and towels. She located the proper drawers for each item, took the sheets and towels to the linen closet, and took the laundry bag back downstairs. In the lower-level bathroom, she located the bottom of the laundry chute and placed the bag, ready to receive more.

When she returned to her desk, Jacqueline smiled at her with her eyes. Erin hoped the smile had also reached her mouth behind the mask.

"Mr. Carver will be finished in the kitchen in five minutes. You'll want to check it to be sure everything is clean, then be ready for the day's orders. Here, I've flagged the pieces of email he needs to see. You should read every item and be prepared to talk about it if he asks. But most of this corporate correspondence really shouldn't have been sent upstairs in the first place. Mr. Duval forwards everything he receives or sends. Pay attention to those, as Mr. Carver will have specific instructions on some of them. Otherwise, use your best judgment."

"I'm allowed to just decide?"

"Yes. The same is true of purchases and purchase order approvals. Check to be sure it is legitimate and if it is for $5,000 or less, make the decision yourself."

"It seems unusual to give a new employee that level of authority."

"We've reviewed your background carefully and know you are qualified. Mr. Carver believes any employee will make at least 51% good decisions. He wants to know immediately if his judgment is off. Believe me, he *will* know if you make bad decisions."

Erin settled in for her first day of real work, continuing to get instructions from Jacqueline throughout the day.

Chapter Eleven

"**M**S. SCOTT," PRESTON said on Thursday morning. "I have a standing engagement on Thursdays, so I would appreciate it if you would leave early and take a long lunch. Plan on being back about two o'clock."

"Certainly, Mr. Carver. I've looked over your grocery list and noted a couple of items that we should have added. I'll take care of that over my lunch break."

"Hmm. Well, that's what I depend on you for. After lunch, let's plan on finishing the hotel model and positioning it on the map. You are doing a good job on the painting."

"Thank you, sir. Have a good lunch."

Erin picked up her jacket and headed for the elevator. Jacqueline had told her to expect this. When she'd looked at Mr. Carver's grocery order, she recognized two of the dishes he was planning. She quickly checked his kitchen and discovered he was missing two ingredients that she would normally use if she was cooking. It was a little cheeky, she supposed, but better to have the ingredients on hand than to reach a critical part of the recipe and not have them.

Mr. Carver's routines were rather comfortable, even though she'd only been in his office three and a half days. She didn't mind the domestic work and found some of the office work challenging. She'd started with editing drafts of an outline for a presentation that would soon be given to the board, and forwarding them to Mr. Duval. Then Mr. Carver had shown her the model painting supplies and she'd begun painting the miniatures that would be placed on the terrain map. It was almost like working on handcrafts, and she'd always enjoyed that.

She ate her lunch in the deli section of the supermarket. She figured she might as well get her own groceries while she was there. She had plenty of time to take them home before returning to work.

While she cruised the aisles, she saw a guy in a gray hoodie sweatshirt and caught her breath. No. It wasn't Jerry. Under the open front sweatshirt, the guy was wearing a tie-dyed T-shirt. He wore no mask, and had a full gray beard. It reminded Erin that her regular lunch customer would be at the diner today. She should have gone there to greet him and tell him of her good fortune in landing the job. She knew Dolores would take care of him and tell him where she was, but it would have been better if she'd told him herself.

She would consider going to the diner next week. It wouldn't be too late to tell him then.

She got back to the office right at two o'clock. If she judged him correctly, punctuality was important to her boss. He was at his desk, head down over his project. She quickly hung her jacket and took the spices to the kitchen. She'd taken time while brewing coffee in the mornings to check the organization of the space. His spice drawer was unsurprisingly in alphabetical order. She carefully moved the bottles to insert the two she'd purchased. Then she hurried back to her desk.

"Miss Scott!"

"Yes, sir."

"This is ready for you to paint."

She went immediately to his desk and he pointed to a model of the hotel. He had a sheet of color samples and bottles of paint.

"This is the color of the logs I want on the bulk of the hotel. You should be able to tell what is concrete and should paint the windows so they have the appearance of glass."

"I can do that."

"Of course. Take it and g-go!"

"Are you well, Mr. Carver?" Erin asked, concerned at the tone of his voice. "Can I get you anything?"

"J-j-just take it. I'm going up... stairs to r-r-r... sleep."

"Yes, sir."

Erin gathered up the model and the paints and took them to a secondary work table next to the larger model. The light was better on this table than at her desk, so she was able to carefully examine the tiny lodge-type hotel and the paints. He'd spent some time the previous day carefully explaining the painting process and color palette, showing her some of his techniques. He'd even supplied a kind of lab coat she could wear to protect her suit. He'd been remarkably patient, not at all the short and grumpy attitude he'd just displayed. She supposed his luncheon engagement must not have gone well.

She watched out of the corner of her eye as he climbed the stairs to his bedroom, conscious that at any time he could come to the railing and look down at what she was doing. She quickly checked her calendar to be sure he had no appointments or virtual meetings this afternoon. He was clear. She started painting.

About thirty minutes later, he came back down the stairs looking far more refreshed and pulled together. He looked over her work and nodded, then returned to his desk where he had drawings open on four screens.

They worked on in silence until five o'clock. Erin cleaned her brushes and made sure everything was in its proper place, then circulated around the room resetting cubes and making sure everything had been wiped down once again. In his bedroom, she smoothed out the bedding where he had apparently lain down on top of it.

"Good evening, Mr. Carver," she said once she'd retrieved her jacket and turned off her desk light.

"Yes. Good evening. Better day tomorrow."

Erin left.

HE HADN'T MEANT to be so short with his assistant, but... *Damn it!* He'd gotten used to his once-a-week lunch in the diner and actually liked the waitress, Maizie. They didn't talk much, but it was... comfortable. He'd even imagined that he might ask her out that day.

But it had been a disappointment. Another girl—a bumbling trainee—had been wearing Maizie's nametag. The owner of the diner did her best to fill in and told him Maizie had succeeded in getting a new job and was no longer at the diner. He knew she'd gone through some rough times, including a divorce and selling her house. He wished her the best in the future. But he just hadn't considered that would mean he would no longer see her.

It had ruined his lunch. He wasn't sure what the special of the day was. He'd eaten it, head down and eyes shaded. It would have been much better if Maizie had served it. That wasn't even her name! Well, it was the end of an era. That was all.

Preston had resolved last fall that he would make some changes in his life. He would conquer his irrational anxiety over being out among people. It was why he'd agreed to the one disastrous date his mother set up for him. And it was why once a week, he pretended to be someone else and went out to eat the special at the little diner. He'd intended to choose a different restaurant each week, but having met Maizie and discovering how accommodating she was to his quirks, he'd never gone anywhere else.

In all this time, he'd learned very little about her. She'd mentioned planning to start a family, but then her disastrous divorce changed her plans. Her husband must have been a real idiot to cheat on a treasure like Maizie—or whatever her real name was.

If she'd been my wife, I'd find a way to show her how important she was every day.

That was a laugh. As if she'd even consider dating him unless she knew how rich he was. If he could just be Jerry, like he'd told her he was, maybe he'd stand a chance. If he could find her. Perhaps he could get Ms. Scott to search for her. He thought she would just consider it part of her job.

Not that Ms. Scott wasn't pleasant company in the office, but she was an employee. He'd automatically erected some mental barriers against thinking of her in any other way. She was a good co-worker. She liked things perfect, just like Preston did. If he could keep from blowing up at her whenever something went wrong, maybe he could keep her as an assistant.

He hadn't wasted time on niceties with her. In fact, he'd given her tasks he wasn't sure Mrs. Armstrong could have handled. In her first week, she'd been his interface with Duval and compiled his notes on the upcoming board meeting. She'd proven herself capable in painting the models he gave her. She'd spotted a missing ingredient for his Saturday meal, and had replenished his moisturizer, even though he hadn't mentioned it was running low.

His mother had either done an extraordinary job of training her, or Ms. Scott was a natural. He could even imagine them becoming friends, sort of. Nothing more, of course. She was an employee first and foremost.

He thought of Maizie again. It was silly. He didn't really know what she looked like. She wore a mask in the restaurant, just as he did. He thought her hair was blonde, based on a few strands that escaped from her little waitress hat. She had nice legs. The diner uniforms stopped about mid-thigh and showed an expanse of lovely bare leg down to her ankle socks and tennis shoes. The waitress uniforms were not form-fitting, but Preston had immediately jumped to the conclusion that she was pretty.

So few clues about the real Maizie. They'd simply hit it off and he liked her. He had no idea if she shared an attraction to him. After all, she'd been married when they met.

"WE STRUCTURE IT as a limited partnership," Preston said to his mother and grandfather during their Sunday dinner together. "Interlake Land Holding brings the property to the table. You've done a great job keeping it debt free. That means the partnership can borrow against the land to establish the infrastructure. By the time water, sewer, electric, and streets are begun, we'll have enough evidence to attract a major investor."

"The board is going to complain the site is too remote," Lawrence said. "They'll want to leverage the land to acquire something nearer to Jerico City."

"We've ample evidence of traffic past the site now," Preston answered. "And we have the State forecast for expanding the highway between Jerico City and Falmouth. That is our major access route. The one thing that makes this stand out is that it is designed for remote workers. Everything online will have rapid interface. Workers could live in paradise and not leave home to go to work."

"Are you going to allow your employees to become remote digital employees?" Jacqueline asked.

"We currently have fifteen percent of our general office employees working remotely," Preston said. "It's trickier to convince the management staff. They wanted to cut those positions first when we had layoffs. I'm thinking we'll even give a bonus or purchase credit to any employee who decides to buy in Cloudhaven and work remotely. Of course, there are some jobs that simply can't be done from home. Construction is the big one. But you could consider everything they do to be remote since they don't come to the office. They go to wherever the jobsite is. There are sales people who will need to be face-to-face in order to close the deal. It's still likely they will be able to work as much as 40% remotely. Say three days a week in the office."

"And you?" Lawrence asked.

"I live as if I were remote already. The toughest part for me is having a dependable assistant. She needs to be hands-on."

"Speaking of which, how is Ms. Scott working out?"

"I'm still waiting for a huge disappointment," Preston laughed. "She's stubbornly not giving me one. Utterly dependable. I have the feeling she is able to project herself into my shoes. She tries to anticipate what I need. This week, she even spotted two spices I needed for my Saturday cooking, and had my moisturizer replenished before I asked for it. Her work on the model has been meticulous. I've reviewed her intraoffice emails and she's been right on. She chose exactly the right ones to forward to me."

"We promised her a better job if she could last six months with you," Jacqueline laughed.

"Maybe I can convince her there isn't a better job," Preston sighed.

The doorbell at the mansion rang and Jacqueline stood. "Now you two just stay seated where you are. I invited my friend Gina Gabriola for dessert. I just thought we needed to expand our horizons."

Preston rolled his eyes and Lawrence chuckled.

"Buckle up, son. Your mother's friends are unpredictable."

"Don't I know it. I wish she wouldn't do this." Preston pulled his mask from a pocket and put it on before Jacqueline got back to the dining room.

"Gina Gabriola, this is my father, Lawrence Jerico," Jacqueline said to introduce the two. "And my son, Preston Carver," she continued. Gina offered her hand to each of the two men and Lawrence pulled out a chair for her. "We're just getting ready to sit down to dessert. Matilda made a wonderful strawberry rhubarb pie and we have coffee. Please join us."

"Thank you, Jackie. How lovely."

What was his mother thinking? Gina was at least as old as she was. Preston tried not to be ageist, but dating someone as old as his mother was not on his bucket list. He lowered his mask to eat the pie. It was good. He relaxed and listened to the older people chat. He really didn't need to say much. Occasionally, he answered a question. Mostly he enjoyed the dessert and then rose to leave.

"Oh, Preston do you have to go so soon?" Jacqueline said.

"Mother, you know I have more work to do to get ready for that presentation. It was nice to meet you, Ms. Gabriola."

"Ah, perhaps I should be going, too," she said, extending her hand.

"Oh, please don't rush off just because Preston has to leave," Lawrence said. "Why don't we relax in the sitting room with a glass of cognac?"

"That would be lovely, Lawrence," Gina said, taking his hand to be led to the sitting room.

Jacqueline smirked.

"Not every woman I bring home is for you, Preston," she said. "I think I'll take a little walk outside."

Preston chuckled and headed back to his office/apartment.

ERIN'S WEEKEND WAS not as peaceful and relaxing as she might have hoped. After making sure Mr. Carver's laundry had been picked up by the service and putting his groceries away when they arrived, she collected the entire Cloudhaven development prospectus to read over the weekend. She'd gathered bits and pieces of the plan during her first week at work, but she hadn't yet managed to get the big picture.

What she read amazed her. She tried not to compare it to Utopia, but it certainly possessed near-perfect qualities for the people who would reside there. She could imagine herself in such a community. Living and working remotely, but still having access to services, shopping, restaurants, and recreation.

As she read the thick book, she highlighted passages and penciled in notes in the margins. There were things she questioned, things she saw that simply wouldn't work, and things that got her excited to see they had been included.

"WELL, HOW WAS the first week?" Dolores asked when the two sat down Sunday afternoon for a glass of wine and chat.

"Interesting, exciting, amazing," Erin said. "You know, I worked for a pretty progressive company up in Cleveland. But it was really only concerned with itself. That's what most corporations are like. There are owners—shareholders—and the purpose of the company is to make money for the shareholders. That's what business is. But I'm finding out there is a company that wants to affect far more than the shareholders' profit. If what I've read and experienced so far is true, JeriCorp wants to improve the world—or at least their corner of the world. Not just for their shareholders, but for their employees, for the community they serve, and for the employees of other companies as well."

"My! You sound like a walking advertisement," Dolores laughed.

"Well, don't forget I was the senior marketing exec at the last place I worked. I suppose I tend toward flowery descriptions."

"No problems?"

"I saw a hint of my boss's famous temper once, but he almost seemed embarrassed by it, if not entirely repentant. I'd like to know how much of this document I've been reading is actually his work and how much comes from someone else in the company."

"Well, watch your back. Remember, your husband was enthused about his new job there at first, too."

"That's a good reminder!"

ERIN WAS ENTHUSED and understood better what Bruce had seen when he first went to work at JeriCorp. How easy had it been to be seduced by a coworker in that environment?

She couldn't see herself being targeted by Mr. Carver. She didn't think she'd heard more than a dozen sentences from him all week. Still, he managed to communicate just fine. He'd given her a thumbs up by email Friday afternoon and actually said 'thank you' when she'd put away the groceries.

She found editing and revising the presentation outline for Mr. Duval to be challenging, but was surprised that Mr. Carver wanted her to send the messages from his email account. Mr. Carver also wanted to be kept informed of certain numbers and progress. She summarized account balances—both personal and business—in a spreadsheet each morning. She'd learned how to read the project planning software so she could quickly identify whether any segment was falling behind.

Erin felt as though data was being shoveled into her brain at a faster rate than since she'd been in school. And she was learning the business. Far from being exhausted by the work, she was energized and ready for the new week.

Chapter Twelve

MONDAY MORNING PROVED to be a much busier day than Erin had experienced in the past week. She brought Mr. Carver's laundry up in the elevator and set it beside her desk until he came downstairs. She made coffee and circulated through the office, wiping down surfaces and resetting cubes from the weekend. There wasn't an unsolved cube in the office.

When Mr. Carver came downstairs, they greeted each other and he went directly to the kitchen. Erin went upstairs to put away his clean clothes and make sure everything was neat and clean. She'd stayed a while on Friday evening to meet the cleaners and make sure they carefully vacuumed under the project tables. These cleaners really had an easy job of it, considering that Mr. Carver kept his home very neat and Erin circulated through it each afternoon and morning to wipe down surfaces and make sure wastebaskets had been emptied.

She heard the elevator bell and hurried downstairs to see an older man stepping off to head for the kitchen.

"May I help you sir?" she said, stepping in front of him before he got to the kitchen door.

"Ah. You must be the new assistant," Lawrence said. "I'm Mr. Jerico, Mr. Carver's grandfather. We're meeting for breakfast. Smells delicious, doesn't it?"

"Yes. I'm sorry, but I was unaware that anyone else had a key to the elevator to arrive unannounced. Please excuse me while I let Mr. Carver know you are here."

Lawrence had never been so effectively cut off. It was not unusual for him to visit his grandson, especially as they approached a critical part of a project as they were now. Other assistants had been too awed to stop his progress into the apartment.

"Mr. Carver, Mr. Jerico is here to see you. Shall I show him in?" Erin asked at the door of the kitchen.

"Well done, Ms. Scott. Yes. Please show my grandfather in. I'll try to remember to inform you the next time I expect a guest so you aren't surprised. We decided on this meeting over the weekend."

"It's no problem, Mr. Carver. Mr. Jerico, please come in. If you gentlemen need anything, please let me know."

Erin retreated to her office area, then realized she still had the laundry bag in her hands. She went to the downstairs bathroom and put the bag under the laundry chute. Then she started her day's review of new email, correspondence, and phone messages. She didn't think Mr. Carver ever answered his phone directly, so she wasn't surprised to find messages from Mr. Duval on the voice mail.

She responded to Mr. Duval with email over Mr. Carver's signature, confirming his meeting in Mr. Carver's office a week from Monday at one. He would not be arriving for breakfast.

"MS. SCOTT, MR. Jerico and I will be going through the plans for the presentation next week. Please keep notes and if you spot something missing, bring it to our attention."

"Yes, Mr. Carver." Erin got her tablet and joined the men at the table to begin their brainstorming.

"I'm not sure Royce fully understands the project yet," Preston said. "He still has in mind a standard resort and conference center with everyone only temporarily in the community and paying exorbitant fees to fund everything. He's missed the concept of the remote worker and the local worker living in the community. That's why there are residential districts. The way it's laid out, we can ultimately support a resident population of 20,000, plus around 5,000-8,000 guests."

"This is what digital nomads are looking for," Lawrence said. "What do you think about enhancing the call to tourists to come to a place where they can both work and play?"

"Yes. Full coverage of the entire community with high-speed wireless communications. Comfortable workspaces, even on the lakeshore. Secure lockers for valuables like computers while the guest is playing tennis," Preston said.

Erin stepped around the project table and stared at the different regions, imagining being a remote worker on the site.

"Ms. Scott, did you spot something?" Lawrence asked.

"We've been very detailed about every feature of the community," she said. "But I don't see any cell towers. Do we know there is dependable cell coverage for the community? Landlines are pretty much a thing of the past. I saw that mentioned in the project plan document."

"Yes! All powerlines will be buried. Cell towers are vital," Preston said. "Make a note to have Duval establish contact with the local carriers and make sure they are on board with providing service out here. We might even need to subsidize additional towers along the highway to ensure seamless coverage as people drive from Cloudhaven to Jerico City or Falmouth."

He nodded his approval and he and his grandfather returned to their brainstorming.

The session showed a new side of Mr. Carver to Erin. He had no hesitation in his voice when talking to Mr. Jerico. He was enthusiastic and animated in his descriptions. There were times when Erin was writing as fast as she could to keep up with him. He was brilliant, but Mr. Jerico was with him every step of the way. She could see how comfortable the two men seemed to be working with each other. A couple of times every hour, they turned to Erin for her observations. She was pleased to be able to offer suggestions on the organization of the presentation, even though she had fewer comments on the development itself. She was especially glad she'd taken the time over the weekend to read the massive development prospectus.

"Ms. Scott, please join us for lunch," Mr. Carver said. "It's simple, but I know my grandfather and I will continue our talk over our sandwiches and it will be helpful to have you keeping track."

"Certainly, Mr. Carver."

The three went into the kitchen for a simple lunch of soup and sandwiches. Erin made fresh coffee, and for the first time, all three dropped their masks to eat.

Mr. Carver was really quite handsome, in a kind of geeky way, Erin thought. One could easily see the resemblance between him and his grandfather, whose once-brown hair was mostly gray now. The real attraction to Mr. Carver, however, was that he was so smart. She had wondered while reading the prospectus who had a hand in its creation. After listening to Carver and Jerico for the morning, she could tell it had come straight from them. Mr. Carver envisioned a new kind of society when it came down to it. His dream was of a place that attracted people who didn't need to commute and sit in an impersonal office space each day. Those people would automatically have more time for leisure activities, of which there would be plenty in Cloudhaven. Well, in theory.

Erin would have been surprised to find Preston's assessment of her ran in the same direction. He knew she was nearly as old as he was, but she had a fresh young look about her that was reflected in her attitude and comments. He felt she really got it, and couldn't believe she'd spent her weekend reading the prospectus. She would be a big help getting Duval on track with the presentation.

ERIN WORKED LATE in the evening, even after Preston and Lawrence had left to go to dinner. Listening to the two men had been a real high as they painted a picture of the new resort development, and turned to her for comments as well. She felt almost as much a part of the team as she had in her former job in Cleveland. She made a note to mention the need for common social areas that could also be used for several workers to get together on projects or for simply sharing a workspace.

She was up early the next morning and returned to the office to make coffee and prepare the space for a continuation of the brainstorming session. She was compiling pages of notes and had distilled a few into slides for the presentation.

Lawrence and Preston were pleased with what she'd accomplished, and after a brief review, they were right back in the thick of it. She was invited to join them for lunch once again.

This continued until Thursday. As they approached lunch, however, Mr. Carver became agitated.

"You need to take a break?" Mr. Jerico asked. "Special place to be?"

"I... No... It doesn't make a difference anymore. Let's just... Ms. Scott, I didn't prepare a lunch today. Please take petty cash and get all three of us something so we can continue."

"Yes, sir. Do you have any preferences?"

"No."

"I'll eat whatever the two of you eat," Lawrence said.

This was a decision-making process Erin wasn't familiar with. In even the lowest-level meetings at her former employer, everyone had an opinion on what to have for lunch. A person could starve to death waiting for them to make up their minds. Meat? Vegetarian? Fast food? Chinese? Mexican? All the same options were available in Jerico City. She grabbed her jacket and left the office.

Both Carver and Jerico had been decisive and unhesitating about nearly everything they had discussed over the past few days. Yet neither of them had an opinion on what to have for lunch. It was mildly disturbing.

Erin allowed her footsteps to carry her back to the diner. Perhaps she would see Jerry there and could say hello—apologize for not saying goodbye before she left.

Jerry was not at the restaurant, but Dolores was running herself ragged.

"Are you okay?" Erin asked.

"Like the old days when I had to do everything myself. The girl I hired to replace you quit when a customer got upset. She was simply not prepared for the rigors of waiting tables. Are you here to work or do you want a seat?" Dolores asked.

"Neither. Three specials to go. Has Jerry come in?"

"Your vagabond? No. Not since he got upset last week because you weren't here."

"Oh, I hope he wasn't the reason your new girl quit!"

"No. You know he's always gentle and polite. But he was unhappy and said he'd come back again in a few weeks maybe. Probably hopped a train for the West Coast," Dolores said. "Order!" she called to the kitchen. "Here, honey, have a cup of coffee while you're waiting." She set the coffee down in front of Erin and ran off to wait on her other customers.

She was definitely short-handed and was covering twice the customers her other waitresses were, but she was efficient as only an owner could be. Orders were taken, coffee cups were filled, and food was delivered hot. Erin watched, hopeful that Jerry would walk in, but he didn't.

"Anything else?" Dolores asked when she brought the bag with containers of food.

"Maybe I should take three slices of apple pie, too," Erin suggested. "The guys have been working hard."

"Hmm. So have you, if I detect correctly. Here you go, Hon. $39.75."

"Here's a fifty. Keep the change, Dolores. It's my boss's."

Erin hopped off the stool with her packages and rushed back to the office. She didn't know for sure whether her boss would have been as generous as to leave a ten-dollar tip, but being in the diner she was constantly reminded of how Jerry had always left her a generous tip. It had made her day and she always looked forward to serving him.

Mr. Carver and Mr. Jerico were bent over the map, placing a row of townhomes.

"Lunch in ten minutes, gentlemen," Erin called as she went into the kitchen to prepare their plates and make a fresh pot of coffee.

She couldn't imagine either Mr. Carver or Mr. Jerico eating out of Styrofoam containers. She gave each plate a thirty-second temperature boost in the microwave and set the plates on the table, along with the separate dessert plates for the pie.

"Come to the table, gentlemen," she called. Preston and Lawrence came immediately to sit at the table for lunch.

"One of my favorites," Preston said. "Stuffed pork chops. I've never had them at home before. This looks just the way M…" He cut himself off and looked curiously at Erin as she lowered her mask to eat. "Isn't this a nice presentation, Grandfather?"

"Excellent. I suppose I won't get fat from one piece of pie. If she brought us lunch every day, we'd waddle around the office."

"I've always tried to limit myself to one midweek meal and one weekend meal to splurge on," Preston said, cutting into the pork chop. "Of course, I can't help what mother fixes on Sundays."

"Your mother couldn't cook any of this. We owe our excess weight to Matilda," Lawrence said. "Now, Ms. Scott. Tell us about your observations from this morning."

"Hmm. We seem to have material for about three hours of presentation," she said. "I think I need to do some work tightening up the slide deck. We can present more in the paper version than Mr. Duval will be able to cover during the board meeting. I think I can reorganize the phases so the first phase is clearly painted and the second and third phases are left a little more in outline. We'll be able to maintain the impression of completeness without going into as much detail—especially where the details are the same or similar. It will be most important to sell the concept of the working resort—a place where remote workers can achieve a healthy work-leisure balance."

"Good," Preston said. "I'd like you to have it ready to present Monday afternoon."

"Monday afternoon? I was under the impression that the board met the next week," Erin gasped.

"Oh, you're quite right. We have two weeks to continue our preparation. But I'd like you to present it to Duval Monday afternoon. After all, he is the one who will need to present it to the board."

"Wouldn't you present it to him?" Erin squeaked.

"Mr. Jerico and I will jump in with details when we feel it is necessary, but I don't present. Not even to Duval."

"Yes, sir. Of course."

ERIN UNDERSTOOD THE concept of a stand-in for a presentation perfectly well, even though she'd never acted in that capacity. In her experience, one of the people preparing the presentation would read it for the other person or people so it could be critiqued before being launched. Nonetheless, she had the weekend to prepare and would be using it to practice so she didn't embarrass herself in front of the president and chairman.

She'd always been the type of person who overprepared. She kept far more notes on their meetings than were required for the presentation, but she found that miscellaneous things the men said were informative regarding what they considered most important—even the terms they used. She printed everything out Friday afternoon and took it home so she could practice in the privacy of her home with a bottle of wine. She wanted to call Dolores and have her listen, but she was pretty sure that would be a breach of confidentiality.

She practiced as she cooked and as she sat in the living room. She practiced in bed and in front of a mirror. She was nervous, but confident about making the presentation, even with the interruptions she knew would be made.

"OH, GOOD SHOT!" Preston called out when Gene hit a long three-pointer Sunday morning. He laughed as he went to retrieve the ball.

"I have to say you're in an extremely good mood this morning," Gene said. "What's got your engine running?"

"Oh! You wouldn't believe it. I'm a blind idiot, but it seems I'm not the only one. I just realized something that should have been obvious two weeks ago."

"Some great revelation with the new project?"

"Not really, though it certainly benefits it. Remember when you told me to disguise myself and go out to lunch once a week?" Preston asked.

"Don't tell me you actually did it!"

"Oh, I did. Have been doing it all winter. It was great."

"You must have eaten at every restaurant in town by now," Gene laughed.

"No. Just one. I liked the Top Knot Diner, so I just kept going there every week on Thursday."

"Well, that's better than not going out, I guess."

"Well, it wasn't just the food. I had a very sweet waitress. I mean, I have a pretty high expectation about what restaurant service should be, but she exceeded everything. She even wiped the plastic menus down with a disinfectant wipe when I got to the diner. And I did what you suggested mostly and just pointed at what I wanted. Only said a few words to her, but gradually we got to know each other better."

"Tell me you asked her out and you're dating now!"

"No. Both better and worse. A week ago Thursday, I went to the diner and discovered she'd quit to take a better job. Turns out, I didn't even know her name. I thought it was Maizie, but that's just a name tag they use in the diner. It really got me pissed off and I decided not to go back."

"That's not a reason to be in such a good mood now."

"No. This week, G-Pop and I have been working every day on the presentation for our new project. The one I won't tell you about until the board meeting. Thursday, I sent my new personal assistant out for lunch and just told her to get anything. When she got back, she arranged the entire meal on plates, complete with dessert and coffee. Seated G-Pop and me, and served our food. It was a special from the diner. I had the sudden realization that my new assistant used to be my favorite waitress!" Preston laughed.

"How bizarre is that? Did you have a sudden warm reunion?"

"I didn't say a thing. How can I? I mean she works for me now. It's not like I can ask her out. And I don't know if she knows I'm the guy in the sweatshirt and dark glasses that used to come into the diner. I mean, she could have come after this job just to stalk me, you know."

"Oh, don't be paranoid. I bet she doesn't even know it's you. I remember that old sweatshirt. You probably looked homeless."

"Well, there were always people from the office in the diner. I tried to make sure I was as invisible as I could be. And I never really said that much while I was there. Just general 'How are you?' kind of things. And we didn't talk much in the office because... well, because I don't. Not until this week when we've been working on the presentation."

"Is she good at her job?"

"Amazing. I wrote a 300-page prospectus on this project and found out Monday she'd taken it home over the weekend and read it and marked it up. She's been contributing ideas and revising the book all week."

"Wow! So, you just saw the presentation of the food and knew it was her?"

"I thought it was, but I cheated a little to confirm it. You know, Mother hired her and just told me her name and that she was qualified. It didn't take long to realize she was *really* qualified. After she left on Thursday, I called up her application and resume from Human Resources. It showed that her previous employer was the Top Knot Diner. But, my gosh! Before that she was a regional vice president of Allard Holding. She has a BA and MBA. She's probably more qualified for my job than I am!"

"I think one of my people interviewed her and came to me begging to create a position for her. Just wouldn't have been smart, though. Is she pushy? Trying to control you?"

"No, not at all. Not afraid to say something when it's appropriate, but I don't think she'd have said anything if I didn't open the door for it," Preston said. "Maybe. If I was about to do something really stupid."

"So, what now?"

"Now I just do my best to keep her as my assistant."

"Ask her out?"

"Heavens, no! That would ruin everything. If she thought I was putting the make on her or wanted something non-professional from her, she'd quit. I can't risk losing her."

"I don't know how you manage to get yourself into these situations," Gene laughed. "Just ride with it and it will work out."

Chapter Thirteen

NO **MATTER WHAT** the day held, she had routines to begin. When she arrived at the office Monday morning, she went about her usual routine and then prepared the presentation area so she could project from her computer.

When Mr. Carver came downstairs, he seemed in a particularly good mood.

"Good morning, Ms. Scott. Ready for your big presentation today?"

"Good morning, Mr. Carver. As ready as I am likely to be. I'm not accustomed to making this kind of presentation, but I will give you my best."

"No doubt! I put together such a fabulous meal on Saturday that I'm still floating. You remember the salmon filet I got in last week's groceries? I poached it in parchment paper with vegetables and it was perfect. Just a bit of rice with it. Clean-up was not at all difficult," Mr. Carver said. Erin was thrown by his unexpected familiarity. "That reminds me, speaking of clean-up."

"Did I do a poor job, sir?" she asked.

"Oh, no! Not at all. I wanted to tell you that even when you go out to get our lunch for us, you are not on the hook for cleaning the kitchen. Mr. Jerico and I would have taken care of it had you not been so efficient. It is actually a part of my routine. When I've eaten,

I feel compelled to clean something. I even do it after Sunday dinner with my mother. I fear my grandfather grew impatient with me while you were cleaning the kitchen. You would have done much better than I did at entertaining him until we were ready to start working again."

"I'm sorry I didn't do as you wished."

"You have been with me two weeks and I can scarcely find a thing to criticize about you. Allow me one little item. Human Resources will think I am ill if I don't have anything to complain about. Still, you make complaining very difficult," Mr. Carver said. "Please come in and sit with me in the kitchen while I eat breakfast, and tell me how you like your first two weeks of work."

"I should check upstairs and make sure everything is tidy, sir." To Erin this was almost as important as cleaning the kitchen seemed to be to Carver. She'd quickly adapted to the routine and missed it if something was out of place.

"I'll give you time while I wash my dishes. Here, have a cup of coffee."

"Thank you, Mr. Carver."

He sat with his breakfast and waited for her to begin.

"Ah. The work," she said. "I find I've been challenged. I expected to be invisible in a corner as I kept notes rather than being brought in on the planning process. I practiced the presentation the way we wrote it all weekend. I can see places where we need to make small adjustments."

"I've never worried too much about that, as Mr. Duval will spontaneously rewrite it when he is in front of the board. His presentations, while effective, have never been pleasing to me. He's a snake oil salesman and I need to make sure the snake oil is real. It will be a small miracle if the project we have designed is the same as the project he sells. But he will sell it. He reads people extremely well. We must do our best to see that he understands the project."

"Will you want lunch with Mr. Duval?"

"Heavens, no! He considers lunch a social invitation and I am rarely social with him," Preston laughed. "Order Thursday lunch for the two of us. I'll let you know if Mr. Jerico will join us."

"Yes, sir."

"Now, how about the routine parts of your job? Bored to death?"

"Oh, no. Relieved to have some less mentally challenging tasks occasionally. Much as you find washing up after your meals to be a means of establishing your space, I find the menial tasks of the office to be just as peaceful."

"Don't become so attached to them that you consider them the *primary* part of your job," he said. "That's happened to me on a couple of occasions in which important tasks were overlooked in favor of putting away my socks. I admit to being difficult, but the company is my number one priority."

"I detected that in preparing this presentation. Are you sure you wouldn't prefer to do it yourself? I know you are passionate about the material."

"First, don't underestimate your own understanding of the material. Duval will get hold of it and will hear only a portion of what we present. That's okay, because he'll sell it anyway. Second, don't ever suggest to anyone—especially to me—that I do a presentation. I find that I can talk to you in the office and rarely become flustered. Same with my grandfather. But I'm quite sure the board of directors would object to a frozen statue at the head of the table. Or to being regurgitated upon."

"I won't mention it again."

"Good. I'll wash my dishes and let you get on with your work. Have a good day today, Ms. Scott."

He sounded almost as if he wasn't going to be there. It was a little frightening.

One of the things Erin had become aware of in these past two weeks was that Mr. Carver thought along several lines at once. She saw it in the way he used a Rubik's Cube. He could solve a cube while working out the most complex design problem in his development. It was the same with his washing dishes. His mind was likely designing the power grid for the community. He actually needed secondary and tertiary trains of thought in order to bring ideas together.

He'd once mentioned water treatment in the early part of the previous week as he and his grandfather were talking. Erin had made a note of it to bring up later. But later in the week he'd been discussing the problems of garbage removal with a particularly unique solution, at the end of which he simply looked up and declared, "And that is how we handle water treatment!" The entire treatment facility and system design rose from his voice and fingers as a complete design.

She completed her maintenance tasks, relaxing her concern over the presentation. Mr. Jerico arrived at noon and the men asked her to join them for lunch in the kitchen. She ate sparingly. She had made presentations before and was comfortable making the presentation to Mr. Carver and Mr. Jerico. But she'd had little to do with Mr. Duval beyond forwarding the spec for the cell towers and drafts of the presentation. She thought it was likely that he didn't read the drafts. She'd arrived independently at the conclusion that Mr. Duval was all packaging and no product.

He arrived promptly at one o'clock.

"Preston, Lawrence. How are you, my friends? Ah, Erin, it's good to see you again. I trust you are getting on well."

"Thank you, Mr. Duval. Mr. Carver keeps me very busy. It's good."

Erin reminded herself of Mrs. Carver's warning that those who leaped to using first names with Mr. Carver, or herself, were pretending to a degree of familiarity that had not been offered.

"Well, so this is the model? My God! How are we going to get that thing into the board room? Well, maybe we can just take some pictures of it and put it in the slide deck. Do I have a fresh deck?" Duval rattled on. Preston just stared silently at the man.

"Have a seat over here, Duval," said Mr. Jerico. "We're going to give you the works. All you'll need to do is add your personality to it. This is exactly what the company needs."

"Whatever you say. You're the boss," Duval said.

"Carver is the boss. I'm just consulting on this," Lawrence said.

"Oh. Yes. Of course. No offense, Preston."

Carver nodded and pointed to a chair where Duval sat. Erin gave each of the men a copy of the presentation and made sure they had their favorite marking tools. She pulled the curtains across the windows to the rooftop patio, and pulled down the screen. She pressed a button on her remote control and the screen lit up with her title slide.

"Gentlemen, welcome to the future of JeriCorp Architecture and Development. Over the past two hundred years, our company and its predecessors have made their mark on Jerico City and on businesses as far afield as both coasts. We've struggled in the past months due to economic realities for some of our clients. I'm here to tell you it is time to take control of our own destiny and leave our mark on the future. I present to you Cloudhaven, a resort and employment community united by digital servers and high-speed communications."

Erin had taken her mask off to make the presentation, but all three men continued to wear theirs, making reading their expressions difficult. She did see them nodding, though, as they followed in their notes.

"WHY DO YOU need me?" Royce asked after the presentation.

"What do you mean? It's your job," Lawrence said.

"It looks like I've been replaced by a demo dolly. She did fine with the presentation."

"Y-you know you aren't here to do a good presentation," Preston said. "You're sup-p-posed to sell it. We always write the presentation. You sell."

"Yeah. It's not usually this polished. I can add the zing to this, but I might want to rearrange a few slides. Do we really need all that about water purification? They'll buy glamour and the romance. It's a resort. No one wants to deal with water purification," Royce said, marking in his copy of the script. Erin kept notes in her copy.

"Not just a resort, remember," Lawrence said. "It is an entire planned community. You need to use this presentation as a launching platform to sell the community concept to the public. We'll need shops, restaurants, and wireless communications, in addition to the resort. All those things require the right infrastructure and your ability to get the marketing people behind it."

"Okay. I get that. We really want to make this a work from home resort? You know the only people interested in working from home are the lazy ones. They can't even be bothered to dress in the morning and go to work," Royce said.

Preston cleared his throat.

"Present company excepted, of course," Royce continued. "You're a special situation, Preston. Every Tom, Dick, and Harry in the office wouldn't be productive if we let them work from home."

"P-Pr-Prod... Results during the shutdown s-s-say th-that's false," Preston said. "We had productivity as high during sh-sh-sh... quarantine as we had before. Better in several areas. That's why we need the entire town preset for fast internet service. Rapid communications. Those are some of the people you need to sell."

"I didn't like it. I like to see an office full of busy people. Having meetings. Getting things done. Working," Duval insisted.

"There would still be people who would work in the office. You wouldn't be abandoned," Lawrence laughed.

"Yeah, like Carver's assistant. Bet you aren't willing to have Erin work remotely."

"If we worked something out, I'd consider it."

"Please," Erin said. "I agree that some jobs require presence, at least part of the time. An earthmover driver can't work from home. But you might as well call him a remote worker. He doesn't come into the office. We depend on him to go to his equipment and do his job. There is nothing beyond a computer and a connection that an accountant needs to do his job. He should be able to do it from anywhere he wants."

The three men turned to look at Erin. She flinched. She was a presenter, here to provide the prototype presentation. She wasn't part of the planning team. Not really. She'd jumped in as if she was part of the conversation.

"You're right," Lawrence said. "If Mr. Carver suggested you work from home, I'd encourage him to rethink it. You add a great deal by being present."

"Mmm, yeah," Duval chuckled. No one joined him. "Can you work that illustration of the earthmover operator into the presentation? Deliver the whole thing again. I want to refine my notes. Or do you guys want me to take her downstairs to practice instead?"

"This is where we'll do all the practice sessions," Preston said.

Erin was relieved. She started the presentation again, folding in the notes she'd taken during the first run-through and discussion.

THERE WERE MORE practice sessions during the week as they refined the presentation, including having Duval deliver it to the other three. By Friday, they felt they had a good presentation and turned it over to Duval to work on from there on.

Lawrence and Preston left Friday afternoon to have dinner together and Erin sat to type the final draft of the slides and notes. After she'd sent the laundry out and put away the week's grocery delivery, she gathered her things and headed down the elevator. When the doors opened, she was surprised to find Duval waiting.

"I was just going back up to ask you to join me this weekend," he said, putting a hand on her upper arm.

"Excuse me, but join you for what?" Erin demanded, shrugging his hand off her. He'd used every opportunity all week to touch her and move into her space.

"I'm thinking we could both benefit from a direct inspection of the jobsite. Looking at the model in Preston's office is all fine and good, but to understand the scope and reality of the project, I need to see the site. You've obviously become indispensable to Preston and Lawrence. This will give you a better understanding of the project and scope as you work with them in the future. And you can rehearse me on the presentation as we go," Duval smiled.

"Really?" Erin wasn't sure if this was such a good idea or not, but she was sure that seeing the site would help her help Mr. Carver. "I could drive out and meet you there, I suppose."

"It's eighty miles. No sense in taking two cars. Let's drive out tomorrow morning, say at nine. We can get back in time for dinner at La Boheme."

"Dinner is unnecessary, but I guess I can be ready to go out to the jobsite at nine. It would be good to see it in life size instead of the model. I understand the surveyors have already been working to stake out some of the infrastructure," Erin said.

"Splendid. I have your address. I'll pull up at your apartment at nine. Probably want a pair of boots for walking around in the wilderness. Maybe even a change of clothes."

Erin slipped away and headed toward her apartment, wondering how he had her address. Was it common for a company president in this area to know where his employees lived?

ERIN TOOK GREAT care of her appearance when she went to work with Mr. Carver. She considered herself to be an extension of his presence and wanted to represent him well. She'd even set aside money to buy a new suit this week. But going out to traipse through open land with Mr. Duval didn't strike her as an activity that required makeup or business clothes. She had her hair pulled up under a baseball cap, wore no makeup, and dressed in her gardening jeans and a heavy shirt.

"You certainly dress down well," Duval said when she got in the car. He headed out of town to the southeast.

"I dressed to walk the property. That is what we're doing, isn't it?"

"Oh, yes, yes. It's just such a shock to see you when you aren't in your professional wear. Quite... quite a difference." He sounded disappointed.

"I didn't know you had seen me enough to form an opinion."

"Well, you did instruct me repeatedly this week on how to deliver the presentation. Very professional."

"Why don't we practice on the way to the property," Erin suggested.

"I thought we could use the time to get to know each other better."

"I'm good. We can practice."

That was obviously not the response he wanted from Erin. Seducing her didn't include reciting lines like a school play. Erin sighed and moved his hand away from her leg. This could be a long day.

"NO, WE CAN'T move that slide," Erin said. "The efficiency cottages are part of phase one and need to be constructed before the hotel is completed."

"That doesn't make sense. Who is going to rent a cottage before the hotel and services are available?" Duval complained.

"Who is going to drive seventy miles a day to go to work?" Erin asked. "Consider the efficiency cottages as temporary housing for employees. Once the second phase is underway, the cottages can be rented as resort property—specifically for weekly, monthly, or seasonal rentals."

"So, I'm supposed to sell a program of employee welfare to the board? Are we going to feed them as well?" Duval was getting surly. They'd only been on the road half an hour and she'd insisted he start practicing the presentation immediately. Erin guarded the presentation as if it were holy scripture.

"It remains to be seen how many other services are provided to employees. However, don't sell it as employee welfare. All benefits will be included as part of their compensation package."

"So, if these are seasonal cottages, why the extensive weatherproofing? Heating and cooling shouldn't be necessary for the grunts who are making beds in the resort."

"The resort, don't forget, is also a digital employee community. While digital nomads may only be resident seasonally, that doesn't mean summer only. With the range of services available, we want to attract people for retreats year-round. The resort will double as a moderately-sized conference center where corporations up to the size of JeriCorp may hold business meetings and retreats. Everything needed will be provided."

"Okay. Let me go through this in my head again. Just be quiet for a few minutes while I organize it in my mind."

Erin sighed. She wasn't sure what additional organizing Duval needed to do. She'd presented the material to him, Jerico, and Carver seven times in the past week. Each time, she'd made the changes and adjustments they'd settled on during the review cycle.

Mr. Duval had an objection for nearly every aspect of the project and presentation. He felt the best design would be a modern all-glass tower overlooking the lake. He disliked the more rustic lodge-style construction Mr. Carver proposed. She'd carefully painted each log in the model of that structure and had grown quite fond of it.

She removed Duval's hand from her thigh again, where he'd casually placed it as he drove.

"Knock it off," she spat at him.

She was having second and third thoughts about making this trip with him. She was getting the impression he didn't want to practice the presentation at all.

"Here's what you don't understand about this business," Duval said at last. "Carver and Jerico don't understand. They figure the idea—the concept—is what's important. It flew full-grown from Jerico's head."

"Carver's."

"Yeah, right. It makes no difference. I'll start off selling exactly what they put in their little model. It will be better if the model isn't even in the room with us. It will distract people. They see something like a log structure, and if it doesn't happen to tickle them, they fixate on it. The whole project is doomed because all they see is logs. And let me say, we'd risk the same thing if we showed a model that was all glass and steel. At this phase we need them to buy into an idea: a resort community at a lake seventy miles from the city. That is where the money is waiting for us. If they start to object to the idea of high-speed internet capacity for the entire community, then I need to de-emphasize that concept as just another detail we can work out. If they don't like the idea of employee housing, then I switch it out to luxury cabins for busy executives."

"I thought you could sell anything. Why can't you sell the high speed internet and rustic lodge design?"

"You don't... Carver and Jerico don't understand that I never sell the product. Everybody knows what a steak is. You can't differentiate yourself by selling a steak. You have to sell the sizzle. What's their hot button? We'll add the lodge and the internet as supporting features at the next meeting."

"There doesn't seem to be any sense in selling them on something just to sell a change thirty days later."

"That's why I'm president and you're a secretary."

Of all the insulting things the SOB could say, that was one of the worst. As far as Erin was concerned, three-quarters of her job went far beyond being a secretary. Yes, she took care of correspondence, the phone, and running errands. But she'd come to consider herself a part of the team in the project Mr. Carver had designed.

No matter what Duval said about it not being his idea, Erin knew differently. Mr. Jerico, for all that he was twice as old or more, deferred to Carver on everything. This entire community had come from an idea Mr. Carver had while still in high school, almost twenty years ago. Just because he wasn't good at presenting or dealing with groups didn't mean he wasn't the brains of the company.

Duval pulled to the side of the road and Erin looked over at him in alarm. "This is the entry," he said. "If you look at your map, phase one is generally all the area on our right, down to the water's edge."

The lake sparkled about a mile away. Erin could see that as soon as they descended from the rise they were on, the lake would disappear from view until they reached the top of the next rise, over half a mile ahead. She got out of the car and stood looking at the terrain. She could instantly see why Carver wanted the entry at this point rather than after the property of the holdout. Down there, the lake would be hidden behind the hill.

Chapter Fourteen

SHANNON WAS UNHAPPY.

That wasn't an unusual state these days. Her husband was the kind of guy who could use his wealth, good looks, and charisma to get nearly anything—including any woman—he wanted. Shannon had identified that characteristic years before and decided to use it to her advantage. His affair with her had led to his divorce from his first wife.

As a result, he'd forced her to sign a prenuptial agreement that would lock Shannon out of whatever wealth he had when they married. She'd been fine with that, since wife number one and child support had stripped Royce of most of his wealth. They started out far closer to even than he suspected. But he had a high-power position in JeriCorp and she had good prospects in the finance department. It turned out he needed her as much as she wanted him.

The prenup had no restrictions. Any divorce, initiated by either party, for any reason, would result in an even split of assets and liabilities, excluding anything either brought to the marriage. Royce didn't want to be on the receiving end of an infidelity suit like he'd been with wife number one. He hadn't quite realized at first that it gave wife number two equal immunity to such a suit.

Shannon still wasn't happy that her husband had arranged to have Bruce laid off after her affair with him.

But she was also smart. Her strength in finance was that she could spot opportunities and capitalize on them. Building up the Duvals' financial standing had been mostly her management. Creating the consortium that bought a quarter section in the property Lawrence Jerico was snatching up was her idea and she'd kept the lid on the deal through any means necessary.

Now, Royce wanted to go 'walk the property.'

Shannon offered to go with him, but he had a reason she shouldn't go for every offer she made.

"I'll come and help," she said. "You always practice best with an audience."

"Don't be silly. You'd be bored to death. And you hate nature. I'll be fine and I'll be home for dinner. Or, if not, I'll call you as soon as I have a signal," Royce said.

"You won't have a signal?"

"That's part of what I'm checking on. I'm told we have to have five bars of service through the entire property, or I need to contact the cell companies and negotiate new towers. You know, it all falls on me. Nothing in this company would ever get done if I didn't go out and do it."

"Yeah. How well I know."

He'd packed an overnight bag, just in case he got muddy and tossed it into his car. Shannon kissed him goodbye and went directly to her car to go get groceries. Not that she ever cooked anything, but it was always nice to have something sweet to go with coffee in the morning. As soon as Royce turned the corner, Shannon reversed and followed at a safe distance.

This trip and Royce's ready list of reasons she shouldn't join him had all the markings of an affair. She was beyond caring if Royce found someone new to sleep with, but she wanted information. Knowing things, like who he was meeting, gave her leverage.

He didn't head straight for the highway. She wondered at first if he'd left something he needed at the office. He stopped at a down-town apartment complex and Shannon watched as Erin Scott came out of the building with a large notebook, and tossed an overnight bag in the back of the car. She didn't look like she was on a date, dressed in blue jeans and a flannel shirt, but some women looked spectacular no matter what clothes they threw on.

Seeing Erin Scott leave with Royce gave Shannon an idea. This would help undermine Preston Carver and move her husband up the corporate ladder. She turned toward the high-end market on the north side of town. They would have everything she needed.

SHOWCASE FOODS COULD always be depended on to have gourmet meals ready to take home and eat. Shannon checked to see she had everything together, including two bottles of wine, then entered the code for Carver's private elevator. She'd worked with the security company when they set up this elevator and knew the override code to enter on the keypad without needing a matching card.

When the elevator arrived at the penthouse, she had to move two batches of things before she could let the door close. She looked around and set her bags on Erin's desk.

"Oh, Preston! It's Shannon. I've brought you a surprise."

"What? What?" Preston said, sticking his head out of the kitchen. "What are you doing here? How did you get up here?"

"I took the elevator. Apparently, my key card works. Doesn't everyone's?"

"N-n-no! Access strictly l-l-limited. P-p-please g-g-go."

"Oh, but Preston, Royce has told me how hard you've been working this past week. I've just brought you lunch so you can relax for a while," Shannon persisted.

"I-I-I have lunch. I c-c-cook."

"Really? Things smell delicious. What are you making?" Shannon asked as she entered the kitchen.

"It-Italian roulade with r-r-red sauce and pasta. I-I-I'm a little far along to switch to a different lunch. P-please. L-I-I... Go!"

"Well, we can share. You wouldn't turn a poor wayfarer away, would you, Preston? My husband and your assistant have gone off for a weekend together and I'm feeling abandoned."

"Th-they what? Together?"

Shannon knew exactly what she was doing. Royce had talked all week about how Preston doted on his new assistant. There was no reason for the CEO and Chairman of the Board to have such a buffer from reality. Preston couldn't function in public without panicking. A good assistant was a cushion he could depend on. Royce was supposed to be the only one he depended on.

"Yes. You know Royce. He's never been able to keep his pants zipped when he's around a willing woman. I try to ignore it most of the time, but sometimes I just get so lonely when he's off playing with another toy."

Shannon tossed off her assessment so casually that it caught Preston by surprise. He paced across the room shaking his head.

"N-n-not Miss S-S-S... Maizie."

"Oh, I could tell the day she applied for the job that she intended to nail a company exec. Those gold diggers always give themselves away. She must have gotten tired of waiting for you and decided to dig her nails into Royce. Have you dated?"

"N-no! She's my p-p-p... assistant. We work! She... we... couldn't..."

"Oh, I'm sure that whatever you have for her to do would still leave time for romance. You don't have much work up here. She's that kind of girl, you know. I wish Royce was made of sterner stuff, like you are. He's always been an easy target for a sneaky woman."

"L-l-like you," Preston managed.

"Oh, I'm not sneaky. Royce knew what I wanted from the first time he met me. I told him as much. Like I'll tell you that if you need a little comfort this afternoon, I'm available."

"N-n-no."

"When I started here, I was a broken woman—recently dumped and trying to find my way on my own. I was vulnerable and Royce saw it. Nonetheless, I told him right off that I was only interested in marriage and if he wanted me, he needed to be single. But he saw my vulnerabilities and before I knew it, I was married to a man with roving eyes."

Preston was wandering around the room, gasping for breath under Shannon's assault. She had him right where she wanted him. If she slept with him, he'd feel guilty and want to give something to Royce. Even if she didn't his head would be full of images of Royce with the Scott woman.

"Let me help you, Preston," she said, stroking his arm as he passed. He jerked away, looking like a deer in the headlights.

"Roulade..." he managed, stumbling to the kitchen. He pulled the tray out of the oven and set it on the unused part of the stove. Shannon put a wine bottle in his hand and had him sit at the table.

"I see that little gold digger had her hooks in you. If I'd known you cared about her, I'd have done my best to hold Royce back. Drink a glass of wine. I'll get the roulade ready. Oh! Fresh pasta. How nice."

She put the pasta in the boiling water, careful not to let Preston see her smile. This was working out better than she'd hoped. Whether Royce seduced Erin or not, Preston would never trust her again. She transferred the roulade to the waiting cutting board. She had no idea how this was supposed to be served, but it was obvious it needed to be sliced. Everything was out and ready for serving, so all she needed to do was add a place setting for herself. There was plenty of food.

"Relationships these days are all so complicated," Shannon said as she set the table. Preston hadn't moved to open the wine. He was fidgeting with one of those cube toys. Stupid thing for a grown man to do. She took the bottle of wine and opened it, pouring generous glasses for each of them. She drained the pasta and served the sliced roulade, pasta, and red sauce. Preston stared at the plate she set before him.

"This is a lovely meal, Preston. Thank you so much!" He just stared at his plate. "Do I need to cut your meat for you?" she asked, trying not to let disdain creep into her voice. Preston looked up. He stared at the food and at Shannon.

"I don't like you. P-p-please leave."

He stood from his place and went upstairs to stretch out on his bed. He lay on his back staring at the ceiling until he fell asleep.

Shannon took another bite of the roulade. It was pretty good. Too bad Preston was stuck pretending to be a corporate executive. He'd make a good chef. If it wasn't for Royce, the company would go down the drain. And she'd just made Royce's next step easier. Preston would never trust his assistant again and without her, Shannon was certain Preston was little more than a gibbering idiot. Royce wasn't a deep thinker, but he was a great leader. She had a plan for her husband and it didn't need Preston Carver as CEO or Chairman.

She finished her glass of wine and left the table. In the living room/office area, she picked up a cube and fiddled with it. They always got stuck when she tried to work them. She forced it to turn and a piece fell off. She looked at it and then pressed it back onto the corner until the magnets caught and it snapped into place.

She tossed it on the table with all the little buildings on it, then grabbed her coat and called the elevator. She snatched up the second bottle of wine she'd brought and took it with her as she left. She could save something from this wasted day.

ROYCE GOT OUT of the car and circled to join Erin, who moved a step away.

"That would be the property of the holdout," she said, pointing across the road. "Seems silly to try to prevent the project with a quarter-section of land. It won't even be that valuable after all the other parts are under construction."

"I wouldn't say that. Besides, it isn't really a holdout. It's what we'd call a silent partner. When they're ready for the project to move forward, the land will be available for a share of the total project, just like Interlake Holdings will become a partner with JeriCorp."

"How do you know that?"

"Oh, I'm a part of the consortium that owns it. We acquired it way back when Jerico started making his move. Sometimes you have to follow the trend in order to find the money. I could see it was going to be big from the very beginning. Have had to keep a lid on my partners who were ready to take the first offer Jerico made."

"So, you are the one holding out and making the planning process difficult?"

"It's not that difficult. We'd have bought up more if Jerico hadn't moved so aggressively in acquisitions. But being a minor partner is still more profitable than having stock options." Royce moved close to her again and she edged slightly away. "Maybe I could find a way to bring you in on the deal. That would be better than anything you get from Carver. We can have our own little private partnership."

Erin snapped around to look at him as she edged back farther into the field.

"Whatever you are proposing, forget it! I'm not interested in any kind of partnership or liaison with you. Coming out here was supposed to give you an opportunity to practice the pitch and to get a clearer idea of the terrain, which I see you were already clear on. I'll walk from here down to the lakeshore. When you've absorbed enough of your self-satisfaction, you can drive down and pick me up so we can return to the city."

Erin headed off across the field, generally toward the lake. It was about a mile away and she felt she knew the terrain fairly well from the map in Mr. Carver's office. The snow was off the ground, but it was muddy in spots. She was glad she took the idea of hiking boots and jeans seriously.

Royce watched her go and considered just turning around and leaving her. Serve the bitch right. But that would be sure to backfire. He checked his cell phone to see if there was any service. There was basic service up here on the rise. He guessed that by the time Erin reached the bottom of the dip, she'd be out of service completely. He saw her lifting her phone and taking pictures.

It was going to be a long afternoon.

ERIN DIDN'T SEE any sign of Duval down by the lake when she emerged from the little grove near the water. The walk renewed her enthusiasm for the entire project. It was just so beautiful. Little flags marked locations for the lodge and townhouses. She could see Mr. Carver's vision taking shape before her eyes and understood every rise and fall of the terrain. She made notes on her phone as well as taking photos.

She walked along the shore toward where the road curved and went one way along the shore and the other way out of the proposed resort. She still didn't see Duval and thought it would be just like him to leave her. Put out or get out. She knew his kind. No thanks. She'd had enough of cheating men in her life and didn't intend to have another.

She started walking up the road away from the lake, contemplating how long it would take her to walk all the way back to Jerico City. She wasn't enthused about hitchhiking, but figured once she reached the main highway, if she hadn't seen Duval, she'd stick out her thumb.

She was just over the first rise and out of view of the lake when she heard an engine coming up the hill. She stopped and turned to face the traffic. A pickup truck came over the rise and hit the brakes as soon as the driver saw her beside the road.

The passenger window came down and Mr. Jerico leaned over from the driver's side.

"Ms. Scott? Are you okay? Broken down somewhere?"

"Mr. Jerico! You're a lifesaver. I was about to stick out my thumb. Can I get a ride back to the city?"

"Certainly. Certainly." Erin opened the door and climbed into the cab of the deluxe crew-cab truck. It was fancier inside than her car. She buckled up. "How did you get out here? Do we need to tow your car?"

"Mr. Duval talked me into viewing the property in person. I've been walking around for a couple of hours. It looks like he decided I wasn't coming back and left."

"Even for Duval, that sounds harsh. Why don't you text him and let him know you have a ride back to the city."

"Good idea. There was no signal down by that end of the lake, but I'm getting one up here."

"So, tell me frankly. What do you think of my grandson's grand idea, now that you've been here to see the area yourself?"

"I think it's even more brilliant than I did while working on the model. Walking through the fields and woodlots, I could really see what he had in mind. I missed the idea of the wooded area around the lodge and how that would give it a wild feeling, but once I had a cell signal, I realized how important the communications infrastructure would be. And the area is incredibly beautiful. Breathtaking."

"I brought Preston out here when he was twelve years old," Lawrence said. "There's a little fishing cabin up the lakeshore about half a mile. The moment I saw what a difference the place made in him, I made up my mind to buy it. And then he started drawing maps of the area, and got me interested in its potential. I worked with him to understand the terrain, water tables, drainage, and everything that goes into a development. But the entire idea was his."

"It's amazing," Erin said. "Beautiful."

"That's when I realized what a gift he has. Our family has a long history of talented artists and architects. My great-great-grand-father designed the original part of Jerico City back in the 1830s. I don't think there has been a talent equal to his until Preston," Lawrence said.

"It's too bad he has difficulty communicating his ideas," Erin mused.

"Well, that's a matter of perspective. You stepped into his office and hit the ground running. You did all the menial tasks, but you handled the critical review tasks as well. You've only been here, what, a month? Five weeks? Your ability to communicate the ideas on his behalf in the practice presentations was phenomenal. So, obviously, he doesn't have difficulty communicating to you. Presentations? Groups? Question and answer? Those are things beyond his ability. Anxiety and panic attacks just ruin him. But when he's surrounded by the right people, he's unstoppable."

"I'm glad I have the opportunity to work with him. I really appreciate his talent and vision. I'm looking forward to the next months as the development gets underway."

"How about a sandwich? Did you pack a lunch when you came out here with Duval?"

"Oh. No, I didn't. I wasn't expecting the day to take quite the turn it did."

"There's a truck stop up at the next exit."

ERIN ENJOYED HER time with Mr. Jerico. While they were eating, Duval entered the truck stop and spotted them.

"Thanks for letting me know you got a ride," he said a little brusquely. "Lawrence, did you just happen upon a lady in distress?"

"Yes. She was hiking up the road when I happened by. Where were you?" Lawrence asked.

"I found a little stream running down from the west toward the lake as I was exploring," Duval said. "Unfortunately, it surprised me and I was soaked by the time I made it back to the bank. I drove out the south end of the lake road and stopped to get a Coke at the service station out there and change clothes. That's something we should mark in our notes as being a service already established within ten miles of the development. The good thing was that I had a cell signal out there and heard her text message come in. I just stopped here for lunch. Erin, I planned to stop here with you on the way back anyway. I anticipate this will become a major stopping point for people between Jerico City and Cloudhaven."

"Have you invested in it?" she asked snidely.

"No. But that's not a bad idea."

"Mr. Jerico came by as I was walking up to where I'd left you. I thought I might find you up there. I figured it was prudent to take a lift back and let you know I was okay."

"Yeah. Good. Uh… You want to switch back to me, or are you making the old man feel young again?"

Erin cringed at the implication.

"Really, Duval? Can't you think for five minutes without your dick in your hand?" she snarled at him.

"Now just a minute, girl…"

"I'm a woman and I've had it with your condescension and innuendo. Mr. Jerico, can I have a lift on into Jerico City?"

"If you don't mind sticking with me, I've got some more questions on your observations," Lawrence said.

"Of course. Mr. Duval, if I could retrieve my bag and notes from your car, I'd appreciate it."

"Sure. Sure. Here's the keys. You know the car out there." Duval handed her the keys and then quickly covered a sneeze.

Erin went to get her bag and the presentation notes. She wanted to make some more notes on the way back to Jerico City.

Chapter Fifteen

PRESTON DIDN'T SHOW up to play basketball or for Sunday dinner at Jerico House. It wasn't unheard of. He often got caught up in a project and forgot about the weekly gathering. Lawrence wished he was there. He'd found out some interesting details about Erin Scott and her life in Jerico City. He filled Jacqueline in as they ate.

"Fascinating girl," Lawrence said. "Picking herself up by the bootstraps after a nasty divorce. Well, nasty as all divorces are. Husband brought her to Jerico City to start a new life and family, then cheated on her. They divorced and he left town, leaving her to figure out what she'd do by herself. She was waiting tables before she came to us, but she's a natural at what she does. Perceptive. Compassionate. Perfect for Preston."

"It's too bad. You know there isn't a chance he'd consider his personal assistant for anything more than the work environment," Jacqueline said. "Did you find out about her background at Allard Holding? She's not only competent at the level we have her, but she was being groomed for the top position in the company."

"We should keep an eye on her. She could add stability to the company that it doesn't have at the moment." Lawrence sat back to contemplate a moment. "You know, I've seen a bit of a spark between the two this past week. Not a flame, surely, but a spark. Something changed on Thursday afternoon a week ago. It was like he suddenly saw her for who she was. When have you ever heard of him asking his assistant for an opinion, or turning a presentation over to her to test? She handled Royce in no uncertain terms. I'd be surprised if he shows up for work Monday."

"I'd bet he was practicing his propositions," Jacqueline laughed. "That man is impossible. He propositioned me once."

"I found her wandering on the road after walking the property all around the site for the lodge. He didn't catch up with us until an hour later at the truck stop. He said he'd fallen into a creek and had to go change clothes. She was definitely not interested in returning to his car."

"Preston laid down the law a year ago when Duval started messing with Ellen in HR. He told him no more employees. Duval is supposed to keep his male member out of the female employees," Jacqueline said. "I'm sure Duval didn't pay attention. You know he wouldn't take Preston seriously if you weren't there to scowl at him."

"That's another thing I observed about Ms. Scott. She recognized the value of Preston's plan, and whenever Duval varied, she put him back on track. If he asked her a question, she turned it back to Preston. She was very effective."

"Let's keep an eye on her. If she's really all that, maybe Preston will see it for himself."

PRESTON SPENT THE better part of his day cleaning. The regular cleaning service had come Friday afternoon, but he felt his space had been violated Saturday. He needed to scrub everything. There were bags of food on his assistant's desk. He didn't bother to open them, but loaded a large garbage bag with everything, including the carefully prepared roulade and pasta. It was ruined. The slices were too thin and fell apart. The sauce was stuck to the bottom of the pan. The pasta was mushy. How could one woman so upset his personal space?

It was all Ms. Scott's fault! If she hadn't gone with Duval, Shannon Duval wouldn't have invaded his space. None of this mess would be here. Perhaps he didn't know Ms. Scott as well as he thought, but he felt as though he'd built a kinship with Maizie and he was positive they were the same person. He couldn't believe anything Shannon had said.

He scrubbed the oven, even though nothing had spilled in it. There was pasta sauce on the counter and under the edge of the cooktop. When he finished the kitchen and moved to the office, he discovered where Shannon had tossed her jacket on the model, knocking around and breaking some of the pieces. The grocery receipt was under the table and Preston made a note to reimburse Shannon. He didn't want even a hint of obligation to the woman. He knew she'd complain about the situation regardless.

A Rubik's Cube had been all but solved and he twisted it into a random setting so he could work on it Monday. It wouldn't be as good as if Ms. Scott reset the cube. He couldn't look at the cube he'd reset and not see the solution as he'd created it. And Ms. Scott took resetting the cubes seriously.

Stuck in his obsessive cleaning mode, Preston washed the large windows that opened to the rooftop patio. Then he moved outside and got his patio furniture out of the storage bin, wiping each piece carefully, and checking for any damage or insect larvae.

Why had Ms. Scott chosen to go with Royce Duval? That question continued to plague him. There had to have been some other reason than seducing him or allowing herself to be seduced. She'd shown no signs of being overly interested in wealth, or any kind of success that wasn't directly proportional to her own efforts.

Why is this so important to me? He had no interest in Ms. Scott other than as his very capable assistant. Except that if he'd found her when she was Maizie, he would have asked her out. It was getting harder to keep himself from letting his fledgling feelings for Maizie be transferred to Ms. Scott. Why did he feel so betrayed?

That was it, really. His ego was bruised. He accepted that everyone in the company assumed Duval was the brains behind the organization. He simply couldn't accept that Erin Scott might think that.

When Preston had finished cleaning, he took a shower and then cleaned the bathroom again. Finally, he lay down in bed and fell into anxiety-ridden sleep.

"THE SLIMEBALL ACTUALLY put his hand on my leg!" Erin said as she and Dolores sat together with a glass of wine Sunday afternoon. As usual, it would be an early evening since Dolores had to open the diner at five.

"I told you to be careful. Your boss has a reputation as a real womanizer," Dolores advised.

"Not *my* boss. He's a sweetheart. The president of the company, Royce Duval."

"I thought your boss was the president," Dolores said, confused.

"No. My boss is the head guy, Chairman of the Board and CEO. Duval is President and COO, but Mr. Carver is the brains of the company. He's really brilliant. A little socially awkward, but a mind that is incredible," Erin said enthusiastically.

"That's news. I didn't know there was anyone above Duval in the company. He's the only person you ever see or hear about."

"Just a pretty face to deliver the news. He's the visible one, so everyone in the company thinks he's the reason it's successful. I spent the entire trip yesterday—I mean the part where I wasn't fending off his hands—correcting him regarding how the project is supposed to be presented. I'm sure even now, when we go before the board on Wednesday, he'll change something significant. Positioning things so they are attractive and sellable is an art and Duval has mastered it. But he doesn't really stick with the product."

"And here I thought he was a genius."

"He's a salesman. You wouldn't believe the number of emails I get from him on a daily basis. I mean email Mr. Carver gets. I screen all his email. Half the time the questions are so inane that Mr. Carver just tells me to handle it. I've got more authority in the company than the company president has."

"You've only worked there a few weeks. You must be a superstar," Dolores said.

"Not really. No one knows who I am. I'm fine with that. You know one of the things I was told when I first started was that I was expected to make correct decisions 51% of the time. As long as my balance stays positive, I'm golden," Erin laughed.

"The higher the percentage the better, I'm sure. If you were still with me in the diner, you'd be managing it by now. But I can't offer anything near what you make at JeriCorp," Dolores said.

"I loved the diner, but I was really trained and educated for what I'm doing at JeriCorp."

"Well, not to be a spoil sport, but I have to get up at four in the morning. No more wine for me. I'm headed home."

"You know, Dolores," Erin said as she walked her friend to the door, "I had no friends in this town before I met you. I can't thank you enough for helping me work through my problems and enjoying my successes. You're really great."

"Just keep Duval's hands out of your panties," Dolores said. "The best thanks you could give me would be to file a harassment suit against him."

ERIN FOUND MR. Carver to be quieter than usual Monday morning. He came downstairs and went straight to the kitchen for coffee and breakfast. She went upstairs and found the bathroom and bedroom to be even cleaner than usual. The 7x7x7 cube had been solved, so she spent a few extra minutes making sure she had reset it to as random a combination as she could.

It was more difficult to set a cube of any size to a random setting than one might think. If she looked at the cube while resetting it, she couldn't randomize it. She had to disconnect her mind from the process, making the moves while thinking of something else. If she looked at the cube when she'd finished and could see a solution take shape, she hadn't done a good enough job. The program Mrs. Carver had showed her helped the process immensely.

When she returned downstairs, she went to her desk and began working through the morning's email. Most she handled, but there were a couple of messages from Mr. Duval that she forwarded to Mr. Carver. He wanted to change a significant point in the presentation.

"Are you no longer able to make a decision like this?" Carver asked, pointing to the email.

"With the board meeting coming so soon, I thought you might want to respond," she said. "If you have no comments, I'll handle it."

"I really have nothing to say to Royce Duval. If I never see another message from him again it will be too soon."

"Yes, sir."

That was considerably more vehement than Erin was accustomed to. She knew Mr. Carver was not fond of Mr. Duval. That had been obvious from their meetings all last week. It sounded like he wanted nothing more to do with the president of the company and that couldn't be good.

"And please make a personal check from me to Shannon Duval in finance to cover this receipt," Preston said, handing her the grocery receipt Shannon had dropped over the weekend. Erin scanned the receipt.

"Was there something I should have had on the grocery order last week, sir? I'm sorry Mrs. Duval had to bring a supplement to the list for you."

"There was nothing missing. I did not invite her attention. Now please do as I asked."

"Yes, sir."

Erin wrote the check and attached a copy of the receipt. At lunch, she went down to the finance office and dropped the check off on Shannon's desk, then left for her break.

"THIS DAMN PUZZLE is broken! What did you do to it?" Preston growled, slamming the cube down on Erin's desk. He didn't often come all the way across the room to her work area. He'd been exceptionally aggravated since the weekend, and Erin was lying low so as not to incur his wrath.

"I'll look at it," she said. "I don't believe I did anything to this one. It hadn't been solved yet."

"It will never be solved. I tell you it's broken!"

Erin examined the cube, working the pieces back and forth as Preston watched. *Fascinating.* She wouldn't win a speed competition working this deliberately, but she wouldn't solve this cube anyway.

He was sure it was broken. Erin set the cube down and reached in her drawer for a letter opener. Most of the mail Preston cared about was paper. Answers were copied to Duval and he took care of everything after that.

"Here we are," Erin said, prying a corner piece off the cube. "Did you drop it? The corner has been dislodged and replaced incorrectly."

"What?" Preston exclaimed. "That's ridiculous. Did you do this as a practical joke?"

"I assure you, Mr. Carver, I don't joke around with your puzzles. I understand your need to occupy your hands as you think through a problem. I have my own puzzles I use for that purpose."

"That bitch!" Preston said under his breath, understanding at once that Shannon must have broken the puzzle when she was in the apartment on Saturday. *What else did she sabotage? Beside my relationship with Ms. Scott.* He took a deep breath to settle himself down. "What kind of puzzles do you use for disconnecting your mind from a problem?"

"I work sudoku puzzles," Erin said. "I usually only use them at night when I'm trying to get to sleep. I don't have problems as pressing as the ones you face."

"I've worked sudoku. It always puts me to sleep."

"That's the objective as far as I'm concerned."

Preston focused on the cube as he continued to stand in front of Erin's desk. In a minute he had it solved. He smiled and set it in front of her as he was presenting a prize.

"I was interrupted this weekend when I should have been working on the model for the meeting tomorrow. I know Duval doesn't want to use it in the meeting, but I'd like to move it to the boardroom this afternoon. They're sure to have questions that will be answered with a glance at the model."

"Yes, sir. Mr. Duval doesn't seem to like being tied to anything that might force him to adhere to the plan. The more he can make up on the spot, the better he likes it," Erin said.

"I'm sure you know better than anyone," Preston mumbled. He began taking the sections of the map apart and Erin loaded each one on a cart to take down a floor to the boardroom.

She hadn't actually been to the boardroom before, but Mr. Carver had told her he expected her to be at the meeting to take notes. He didn't want to be at the meeting himself, but it was expected, even though Duval would handle most of it.

They worked together to assemble the model on the boardroom table. Once it was perfect, they covered it with a cloth so it could be revealed when they were ready for it.

"If Duval never gets around to showing the model, I want you to simply remove the cover at the end of the presentation. I want the board to clearly see what we are planning. I don't want any conditional commitments. We want approval of the partnership between JeriCorp Architecture and Development, and Interlake Land Holding. He'd better focus on getting that agreement."

"Certainly, he won't go so far astray as to not accomplish the purpose of the meeting, will he?"

"I don't know. Will he? I find I don't trust him even as much as I once did," Carver said. "And his wife even less."

"I don't blame you for that. I thought my mistrust was unduly influenced by his attitude toward women. I'm glad to find it is shared so widely," Erin said.

Preston considered his assistant carefully. It did not sound as though she had had an assignation with his president over the weekend. Shannon had been lying to him. He didn't know who to trust anymore.

Chapter Sixteen

WEDNESDAY MORNING THE air in the penthouse was alive with excitement. Erin was at her desk at seven forty-five. She swept through the office and kitchen, wiping things down with a vengeance. The large table in the center of the room was empty for the first time since she started working and she scrubbed it thoroughly. When Mr. Carver came downstairs, she rushed up to his bedroom to reset cubes and clean the bathroom.

He carried a cup of coffee out of the kitchen with him, which Erin thought was odd. He never brought food or drink into the office area unless he was meeting in the sitting room near the windows. He set the coffee down on Erin's desk and she looked up at him in surprise.

"Is something wrong, Mr. Carver?" she asked.

"No! This is the best coffee I've ever had. I had to bring you a cup. Have a taste and let's go to the meeting area and go over the plan for this afternoon. It's a great day!"

Erin breathed a sigh of relief and took her tablet and coffee to the lounge area where the sun was shining through the tall windows. Preston brought a cup for himself and sat across from her.

"Now, I don't do much in the board meeting. I'll call the meeting to order and announce that we have just one item of business to attend to, then ask Duval to address the board. You'll have the computer set up with the slides ready to project at the end of the room. Duval never stays in one place while he's presenting. Motion to him to move when he's blocking people's view of the screen. The vote should be a formality. If Duval does his job, everyone will vote in favor. Of course, the family votes will all be in favor so we actually only need one more. Jerico won't attend the meeting, but Mother will cast his vote."

"So, that's you, Mrs. Carver, and Mr. Jerico? I show six others on the board. Doesn't that mean you need two more votes?" Erin asked.

"Hathaway and Vaughn nearly always vote with the family. That's what has enabled us to maintain control of the company for more than fifty years. Always pack the board with supporters, according to Jerico."

"Okay. I'll record the vote and then what?"

"Then I'll adjourn the meeting. They'll hang around a while. Duval will probably take them all out for a drink. He can't stand to have a meeting end without an opportunity to schmooze. We'll pack the model back up and bring it up here to reassemble. It's likely that we'll have a number of visitors up to the office next week as pieces of the project get sent to different departments. Everyone will want to look at what we are building. I... don't think I'll be here. You can host the guests."

"I'm sure people will want to congratulate you on the plan and design," Erin said.

"Maybe I'll sit at my desk and nod at them. If you need to ask me a question, call."

"Okay. I can do that. It will be nice for you to be present, though."

"The board may want to spend some time looking more closely at the model after the presentation. If they start asking questions there that Duval can't or doesn't answer, you'll answer them. For the past two weeks, I've tried to make sure you are as prepared for this as you can be. I... Ms. Scott, I trust you."

"Thank you, Mr. Carver. I will not betray your trust in me."

The phone rang and Carver waved her toward the phone on his desk since they were at that end of the office.

"JeriCorp, Mr. Carver's office," Erin said.

"I'm sick," Duval said over the phone. His voice was scarcely there at all. "I can't come in today."

"What? Wait. You have to! The presentation is this afternoon," Erin said in alarm.

"Can't help it. Started getting sick after I fell in the creek Saturday. I haven't been in the office all week—not that you or your boss would have noticed," Duval said.

"Just a moment," Erin said, turning to Preston. "Mr. Carver, Mr. Duval is on the line for you. It isn't good," she said. It was less than an hour until the board meeting. Preston went to his desk and Erin handed him the phone.

"Wh-what? What's wrong?" he said into the line.

"I'm sick. I can't do the presentation. I can hardly talk at all."

"But you have to!"

"No amount of having to is going to move me out of this bed," Duval said. "You'll have to do it yourself. If you can't, have the old man come in. I'm out of the game."

"You might be out of a job!" Preston growled, slamming down the phone.

Erin stepped away from Preston's desk, gathered the coffee cups and rushed to the kitchen to clean them up just to be out of Preston's line of sight. She'd never seen him so angry. Preston dialed his grandfather's number. Since handing control of the company to his grandson, Lawrence avoided most board meetings, so people didn't turn to him instead of Preston. Jacqueline, however, attended most of the meetings.

"Duval is sick and can't present to the board!" Preston shouted into the phone when his grandfather answered. "I need you to come in and do the presentation."

"Preston, you know I can't do that. It's a conflict of interest. The presentation is to authorize a partnership between Interlake Land Holding and JeriCorp Architecture and Development. It would confuse the arguments to have me in the meeting at all," Lawrence said.

"What'll I... What'll I... do?" Preston began to hyperventilate. "I... I can't... They wouldn't even listen. I need... need help!"

"Son, take a deep breath. There's no need to panic. What did we find out this past week? You have the answer right there in your office. In fact, I'd bet she's not five feet away, waiting to jump in and help you however you need. Have Ms. Scott make the presentation. She can do it. Put your trust in her."

"C-c-can I?" Preston panted. "Can I trust her? She was with Duval over the weekend."

"No, she wasn't. Oh, he took her out to the site so she could walk it, but I met her there and brought her back to Jerico City. Trust her, Preston."

"Trust. Trust. Trust."

Preston looked up from the phone to the lounge a few feet away where Erin was waiting for him. He could trust her. He had to trust her. He hung up the phone and stepped off his dais to meet Erin. She headed toward him.

"I have everything together you need to make the presentation, Mr. Carver. It will be just like we practiced. You know all the slides and even have the personal insight that makes the project come alive. You can do this."

"No. No, I can't, Ms. Scott. I may need to throw up from even thinking about it. I can't stand in front of them and open my mouth."

"Oh, Mr. Carver. Shall I call the board members and postpone the meeting? They'll understand illness."

Preston gulped in several lungsful of air and collapsed in his chair. Erin immediately poured him a glass of water, which he drank hurriedly.

"Ms. Scott, you'll do it. You've practiced the presentation and know it even better than Duval does. I'm asking… I'm begging you… please make the presentation on my behalf. P-p-please."

Preston was near a complete collapse. Tears leaked from his eyes and he was having difficulty catching his breath. Erin snatched up a tissue and wiped his eyes, handing him another so he could blow his nose. Preston stripped off his mask, which had already become soaked.

"I'll do it, Mr. Carver. I don't know why you think I'm capable, but I'll do anything for you," Erin said. "If you'll give me a few minutes to use the lavatory. I may need to throw up as well."

"WE HAVE JUST one item of business for this meeting," Preston rasped when he called the meeting to order. He was barely audible to the five men and three women in the room. He pushed away from the table to give Erin room. "My assistant, Ms. Scott, will present." She removed her mask as she stood before the board.

"Gentlemen and ladies," Erin began. "As I am sure you are aware, a new virus variant is making the rounds. While both have tested negative, we find that both Mr. Duval and Mr. Carver have lost their voices and are unable to present before the board today. Mr. Carver has asked me to speak on their behalf, as the matter to be brought before the board today is critical and time sensitive."

There was a little shuffling among the members, but they were all curious regarding the draped model on the table and Erin's first slide on the screen.

"Please let me introduce you to the future of JeriCorp Architecture and Development: Cloudhaven, a work and leisure destination for today's digital professional."

Erin launched straight into the presentation, just as she had done in the rehearsals. She knew the presentation better than any of the executives who had been involved—especially Royce Duval.

The board members gasped in amazement when Erin slowly unveiled the completed model.

"We have been working on this plan for ten years," Erin said, though she herself had been involved for less than two months. "Moving ahead too soon would have left it in jeopardy. The effect of the pandemic on our businesses was an unexpected hurdle, but the new work-from-home routines inspired actually advanced the project."

"And how do we afford to launch this project?" one of the members asked.

"First, the land has been acquired through an acquisition project nearly twenty years old. It is fully held by Interlake Land Holding Company, which is ready to enter into a partnership agreement with JeriCorp to make the project feasible," Erin said.

"I see old man Jerico's hand in this. If he's in it, I'm in," said another board member.

"What about this bit at the entrance you've marked as 'not acquired?' It would be a shame if someone built substandard housing right up against our community," the youngest of the men asked.

"I don't believe we need to worry about this, Mr. Hathaway. Obviously, the senior executives of JeriCorp have been aware of this project for a long time. Showing a unique initiative, Mr. Duval joined a consortium to invest in that bit of land some five years ago."

"Duval? So, he's on board with the whole project?" Jacqueline asked.

"Yes, ma'am. His consortium has been lying in wait for the right time to enter into a limited partnership with Interlake Land and JeriCorp. The consortium is a company known for its development of golf courses. The parcel is a perfect size for a course adjacent to the resort, and even provides a bit of a buffer between the rest of the community and land that might be developed in the future by others," Erin said.

"How do you know that?" Carver exclaimed, belying his loss of voice.

"This past weekend, Mr. Duval convinced me to walk the property with him so I could better assist you in planning this presentation, Mr. Carver. When we got to the site, he could not contain himself from bragging about what a good investment he'd made in that property and how it would pay back."

"So, you've walked the entire site?" the oldest man asked.

"The entire site is a little over two square miles—1400 acres," Erin said. "I walked this area described as Phase One in your information packet. While the model before you is accurate in every detail, it does not do justice to the beauty of the future Cloudhaven. Let's all refill our coffee cups and I'll take you on a deep dive into the philosophy and features of Cloudhaven."

The board members turned to talk to each other and Erin put her mask on so she could sit next to Preston and check in with him.

"Am I doing okay? Is there something else I should emphasize?" she whispered.

"Fine. That's why you went away with Duval for the weekend?"

"Away for the weekend? Hardly! I rode out to the site with him while trying to get him to practice the presentation. When I saw the location, I headed out to walk it as I thought we'd agreed. When I got back to the road, Mr. Duval was nowhere to be found. It turns out that he'd wandered across the parcel his consortium owns and fell in a creek. If he'd spent any time studying the map, he'd have seen where it is. As it was, I was lucky that Mr. Jerico came driving up in his big truck. He gave me a ride back to the city."

"That bastard!"

"Mr. Jerico?

"No. Duval. And he's part of the consortium that owns this other parcel? Grandfather will shit. Pardon me."

"I think it will work out. The golf course is a good idea. Hmm. Much better than I'd credit Mr. Duval with. I'm sure someone else came up with it."

"You are doing great. Take us into the dream, Miss Scott. I'm almost sold myself."

Erin returned to the head of the table and called the meeting back to order.

"Let's take a look at the first people who will move to Cloudhaven. If you are curious about the name, think of it as a retreat for people who work in the cloud—digital employees who are not tied to an office to do their work. We are talking about people who live and breathe the internet. These workers have been awakened during the shutdown period. They held jobs in offices and were tied up for hours each day in unproductive meetings, commuting, and office politics when the real work they had to do was done on a keyboard in front of a monitor. JeriCorp still has ten percent of its employee population working remotely. Studies indicate the vast majority of the people who began working remotely never want to return to an office."

That started a discussion about the pluses and minuses of remote workers and who couldn't work from home because of the nature of their jobs. Erin used the discussion to sell the idea that community infrastructure had to include adequate power and high-speed com-munications technology from the get-go.

"Of course, the entire community will be a construction zone for a year before we are ready to open even the first units to the public. And that will only be possible through an intensive effort that will enable us to have residents in the community by mid-summer. Construction crews and equipment operators will have a place to stay while they are building so that they don't need to make a seventy-mile commute each day.

"This is a way of capturing the workforce for greater productivity. I encourage you to look at the cruise ship model. Employees are hired for a period of time to reside on board the ship. Their modest housing and food costs, their uniforms, and even their recreation are included as a part of their compensation package. Nearly fifty percent of an employment package at Cloudhaven will be in non-monetary compensation, making their earnings nearly all profit for the employee. This also keeps our direct cash expenses down."

There was a little debate, but when they cross-checked the distance of the resort to the nearest communities where they might hire people, the board quickly agreed the resident staff model was positive.

"The timeshare model has been shown to be shaky at its best and flat-out fraudulent at its worst, but the investment in timeshares is what pays for the development. We're proposing an alternate model in which people own their property outright. It is not a shared ownership unless the buyers decide to create their own partnerships. We would expect that buyers will want to be the primary occupants of their property and will pay actual maintenance costs annually. We will, however, provide a rental agency that will endeavor to keep property occupied when the owners are not resident. Of course, the resort will receive a percentage of all rental fees. Since all the properties in phase one will be townhomes, a lot is deeded to the property owner."

Since the concept was a unique variant of models they had seen before, there was less discussion of that aspect than might have been expected. Erin launched straightaway into how they intended to attract businesses to the area so that essential goods and services were available as soon as people began to show up.

"Finally, members of the board, it is time to pony up and put money where our enthusiasm has headed. The single order of business before the board today is to authorize the corporate executives to negotiate a partnership and investment with the landholder, and to begin infrastructure at once. You have before you a corporate resolution to authorize the creation of Cloudhaven Partners, LLC with sufficient funding to launch the project. The chair will entertain a motion to approve," Erin said.

The board approved the motion and finally adjourned for dinner after they approved the motion, but they did not all depart at once. Some members surrounded Erin and began prodding her regarding who she worked for and how she had come up with all the ideas for this project.

"Please, I'm not the creative mind behind this. I think Mr. Duval referred to me as a demo dolly. I was simply here to show you why you needed to approve the plan. I have no authority to negotiate or change the contract."

"While that was refreshing, perhaps we should see about getting you the authority. We'll have to see what Carver says about that," Mr. Hathaway said. He was the youngest on the board at about the same age as Mr. Carver.

"I am happy to carry out whatever Mr. Carver wishes," Erin said.

PRESTON LEFT THE boardroom in the company of Gene Hathaway, and Erin stayed to clean up the display materials and presentation notes. Two of the board members, including Jacqueline Carver, paused to congratulate her on an effective presentation. They said they'd be keeping an eye on her. Then they, too, left. Erin was reminded that she was just Mr. Carver's personal assistant. She wasn't an executive.

She carefully broke down the model and loaded it on her cart, then made her way back to the elevator and the penthouse. He wasn't there. Well, she knew what needed to be done. She reassembled the model on the work table in the center of the room, reconnected her computer, and started transcribing what she remembered from her notes regarding the questions board members had asked.

At five, she closed her laptop, put away all her notes, cleaned and wiped down the office, and went home.

"Good job, Erin," she muttered to herself as she turned out the lights.

Chapter Seventeen

"CONGRATULATIONS, MY MAN. This project looks absolutely great! Just tell me that Ms. Scott didn't blow smoke up our asses. This is for real, right?" Gene asked Preston as they sat in a quiet corner of a neighborhood bar. Preston never came into the place except with Gene. No one ever bothered him when he was with Gene.

"If I could speak in front of people, that is what I would have said," Preston said, shaking his head. "It's like she read my mind. It worries me."

"What bothers you?"

"She knew things that I didn't even know," he said. "G-Pop and I have been trying to figure a way to crack this consortium that owns the 160 acres that we haven't been able to get hold of. She identified it, said Duval is a part owner, and said the consortium plans to develop it into a golf course. And to think Duval has held all that back from us! How'd she get him to talk about it? Is she spreading information about me to him?"

"Don't get paranoid on me, brother. Nothing she said leads me to believe any of that was told to her in confidence. You know Duval. He probably bragged about it, hoping to get her in bed," Gene laughed.

"You don't think it worked, do you? I'm such a bad judge of women's intent. If she was in bed with Duval, I'd need to dismiss her," Preston said. "I can't stand the thought of that."

"It would be the dumbest thing you've ever done. Man, you've landed a real treasure as your personal assistant. I know you've read her resume. Where else are you going to find someone with those credentials as a personal assistant? You're the chief executive officer and she's your chief of staff. She's got your back on everything," Gene continued enthusiastically. "If I were you, I'd marry her!"

"I can't do that. She's an employee. It wouldn't be right."

"Don't get so hung up on what's right that you miss what's good." Gene looked over at him. "You're both smart people. It was obvious in every word she said today that she admires and respects you. Didn't you hear how she handled Reinholdt in the meeting when he suggested that they needed Duval's stamp of approval? She didn't tear Duval down, but she made it clear that Duval had your approval and that was all he needed."

"What if it's all a fake? Duval's wife came charging into my home Saturday and told me Ms. Scott was out seducing her husband. Then she proceeded to ruin my dinner and the rest of my day with her prattle. It was all I could do to get rid of her!"

"That's the real problem, isn't it? Shannon Duval started a rumor and you can't shake it. Preston, you know the kind of person she is! How could you fall for a pack of lies she tells to get you upset?"

"Is that all it is, Gene? I need to get myself past this."

PRESTON WAS STILL in a mood when he left Gene and went to Jerico House for dinner. There was nothing he wanted more than to believe Erin Scott was all he imagined her to be. He'd really fallen for the waitress Maizie and knew they were the same person, but the decisive executive he saw as his assistant frightened him a little.

"Did she do okay with the presentation today?" Lawrence asked.

"Flawless," Jacqueline chimed in.

"I'm wondering if Duval had any idea how she would show him up in the meeting today," Preston snorted. "I wouldn't put it past him to set her up for the meeting thinking he could come in later and save the day. His wife showed up at the apartment Saturday and accused Ms. Scott of trying to seduce her husband and go away for the weekend with him. She ruined my meal Saturday."

"Well, she didn't go for the weekend," Lawrence laughed. "As far as I can tell, the only time she spent with him was on the drive to Cloudhaven. He let her off and abandoned her. Then he went off and fell in a creek. I picked Ms. Scott up on my way home from the cabin. Found her walking out the access road."

"Why would she go with Duval at all? Surely, she knows by now what kind of person he is," Preston insisted.

"Preston, love, not everything has an ulterior motive," Jacqueline said, patting his hand.

"It was so much easier when she was my waitress," Preston sighed. "It was simple then."

"What waitress?" Lawrence asked.

"I... um... sometimes... the past few months... I started going out to lunch on Thursdays, so I wouldn't be inside the penthouse all the time. I wore a hoodie and dark glasses. Went to the diner. Maizie waited on me and we... sort of... became friends. She went through a divorce and was alone and applying for jobs. Then I went back to the diner and she was gone. The owner said she got a new job, but wouldn't say anything else. I was going to... It doesn't make a difference. She must have figured out who I was and applied for the job as my assistant to get access to me." Preston was scarcely making sense, but his mother shook her head.

"No. Ellen told me she applied for a job in marketing—which didn't exist. After her initial interview, we put our heads together and worked out a deal where... Oh, Preston, you know you're hard on assistants. We told Erin Scott that if she could put up with you for six months, we'd find a place in marketing for her. She didn't come to us applying for your job."

"She was perfect from the very start. Even her coffee tastes better than what I had before. And the way she goes around the room with disinfectant wipes and makes sure my puzzles are reset. I've never had an assistant who was such a help. She handled all my correspondence with Duval because I really can't stand the man. I keep thinking the other shoe is going to drop and my vision of perfection will disintegrate."

"Maybe you should think about marrying her," Lawrence said. "I could see when I was in your office working on the proposal and presentation that she was a natural fit with you. She could practically complete your sentences for you."

"It was that Thursday when I figured it out," Preston said. "She went out to get lunch for us and then set the table exactly like it's set at the diner. Arranged the food on all three plates just like it would be served at the diner. She had the table wiped down and silverware set exactly the same. Later that night, I looked up her resume and saw that she'd been at the diner."

"And?" Jacqueline asked.

"She's more qualified for my job than I am! Is that it? She was an executive for Allard Holding Company. Do you suppose they're planning a take-over bid? Is that why she took a position she was so overqualified for?" Preston asked.

"Hmm. Things could be worse than being bought out by Allard. They're a good company," Lawrence said. "I haven't heard of them being interested in real estate development before, though."

"The board authorized the executives to negotiate a partner-ship with Interlake Land Holdings. And did Mom tell you what she said about the 160 acres that are held out? Royce Duval is part of the consortium that holds the property. They want to develop a golf course there when the resort is finished."

"Hmm. That could be beneficial to all of us. She didn't mention that when we were talking on the way back to Jerico City. I'd guess she assumed we—or I, at least—knew. That doesn't sound like an idea that Duval would come up with, let alone him forming a consortium to buy and develop the land."

"Sounds more like Shannon Duval," Jacqueline said. "Now there is a devious woman. If you accused her of trying to become your assistant and seduce you to take over the company, I'd believe you."

"I... She... That bitch!" Preston exclaimed. "She brought a lunch and wine to the apartment Saturday. I want her keycard revoked and reissued so it won't unlock the elevator. She completely ruined my dinner. I was making an Italian roulade—a braciole—with fresh pasta. She tried to give me wine and just took over the kitchen. She ruined everything. After I sent her away, I spent the rest of the weekend cleaning my space. It was violated."

"Ah. And it was Shannon Duval who told you your assistant was spending the weekend with Royce," Lawrence said. "You know, if she wasn't so good at her job in the finance department, I'd suggest you get rid of her, but she's likely to be the one who raises the funds we need for Cloudhaven. I understand she had an affair with another employee over the holiday. Duval arranged to have him fired in the cutbacks."

"Affair over the holiday. Fired," Preston said. "Maizie said her husband had an affair and lost his job. They divorced."

"You need to figure out where your head is when it comes to your assistant," Jacqueline said.

"I need more details."

"You've often talked about working remotely. Stay here this week," Lawrence said. "A week or so alone in the office will tell you how she's doing and who she's loyal to."

"Yeah. Good idea."

THE OFFICE WAS quiet when Erin went to work. Everything was exactly like she'd left it the night before. She made coffee and circulated around the office checking cubes, to find none had been solved. When Mr. Carver did not appear to make breakfast, Erin crept up the stairs and saw his room was pristine. The bed had not been slept in. There was no sign Preston had come home the night before.

She returned to her desk and began the daily routine of sorting email and getting the day organized. She sent a couple of urgent items to Mr. Carver, including a reminder that they needed to start negotiating a partnership with Interlake Land Holdings.

About half an hour later, she received a reply from Preston.

"I'm working remotely for the rest of the week to focus on the partnership and process. Please respond to all correspondence and tell Duval to open negotiations with Interlake. Thank you."

Erin had no difficulty handling most items. She knew what Carver would say, but forwarded messages of a certain level to him.

He always responded directly to members of the board, Mr. Duval, the CFO and the CEOs of other companies. Anything below that level was shuffled back to her. She supposed that, in some ways, she exercised as much authority as the president of the company did.

She wrote to Duval, using her notes compiled in meetings with Preston and Lawrence regarding what the partnership should look like. She added her own notes regarding how to integrate the golf course consortium into the mix. She blind-copied all her correspondence to Mr. Carver, knowing he was unlikely to even read it.

Since she was on her own in the office, she began compiling a list of tasks to be accomplished before actual development could begin. Now that the project was approved, relationships with the County Commission needed to be established, with the necessary paperwork for environmental impact. Duval was going to be a busy man in the next two months, just getting the processes in place for Cloudhaven. She suggested that if he felt he needed one, he should hire an assistant to help with the increased work load. She'd see how that panned out.

The project management software on the corporate server was different than what she'd used in Cleveland at Allard, but after a quick tutorial, she grasped what needed to be done. She created a new project and began entering the tasks and mileposts for the development. She found Mr. Carver had also begun a project plan, but Erin's started earlier in the process and had soon passed the point Mr. Carver had reached.

The drawings for each part of the development were completed and marked 'in review,' so it was fairly easy to link from tasks to plans. Erin was tired when she looked up at the window to the rooftop patio and saw it was dark.

She cleaned the kitchen and made sure everything was put away as Mr. Carver liked it. Erin shared his pride in a clean space and was glad she was working with a man who cared about his environment. After double-checking the entire apartment, she left for the day.

Friday was a near duplicate of the previous day. She got the same email message from Carver and discharged all the correspondence and urgent messages. She requested an update from Duval on the status of the partnership and reminded him that he was on the hook for contacting the cell companies to make sure the site had adequate coverage.

She sat for a few minutes in the kitchen to have a cup of coffee while she made notes regarding what needed to be put on the project plan. After she'd washed her cup and put it away, she returned to her desk and began working on the project plan again. She sent several requests to people in the architecture review department for updates on different phases, and to the land development department for information regarding the timing of installing infrastructure.

When it was time to leave at the end of the day, she realized she hadn't eaten since breakfast. She let the cleaning service in and went out to eat at a family restaurant near the waterfront.

"IT'S BEEN AN incredible week," Erin said when she and Dolores met for their weekly glass of wine on Sunday afternoon. "I feel like I've been cut loose to just make this project go. When I started, Mrs. Carver told me I had signing authority of up to $5,000. I found that hard to believe, but this week, I've authorized others to make deals over $100,000. I mean, I didn't sign the PO, but I told the person who could sign it to make it happen. I even told the president of the company to hire an assistant!"

"Erin, you're not being set up, are you?" Dolores asked in alarm.

"What do you mean? How could I be set up?"

"You make a major presentation to the board of directors and convince them to authorize the project. Then your boss deserts you and leaves you to authorize all the pieces. Could they be planning to dump the project and you with it?" Dolores asked.

"I don't think so. If it were up to Duval, I'd be suspicious, but not with Carver. I had a position with a fair amount of authority in Cleveland, and I think I could spot a setup like that. You need to know my boss to understand how he works. I'm getting a lot of input from him on the plan. He merged his project plan with mine and is just sending me the mileposts and timing to enter. We've had a couple of good conversations—brief but good. He wouldn't set me up for failure. He's too decent a guy for that."

"Speaking of decent guys, guess who came into the diner Friday. Your old friend Jerry," Dolores said.

"Oh! How is he? I really miss seeing him each week."

"Still nice, quiet, shy, generous. He asked if I'd heard from you and if you were happy."

"I hope you said yes."

"Mmmhmm. But not too enthusiastically. I think he wanted to know you miss him like he misses you. I assured him you were being successful in your job, but there were things about the diner you missed—like him."

"That's true enough. Mr. Carver reminds me of Jerry's simple joy in life and disdain for excess. You know, most days, we are the only ones we see in the office. I usually go out for a bite of lunch and see other people, but he doesn't leave his little abode. His grandfather joined us there most of the past two weeks. And then President Slimy was in for several afternoons, but otherwise, he doesn't really see many people at all. I tell you, after the president was in the office, I wiped down everything with disinfectant wipes twice. Then I stayed Friday night until the cleaning crew was finished."

"Well, here's a phone number for you. He said if you ever wanted to have lunch together to text him."

"Oh, wow! Do you think he means a date? I have to really think about that. I've only been divorced three months. I don't want to act rashly. Right now, I don't have time for a relationship outside of my job. I'll tuck it away. It would be nice to see him."

"Four a.m. comes earlier every Monday, I swear. I need to head home and get what sleep I can before the work week starts again. You be careful now, okay? I'm really happy you're experiencing such success, but I don't want to see you hurt."

"Thanks, Dolores. You're the best ever."

MONDAY MORNING, THERE was no sign the apartment had been occupied over the weekend. Erin made coffee and sat with a cup before she started on the daily tasks. She absently worked the

3x3x3 cube in the kitchen as she mentally prepared her agenda for the week.

She handled the email and correspondence, picked up the laundry delivered to the elevator, and put it all away. Then she turned to her project file to continue inputting the tasks.

Carver had merged his project plan with hers and it was filled with notes. He'd obviously been busy working remotely over the weekend. He pointed out places where she needed to add time for tasks and filled in several tasks that she had missed. A note directed her to work on the power grid critical path next. He wasn't in the office, but he obviously kept track of what was going on. She focused on the tasks and filling in the chart.

There were several portions of the project she was unfamiliar with, but the software led her through the bulk of the tasks. She forwarded her specs to the Land Development Department for cleanup and detail work. She looked through the rest of the notes and determined she'd need to focus on the sewer and water infrastructure tomorrow, including the water treatment system Mr. Carver designed.

TUESDAY AFTERNOON, AFTER another busy day of data entry and coordination of tasks with other departments, Erin sat back to contemplate what was going on. She was getting a lot done, and apparently Mr. Carver was, too. He'd been at Cloudhaven meeting with the contractors and with the utility people this week. His grandfather had been at the jobsite, as well, and even Mr. Duval had been summoned out there.

She was feeling a little lonely. Since the board meeting on Wednesday, the only person she'd seen was Dolores on Sunday. She pulled Jerry's phone number out of her purse and contemplated whether to call the shy man she used to wait on. No. Dolores had specifically said 'text.' She tapped in a message, erased it, and started over. Was she really suggesting a get-together with Jerry?

"It's Maizie. Drinks after work today or tomorrow?"

She sent the text, expecting an immediate answer. Nothing came back. She did the ritual wipe-down of the office and apartment even though she'd scarcely been anywhere but her desk and the kitchen. Then she went home.

About seven that evening, her phone vibrated and she saw a message from Jerry.

"Out of town. Lunch at diner Thursday?"

Erin breathed a sigh of relief that she wasn't just being ignored. She wondered what he was doing out of town.

"See you at noon," she texted back.

Well, that was done. Meeting for lunch at the diner was far more sensible. People met for lunch all the time. Meeting for drinks after work was too much like a date and she wasn't really sure she was ready to date yet. She missed her weekly encounter with Jerry, though, and this would be perfect.

It helped Wednesday go by more quickly.

Chapter Eighteen

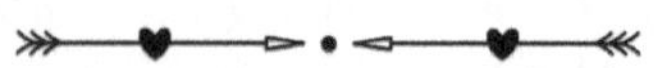

I **HAVE NO** *reason to be nervous,* Erin lectured herself as she dressed for work Thursday morning. She was no longer a waitress getting ready to work a double shift. She was a professional who worked for a respected senior executive. She only needed to dress accordingly. Jerry would be happy to see her looking successful.

Still, she chose the new suit she'd purchased for the board meeting. It looked very good with the mauve silk blouse she wore with it. Her hair... She just brushed it out. Jerry had never seen it to compare to, since she'd always worn it up under her waitress cap. He wouldn't notice it had grown an inch since she last saw him.

She spent just a little extra time with her makeup and then scrubbed it off her face and redid it as she normally wore it. It was always possible Mr. Carver would be in the office today. She wouldn't want him thinking she had a reason to get fancy.

Not that she needed to justify herself to her boss. If she wanted to meet a nice guy for lunch, it was strictly her business. But she was aware that it did make a difference to her. She didn't want her boss to disapprove of anything she did—even if it was none of his business. It wasn't like she was going to date him. She admired and respected Mr. Carver, but she certainly wasn't infatuated with him. She didn't think.

She was almost late getting to the office, hanging her jacket, and quickly checking the penthouse to be sure everything was in order and Mr. Carver was still out of the office. She made herself a cup of coffee and made a list on her tablet of the things she needed to accomplish that day. Having calmed herself, she went about the morning's work and was pleased with the amount she'd gotten done by the time she put her jacket on to go to lunch.

As a last thought, she sent a note to Mr. Carver to tell him she might be a little late getting back from lunch that day. It was just a courtesy.

WHEN ERIN ENTERED the diner, Dolores smiled at her and nodded toward the back booth where Jerry was already waiting. Erin took a deep breath and squared her shoulders to go meet her lunch date.

"Jerry. It's so good to see you. I hope you haven't been waiting long," she said, offering her hand. He took it with a slight squeeze.

He was wearing the same thing he always did when he came to the diner: a college sweatshirt with the hood pulled up, sunglasses and a mask.

"Um... Maizie. I..." He was barely whispering and she leaned forward to hear better. "P-p-please, don't... It *is* you. I m-m-mean, I knew... Not-not for long. I just... I figured it out..."

"What are you talking about, Jerry? You can relax with me. Take your time," she said.

He didn't continue. Instead, he shifted the hood back and took off his sunglasses. Then as Erin watched open-mouthed, he removed his mask.

"M-Mr. Carver!" she gasped. "I... You... I mean... Are you?"

"Yes. I'm sorry. I d-d-didn't mean... to d-d-dec... lie to you."

"You hired me! You didn't need to do that! I'm not a charity case!" Erin practically shouted.

"N-n-no! I didn't know! I only found out you were Maizie two weeks ago. I-I-I didn't know what to do."

"I can't believe I didn't... Well, I didn't really know you that well in the diner. I mean, I would never have applied..."

"Please don't say you quit!" Jerry gasped. "Please."

"I don't know what to do. What do you expect of me, Mr. Carver?"

"When we are just being casual and chatting, can you call me Jerry and let me call you Maizie. W-w-we can leave Miss Scott and Mr. Carver at the office," he said.

"That might work for today. How did you come up with Jerry?"

"Preston Jerico Carver. My middle name."

"Well, can I get you kids your lunch?" Dolores asked, setting water and coffee on the table.

"Two specials, please," Erin answered automatically. "Oh! Er... Is that..."

Jerry just nodded at her. Dolores chuckled as she went to get the orders in.

"I didn't mean to act like I knew just what you wanted," she said.

"But you do," he answered. "You always have. It's how I finally recognized you. You brought specials from the diner for our lunch with Mr. Jerico. You arranged them on the plate just like at the diner and set them down the same way. I didn't know what to do. I was... scared."

"Why would you be scared of me?" she asked.

"I... um... always have a bad time with women. It seems that when they know who I am and that I'm the head of JeriCorp and, well, rich, everything changes. I was afraid you'd figured out who I was and were stalking me."

Erin looked at him with wide eyes and then spluttered in laughter. He was baffled.

"You, rich? That's not really... um... I mean, you aren't poor. You have enough, but no woman in her right mind would pursue you for your wealth. And I wasn't pursuing you. I didn't know who you were until a few minutes ago. I mean, I knew Preston Carver, but I didn't know you were Jerry."

"I'm kind of rich," Jerry said indignantly.

"Not really," Erin said. "You forget I check all your... I check all Mr. Carver's accounts daily to be sure there is no unexpected activity. I flag anything I see for him."

"I ap... He appreciates that."

"Well, you don't have all that much money. I mean, you're comfortable and don't have to worry too much about what you spend—even though you do. Worry, I mean. You... Um... This is diffi-cult. Ms. Scott knows Mr. Carver could move out of the penthouse the company pays for and move back to Jerico House. Either way, it's rent free. But that isn't money."

"I... Mr. Carver owns stock. A significant portion of JeriCorp. He's a shareholder in Interlake Land Holdings. He has other stock in his portfolio," Jerry explained.

"Ms. Scott used to own a Rembrandt," Maizie said. It was becom-ing easier to refer to their office personae in the third person.

"What?"

"When she was single and well-employed, she invested in art. A Rembrandt etching was acquired for $3,500. When Ms. Scott married Mr. Silvers—a day she rues—she liquidated her investments to put the money into a house. The Rembrandt went for $1,500. Investments are where we put our hopes for a better tomorrow. They aren't real money."

"You have an interesting take on wealth," Jerry laughed.

"Who needs more than enough? Ms. Scott left a lucrative career in exchange for what she thought would be eternal bliss. Now she works for a living."

"M-M-Maizie, when I last saw you at the diner, I'd just decided I would... I would... you know... I would ask you out. Then you weren't here the next week."

"Oh, my! That's why Mr. Carver returned to the office so surly! Ms. Scott began to wonder if she'd made a wise choice to work for him."

"I am sorry. I was... He was... really upset. You know how he is about his routine."

"I do."

Dolores arrived with plates of food.

"Here's your lunch. Pulled pork with macaroni and cheese. Peach cobbler for dessert, on the house," Dolores said, setting their plates down. "Don't feel that you need to rush. I've set this table aside for the whole day if you need it."

"Thank you, Dolores," Maizie said. "I still have to get back to my job at a reasonable time."

Dolores left and Jerry smiled.

"You don't have to rush back. When I was coming here for lunch once a week, Mr. Carver always gave his assistant a long lunch break on those days."

"I don't like to seem like I'm taking unfair advantage of him."

"I don't think you... she ever has," Jerry said, taking a bite of macaroni and cheese. "Mmm. I haven't made mac and cheese in ages. What does she do to this? It's different."

"You have such joy for the food. I'm not sure Dolores knows what Jim does in the kitchen. He is a wizard."

"I want to meet him. Um... I mean... Do you think...? I can't just..."

"If you'd like, I'll introduce you and run interference if you need it. He's pretty easygoing, though. I'm sure you'll be fine," Maizie said.

"Food. Yes, I like to eat and try new things. But I like to cook. I experiment. I try something different every week. Sometimes I cook it for Mother and G-Pop. Sometimes, just for myself."

"How did your Italian roulade turn out? The recipe looked delicious!"

"Rrr. It was a bad day."

"Oh, I'm sorry to hear that. Perhaps you could try it again."

"Maybe. That... um... I'm not... Uh... Shannon Duval showed up in the middle of things."

"Just out of the blue? I'll have the elevator rekeyed."

"Let Ms. Scott do it," Jerry laughed. "Mrs. Duval told Mr. Carver that Ms. Scott had gone off for the weekend with Mr. Duval. I... I... I know I... Mr. Carver has no claim on Ms. Scott's social time. But he was very upset that she would go off with Mr. Duval. I... He really doesn't like the man."

"Neither does Ms. Scott," Maizie said firmly. "Off for the weekend? He talked me... her into a field trip to see the site and practice the presentation. It was clear before we were halfway there that he had other things on his mind. I... She left him on the road and hiked the area down to the lodge site by herself. When she was walking back up to the entrance, Mr. Jerico happened by and saved her from having to ride back to Jerico City with Mr. Duval."

"I'm sorry the whole incident affected me... Mr. Carver more than it had any business doing. He felt betrayed. And after Mrs.

Duval's invasion, he spent the rest of the weekend cleaning. I'm sorry if I... he was short with you last week."

They finished the meal and Dolores poured them more coffee to have with their cobbler. When they were finished, they both started to speak at the same time.

"You first," Jerry said.

"Jerry, this has been a very nice time. I always looked forward to seeing you on Thursdays. I'm... I don't think it's a good idea for us to um... make a habit of it. As well as we've kept work separate from our lunch, it is still there. I, Erin Scott, work for you, Preston Carver. Things like that get complicated and we shouldn't muddy the waters. I've only been divorced four months. Even if we weren't working together, that's awfully soon to start... you know. I mean... Maybe you had no intention of that and I jumped to conclusions, but we should keep things professional. Don't you think?"

She might have been expressing doubt with that last phrase. If he'd tried to convince her they could see each other socially, she'd probably have considered it seriously. It was a pain to take the noble route.

"I... was going to say the same thing," he said. "I... When... Before, it seemed possible to see this really nice woman I met in the diner. She didn't know who I was. It seemed safe. Um... I... really wish... Well, Mr. Carver and Ms. Scott will see each other a lot and will enjoy working together. Right? I'd better pay the bill so we can get back to work."

"Yes. Um... Jerry... thank you. This was really nice. I'll see you around."

Erin got up and dropped a twenty next to her plate to pay for her lunch. Jerry did the same. When Erin turned away from the table, Jerry dropped another ten for an extra tip.

MR. CARVER DID not return to the office that afternoon. He sent an email indicating that he was wrapping up a number of things in his office at Jerico House and would be meeting with Mr. Jerico. He would be in the next day.

Erin breathed a sigh of relief. She was sure she could return to a professional relationship with Mr. Carver, but was glad to have a few hours before she had to face the reality. What a great way to screw up a day. Or a life.

She found it difficult to concentrate on work that afternoon. She picked up a 5x5x5 cube and sat in front of the windows for fifteen minutes as she worked it. She finally got back to her desk and began sorting through the reviews of the different phases of the plan. It was a huge project and she organized the pieces so no one had to face the entire plan at once. She assumed, however, that Mr. Carver had it all in that remarkable head of his.

She received an email from Carver with his grocery order for the coming week and was amused to find the ingredients for macaroni and cheese on the list. She ordered it for delivery on Friday and wondered if Mr. Carver would have laundry to send out Friday afternoon. For that matter, she didn't know what he'd been wearing the past week..

She completed her usual end-of-day routine, then went home to try to put her head back together after the surprise of the day.

"IT WAS SO nice to see you with Jerry Thursday," Dolores said when they got together Sunday afternoon. "And to see him finally pull his hood back and take off the dark glasses. Are you going to see him again?"

"It's impossible not to," Erin sighed. "Not that I'd want to avoid him but... Dolores, he's my boss! He started coming here in his hoodie and dark glasses because he was afraid people who work for him would recognize him and make life hard. But then I got the job working for him and when he found out, he freaked out. Which is what I'm doing now that I know."

"Wait. What? He stalked you?" Dolores asked.

"No. Neither of us knew we were Jerry and Maizie. In the office, we're Ms. Scott and Mr. Carver. He figured it out a couple of weeks ago and hasn't been in the office since. I didn't know until we met Thursday. He thought I'd been stalking him. It's such a soap opera!"

"Oh, my goodness. Let me pour you another glass of wine. That one seems to have evaporated," Dolores said. Erin drank again. "So, the chairman of the board of JeriCorp—who, I understand is part of the city's famed Jerico family—decides randomly to go slumming and have lunch at the diner. But to keep from being recognized, he pulls up a hoodie shirt, dark glasses, and a mask and hardly speaks at all for five months while you wait his table. Then your marriage falls apart and you have to start looking for a job. Just when the mystery man decides he should ask you out, you quit here and go to work for him—not knowing it's the same guy. Am I close?"

"Yes."

"And he didn't figure it out when he interviewed you and read your resume?"

"He didn't. I never interviewed with him. And he never saw my resume until two weeks ago. I was hired and trained by his mother. It was like I'd always worked there from the day I arrived."

"Did his mother have plans for the two of you?" Dolores asked.

"I don't think so. No more than a mother sizes up every woman as a potential mate for her son. And she didn't know Jerry was coming to the diner every week."

"You've had every opportunity size him up yourself. What kind of guy is he?"

"Nice. A little socially inept, but well-intentioned. A creative genius. He hides behind a façade of business formality to prevent himself from panicking. It's a way of distancing himself. He is always proper in his behavior and always treats me professionally. I suppose if I took the time to analyze the characteristics of Jerry in the diner and Mr. Carver in the office, I'd have seen the similarities. But it just never occurred to me to imagine they might be the same person. Just as it didn't occur to him."

"So, what are you going to do? Dating your boss could be a little awkward."

"No way. We've agreed we cannot be in a dating relationship. Can you imagine what that would do to both of our reputations in the office? It would be impossible. Half the people would think I got special treatment because I was dating him. The other half would think

I was available for anyone in the office to screw. Oh! That would be just what Mr. Duval needed. I'd never hear the end of it!"

"But that's terrible. You like each other. And you are simply going to sit in the same office all day every day and not have it affect you?"

"It was hard on Friday. It took us most of the day to relax around each other. But we have to be firmly in the friend zone. We can work together as friends. We couldn't as lovers. Ack! I shouldn't even have said that word. It never came up!"

"But you thought about it."

"No! I mean... Maybe. A little. Not seriously."

"So, are you going to quit?" Dolores asked after pouring them each another glass of wine.

"Why would I quit? I have a great job. I like what I do. I like my employer. It's exciting and challenging. Quit? You've got to be kidding!"

"But then there would be nothing between you to stop you from dating."

"Dolores, I threw away a perfectly good career in Cleveland to marry the man of my dreams. My nightmares! I'm not going down that road again."

"You poor thing. I don't know how you'll stand it."

"I'll do my job and do the best I can. That's all either of us can do."

Chapter Nineteen

"WHY SO MOROSE?" Gene asked his friend as he launched a long shot that bounced around the rim and out. "Things are going well. You're spending most of your time down at Cloudhaven, which is where you want to be anyway."

"It's... Ms. Scott," Preston moaned. "I can't make anything work."

"What needs to work that isn't?"

"We agreed to keep our relationship professional, but I'm always messing up."

"Like?"

"Friday, I tossed her a Rubik's cube and challenged her to a contest."

"Don't tell me she beat you!"

"No. But we started laughing and teasing each other and then both became aware of what we were doing and put the cubes down and went back to work. It was embarrassing."

"To whom? I don't understand what the big deal is. Office romances are a common occurrence. You're both single and unattached. If you want to see each other, do it," Gene said.

"I can't. Not while she reports to me. Maybe if she was in a different area of the company, I could justify it. But dating my personal assistant is such a cliché of the boss taking advantage of his employee. I was suspicious of her possibly wanting a relationship because of my money, but she has to be just as suspicious of me wanting to be with her. It's just too complicated."

"Move her to a different part of the company and then start dating."

"I *want* her as my assistant! She manages the business better than I do. Why do you think I've been able to be down at Cloudhaven the past three weeks, since the board approved the project? She's a wizard with the project planning software. She knows exactly how to respond to Duval. She handles all the daily work in the office. She even approved hiring a new assistant for Duval! She has her finger on the pulse of every department in the company. I just nod and tell her to make it happen."

"Hmm. You are in danger of a *9 to 5* situation."

"What's that?"

"The old-school satirical movie, *9 to 5*. The secretaries kidnap and restrain the boss and take over running the company without him. It turns out more profitable. Great Dolly Parton song."

"I don't think she'd..."

"Of course not. She loves you."

"What? She couldn't..."

"I don't mean she's *in* love with you, but she loves who you are and how creative you are. She's just helping to clear you for action where you're needed. I could use an assistant like that," Gene said. "I'm not trying to keep a complex company alive as you are, though. My biggest task is keeping the scientists from murdering each other."

"I don't envy you that one. But it doesn't help me with my real problem. I would like Ms. Scott to like me the way Maizie likes Jerry. We just can't be both," Preston said.

"You could be the one to resign," Gene mused.

"I could what? I don't see how that would help anything." He eyed the hoop and launched the ball. It swished. "G-Pop would kill me," he muttered.

"JERICORP BOARD OF Directors monthly meeting," the heading of the email read. Erin read the memo carefully. Usually, she would be the one to put out the meeting notice. Next week it would be a month since the meeting approving Cloudhaven. She read on: "Order of business: Leadership review. All senior leadership to be reviewed and voted for confidence. This includes Preston Carver, Chairman and CEO; Royce Duval, President and COO; Leroy Masters, CFO; Naomi Dirksen, Vice Chair and General Counsel."

The meeting announcement was signed by Naomi Dirksen, the Vice Chair of the Board. Dirksen, Masters, Duval, and Carver were members of the board by virtue of their positions as corporate officers. Mrs. Carver and Mr. Jerico held ownership positions, but were inactive most of the time. Three men from area businesses rounded out the number: Reinholdt, Vaughn, and Hathaway.

It was just a normal board meeting, but for some reason, it bothered Erin that the announcement came from Dirksen and not from her. Erin forwarded the announcement to Carver, Carver, and Jerico, then decided to pay a visit to Ms. Dirksen. Erin did go through the main offices several times a week, so she wasn't a stranger to Ms. Dirksen's secretary, who waved her in.

"Good morning, Miss Scott," Dirksen said politely.

"And to you, Ms. Dirksen. I wanted to check in with you to see why the board meeting announcement came from your office today instead of Mr. Carver's. It's a little unusual."

"You know, it should be your boss who is knocking on my door."

"He's working remotely at Cloudhaven, getting the infrastructure started."

"Yes, we might want to make some changes to that. The feeling on the board is that the tone of the development should be more upscale. It's such a beautiful piece of property but the design appears to be rather middle class, if you don't mind my saying."

"I do. The board approved the project and it's underway. It seems a little sneaky to call for a review of officers and an unspoken agenda for changing a plan that is well underway."

"All senior executives are being reviewed, including me," Dirksen responded. "It happens every year. The board members feel there is a crisis of leadership. The presentation of the proposal is a case in point. Mr. Duval has indicated that what you presented was not what he would have presented, nor what Carver should have presented, rather than sending an assistant to handle a board meeting. I am vice chair of the board and have conducted ten times the number of meetings Preston has. Now, we've agreed to a $500,000,000 project and no one is convinced we have the leadership to pull it off."

"So, you want to become Chairman of the Board?"

"No. Not at all. Royce Duval will be the leading contender for the position. He is the face of JeriCorp. Everyone follows where he leads."

"He leads where Mr. Carver tells him to. What has Mr. Duval led the company to?" Erin asked.

"The most recent is his foresight in planning a golf course for Cloudhaven. It's hard to believe there wasn't one in the initial prospectus. Then there is the way he closed the Mackenzie Project and cut the company losses. Over the past several years, Duval has led us to good partnerships and profitable projects. He's a natural to lead the board."

"It's ridiculous," Erin spat. "It's hard to believe Duval can so effectively pull the wool over the eyes of the board. All the things you mention were spearheaded by Preston Carver and executed by Royce Duval except the golf course. Even that was Shannon Duval's idea, not Mr. Duval. Duval is an empty suit. A smile with perfect white teeth. He has never made a decision on behalf of the company."

"I understand your loyalty to your boss. Don't become too attached to him. Rumor has it that he wants to become the chef at the lodge at Cloudhaven. He doesn't even want the responsibility of the company. He just sees the development as an opportunity to feed his real passion."

"I would put his leadership up against any ten people in the company. He merely depends on a loyal staff. It appears that trust is misplaced."

"Your words may be put to the test, Miss Scott. Wednesday at two. Let him defend his claim. We can't risk the company on a hermit."

ERIN WAS FURIOUS. She heard much the same story from Mr. Masters. She didn't need to stop to talk to Duval. The senior executives of JeriCorp were launching a coup against their owner and CEO. She calmly dialed Carver's number and was pleased to find him in range of a cell tower.

"Mr. Carver, the board wants to replace you as chairman and CEO. You need to come into the office and prepare your campaign to retain your position," she said.

"Oh. That again. Perhaps it would be better. I'm not much of a CEO and am really in my element out here on the site."

"They want to change that, too. You know it's Duval. He wants it 'upgraded' to something fancier. We can't have Duval with that authority! The man mounted his horse and rode off in all directions."

"Very funny, Ms. Scott. Take care of it. You're much better at it than I am. I give you my authority to set a strategy for the board meeting. I'm almost finished with the street grading and paving plan. I'll try to get back to town next week."

"Yes, sir."

THEIR CONVERSATION DID nothing to ease her upset. Erin sat facing the windows with a 5x5x5 cube and tried to determine what to do about the challenge to Mr. Carver's position. She was absolutely certain that if Duval held the reins, the Cloudhaven development would crash and burn.

The other three senior executives were firmly committed to having Royce Duval promoted to chairman and CEO. There were nine members of the board. Three were the senior executives and three were family members. That meant Duval must have at least one of the three outside board members committed to him. He wouldn't dare launch such an attack without at least four of the nine members and the hope of convincing another.

She called up the bios of the three outside board members and compiled a quick dossier on each. She made her decision and set an appointment for the next morning.

"THANK YOU FOR seeing me, Mr. Vaughn," Erin said when she was greeted by the CEO of Vaughn Home Furnishings. She had interviewed with him when she was looking for a job. Mr. Vaughn was an older member—perhaps the oldest—of the board of directors. He was of Mr. Jerico's generation and had been almost silent during the presentation. His only comment had been, "Jerico has his hand in the project? I'm in."

"How can I help you today, Miss Scott?" Vaughn asked.

"I'm sure you have received notice of the board meeting to be held next week," Erin began. Vaughn nodded. "I have uncovered a kind of conspiracy among the senior executives to make a wholesale change in the leadership of the company and the direction of the Cloudhaven project."

"I think that is obvious."

"I've spoken to Ms. Dirksen and Mr. Masters. They seem to be driving an effort to install Royce Duval as Chairman and CEO."

"Royce is a good man. Flashy, but generally solid. He'd drive the company wherever the board pointed him," Vaughn nodded.

"In my opinion, that could be the problem. Mr. Duval is a salesman. He sells whatever people want to buy, not necessarily what he has to sell. I've worked with Mr. Carver for three months and have found that he is the true creative force behind the company. He has issues that prevent him from expressing himself freely in front of a group—even the board—but having Duval as his salesman has always been enough to drive his decisions. It's a good fit for Duval as well."

"I have to say, Preston is lucky to have you as well."

"I'm just filling the blank spaces where he is unable to. This week, for example, we have been working together on the master plan for Cloudhaven's infrastructure. You can't imagine how complex the PERT chart is."

"Oh, I can. I haven't always been content to limit myself to furniture manufacturing. You'll find half a dozen businesses in this town with the name of Vaughn attached to them. I've divested myself of control as I have no direct descendants to pass them on to. When I go, the only one of the original families left will be the Jericos, and they, of course, are now the Carvers. At the rate Preston is going, he might be the last of the family line."

"I'm sure he'll find his own happiness down the road. What I am most concerned with is changing leadership at this delicate time could jeopardize the design, the construction, and the timeline of Cloudhaven. I believe we need to keep Mr. Carver at the helm, at least until the plans are stabilized and the first phase is complete. Any change before that time will be detrimental to the company and the employees."

"I see. You make a very good case, Miss Scott." He paused and looked out his window as he nodded his head. "When Lawrence Jerico recruited me for the board of directors of JeriCorp, it was more than a business deal. We are the last remaining patriarchs of the city, if you will. Even the family names are fading into obscurity. But I agreed at that time to cast my vote with the family. So, I will give you my proxy to vote with Lawrence Jerico on all matters before the board next week. I will not be at the meeting, so I won't need to face my fellow board members. Let me have my secretary draw up the proxy."

"Thank you, sir."

"Don't be premature in your thanks. You still have one more board member to win over. I suggest Hathaway will be your most likely ally. He's the same age as Carver—went to school together. He's done well in electronics. Took over a company that was making vacuum tubes and then transistors. Now they make silicon components—almost all operated by robotics. Very profitable. If I were to guess, I'd say Reinholdt has already committed to the coup."

"Thank you for the advice, sir. I'll try to get a meeting with Mr. Hathaway before the board meets."

GENE HATHAWAY WAS not available. She was told he was in California for a conference in Silicon Valley. She would have to focus on the family since Reinholdt refused to take a meeting with her. She needed to make sure the Jerico family would vote to retain

Preston. He had a close relationship with his grandfather and unless something drastic had changed in the past month, she was confident Jerico and Mrs. Carver would vote with Preston.

She stopped at the diner and picked up two orders of the daily special, then went directly to the monumental structure of Jerico House.

It was an imposing building, now on the National Register of Historic Places. She thought it was the oldest structure in Jerico City, though another historic mansion was on the east side of town. Eight steps led up from the circular drive to the pillared portico and front doors. She wondered briefly if she should have gone around to a servants' entry, but she was already standing at the door with the bell chiming deep inside the house. She was surprised to find Mr. Jerico opening the door.

"Ms. Scott! What a surprise. Come in."

"I've come to bring Mr. Carver lunch, sir. If you could direct me to him, I'll not bother you," Erin said. She was becoming rather good at simply assuming the close when she wanted something. She didn't ask permission to see Mr. Carver. She didn't care if she was directed to his office or his bedroom. She spent her days with him in isolation. It wouldn't make a difference to her where she met him today.

"Of course. Third floor, top of the stairs. The kitchen and dining room are just to the right when you reach the top of the stairs."

"Thank you, sir."

She headed the direction he pointed and came to an abrupt stop at the dragon staircase. She was on a mission, but this massive work of art required a moment to pay her respects. It was beautiful, sweeping around to the landing on the second floor. Once she had caught her breath, she headed up the stairs.

At the top, she saw the kitchen and dining room to her right and went directly to them. Mr. Carver had a more elaborate apartment here in Jerico House than he had at the office. She could see through another door that he was in an office at the back of the house. She immediately set about plating the food and giving it a brief boost in the microwave. Then she went to his door.

"Mr. Carver, lunch is served. Will you join me?"

"Maizie! What a surprise!"

He wore jeans and an open collared shirt with a gray college hoodie over it. The hood was pulled over his head, but he wasn't wearing a mask or dark glasses.

"I wish I'd had an invitation, Jerry. I had to simply barge my way in past your grandfather," Erin laughed.

"I'm sure he put up no resistance. Now if you'd met Mother at the door, she'd have carried you up the stairs."

The two went into the dining room and sat at the table where Erin had put the plates and flatware. The day's special was Yankee pot roast with assorted root vegetables.

"I'm afraid I'm here on business," Erin said.

"I know. Let's just enjoy being Maizie and Jerry through lunch. Then we can deal with today's crisis."

"It is nice to see you in your other habitat," she said, gesturing at the third-floor apartment.

"The two apartments on the second floor don't have kitchens. That's where Mother and Grandfather live. Matilda cooks most of the meals in the first-floor kitchen and serves in the breakfast nook or the dining room. Living up here is almost like being independent."

"I suppose there is still a stigma attached to a man living at home with his mother and grandfather," Erin smiled.

"Oh, don't you know it! Unlike you, I've never had to go out looking for a home to buy. The nearest I came was the apartment I shared with Gene Hathaway in college. It's one of the reasons I like the apartment in the office. At least I'm not living with Mommy."

"You know, you don't have to stay away. It *is* still your home. I don't infringe on it."

"No, I don't avoid the office because you are there. In fact, I miss you, though I suppose I shouldn't say that. I mean it professionally."

"I miss you, too, Jerry." She left off the 'professional' part of the sentence.

"Having you in the office has liberated me to take care of important issues on the job site. You know, I'm educated and trained as an architect and city planner. After all the initial plans were drawn up, my real job was out on the jobsite. I find I can communicate to the crews without much problem. It's very different than communicating in the office or in public."

"I'm glad to hear that."

They finished their meal and stood at the sink together to clean up the dishes, still joking about where he was comfortable. He hardly ever stumbled or stuttered when he was talking to Erin. She'd noticed that was true in the office as well as when they were talking informally as Maizie and Jerry. But ultimately, it was time to go into Preston's home office and have the meeting Erin came to have.

"I need you to be at the meeting Wednesday to vote to preserve your position. I'm not sure, but I suspect Ms. Dirksen is organizing the senior execs. She talks a good line about having Royce in the true leadership position, but I think she fancies herself as the power behind the throne. Typical of a corporate lawyer. She has the three senior execs and one other board member in her camp. Mr. Reinholdt declined to take a meeting with me, saying I had nothing to say that would change his mind. Mr. Hathaway has been in California, but will be back for the meeting. I'll have to convince him on the spot."

"So, the opposition, as you style them, has four confirmed votes and is counting on one of the other of us five joining them," Preston said.

"That's the way I see it. We need your family to vote as a bloc in order to put the pressure on Hathaway. You need to be seen as the leader of the company."

"I'm not the leader," Preston said. "I'm a manager. I know what needs to be done and I can direct resources to do it. Duval, for all I dislike him, is a leader. He can just point to an objective and people will follow him to it. There's a difference."

"A strong business is more dependent on a good manager than a good leader," Erin said. "A leader will lead people right off a cliff if he isn't a good manager. Knowing what actually needs to be done and directing resources is more valuable than chasing squirrels."

"Even with my mother, grandfather, and me, you have only three votes," Preston said.

"I have Vaughn's proxy to vote with Mr. Jerico," Erin said. "And I believe a word from you is all it would take to convince Mr. Hathaway."

"You have been busy!"

He reached for a cube on his desk and in a minute had it solved. He tossed it to her and she immediately started resetting it.

"I won't come to the meeting," he said eventually. He held up his hand before she could protest. "I think we need to approach it as if it were already decided in our favor. My favor, I guess. I'm the only one who is at risk here. And they can't take away my membership on the board. It is likely that I could mount a proxy fight at the annual meeting and oust all of them."

"Would you do that?"

"No. You know what kind of public presence a proxy fight would require. And I don't believe either Mother or G-Pop would head it up. What I will do is grant you my proxy. I believe we can go downstairs and you can persuade Mother and G-Pop to give you theirs. With Vaughn, that would give you the same number of votes as the coup. You would need to be more convincing to Hathaway than Dirksen is."

"You'll talk to him?"

"If he'll take my call. Let's talk to Jerico and Mother. None of us like to be at the board meetings. They'll give you their proxies. If the board wants to keep me as chairman, fine. But I'm not going to fight them for it."

"You're going to let me fight them for it."

He grinned at her.

"You are much better equipped for this kind of fight than I am."

Chapter Twenty

ERIN FOUND HERSELF at the center of the family confab, being interviewed in a way she had not anticipated. She thought it would be simple to have Mr. Jerico and Mrs. Carver agree to the plan to keep Preston as the head of the company.

"So, why do you think Preston should stay at the head of the table?" Lawrence asked.

"Are you doubting it, Mr. Jerico?"

"You have declared yourself willing to go before the board of directors and fight to have Preston retained as chairman and CEO. I want to know your rationale and how you will present that to the board. My rationale is obvious. He is my grandson and heir to the Jerico business and fortune. Why do *you* think he should stay at the head of the table?"

"I've worked with Mr. Carver for three months. In that time, I have had a more intense look inside an extremely creative mind than I believe anyone else in the company has had in the past ten years. He is not just creative, though. He is a problem-solver. He can look at a very large dataset and reduce it to actionable items. That's the basis of a good manager. My experience with Mr. Duval, on the other hand, is that he is..." Erin cut herself off before blasting the company president.

"Go ahead and say it, Ms. Scott," Jacqueline said.

"Mr. Duval is a valuable component in the corporate culture," Erin said carefully. "He is a salesman and is capable of taking Mr. Carver's ideas and selling them. But in my opinion, he is a vacuous imbecile who gets along on his smile and his backslap. He's a womanizer, and he attempts to seduce his clients the same way he seduces women. But as far as the business is concerned, he hasn't an idea in his head."

"What about the idea for the golf course at the resort?" Lawrence asked.

"Something I am certain will be brought up at the board meeting," Erin said. "Ms. Dirksen has already been vocal about what amazing foresight he had in spotting the weakness in the prospectus. But after looking into the matter further, I have arrived at the conclusion that the idea was actually Mrs. Duval's, and that she arranged the meeting between her husband and the golf course developers to form a consortium. While a golf course will certainly be a draw for some people, it wouldn't have been considered a first phase project if the consortium hadn't proposed developing it themselves. There were other suitable plots in Cloudhaven that would have made equally good golf courses if developed later in the process. The payback Mr. Duval is expecting on his investment is overinflated. I do hope none of you gave him money for his project."

"Ooh. I like that. Do you think any of the other board members have invested in it?" Preston asked.

"Possibly as a token. It's hard to believe people at that level, who deal with money on a regular basis, could be so taken in by Mr. Duval. However, it also would explain why they are enthused about the idea of upscaling the project and trying to draw a more affluent clientele than we have projected," Erin said, making a note to herself.

"How would you approach this differently than Duval would if the decision was thrust upon you?" Jacqueline asked.

"Well, the initial prospectus was good. The destination conceived by Mr. Carver suits the location perfectly. It does not overtax resources, for example—either natural resources or financial resources. The current prospectus represents years of planning and research. It would be foolhardy to change directions when we are about to break ground and throw the entire proposal back into early planning stages again. While I am always aware that new information can alter the execution of plans, I do not see any such new information on the table."

"Very well," Lawrence said. "I'll give you my proxy. Jacqueline?"

"Yes. I'm in. However, Ms. Scott, I believe you should be prepared for a heated contest and you might need to make compromises you would not normally consider to accomplish the larger goals," Jacqueline said. "Most especially, you need to be prepared for a personal attack on your character. Duval will try to position you as a mere secretary and will undercut your arguments, dismissing you as inexperienced and uninformed. Good luck."

"Thank you, ma'am."

THAT'S A STRANGE *family*, Erin mused at the end of the day. Even after they had given her their proxies, they continued to quiz her on every aspect of the business. She had gone to the mansion to convince the three family members to attend the meeting and cast their votes. Instead, they had drawn up proxies and given her power of attorney to negotiate on their behalf. Even Preston had worked with her on areas of the project that could be compromised in order to make it look like they were giving ground to Duval and his cronies.

She wasn't expecting that kind of authority, but it was in keeping with the responsibilities Preston had given her in his absence. She'd stopped on her way out to take another look at the dragon staircase. It was impossible not to. Somehow, the dragon seemed to represent the family's mystery and adventure. One day, she would like to know more about it.

Once she was back in the office the next day, she took care of the usual daily tasks and settled in to compose her arguments to the board. While she had four votes in her hand, she was only one voice among six who would be in the room. She needed to win Hathaway over quickly and her arguments for how the voting should be done needed to be firm enough that Dirksen, the corporate counsel, had to abide by them. She could expect Reinholdt and Duval to be vocal in attempting to drown her out.

Hathaway was not only of her generation, but he had also been Carver's best friend all the way back in high school or possibly before. It was odd to think of Mr. Carver as having friends. He seemed to be such a recluse. But she could certainly see Jerry having a select group of very good friends and was sure that more closely matched the man's real personality.

She allowed herself a few minutes to think about her lunch with 'the hoodie man,' as her fellow waitresses had called him. She and Jerry had so easily suspended their office roles and simply enjoyed having lunch as friends. He *was* a good friend, and she was determined to be a good friend to him.

ERIN WAS NERVOUS and skipped lunch before the meeting. Her stomach did not want to settle down. This was more nerve-wracking than making the presentation to sell the resort concept. She knew why. She was alone. It would be so much easier if Mr. Carver would be sitting next to her. Or even if he'd been in the office this morning. Instead, she'd received four email messages from the four people she held proxies for, wishing her good luck.

She stood outside the boardroom door a minute before entering. She could see the other board members gathering, coffee cups in hand, acting as if the vote were a done deal. She squared her shoulders and went into the room.

The five board members in the room stopped to stare at her as she took her seat in Preston's chair at the head of the table.

"Ms. Scott, this is a board meeting. Are you here to make a presentation like you did last month?" Ms. Dirksen asked.

"No, Madam Vice Chairman. I bear Mr. Carver's proxy for the vote. It is necessary to keep him at the helm as he is the chief architect of the corporation. We have no design for Cloudhaven and no future projects without him."

"Well, it's not likely to do you much good, but we have to keep the business record clean anyway. Shall we vote to accept the slate of candidates for executive positions?" Dirksen said.

"No," Erin spoke up. "The Corporate Bylaws dictate that election of officers and approval of senior executives must be individually nominated and voted upon. Mr. Carver pointed that out and insists that the board abide by the bylaws."

"Are you really going to sort this out and make each individual make his preference known?" Duval asked.

"Yes, Mr. Duval. As there is an alternate slate of candidates submitted here by Mr. Carver, which holds discrepancies with the slate presented by Vice Chairman Dirksen, the vote must be tallied for each position. This will give shareholders the opportunity to express their preferences at the annual meeting when it comes to approving the slate of candidates for the board of directors."

The board members shifted uncomfortably. Simply having a vote carry unanimously for the entire slate of officers provided anonymity that a roll-call vote would not have. There were a lot of family sympathizers among the shareholders of JeriCorp and Erin had just leveled a veiled threat that the family might present an entirely different slate of candidates for the board at the annual meeting. It would be bad form to appear to attack the family.

"Well, let's start with Chief Financial Officer. The only candidate is on both slates. Are there other nominations? Those in favor of Leroy Masters as Chief Financial Officer, raise your hand." She counted the hands quickly. "The nomination is approved and Leroy Masters is confirmed as Chief Financial Officer."

Erin had not exposed her entire hand. When the vote was tallied, she simply raised her hand with the others and it was counted as Mr. Carver's vote. The other three board members were counted as absent. Dirksen moved on to her own nominations and to those of Royce Duval. Finally, it came to the position of Chairman of the Board.

"I request a roll-call vote of all members," Erin said. "And in that matter, I hold the proxies for Preston Carver, Lawrence Jerico, Jacqueline Carver, and Richard Vaughn. All four vote in favor of retaining Preston Carver as Chairman of the Board."

"You've been a busy little beaver, haven't you?" Duval asked disgustedly. "Well, your four votes are not a majority. We vote for the opposition. Oh. That's me."

"Not so fast, Duval," Hathaway said. "Ms. Scott has shown us the family is not absent or unaware of what happens in the company. That means they may well be organizing a new board for approval at the annual meeting. Ms. Scott has shown decisiveness in gathering proxies, and I daresay, her campaign was driven by her boss, Preston Carver."

"Are you voting against the rest of us and for Preston?" Dirksen asked bitterly.

"Maybe. I'll propose a compromise that I believe will be acceptable to the family. I propose we retain Preston Carver as chairman, provided we have a new and decisive candidate for CEO."

"You want to have Preston as chairman and me as CEO?" Royce said. "It seems silly, but I guess I'm okay with that."

"No," Hathaway said. "I'm sorry, Royce, but you just don't have what it takes to run the company. The only thing we've ever complained about since Preston took over the reins is that he can't function in a social or public environment. His management skills are exemplary. We need a CEO who can make decisions and execute them."

"You have a nomination, Gene?" Dirksen asked.

"I propose we approve Preston Carver as continuing chairman of the board, under condition that we also accept the nomination of Erin Scott as our CEO."

Erin caught her breath and sat back in the chair. *What on earth was Hathaway playing at? I can't be CEO!*

"Are you out of your mind, Hathaway?" Reinholdt asked. He was the board member voting with the senior execs and was about the same age as Dirksen and Duval. He didn't say much in meetings, but was a frequent golfing partner of Duval. "We don't know a thing about her! I'd sooner have the company run by an orangutan."

"Which explains your alliance with Duval," Hathaway shot. "It's not true that we know nothing about Ms. Scott. I investigated her thoroughly. Her former CEO at Allard Holdings had her on a fast track, grooming her for senior management. In her eight years there, she led her division to record profits and oversaw the expansion of the Cleveland Regional Center. Marriage brought her to Jerico City, and divorce brought her to JeriCorp. We are lucky to have her and should carefully consider what a merger with a company like Allard would look like."

Erin just stared at him. The idea that she was leading Allard to JeriCorp for a possible merger was a shock to all the board members. It had never even occurred to her.

"I disagree," Royce said. "We should be preserving our positions and company, not preparing it for a takeover." He looked at his co-conspirators. They looked away and subtly shook their heads.

"It's really up to Ms. Scott," Hathaway said. "Will you accept this compromise? One vote for Preston Carver as Chairman of the Board and Erin Scott as CEO. I move this new slate."

"I... did not come here looking for this," Erin began as if she was talking to Mr. Carver. Then she sighed. "I cast four proxy votes in favor of Mr. Hathaway's new slate of Carver and Scott."

"That's five in favor," Hathaway said. "We made all the other candidate elections unanimous. Shall we do the same with this one?"

The other four board members raised their hands, though Duval looked daggers at Erin.

"Congratulations, Miss Scott," Ms. Dirksen said in a sweet voice. "We'll all be looking forward to your leadership. I don't believe we need to revisit the plans for Cloudhaven in view of this decision. Meeting adjourned."

ERIN STEPPED BACK into the penthouse office and looked around. She wondered if she would have to leave it to execute her new responsibilities. She would need to meet with HR and find out what the salary and benefits of her new position were. If she survived her next meeting with Mr. Carver. She knew very well he could still fire her.

Since she'd taken her first college internship, Erin had dreamt of sitting in the corner office of a major corporation. She'd been fortunate to have exemplary bosses over the years—men and women who mentored and prepared her for authority and responsibility. When she was given the responsibility of opening a full regional office center in Cleveland, she'd happily taken the opportunity and proven herself more than capable. As a reward, she was named regional vice president.

Perhaps it had been too satisfying for her to reach that level. After her parents' death and Bruce's proposal, she started thinking about having a family and devoting herself to raising her children. It hadn't been a difficult decision to leave her position and go to Jerico City with her husband.

She wondered if that was still her dream. She didn't trust men easily these days. Perhaps in a few years, when she was satisfied with her life and success again, she would find a nice enough guy who would get her pregnant so she could raise her child. She didn't need the man for anything else. She could easily consign Duval, Reinholdt, and Masters to the same mental flames she thought for her husband. All men.

Maybe not Carver. She thought she knew him pretty well after working for him for three months. What did she really know?

She wouldn't be thinking about that for a while. She was now the Chief Executive Officer of a mid-size corporation. She needed to more fully understand the financial standing. She'd thought for some time that the Mackenzie project in St. Louis didn't need to be a complete loss. In fact, Carver had directed the company foreclose on the property and acquire it out of receivership. They could proceed with the construction and either sell the building or lease it.

In fact, Hathaway had planted an idea. It was ridiculous to imagine she had come to Jerico City as a vanguard to prepare for a corporate merger. Allard was much larger and diverse in a different way than JeriCorp. But she wondered where they were in their westward expansion. They might well be ready for that new regional center in St. Louis. She would make a note to check into that in the next week.

She fixed coffee and went to sit on the sofa looking out over the rooftop patio. She hadn't meant to take part of her boss's job. It was a tradeoff. It was the only way she could preserve his position. Besides, she supposed it really didn't change anything. Mr. Carver was still in charge as far as she was concerned. If she relayed his orders through her own office, it would be just like it was now. She'd been handling more and more of the daily job responsibilities anyway. She'd even initiated the planning document because it needed to be done. It was what an assistant should do. How on earth did any of his prior assistants function?

It had been an exhausting day. She decided to just close her eyes for a few minutes, and then she'd take care of preparing the penthouse for the return of her boss.

Chapter Twenty-One

LAWRENCE WAITED TO tell Preston what he'd done until he was sure the board meeting was underway. He'd called Gene Hathaway with an off-the-wall idea that Erin Scott should be CEO of the company. He wanted to give the board a wake-up call that they weren't as all-powerful as they assumed. Some corporate officers needed to get back in line where they belonged.

Preston wasn't sure how to respond to his grandfather. Putting Erin in a position of power like that just played into the scenario that she was a gold digger, stalking him for his money and position. But that didn't hold water. She just wasn't that kind of person and Preston had to face the possibility she was really as nice and kind and… downright attractive as she appeared to be.

"You've read her resume," Lawrence said. "Gene called her references at Allard. And I think it was you who suggested dropping the hint that Allard was thinking of a buyout."

"I suggested… I was afraid that was why she got the job in my office. Do you really think Allard would want to buy us out?"

"I doubt it. We aren't in the sweet spot of their holdings. Actually, we're a little small for them. That Cleveland Regional office that Erin was Vice President in charge of? She had more employees there than we have in Jerico City. But Duval, Dirksen, and Masters haven't paid attention to what's out there. They still think she's just a

glorified secretary. You know, having her get your laundry and groceries just amplifies that message."

"I think she could have talked Gene into voting with us without
the added incentive," Preston grumbled.

"Maybe. But the family is sending a message here, son. This is
our company and we choose who runs it."

"Yes, sir."

Preston's phone rang and he saw Gene was calling.

"Well, did you oust me from my office?" Preston barked into the
phone.

"Only halfway," Gene laughed. "I take it your grandfather filled
you in on the plan. I'd have to say it was successful. Duval, Dirksen,
and Masters folded up their tents and crept quietly away. And now
they are all thinking about what they can do to make their shares in
JeriCorp more valuable in case of a buyout."

"And Ms. Scott went along with it?"

"I didn't give her much choice. She was committed to preserving
your position on the board. I held the fifth vote she needed. I think
Reinholdt is going to resign from the board, by the way. It will be a
good timing to get another independent board member signed up."

"Erin Scott."

"Well, unless you change the bylaws, she'll have a position on the
board by virtue of her office as CEO. No. I'm thinking you should
look at one of the younger execs in town—or even out of town.
Nothing says we're growing like having a board member or two who
are from larger companies outside of town."

"I don't think we need to be too heavy-handed about it. If your
plan worked as well as you say it did, we've reasserted control. If Ms.
Scott will let us have it."

"If not, it's in good hands. She's probably celebrating in your
office now."

"I should go over there."

AS PRESTON DROVE to the office, he realized he felt rather light
of heart. He'd never really liked the responsibility of running the

company, even though he shuffled all the public aspects of it off to Duval. He wondered how much of that Ms. Scott would wrest from Duval. As far as Preston was concerned, it was a burden that kept him from thinking about the real work of architecture and development. He wanted to create things. He wanted to build a wonderful resort city where people could fully realize their dreams of a true work-life balance.

If Duval had become chairman and CEO, the entire shape of Cloudhaven would have been changed. Duval's vision—what he had of it—was completely commercial. He wanted a thousand hotel rooms in a glass tower while paying no attention to what would attract people to the resort. A thousand-room hotel would just sit empty until he could sell rights to develop a big casino and some recreational facilities to augment his golf course.

And, if the project failed after Duval took over, he would see to it that Preston was blamed for the whole bad idea. It would be the end of the Jerico family involvement in JeriCorp.

At least Erin understood and bought into the concept. Yes, Preston could get along quite well with Ms. Scott as his CEO. And he'd find out soon enough if she wasn't true to the colors she'd shown.

He stepped off the elevator into his penthouse and took his groceries to the kitchen. He hadn't had groceries delivered recently because he'd stayed at Jerico House or down in Cloudhaven. The coffee pot was cold and the grounds had not been emptied and cleaned. Was that the first sign she was not all she appeared to be? He decided to look through the rest of the apartment and check to be sure she'd done her job the past weeks.

Nothing else seemed out of place. Puzzles were all reset. His laundry had been put away. The cleaners had done their job. He stepped around to the sitting area, looking out on the rooftop patio, and saw Erin Scott asleep on the sofa.

What on earth is she doing here? Well, he supposed she had been working pretty hard this week. He could hardly blame her for falling asleep. He'd slept a while in the afternoon himself.

He sat in a side chair and looked at her. Her glasses were clutched in one hand and a coffee cup sat on the table next to her head.

She was truly lovely. Oh, not one of the false beauties his mother had arranged for him. Erin didn't wear too much makeup. Or he was very bad at being able to tell if she was wearing makeup. Most of the time, she wore a mask when she was with him—it was a rule of the office. He supposed that obviated the need for most makeup. She had a pleasant heart-shaped face. Her shoulder-length blonde hair tended to fly away in all directions. He'd often noticed her blue eyes.

That should have been a clue to her identity when he first met her. He'd noticed her eyes in the restaurant and thought they were striking, but he'd never really looked into her eyes after she came to work for him. How many other things had he not noticed?

Well, he needed to put those romantic thoughts out of his head. Not only was she his assistant, she was now the CEO of his company. He had to wonder how that was going to work. Would he need to find a new assistant? They had worked so well together remotely over the past two weeks, perhaps they needed to stay separate. She'd done an expert job of starting and organizing the project plan and distributing the parts to the people who would need to contribute.

He smiled, just appreciating the woman across from him. His own eyes drifted shut.

"JERRY? MR. CARVER? Oh, my! I fell asleep! I'm so sorry!" Erin said when she opened her eyes. Carver jolted awake and looked at her.

"It was very peaceful," he said. "I nodded off myself."

"I didn't mean to wake you. I was startled is all. I'll clean things up and leave. I didn't mean to infringe on your personal space. It was... an exhausting day and I didn't sleep well last night."

"Please, Ms. Scott. Don't rush. How about joining me for dinner? I stopped at the market on the way home, since I hadn't been here for a while. It will be a simple meal. I usually cook my fancy meals on Saturday."

"Mr. Carver? Is it okay for me to stay? I wouldn't want anyone to think something inappropriate was going on."

"Maizie, your friend Jerry is inviting you to dinner. You've never tasted my cooking. And no one really watches the elevator over the weekend."

"Well, then, I suppose it would be okay. Thank you for the invitation, Jerry."

"Was Maizie a name based on anything?" Jerry asked.

"No. Dolores has a bunch of nametags of kind of fifties-sounding names and that was the one I drew when I went to work there. It's funny, you know. I could have been a Jeri. My middle name was Jericho. Spelled differently than your family name. I mean, my mother was a Jericho and insisted that I bear it as my middle name. I only ever used my initial, J. When I married, I dropped it, and when I divorced, I regained my maiden name, but didn't reaffirm my middle name."

"There aren't that many Jericos in the country," Jerry said, leading the way to the kitchen. Erin went immediately to clean up the coffee pot and her cup, washing and putting them away. "I have a couple of chicken breasts. I thought I could poach them. I have a very good recipe."

"It sounds delicious. What can I do?"

"Why don't you start the rice as I get the oven heated and the chicken ready to wrap in parchment?"

The two worked companionably beside each other and managed not to get in each other's way. They talked lightly of all things that were going on in their lives.

"I usually have a glass of wine on Sunday afternoon with Dolores and we run through how our week went. We've become very good friends. In fact, she was the only friend I had in town until we joined a bowling league. Can you imagine me bowling on Thursday nights?" Erin said. "Dolores will not believe what's happened to me this week."

"I haven't bowled in years. In college, Gene Hathaway had quite a ruse going. He played the part of the wealthy playboy and I was simply his wingman. Not a very good one, I'm afraid."

"Hmm. When I was working in the diner, there was a nice guy who used to come in while I was working. We had some nice conversations. I lost track of him when I quit to come to work here."

"I really enjoyed that. You know I only went back once after you left. It just wasn't as much fun," he said. "I kept kicking myself for not having tried to get your number before you left for your new job. I thought I'd just missed my chance."

"Chance at what, Jerry?"

"Um... Th-the chance... um... I-I-I mean... to uh... get to know you better."

"Jerry, relax. I'd like to get to know you better as well. We don't need to press things. Besides, I got your number from Dolores and it was me who made the call."

"Oh! Wow! Um... Maybe... you know... I'm just after your money!"

"What money? Do you think you pay me enough to share?"

"You're the CEO now. You need to go down to HR and have them explain your benefits and new salary. Things will change for you, Ms. Scott."

"I don't know how they can. Surely, the board didn't intend for me to share your salary. I'm just your assistant."

"Well, about that. The CEO is a paid position in the company. Chairman of the Board is not a paid position. No one is paid to be on the board or have a position on it. Those are honorary roles. We set that up years ago so the board wouldn't be dependent on the company for its income. That means you will be paid as CEO. I will not be paid as Chairman. I hope they let me keep my apartment. I don't want to move back to Jerico House. It wasn't bad for a month, but I wouldn't want to stay there permanently."

"Jerry, we need to make sure you are employed here. This is your home as well as your office. They certainly couldn't expect *me* to live here. That would be ridiculous. How could they think such a thing? And besides, Chairman doesn't describe your real job in the company!"

"What does?" Jerry laughed. "Corporate recluse?"

"I actually mentioned it during the meeting today. Didn't realize I was creating a new position. When they asked for a reason you should be kept in this role, I said, you are the chief architect of the company. It's important enough that we should establish the position. This apartment office should belong to the Chief Architect."

Erin was satisfied with her rationale and nodded her head, not noticing how silent Jerry had become. He removed the poached breasts from the oven and put them on the plates with the rice Erin served. The poached chicken included onion, peppers, and asparagus spears. He carefully spooned broth from the pan over the chicken and the rice.

"This is such a lovely meal, Jerry. Thank you for inviting me."

He held up his hand and went to the refrigerator to get a bottle of white wine, which he quickly opened and poured into two glasses. He sat and raised his glass. Erin joined him.

"Madam CEO," he said. "When Grandfather told me he'd talked to Gene and what they'd agreed to, I was momentarily angry. He convinced me handily. But nothing has convinced me more than spending these few minutes with you cooking dinner. Erin, you are not in the position of CEO as an honorary executive. If there is anything regarding aspects of the business I can help with, I will. You know, specifics about architecture and development. But you are the CEO of JeriCorp. I will take whatever position you find for me."

"Uh... Jerry... I mean... I didn't come here to try to take over the company from you. Really. I think Mr. Hathaway made that up to scare the others. Please don't think that of me."

"You were really given no choice. You're the right person for the job." They sampled the chicken and both made exclamatory remarks about the flavor.

"Mr. Carver, I need to ask you something. We've worked closely for the past three months. I like the office up here. I even enjoy the menial tasks I've done. This space... being here with you... I like it. Do I need to move to a different office? May I please continue to use my office space here."

"Hmm. We might need to hire another assistant. That would make it difficult for you to use that office space. Why don't you consider taking my grandfather's space on the other side of the conference area? He doesn't really use it, even when he comes into the office."

"If you don't think he'd be offended, that would be wonderful."

"YOU SIMPLY WOULDN'T believe what they did to me," Erin said when she met Dolores for their Sunday glass of wine together. "Dolores, I worked toward this at my previous company and suspended it all to get married and have children. Then that all fell through. Now I have what I worked so hard for in Cleveland. I'm the CEO of the company!"

"How on earth did you get that? You aren't sleeping with anyone, are you?" Dolores asked her young friend.

"How could you think that? I was part of a compromise deal. The Board of Directors would keep Mr. Carver as Chairman of the Board only if I agreed to become CEO. The CEO, by the way, also has a position on the board, so I'm now on the Board of Directors."

"Oh, Erin, honey, I'm truly trying not to be negative, but it all sounds like some fantasy. I suppose you'll marry the billionaire chairman now," Dolores laughed.

"Um... I need to be really careful about how people think of that. I mean, I like Jerry. I've liked him ever since he started coming into the diner. We're friends. But now, he's my employee. The first thing I did as CEO this week was create the position of Chief Architect and hire him for it. It's kind of circuitous. As CEO, the Chief Architect reports to me. But I report to the Chairman of the Board. Sort of. It's confusing."

"Let me see. In all that dissembling, I didn't hear you say you wouldn't be willing to marry him," Dolores said.

"It's so complicated. Why am I even considering whether I would marry him? We aren't dating. We had dinner together this week. It was nice. Mostly, we just talked about life and how we came to be where we are. Did you know he wanted to be a chef? Maybe eventually he will be. The poached chicken he made was heavenly. But we need to work together, too. We can't let a relationship interfere with the jobs we have. The Board will watch us like a hawk."

"Speaking of which, what are you going to do about the rebels who tried to overthrow the regime?" Dolores asked.

"Good question. AS CEO, the Chief Operating Officer, Chief Financial Officer, General Counsel, and Chief Architect report to me. I have to consider three of them hostile, or potentially hostile.

I think the CFO was embarrassed that he joined with Duval. I don't want a massive walkout because of something I do. If Royce Duval has hurt feelings and needs to go to a corner and lick his butt, I won't stop him, but I will demand he does his job. I plan to call an executive meeting for later in the week so there's time for the dust to settle. That will also give me an opportunity to talk to Mr. Jerico and the Carvers so I'm sure we are in alignment."

"You'll be lucky if your officers are the only people in the company you have to manage—even if they are the only ones on your org chart. I know you like your office with Mr. Carver, but you should consider getting an assistant yourself. You'll have your hands full of executive things."

"Executive things. I wonder how many of those are stacked up waiting to fall on me."

"I DIDN'T LIKE the idea when you told me what you'd done," Preston said at his family dinner table Sunday. He'd had a good game of basketball with Gene early in the morning and was feeling fresh and invigorated. Lawrence and Jacqueline were at the table, of course, but so was Gina Gabriola. She and Lawrence had become quite a pair. She wasn't being pushed at Preston, so he found her quite charming.

"You're adapting," Lawrence said.

"Maybe too fast. By the way, you don't have a desk in my office any longer. I gave it to the CEO," Preston said with a smirk.

"Well, that was…" Lawrence started indignantly. "That was a smart thing to do."

Preston looked at Gina and then his mother.

"Erin and I had dinner together."

"Please don't tell me it was a disaster," Jacqueline said.

"It was… stimulating," he said. "I like her. I've liked her from the day I met her in the diner. I just didn't know the girl in my office was the same as the waitress in the diner."

"You called her a girl?" Gina asked.

"No. Of course not. She's a woman. Really… a nice… woman."

"Just take your time. Things will sort themselves out," Jacqueline said.

"What are we going to do about Duval, Dirksen, and Masters? I don't much blame Reinholdt. He's likely to go with whomever he thinks is most powerful," Lawrence said.

"It's disgusting that they tried to displace you from your own company," Gina said, shaking her head. "Don't they hang traitors?"

"Not in many years, dear," Lawrence chuckled. "I can imagine my father or grandfather dealing with them quietly and permanently, though."

"We need them," Preston said.

"Yes, but there is going to be some doubt regarding how badly they are needed. They were outmaneuvered, seemingly, by a woman they discounted as nothing more than a secretary. They will be wary. It will be best if you just quietly sit back and support Ms. Scott."

"As if I would say something," Preston snorted. "But I'd like to get a reading on how she wants to deal with them. It will tell me a lot about what the future will look like."

"How do you feel about becoming Chief Architect?" Jacqueline asked.

"It's brilliant! It's all I've ever wanted to be in the company, really. I appreciate needing to keep the chairmanship in the family, but I was never very good at being CEO."

"It was good experience for you anyway," Lawrence said. "Especially now that you may need to help and guide our new CEO. I admit, naming you Chief Architect was an excellent first step on her journey. The biggest threat we have is losing control of the design of the project. This puts you in a position to guard dog the entire Cloudhaven development."

"I promise I'll make it successful," Preston said.

Chapter Twenty-Two

ERIN WAS IN the office fifteen minutes earlier than usual. The previous week, she and Carver had set up her office in the space that Jerico had graciously relinquished. They'd spent the time reviewing all the reports and status of projects for the company. While Cloudhaven was the focus of their energy, it was by no means the only project going on in the company. The residential construction group had recently begun building a new neighborhood on the west side of Jerico City and the real estate division was reporting an uptick in home sales consistent with expectations for spring. The one item Erin was unhappy with was the status of the foreclosed Mackenzie project in St. Louis.

Before she started on her regular morning routine, she sat at her computer and sent several messages and meeting requests. Rather than starting with her COO or General Counsel, Erin began with the PR department. Her new position needed an announcement with some fanfare. Then she would meet with the Director of Human Resources and get the new position paperwork taken care of. She'd already sent the personnel request to have Carver named as Chief Architect.

When she had those few items taken care of, she moved to the kitchen to make coffee. She could hear Carver moving upstairs in his bedroom and bathroom.

Preston came downstairs and headed for the kitchen.

"Will you join me for breakfast?" he asked.

"Oh! Is that allowed?" she laughed. "I'd love to have a cup of coffee with you."

"Hardly enough to start your day as CEO of this prestigious company. Let me fix you something hot," he said.

"Thank you, Jerry. I'll just print out the schedule for the day."

They sat to eat a light breakfast and talked about the agenda for the day. He fully agreed with her assessment of what was important. She scheduled an executive staff meeting for Thursday, with location to be announced. The PR person would be in the office at nine o'clock. Before that, the elevator chimed and Preston's laundry arrived from the weekend. Erin jumped up to get it and put it away.

"I don't think the CEO should have to put away my laundry," he sighed. "Maybe I should learn to put my own clothes away. It's rather pretentious of me to have an assistant do menial tasks, don't you think?

"I took them on as part of my job," Erin said. "I never felt demeaned by doing what was my job to do. I suppose we might need another assistant, though. Let's see how the day plays out and decide later if we need to do more work ourselves or to have someone else pick up some for us. HR might have something planned already. Technically, the workload in the room remains the same. We still have the Chairman and the CEO. I'm not sure it requires another pair of hands."

"You might be surprised. You know, I have simply ignored a lot of the job. I don't respond to a lot of messages and you pick that up. I don't go out to social or public events, which the CEO might normally be expected to attend. I've left that to the President. I can't really blame the other execs for rebelling. I ignored a lot of what people consider the normal tasks of the chief executive."

The elevator chimed and Erin greeted a person from the marketing department assigned to interview her for a press release, while a second person carted in a camera and began figuring out where she should pose the new executive.

It took longer than Erin had allowed, Preston sitting behind his computer monitors the entire time. He never said a word. After the meeting and interview, she had time to check the new messages, one of which was the company-wide announcement from the PR person. Erin followed it up with her own company-wide greeting.

At ten-thirty, she left the sanctity and sanity of the penthouse office and went to the second floor to visit Human Resources.

"ERIN! MY GOD! You didn't waste any time clawing your way to the top," Ellen said when Erin appeared in her office.

"I started at the top when you sent me to be Mr. Carver's assistant," Erin said. She didn't much like Ellen's casual way with her. They weren't friends. "Mr. Carver established a culture that treats executives with a degree of formality. You can refer to me as Miss Scott or Ms. Scott. I'll expect the same treatment for Mr. Duval, Mr. Masters, Ms. Dirksen, and Mr. Carver."

"Yes, ma'am," Ellen said. *Who does this upstart think she is?* "I suppose we should get your paperwork taken care of. It should only take a few minutes to adjust your employment record with the new salary and benefit schedule. Then there is the matter of stock options."

"Has Mr. Carver's new position as Chief Architect been finalized? And I will need to hire a new assistant who can serve both the Chairman and the CEO. I do not have enough hands to juggle the work put on my desk this morning."

"We have an office and assistant prepared for you on the fifth floor," Ellen said. "I assumed you would be moving to that location."

"We'll hold that option open. For now, I'll be occupying Mr. Jerico's space in the penthouse. Let's schedule IT to make whatever changes they need to in phone directory and computer connections this afternoon. Keep in mind the level of tasks you asked me to perform when I started here. That will also be the starting level for our new assistant."

"Yes, ma'am. Will there be anything else this morning?"

"No. I'll stop on the fifth floor and interview the assistant there to determine if he or she will be suitable for the penthouse position."

Erin finished signing her forms and left Ellen's office as the HR person stared after her. Ellen immediately called Shannon.

"HI. ARE YOU the admin for the new CEO?" Erin asked when she approached the woman sitting at the fifth floor desk.

"Yes, ma'am. May I help you? Mr. Duval isn't in at the moment."

"I see. I'm Ms. Scott. I am the new CEO. I'll meet with Mr. Duval later. Please give me a tour of this part of the office and show me to mine."

"Oh! Okay! I was... I mean last week... Mr. Duval said he was going to be the new CEO. He told me if I... I mean..."

"If you what? Uh... Miss Anders?" Erin read off the desk plate.

"Please, ma'am. I really need this job. Don't make me say things that will lose it for me."

"Miss Anders, I don't intend to lose your job for you. I will tell you that if you are being sexually harassed by Mr. Duval or by any other member of our staff, that person will be dealt with immediately and harshly. Let's step into the conference room here and have a little chat."

Cheryl Anders was in her mid-twenties. She'd gone to community college to get an associate degree in office administration. She wasn't stupid by any stretch of the imagination. It wasn't completely clear if Duval had pressured her or if she had simply made herself available, though Erin doubted that.

When she heard the job responsibilities as assistant to the new CEO and Chief Architect, she thought they were a bit strange, but not difficult and certainly not exploiting her—sexually or even intellectually. Erin explained how the job could be expanded beyond the mindless, but that the basics were firm. Cheryl seemed excited, especially when told she would be taken to the penthouse for her job.

"This is a lot better than pretending to be attracted to Mr. Duval," Cheryl confided when she'd been introduced to the office upstairs.

"You'll probably do a fair amount of running up and down, as we seldom bring people up here. The first thing I'd like you to do is arrange my meeting with the four officers of the corporation on Thursday. We need a location, coffee, and rolls. And general meeting supplies, of course. I've scheduled it to start at nine. In the past, Mr.

Carver held very few meetings, so I really don't know what facilities are available. I'll be sending a slide deck to you to polish. You're good with that?"

"Yes, ma'am. Can you show me any tricks to resetting the cubes? I've never worked one before."

If that was the biggest problem she had adjusting, Erin was sure she would work just fine.

WHEN PEOPLE HEARD the news that they had a new CEO, eyebrows went up. Most employees just assumed that since Royce Duval was President, he was also the CEO. No one thought of Preston as holding an office at all.

Erin hoped the transition would be quiet and was content to let Duval continue to be the public face of the company as long as he could do so in a supportive and positive way.

By the time of her meeting with the execs on Thursday, Erin was already feeling pressed by the demands of her new job. The executives had apparently decided they should make no decisions without consulting her. She had requests to approve the board meeting minutes, sign off on the partnership draft with Interlake Land Holdings, and decide on a cellular company. She knew these were normally things Duval handled, and in her mind, they were clearly the responsibility of the COO.

She'd also received an invitation to speak at the local Chamber of Commerce next week, and had Cheryl accept the invitation, even though it was short notice. She'd talked it over with Carver and he said he always ignored such things, but it was probably a good idea for her to accept the invitation.

"THE QUARTERLY FINANCIAL reports look good. Mr. Masters, did you note anything out of the ordinary?" Erin asked in the meeting with her senior officers.

"Not really, Ms. Scott. We are seeing the waning effect of our January one layoffs. That will put us in an advantageous position going into Q3. We've been watching our subsidiaries more closely. Most of the construction wing we had active in St. Louis has been shifted to other projects. Some have been laid off."

"We acquired the Mackenzie property in the foreclosure, did we not?" Erin asked.

"Yes, Ma'am. The property itself could be sold or held for a while."

"Mr. Carver, is the building worth salvaging as a JeriCorp property if we could locate a tenant or buyer?" Erin asked, turning to Preston. He looked momentarily like a deer in the headlights.

"Y-yes," Preston answered. "It's g-g-good."

"Good. We have interest from a potential tenant. Mr. Masters, please prepare a financial analysis of the project and what would be needed to reopen it. We'll need to put together both a lease and purchase projection with any potential impact the project might have on Cloudhaven."

"Yes, Ma'am."

"I'd also like to start my tenure with a clean slate, so to speak. I'd like you to arrange a full audit of our corporate finances from top to bottom, including all subsidiaries," Erin said.

"That could take three months to complete."

"We should get it underway as soon as possible, then. We'll want certified numbers to present at the shareholders meeting in September."

Masters puffed a sigh and just nodded. It was clear he wasn't happy.

"Status of negotiations for the partnership and contract progress for Cloudhaven. Mr. Duval?" she said.

"Right. Well, we're just skipping right along. You have the partnership papers to sign," Duval said.

"That's within your purview as COO, as it has been in the past," Erin said. "If the partnership is solid and the contracts are within our parameters, sign them. Don't sit around waiting for me to pat your head."

"Yes, Ms. Scott," Duval growled bitterly. He'd need to go through the papers again if they were going to have his signature on them. He didn't want any surprises that he would have relished if Erin signed the papers.

"Mr. Carver, status of the planning documents for Cloudhaven Phase One."

Preston read the statement he and Erin had prepared. This was more about Erin managing her team than Preston being told to make a presentation.

"Infrastructure plans have all been drawn and approved by the Land Development Department. Cloudhaven is in an unincorporated region of Lewis County and has little in the way of building codes or a planning commission. We have offered the county assistance in putting together a mutually beneficial organization. Soil tests and environmental impact studies have been completed. Surveys are complete and we are clear to begin grading."

"Excellent. I appreciate you keeping me informed as the project progresses. Ms. Dirksen, is there any legal fallout to our repositioning in January? Any other issues to be handled?"

"The layoffs were handled according to policy in January and most affected employees received a substantial severance package. The reorganization of the subsidiaries to consolidate operations was fairly smooth, though we have a continuing negotiation with Local 494 regarding the Mackenzie project. If we return to development and get them back on the job, those problems should disappear."

"Very good. Please keep me in the loop should any new developments arise. Also, I would like a review of the board structure: Who is automatically granted a position, any record of compensation for board-related activities, and the process for board nominations to come before the shareholders' meeting. I want to be sure we have a solid plan and slate of nominations according to the bylaws. Please understand, everyone, this is not a precursor to shaking up the board any more than it has been in the past week. This is an effort to have a unified slate of candidates to present to the shareholders. We need to be looking at every way we can have our company dressed and pressed for the shareholder meeting. Any questions?"

"Is that all we're meeting about?" Duval asked.

"Do you have another agenda item?"

"Well, no, but usually executive meetings are day-long. We've been at it less than an hour. People will wonder if we did anything," Royce said.

"I have no interest in meetings that drag on and on. If you have issues that need to come before this executive committee, bring them. If it is just something you need to cover with me, make an appointment and let's hash it out. I think that's everything for today. We're adjourned."

Erin got up and left the board room where the executives met. Preston made his goodbyes and hurried after her to the elevator up to their office.

"WHAT A BALL-BUSTER," Royce growled at the other two senior managers. "What are we going to do?"

"Our jobs," Masters said. "I'm not particularly happy about having a full corporate audit done, but it's not a bad idea. I don't believe we've been audited in three years. There's nothing to hide. And it's a good business practice. I can't really complain."

"I expected her to latch onto every symbol of power, like the contracts and partnership papers," Royce said grudgingly. "She might not be as hands-off as Preston, but she does give us room to do our jobs."

"Just make sure you do it well," Dirksen said. "She's also the kind who will hold you responsible."

"MS. ANDERS, PLEASE go ahead and send the meeting summary I gave you before I left. I don't need to make any revisions to it. Make sure the action items for each manager are clearly called out," Erin said when she returned to the penthouse.

"Yes, Ms. Scott."

Erin didn't stop at her former desk. She'd added two large monitors to her desk. She kept the Cloudhaven project plan open on one so she could respond quickly to updates any of the departments made to it.

Miss Anders was adapting well to the environment and the tasks she was given. She'd been well-trained in administrative responsibilities and Erin was certain she could coach her along to an expanded role eventually.

Erin went into the sitting area between her office and Preston's, where she flopped on the sofa, threw her head back, and sighed.

"I don't think there's ever been such an efficient executive meeting at JeriCorp," Preston said from the chair next to her. For a long time, they just stared out at the sunny day on the rooftop patio.

"I love looking out at the patio," she mused.

"How about lunch there on Saturday?" he asked.

"Mr. Carver?"

"No. Jerry. Seems like we might both need an afternoon forgetting about the company," he said.

"In that case, I'd be delighted," she chuckled. "I suppose, however, I'd better start working on my presentation for next Tuesday. Any suggestions regarding the topic?"

"I'm hardly the person to make speaking recommendations," he said. "I'll... uh... be happy to help if you need technical information, but you're already a better executive than any of your officers."

"I talked to my mentor in Cleveland Tuesday to find out if Allard would be interested in opening conversations on the Mackenzie building. Perfect timing. They're looking at a spring announcement of their regional expansion to St. Louis. She said she had been certain I wouldn't stay with her company long enough to take it over, but she'd done her best to prepare me for that job somewhere else. It was so stupid of me to believe Bruce was worth throwing away my career. I had such high romantic hopes."

"There's nothing wrong with romance, I guess," Preston said. "It's just always evaded me. Um... You know... Y-y-you could hire him back. If you wanted to."

"What?"

"Your husband was coordinating the Mackenzie Project. He probably knows it better than most people here," Preston said.

"No. Not just no. Hell, no! It would be bad business to bring him back into a situation where he still had to interact with all the same people and have his ex-wife at the helm of the company. And it would be bad personal relations to suggest to my ex there was any possibility for him to reconcile. I am not going there."

"I... uh... should get the grading contracts sent out," he said, jumping up from his chair. Erin smiled after him as he went to his desk. Then she pulled herself off the sofa and went to her own desk.

Chapter Twenty-Three

"ARE YOU HERE, Jerry?" Erin called when she stepped off the elevator Saturday.

"Kitchen!" he called back. She went to join him and found him rolling out pastry dough.

"That looks interesting," she said. "Red wine or white?"

"Chicken pot pie," he said. "Almost ready to assemble and put in the oven. White, I guess."

Erin opened and poured the wine. She handed him a glass and they touched the rims.

"Salud!" he said.

"Are we still good for patio dining?" she asked. "It felt nice and warm on the way over."

"Unless it's suddenly gotten windy, we should be fine. It was beautiful when I went out a little bit ago."

"I'll set the table."

Erin selected the dishes and silverware to take outside, then got a clean cloth and hot water to wash down the patio table and chairs. She couldn't help but smile about how terribly domestic she felt. She hummed a little tune as she prepared the table. Back in the kitchen, Jerry was cleaning up, now that the pie was in the oven.

"It's a small pie, so it should only take about forty minutes to bake. Shall we go relax on the patio?" he asked.

"It's beautiful out. Perfect for the patio."

"I love the space out here," Jerry said as they settled in lounge chairs. "Sometimes I come out here with a couple of cubes and spend all afternoon. It's harder when I reset my own puzzles. I end up trying to fool myself with blind twists. It never works."

"I don't trust my ability to scramble a cube randomly," Erin said.

"But your cubes always seem to be scrambled better than mine."

"I use the computer. There's a program that will generate a random sequence. I carry around my tablet and just follow the instructions the computer gives me for each cube. I learned a long time ago it was difficult to reset your own cube and make it feel random," Erin said.

"You are so devious! I can't believe you've been using a computer program all this time."

"Your mother taught me my first day on the job. I don't think I'm particularly clever about it."

"My mother is sometimes too smart for me. I wonder how long she's used a program. I'd guess soon after she figured out that the cube had a calming effect on me. I was really quite a terrible teenager."

"Really? Why do you think that?"

"I was constantly frustrated. And I couldn't express myself. Words just got tied up in my mouth and that made me more frustrated."

"You don't seem to have any problem communicating with me. I'm glad."

"When we met in the diner, I was trying a great experiment that Gene suggested and my therapist approved. I would hide behind the anonymity of my sweatshirt, mask, and shades. Since no one would know me, I was free to mess up. I didn't need to go back. The first time, I was still afraid I'd make a fool of myself, but this very sweet waitress didn't try to rush me or finish my sentences for me. She encouraged me to take my time. She asked questions I could give simple answers to. Over time, I was able to relax enough not to feel threatened by the situation."

"I don't recall that you had much difficulty when I came to work here. And you say you only figured out I was the same person when we were working on the presentation."

"I tried not to say anything to you for the first two weeks," Jerry laughed. By then, you were so well established in the office you weren't a threat or someone I needed to impress."

"I'm glad of that."

"The pot pie should be done. I'll go get it."

THEY HAD A good time as they ate the pot pie and talked more than Jerry had talked… ever!

"What else do you enjoy doing?" Maizie asked.

"I like sports. Gene and I played basketball in high school. He's the total opposite of me. Talkative and outgoing. I used to depend on him to get us both dates and I'd just ride along. I guess the main thing I like is cooking. I try to cook something special every Saturday. It's my time in the kitchen. Sometimes I experiment with new recipes and sometimes I cook an old favorite like this pot pie."

"I enjoy the social aspects of cooking and eating," Maizie said. "I'm afraid, left to my own devices, I eat a sandwich in front of the television rather than cook for just myself. Aside from that, I read quite a lot—mostly business and biography. Occasionally, I'll relax with a good novel."

"Rather sedate," he laughed.

"Don't believe that. Remember, I joined a bowling league!" she laughed. "I had a great time traipsing all over the Cloudhaven property in my boots and jeans. I really love it out there."

"I'll take you to our cabin sometime," Jerry said enthusiastically. "I want to build a regular house out there, but that probably isn't until phase three. It's at the far opposite end of the project from where the lodge will be. I could take you out fishing and we… um… uh…"

"What is it, Jerry?"

"I realized I was just painting a picture of things I've always wanted to do with a… girlfriend. I didn't mean to… you know… imply… er… Do you think I put too much tarragon in the pie?" he asked abruptly.

Erin responded to the question and analyzed the other herbs he'd used. All the time, she was examining her own feelings. How did she feel about that? When he was really just Jerry in the diner, becoming friends and flirting a little after her divorce seemed natural. She didn't ever consider the possibility of dating when she came to work for Mr. Carver. Even over the past few minutes relaxing over dinner, she thought of him as Jerry, rather than the sort-of-rich recluse and master architect. Other couples managed to work out a professional and a personal relationship. She was sure Jerry wasn't suggesting anything just now, anyway. They were just two friends having lunch on a Saturday afternoon.

"Perhaps you'd consider showing your *friend* Cloudhaven from your perspective sometime," she ventured. "I think that would be okay."

He smiled at her and nodded. After lunch, she convinced him to listen to her presentation prepared for the chamber. He was very helpful and pointed out a few things she might not have known before.

"THANK YOU FOR inviting me to speak this evening," Erin said Tuesday evening. "As Mr. Duval indicated in my introduction, this is my first official appearance since joining JeriCorp."

It wasn't a big group, but Erin had been surprised to find that Duval was host of the Chamber of Commerce meeting. He'd given her a decent introduction as their speaker and she stood to deliver the fifteen-minute talk. She gathered there were several people who interacted regularly with JeriCorp as suppliers, contractors, clients, and business partners.

"We are facing a new era in our relationships with our customers and our business partners. We all had a wake-up call when the pandemic hit, and many struggled to adjust to new ways of doing business. But we learned. Let me describe a few of the ways we are moving forward in this post-pandemic work environment."

She had spent most of Monday and Tuesday working on the presentation. She'd even talked to Dolores about it on Sunday. She decided talking about the effect of the pandemic on business relationships would transition nicely to an announcement of their new project and plan to attract digital natives for remote work in a resort environment.

"Why, after all, should a job be defined by four walls, or a cubicle? Many employees who work in cubicles have no real reason to be held captive in order to do their jobs. The equipment they need is not restricted to a single location. If we can provide an experience that improves work-life balance, so much the better.

"Think about how attractive our companies would be if our employees learned their jobs are compatible with a great lifestyle. I foresee us making the same changes in the larger community. Consistent wireless communications from anywhere in our town. Anywhere in our state or broader area. Comfortable places to work that are within community enclaves where childcare and activities are as convenient as another cup of coffee. Environments employees can customize with their own art, music, and services.

"We have built wonderful technology for humanity. It is time to make it serve our employees and each other. Thank you."

There was polite applause. Erin didn't expect anything more. She was proposing something that was still controversial. Many employers believed workers wouldn't work if they weren't in an environment controlled by the employer. They would find out, eventually.

"Thank you, Ms. Scott," Duval said as he stood to conclude the meeting. "I've been at JeriCorp for over fifteen years, and I'm amazed that someone so new to our industry—and so cute—can be so articulate about it. Thank you for enlightening us regarding the future. You're all welcome to stick around for another cup of coffee and to chat with our new JeriCorp CEO. The Tuesday meeting is now adjourned."

Several people did stop to chat with Erin, but her mind had gone elsewhere with Duval's remarks. She was furious. She smiled and shook hands, meeting executives and managers she knew she would be meeting again, and all smiling at her because she was cute.

"IF YOU EVER undermine me in public again, it will be your last day at JeriCorp," she stated levelly at Duval when she walked into his office the next morning.

"Whoa! I was trying to give you a platform where you could meet a lot of important people and get started on the right foot. I wasn't undermining you!" Duval sputtered.

"Comments about how amazing it is that I'm articulate for a newcomer and that I'm cute are totally inappropriate. In a sentence, you revealed your true colors. I was promoting the official position of our company, about to embark on a new project. A position you are tasked with promoting and supporting to our partners and employees. Instead, you treated it like it wasn't serious. I know you announced at the last meeting there would be a new CEO to present at this meeting. That was before I was hired, so you expected to give this presentation. From now on, I expect you to be supportive and to do your job. Do not ever undercut me again."

"I should have stuck with my opinion that you were a ball-buster," he snapped.

"You have no idea how thoroughly I'll bust them if you ever cross me again," Erin spat. "You've been warned." Duval stared at her.

"Now. How soon are we ready with the partnership and initial contracts for Cloudhaven?"

Her abrupt change of subject threw Duval.

"The partnership is signed. We'll have an official ground-breaking next week. I have a call in to the governor's office to request his presence. PR has a release ready to distribute today. We might not be able to get television cameras out there, but we should have good print media representation. We'll break ground on Thursday," Duval said.

"Good work, Mr. Duval. Mr. Carver and Mr. Jerico should be there with you, of course. There is an organization called Digital Nomads. You might see if someone from their group could cover the event on social media. I'll have Miss Anders send you the contact info," Erin said.

"You'll want to speak again?"

"No. This is your environment. Make it look like you invented the entire concept, but don't shortchange either Mr. Carver or Mr. Jerico."

"Of course."

"Carry on, Mr. Duval."

Erin turned and left his office as quickly as she'd arrived.

"SHE CAME CHARGING in and lambasted me for the way I introduced her and concluded her presentation, then switched gears and got me to tell her about the groundbreaking and the contracts. She told me it was a good job. Doesn't even plan to attend the groundbreaking. Said it was my event!"

Royce Duval frankly didn't understand Erin Scott at all. He was pacing around the dinner table while Shannon tried to get him settled down. When Erin had stormed into his office, he expected her to harangue him for an hour. That's how women worked. They never let a subject go. Erin had criticized him, threatened him, and then dropped the entire matter. What was wrong with her?

"Maybe she's actually a good executive," Shannon ventured, trying not to trouble the waters further. "Masters is sending me to St. Louis with a revived Mackenzie team to put together a plan for reopening that project."

"I can't stand it! She's a usurper. I should have had that position. But damn it, she's good."

"I kind of regret screwing up her marriage," Shannon said.

"What?"

"I assumed you knew. That guy you managed to fire as part of the cutbacks in January was Erin Scott Silvers' husband. I've always felt a little bad about getting him fired," Shannon said.

"His project was cancelled. Probably could have used him on the new one, but I won't have a guy sneering at me because he slept with my wife," Duval said. "If it wasn't for you sleeping with him, Erin Scott would never have come to work for JeriCorp."

He walked around the table to Shannon's chair and pulled her to her feet so he could kiss her thoroughly.

"I don't want any guy sleeping with my wife."

"Oh my, big guy. Where did this sudden possessiveness come from?"

"I don't know. I just know... I'm forty-seven years old and I'm tired of the games," Royce said.

"What if I told you the same thing? I don't want any other slut sleeping with my husband," Shannon shot, not letting go of him.

"We could... We could try that," he said. "God! A reformed Royce and Shannon Duval? It could work."

"You could be all I want. All I need," Shannon said.

"I'd like to be all you need. I don't want anything but you anymore."

"Dinner will get cold."

"I'm not hungry."

"Then take me to bed."

"TWO MEN, MORE than any others, made this innovative project possible. It started with a boy's dream when his grandfather took him fishing on this very lake. For twenty years, they have quietly planned and prepared for today. I am talking, of course, about the Chairman Emeritus of JeriCorp Architecture and Development, Lawrence Jerico, and his grandson, the current Chairman of the Board and Chief Architect of JeriCorp, Preston Carver," Duval said at the groundbreaking.

He'd managed to get much wider coverage of the event than expected. The governor was next to him on one side, with Jerico and Carver on the other side. A television crew from Jerico City was on hand, and so was the network crew from the state's capital. Behind Duval stood executives of a cellular company committed to covering Cloudhaven with high-speed access, and the president of a luxury grocery chain announcing plans to build a store and service station nearby. The senior partner of the consortium Royce and Shannon had joined was there with an announcement regarding the proposed golf course, and the various contractors hired to excavate the streets and infrastructure were also present.

"It's all about vision," Duval continued. "And vision is not always the same as economic forecasting or political prognosis. Four hundred years ago, vision looked across the ocean to a vast untamed land and saw the rising of a great nation. The vision of twelve men looked at a confluence of two rivers and saw Jerico City take shape two hundred years ago. Vision led that great nation to plant its flag on the moon sixty years ago. And vision brings us to the shore of this lake to create a refuge where office workers in many different industries can perform their duties free from the shackles of a steel and glass tower in the city. This—this new community of Cloudhaven—is the future of the white-collar work force. It is the culmination of the techno-logical dream. This is where we turn a shovelful of dirt to commence Phase One of the Cloudhaven digital native resort."

There was a lot of applause, even though there weren't that many people present in the remote location. The governor spoke about new frontiers still being available in their old state. The businesses represented made their announcements. The principals gathered with shovels to join together in turning the first bit of dirt where the lodge would soon rise.

Under a tent nearby, the model of Cloudhaven had been unveiled and the television crews were as intent on it as on the actual land.

ERIN WATCHED THE feed in the company auditorium—a room that would hold about a hundred people comfortably. Far more were packed into it. It had been tricky getting set up, but the cell company brought a portable tower to Cloudhaven for the event so people would be able to report on it. One of the marketing people had agreed to set up the laptop and camera to get a reasonable feed that was played at the office.

She smiled at Duval's message. Something had clicked with him. Previously, he could have been expected to talk about how the idea had come to him in a dream and he employed the best people he could find to realize it. In this groundbreaking ceremony, one might almost have considered him humble. She watched the response of the employees in the room and saw it had done nothing to reduce his image. As they returned to their desks after the stream, she heard comments about how wonderful Royce was and how he would lead them to prosperity through this development. She would still need to monitor him carefully. She didn't entirely trust his change of spots.

That suited her fine. This was where Duval truly shined. He could position the message in such a way that people—especially employees—were enthused and in awe. Dirksen and Masters stood with her in the back of the room, so employees lumped them all together as 'the execs.'

Erin returned to her office with Miss Anders.

"Mr. Carver suggested you use his car for your trip to St. Louis," she said. "I've had it serviced and filled with gas. Your bag is already in the car. Mrs. Duval will join you there as soon as I tell her you are on your way."

"That's great, Miss Anders. I think it's time to go, so let my traveling companion know. This should be an interesting trip."

She headed to the elevator.

Chapter Twenty-Four

ERIN WAS NOT particularly keen about spending three hours in the car with Shannon Duval. She'd had very little interaction with the woman, so her only real basis for judging her was that she'd had an affair with Erin's husband, which cost him his marriage. She doubted Mrs. Duval was any more enthused than she was.

"I… My car is gassed up and ready to go if you'd prefer for us to travel separately," Shannon said when they met in the garage.

"I think that would be wasteful. There's no need to take two cars," Erin said. "I need to adjust the seat and mirrors, though. I've not driven Mr. Carver's car before."

"He's still driving the same car he bought when he first became Chairman of the Board," Shannon snickered. "Mine's a little newer."

"Six years isn't terribly old for a car that's well maintained. It only has 35,000 miles on it."

"Only driven by a little old lady to church on Sundays."

"It is rather a cliché. But it's a comfy car. Seat warmers if you want one," Erin said. She backed out of the parking space and headed toward the freeway. She wasn't very happy with Shannon's implied insults to Mr. Carver, but she'd determined to make the best of this trip.

They rode in silence until they'd crossed the river and headed north. Erin considered turning on the radio, but that seemed rude.

"Tell me about the financial status of the Mackenzie project. How deep are we and what does it take to make it profitable?" she finally said. She took Shannon by surprise, but the controller opened a folder and began summarizing the numbers. Erin had already read the formal report that came from Masters and assumed correctly it had been written by Shannon. Hearing the woman explain the details helped sharpen Erin's understanding and told her a lot about Shannon's expertise.

"So, even though we have clear title to the property and the plans, we still have a heavy debt to cover the excavation that was done in November and December, before Mackenzie filed Chapter 11," Shannon said. "We managed an agreement with the union local and the general contractor to stretch payments out over twelve months, which we've done by mortgaging the property."

"How much of a commitment do we need to get from Allard, or a tenant, to clear us to resume construction?"

"A company like Allard might want to simply acquire the property and take over the whole project without us. We'd need to clear $1.7 million to be able to walk away. We could take that on a build to suit lease agreement and the union would be happy because they'd be back at work and we could get joint financing fairly easily."

They continued to talk and strategize the meeting with Erin's former company until silence finally fell in the car again.

"Don't you want to talk about what happened with your husband?" Shannon finally asked.

"Is there something you need to say about it?"

"Only that I'm sorry I screwed life up for you. I'm trying to reform."

"I'm divorced," Erin said. "It's past. I'm divorced because my husband was unable to keep his word to me. I don't blame the other woman. There are always willing women if a man is willing to break his vows. I'm glad to have found out before we had children."

"You're very pragmatic about it."

"I have a standard. Some would say it is a high standard. I think it's fundamental. In business, I expect everyone who works with me to strive to adhere to that standard. In my personal life, I want to share my life with people who have a compatible standard. I have a hard enough time following my own standard to assume everyone else in the world is going to follow it."

"But you divorced your husband because he failed?" Shannon asked.

"He wasn't trying to live up to the standard. He failed in the most basic part of a relationship: trust. Once that was broken, there wasn't anything else," Erin responded. She was already tired of this conversation, but Shannon seemed determined to pick at it.

"Reprimanding my husband for dissing you wasn't related to his firing your husband?"

"By the time Bruce lost his job, we were already headed for divorce. But Mr. Duval was not yet clear on what the standard is. He thought I operated on a principle of one-upmanship. Once I was clear with him that I would not tolerate that, he then had to make decisions and statements based on the standard of mutual support and promotion of the company. He did a great job with the ground-breaking at Cloudhaven this morning."

"He's a good man."

"I hope you encourage it," Erin said, ending the conversation as they crossed the Mississippi into St. Louis.

"WHEN YOU LEFT to move to the boondocks and have babies, I never thought I'd be facing you across a negotiating table," Dee said as she and Erin left the meeting. They waved their team members off and headed out to dinner together.

"Believe me, I thought I'd left this life far behind," Erin laughed.

"You know, if you'd called Allard when you divorced, you'd be on the other side of the table today. I was always second choice for this position."

"You're perfect for it, Dee. I'd never want to take it away from you."

"It helps coming to a negotiation with a person I know and trust. So, tell me how you came to be the CEO of JeriCorp. This has to be quite a story."

Erin was fundamentally honest, but didn't feel it was necessary to go into the details of her Board's attempt to overthrow the family and that she was a compromise.

"They promised me a better position if I could put up with being the Chairman's assistant for a few months. I had no idea they'd make me the CEO. When it comes down to it, though, Mr. Carver is brilliant and being his CEO is still almost like being his assistant. I just get to do the fun things like this."

"When do you think you'll be ready to return to the big show? No doubt being CEO of a midsize company will definitely look as good as being a regional VP at Allard, but the next step for you has always been into the executive suite of a Fortune 100 company."

"I don't know that I'll ever return to that path," Erin said. "Not that I'm likely to return to the happily married mommy path again, but I'm learning a lot about balancing my work and life. Part of that has been working on this new community we're developing. It could really change things for a lot of employees."

"Do you think you'll lose a lot of your office workers to the new remote community?" Dee asked.

"No. I'm sure there will be a few, but we're not moving the company headquarters to Cloudhaven. I don't see it becoming a headquarters for any company. The idea is to attract a cross section of workers who are from many different companies and industries. They'll still have their strong connection to the people in their own companies, but they'll work beside people from other companies. They won't be competing for a promotion with the person in the office next door. If it works well, they'll be doing more collaboration and partnering."

"It sounds a little utopian, but I'd love to see it actually work," Dee said. "Now tell me about your love life. Have you found anyone special in this new company?"

"Oh. Well... um... no... not really. Working in a penthouse like I do, I really only see the Chairman and our assistant on a regular basis. Even he is often down at Cloudhaven, since he's also the Chief Architect. I don't think it's that good an idea to shop in the company store, you know? I'll try to get out a little more this winter. Meet more people."

"But you share an office with the Chairman, who also happens to be the Chief Architect and principal owner of the company. And you think of yourself still as his assistant. Sounds like a recipe for romance."

"You are the third or fourth person to suggest that," Erin giggled. "Why can't anyone believe we're just good coworkers?"

"Maybe because of that little giggle," Dee said. "Just remember, you don't *have* to marry every guy you sleep with. You could just take him for a test drive."

"You're wicked, Dee. Wicked."

THE EXECUTIVE COMMITTEE was meeting in the penthouse. Erin had decided that since the model of Cloudhaven had been moved to the portable building at the worksite, it would be appropriate to bring the execs into the penthouse to gather around the central table.

"Well, the contract with Allard is solid," Masters said. "Mrs. Duval succeeded in getting a letter of commitment from First National in St. Louis for construction financing. The crews are back on the job and we should have footings poured by September 1. I am also informed that we owe the contract with Allard to our CEO who successfully negotiated with their regional Vice President. Well done, Ms. Scott."

"Thank you," Erin said. "I had an advantage. She used to report to me. Let's move on to the status at Cloudhaven. Mr. Carver?"

"The street grading is nearly complete in the phase one section. Utilities have begun laying the water, electric, and sewer lines. Of course, grading is only the first step. They'll start laying the sub base. Trucks will be lining up with gravel starting in two weeks. We will drive on the sub base for the winter. That will improve compaction and make a more stable base when we are ready to pave next spring. By that time, most of the heavy excavation equipment should be off the site and road damage during building construction next summer should be minimal," Carver read from his notes.

"This number for the sub base," Duval said. "Do we really have to go that deep? I had my driveway paved and they only used a four-inch sub base."

"Um… You only drive your Lexus on that. The kind of traffic the street will bear requires a better foundation. Otherwise, we'd be spending every spring filling potholes," Carver answered.

"Good. I want to review the assignments for the annual shareholder meeting and make sure we're all on the same page. Mr. Duval, most of this falls on your plate. How is your new assistant working out?"

"I'm pleased," he answered. "I have to tell you I doubted the need for an executive assistant. I've always handled everything just fine. But this gal is just always a step ahead of what I need. I honestly didn't know people like this existed. Leva… Mrs. Hamilton… came to work for us after having raised her family and wanting to get back in the workforce. I was doubtful, but having seen your success, I decided to try her out. Stellar. The notes you have in front of you for the annual meeting are some of the work she's done. Just the work she does keeping my calendar is worth her wage."

"I'm glad to hear that."

The meeting continued with the reviews and everyone felt that in an hour and change, they'd covered all the business and were on track. Dirksen, Masters, and Duval left and Miss Anders went directly to her workstation to type up the minutes.

"I could use a cup of coffee. How about you?" Erin asked Preston.

"After that, I could use something even stronger. Coffee will do, though."

The two went into the kitchen and Erin made a pot of coffee and poured a cup for each of them.

"I'm really proud of the way you handled that. Even the question from Duval. You sounded calm and confident. You know he was just trying to throw you. He hasn't really changed all that much," Erin said.

"It's all because you're there," Preston said. "Duval always knew he could stall me or make me look like an idiot by asking a question, even when he already knew the answer."

"Old habits die hard, though. I'm counting on Mrs. Hamilton to help rein him in. The more he discovers he can get done with brains and hard work instead of good looks and charm, the less abrasive he'll become."

"Having an assistant sure helped me. Once I got the right one. I'm... um... still a little awkward around Miss Anders."

"She's mostly harmless. That doesn't mean you should be careless around her. She could take a kind gesture as meaning more than you intend. Just don't be mean to her either."

"I'm not interested in anyone else," he said. Erin raised an eyebrow.

"You're interested in Miss Anders?" she asked. She quickly calmed herself.

"Who? No! I mean anyone else... um... other than... um... you know."

"I'm flattered, Jerry. Really. I'm just... let's get the company sorted out and maybe one day we'll be ready to look at what a relationship would be like. I'm not saying uh... never. Someday."

"Someday," he agreed.

AS THEY HALF expected, Reinholdt tendered his resignation from the Board of Directors and they began a search for a replacement. Much to their surprise, Vaughn also said he was retiring. He was nearly eighty years old, so it was understandable.

Preston and Erin used the opportunity to nominate two younger people who would firm up their voting bloc. It wasn't contested by any of the other members of the board. Erin convinced her former boss and mentor to join the board by indicating that she could attend meetings remotely. The new president of Vaughn Home Furnishings, taking Vaughn's place in management of the company, had also agreed to take Vaughn's place on the Board.

At the annual shareholder meeting, Duval turned the meeting over to Erin for the next item of business.

"I'll ask our CEO, Miss Erin Scott, to introduce the next item of business," Duval said.

"Thank you, Mr. Duval. Our next item of business is election of the Board of Directors," Erin said. She hadn't realized how many shareholders there were in the company—many of them employees—who came to the annual meeting. While the family controlled the largest portion of the stock, it wasn't a clear majority. Now, as part of her compensation package, Erin was a shareholder, too.

"As you can see, there are some new names on the slate of candidates for the board. These have all been vetted by the current board and the principal shareholders. We place these names before you this afternoon."

"I move the election of the slate of directors presented by the board," one of the shareholders called out.

"Second!" another called.

"Moved and seconded. Is there any discussion?" Erin asked, scarcely pausing before she moved directly to the vote. "Those in favor say aye."

The motion carried and she officially became a member of the board of directors instead of being merely an ex-officio member as CEO. She turned the meeting back to Duval. Duval introduced Mr. Masters, the CFO.

"We initiated a full internal audit this spring," Masters said. "With changes in Board membership and executive management of the company, this was a prudent move so we could be fully transparent. The audit was completed by Jefferson-Mahon Accountants and we are pleased to inform the shareholders that we have a completely clean slate going into the next fiscal year."

There was much more and Masters fielded several questions regarding the previous January layoffs and the revival of the Mackenzie project, which had been renamed 'The Allard Midwestern Headquarters.' The response was positive and the report was accepted.

The model of Cloudhaven had been moved into the hall for the meeting, so shareholders could see exactly what had been committed to. Mr. Carver had continued to develop the model as more features had been added to the spec. He now had thirty architects and draftsmen working on the plans as development picked up speed.

His presentation was short and to the point. Erin did not allow time for questions, but moved directly on to the next division of JeriCorp.

She'd been out to the jobsite with Carver and Jerico on several occasions, riding between the two men in the front seat of their rather luxurious truck. She was always pleased with what she saw. The community was going to be wonderful. She even considered the possibility of moving to it herself.

At last, the annual company meeting was adjourned and she greeted many of the shareholders afterward, learning more about the business from those who owned it. Of course, Lawrence Jerico and Jacqueline Carver were very popular among the shareholders who had known the family for many years.

Finally, she left the auditorium and went to the penthouse. Mr. Carver was already there.

"Congratulations, Ms. Scott," he said when she stepped off the elevator. "I'm impressed with the way you've managed your executives. Everyone did a good job today."

"Including you, Mr. Carver," she said. "I'm glad you gave the introduction to Cloudhaven. That meant as much to the shareholders as anything that was discussed. It was okay to leave the flowery speech to Duval, but people really needed to see the person who conceived it. Congratulations to you."

"It was only having you standing beside me that gave me the courage to speak. My heart has only just begun to slow down."

"Thank you for doing it. I know you only did it because I asked. I appreciate it."

Without really thinking of what she was doing, she impulsively reached up and kissed him softly. Then she jumped back with a gasp as he looked at her with wide eyes.

"I... um..." she started.

"Please don't say you're sorry!" Preston said.

"Well... No, I'm not," Erin breathed. "I didn't plan that. I... But I'm not sorry."

"Good! I've wanted to kiss you for a very long time now."

"I kind of jumped away from you because I was so surprised by my brashness."

"Could we... um... try again without jumping away?" he asked.

"Yes," she squeaked.

They moved together and joined their lips. It couldn't be considered a passionate kiss, but was certainly one that held promise of something more to come. When the elevator bell rang they pulled away from each other slowly.

"Miss Scott. Mr. Carver?" Miss Anders said. "Um... I should probably go back downstairs." She started to back onto the elevator.

"Nonsense, Miss Anders. It's office hours," Erin said. "Uh... We'd appreciate it if you kept our little celebration of the annual meeting quiet. I assume Ms. Dirksen has set a time to go over the minutes with you?"

"Yes, Ma'am. I think we'll have everything by the end of the day on Monday."

"Do we have anything else on our agenda for today?"

"I'm told there is a traditional gathering of attendees at the Dragon Wing Bar on the waterfront after the meeting. I thought I'd go there to see what it was like."

"Sounds interesting. Why don't we all go down and mingle. Mr. Carver? Will you join us?"

"Um... uh... y-yes. If it's okay."

"I think so."

Erin hooked an arm through his and the three of them left the office.

Chapter Twenty-Five

IT WAS THE beginning. Erin had to face her own feelings about her attraction to Preston. He had declared his longstanding desire to kiss her and both understood that meant far more than being best friends. But was she ready to move on to this phase of life?

"I don't know what I should do," she confessed to Dolores later that evening. "I like him. He's smart and kind. And creative. And handsome. And... I like him."

"Why are you arguing with yourself about this?" Dolores asked. "The whole argument seems one-sided."

"Sure. Everything sounds great. He's socially inept and suffers severe attacks of anxiety. But the negatives aren't really about him. They're all about me. I've only been single for eight months. I've just paid off the debt I incurred from my last marriage. And in that regard, I'm batting zero when it comes to choosing a partner. Add to that, I manage the company he owns. We have a professional business relationship. If I'm romantically involved with him, do I even have a job anymore? I'm not going to give up everything for the idea of love again."

"Ah, yes. The *idea* of love. Don't you think you've learned something from that experience? You didn't give things up for love. You gave them up for the *idea* of love. For the *idea* of having a family and becoming your *idea* of a perfect mother and wife," Dolores said.

"That paints a rosy picture of it, doesn't it?" Erin sighed melodramatically. "And accurate. Maybe I'm not capable of that kind of relationship. Maybe if I'd been a better wife, Bruce wouldn't have strayed. Maybe if I get involved with Jerry, it will just be a precursor to him finding someone else, because I'm not enough for a man. I should just steer clear of relationships."

"Liar," Dolores laughed at her. "You don't believe any of that. First off, Bruce would have strayed no matter who he married. You could have been the matron saint of the marriage bed and he'd still have looked elsewhere. And you don't believe any of that about Jerry. What are you really afraid of?"

"What am I afraid of?"

Erin poured herself another glass of wine. She'd had a drink at the bar with the shareholders and said goodnight to Jerry. Then she'd come to Dolores to share a bottle of wine, which Dolores barely touched because Saturday was still a work day for her. Erin was feeling the effects of the alcohol, but it was sending her deep into her own thoughts.

"He's a nice guy. I like him. He'd probably welcome me if I just went back to the apartment tonight. Maybe. He's a little scary. I mean, am I really capable of being calm if he's in the middle of a panic attack? Not just the first time, but the fifth and tenth times? It seems like a lot of responsibility. Would I be a stressor? Would having me around make him more prone to attacks? Would I be... good for him? As good as he is for me?"

"Those are serious questions, Erin. And they aren't about Jerry. You're the only person who can answer the questions about you."

"What should I do?" she repeated. "I like him."

"My opinion, which is worth every penny you're paying for it, is that you should take it slow and easy, but let it progress naturally. It's definitely not a good idea to go back to the apartment tonight. Don't rush things. Even when you feel like rushing. Get to know him better. Think about going out someplace that is neutral territory. Get to know him there."

"You need to get to bed so you can go to work in the morning," Erin said, standing. "Thank you for listening. I won't do anything stupid. At least not tonight. I don't even need to drive home. I live close enough to walk. Thank you, Dolores."

"Get home safely, dear."

ANOTHER BOTTLE OF wine waited at home for Erin. She shut her cellphone in a kitchen drawer and took the bottle to bed where she watched old sappy movies on the television. At least she wouldn't be drunk-texting anyone. It only took another glass of wine before she faded off to sleep with the television still playing.

She was not used to the volume of alcohol she'd consumed, and woke up slowly on Saturday. It was a day of nursing a headache and putting herself to work. She cleaned her apartment from top to bottom, even sorting kitchen drawers and reorganizing her closet. She wondered absently how her cellphone ended up in the kitchen junk drawer.

She over-indulged in black coffee to the same extent that she'd imbibed alcohol the night before. As a result, she was shaky by the time she left her apartment to go to a family restaurant at the shopping center for dinner. She ate the commercialized Italian food, and purchased the extra meal they offered at a discount to take home.

She looked at the open bottle of wine from the night before and poured it down the sink. She certainly didn't need a repeat of that. She made herbal tea and turned on the television, but sat in bed with her laptop and reread all the reports from the previous week.

"Why isn't there a book called *Running a Company for Dummies?*" she sighed. Maybe she should write it.

Instead, at about one o'clock, she got out of bed, dressed in her bowling clothes, and went to the bowling alley.

SEVERAL LANES WERE in use at the bowling alley but Erin didn't really care where she was assigned. She just wanted to throw something heavy at something that made a lot of noise. Frustrations. She picked up her score sheet and shoes, then went to the area where she knew there was a ball that was decent for her to use.

She set the ball in the ball rack and sat to pull on her shoes, then lined up for her first throw. She took a breath and relaxed. Five steps and release. The ball sailed down the lane, nearly in the right gutter but curving directly into the pocket. Strike!

"Wow!" said the bowler in the lane next to her.

"First frame luck," she laughed, turning to him.

They both stopped and stared.

"Jerry?"

"Maizie?"

"How...?"

"Why...?"

"Do you...?"

"Sorry! I didn't mean..."

"It's okay. I mean..."

Both stood and just stared for a moment.

"Um... Hi! Fancy meeting you here," Erin said.

"I didn't think I'd see anyone I knew at this hour," he responded.

"I'm not stalking you. I just couldn't sleep tonight and needed to hear some pins fall."

"Sure. I didn't think you were. I mean... I'm not either. Stalking, I mean."

"Do you... um... come here often?" she asked.

"No. I've never been here. Well, I mean, not since I was in my teens. Not in a long time."

"How strange that we both show up at one o'clock in the morning," she said.

"I didn't mean to run into you, but you're why I'm here."

"What? Why?"

"Well, I knew you bowled. I mean, you've talked about your league and team. And I thought... Oh, geez!"

"Jerry, what is it? I was inspirational in getting you out for some exercise?"

"Inspiration. Yeah. Um... I wanted to ask you out and I tried to think of something you'd enjoy. So, I thought I'd try bowling to see if I could do it without making a fool of myself so I could ask you out sometime to go bowling," he explained. He was blushing brightly and went to the bench to sit with his head in his hands.

"Jerry, that's sweet. In fact, it's very thoughtful. Thank you. I mean, we're here and each have a lane with pins set up, we might as well use them. Maybe we can talk between frames. You know?"

"That's kind of what I thought we might do if we were on a date. I don't mean to force you into thinking we *are* on a date. I just... Yeah. I'd like that."

"HOW DID YOU first get interested in bowling?" Jerry asked. "It doesn't seem like the kind of game a high-powered executive up north would be into."

"I guess that's true in part. But I went to college in Ohio. I don't mean to be derogatory, but it was very working class. I think that the enjoyment of simple activities extends through all labor classes. And I'm a little competitive. Having something that I could compete with helped me deal with the stress and frustrations of college," Maizie said.

"I understand that. When I look down the lane, I can see certain faces on each pin. I don't care if I get a strike. I just want to hit as many of those people as possible," Jerry laughed.

"You found me out. That's why I got up in the middle of the night and came to the alley. I just wanted to hit something with a heavy ball."

"I hate to ask how many of those pins have my face on them."

"And I'm not going to tell you!"

They looked at each other and started laughing.

"Can I get you a Coke?" he asked.

"Oh, thanks. I'll walk up to the concession stand with you."

They went to the snack bar and Jerry ordered them soft drinks as they continued to chat.

"I forgot how heavy bowling balls are," he said. "I think I'm going to be sore tomorrow. How do you stand it?"

"I'm using a lighter ball than you are," she laughed. "I have to say, though, I felt it the first few times I went bowling with the team. If you compare your mass to my mass, I think twenty-five percent less weight is appropriate for me."

"Twenty-five percent? What does my ball weigh? It's the same size as yours, right?"

"Same size, different materials. Yours probably weighs sixteen pounds and mine weighs twelve. To be honest, I would probably bowl better with a fourteen-pound ball, but they don't have one on the racks that I've found to fit me. If I were serious about this, I'd order my own ball and shoes instead of using what's available at the alley."

Maizie and Jerry rolled again and both left a split on the corners.

"Um… What do you do with this?" he asked.

"I usually roll one right down the middle and miss both of them," Maizie laughed. "I aim for the inside edge of the left pin and hope it bounces back across the lane to hit the one on the right. That's one of the disadvantages of using a lighter ball. You don't get as much pin action as with a heavy ball."

She rolled for the spare and knocked down only the seven pin. The frame reset. Jerry rolled. The ball went into the left gutter, jumped back onto the lane and rolled down to drop into the right gutter just before it got to the ten pin.

"Wow!" she said. She looked at him and they both sputtered out laughter.

"I don't suppose I could interest you in a game of basketball, could I? Something I don't completely suck at?"

"Sometime," she said. "Don't be too hard on yourself, though. There was a lot of power behind that ball. Try rolling a little easier the next time. The pins are already dead. You don't have to kill them."

He did go a little easier the next time and left three pins standing. She rolled and left one.

"I'm going to mark this down as one of the many things I can learn from you," he said. "What do you suggest to get this?"

They talked for a few minutes before bowling for their spares. She told him about the arrows on the floor and how he held the ball. When he rolled again, he hit all three pins. She missed her single.

"Did I make you do that?" he asked.

"No. I'm just not focusing very well. Besides, I'm not that great a bowler. I just like to see the pins fall down."

"Tell me what has you frustrated enough that you wanted to come to the bowling alley in the middle of the night and throw a heavy ball at inanimate objects," Jerry said.

Maizie sighed and sat beside him at the scorer's table. She took a deep breath and decided to plunge ahead.

"Something I haven't had a problem with since high school," she said. "Boy trouble."

Preston was taken aback a moment. He'd never considered that Maizie—or Erin—might have a relationship with someone else since her divorce.

"Uh... Wow! I mean... that's really... um..."

"You see," she said, uncharacteristically not allowing him to regain his composure and finish the sentence, "there's this guy at work that I kind of like. And I think he kind of likes me, too. But I'm worried that if I got involved with him, it would ruin our working relationship. And friendship. Because I think we are friends, you know?"

Preston recaptured his composure. She had to be referring to him. Right? He wished he was better at talking about personal things with a woman. For all he'd grown comfortable with Erin since she came to work with him, he really didn't understand women that well.

"He um... probably worries about the same thing. Intraoffice romance can be tricky."

"I suppose I could just do nothing, but that could harm things, too. We'd constantly be feeling like we were hiding something from each other. At least, I would. But there's all the problems of office gossip and people misunderstanding. I mean, we work really closely together."

"I suppose the first thing would be to keep the romance out of the office," he said. He was beginning to get the picture. Erin had all the same problems with an office romance that he had.

"That's true. But you know, if I was going to date someone, I wouldn't want to sneak around about it. Not like I'd need to send out an office wide email announcing it—or even put it on social media. I just wouldn't want to be embarrassed to be seen in public with him."

"I know if I was in that relationship, I'd want to do things other than meet in secret. Like, I'd love to cook her a meal, but I wouldn't want to feel like my place was the only place we could go or meet. I really like concerts and theatre," he said.

"Oh, I do, too. And bowling. I could even get into traveling a little to see a professional ball game of some sort. I just wouldn't want to spend every Sunday afternoon in front of a television watching one."

"There are lots of things to do that could get people out of the house. I like to go for a hike, or boat, or fish. One of the things I like about going down to Cloudhaven so much is just walking around the property and imagining what will be there in a few years."

"I really enjoyed the one time I went down to walk the property. After looking at the 3D map in the office, I felt like I already knew the territory, but feeling it, smelling it, walking on it—those all made it much more real to me."

"I can't believe I was upset because you went there with Duval," Jerry sighed.

"I was so thankful when your grandfather came by in his truck. I was dreading getting back in Duval's car with him."

"You know, we have a school for the arts here in town and they often have plays, exhibitions, and concerts. I played basketball when I was in high school here and I'd still like to go to a game there occasionally," Jerry said.

"Did you ever think about taking a class just to learn something new?" she asked. "I read about a nature class that was just focused on learning to identify local trees and flowers."

"I thought about taking an art class once. Not to learn to be an artist, but to appreciate art more. I know there are cooking classes. And there's a brew pub in town that sometimes has a comedian or a musician entertaining." Jerry was getting excited about the kind of things they could do together.

"I think the most important thing about it, though, is not to hide it. If we saw someone from the office or that we knew from school or bowling, we wouldn't be embarrassed about it and try to pretend we weren't together."

"We wouldn't pretend to *not* be together at the office, either," he said. "We just wouldn't make an issue out of it. We'd have to be careful of PDAs in the presence of other employees, but if someone in the office knew we were seeing each other, we wouldn't get embarrassed or try to hide it."

They grinned at each other and realized they'd been sitting at the scorer's table for some time without having actually bowled. They laughed a little and got up to bowl another frame. Both, by some miracle, rolled strikes. They slapped hands in a high five and held them together as they looked into each other's eyes.

"We were... talking about us... weren't we?" she asked a little uncertainly.

"I was. I... I hope you were."

"Yeah."

"Not to rush things, but would you like to go for a walk by the river tomorrow? The leaves have begun to turn."

"That sounds like fun. Maybe two o'clock? I think I'd better go home now and get some sleep."

"Yeah, me too. I think I have a date tomorrow afternoon. I'll stop and pick you up at two."

They pulled their score sheets and changed shoes, taking them back to the cashier. It had been an inexpensive night out. They walked out together with hands lightly brushing against each other. At her car, she paused to look at him and met his lips with hers. They both grinned and went their separate ways.

Chapter Twenty-Six

PRESTON AIR-BALLED HIS shot and Gene grabbed it on the bounce.

"What happened to you, sharpshooter?"

"I didn't get much sleep last night," Preston laughed.

"Up late planning a new magnificent project?" Gene asked.

"Bowling."

"Wait. What? You were bowling?"

"There aren't too many people at the bowling alley at one in the morning."

"I don't remember you ever bowling before."

"It was my first time since high school. Remember when I took Sue Williams out? Not only did she cream me at the alley, she humiliated me at school by telling everyone how bad I was."

"I think you're the only person in Jerico City who remembers that. How did you do last night?"

"Better than you can ever imagine."

"What was your score?" Gene asked.

"I have no idea."

"Preston, what the hell are you talking about?"

"Maizie... Erin was there. We sort of had an impromptu date."

"You dog! You didn't leave her in bed to come and play basketball, did you?"

"Oh, geez no! We didn't... We each went to our own homes after the bowling alley. We just talked," Preston said.

"I hope you were more erudite than you're being with me."

"We really had a great conversation. I went bowling so I could decide if I could ask her on a date to bowl. I wasn't expecting to see her there. She ended up on the lane next to mine and started with a strike. Then we realized we were next to each other and got to talking. We bowled some, too. It just wasn't as important as talking."

"She goes bowling at one o'clock in the morning?"

"Not usually. She said she was there to work out her frustrations by throwing a heavy ball at inanimate objects."

"Frustration?"

"That's what we talked about. It was all kind of cool. She talked about liking a guy who she thought liked her but she didn't know what to do about it," Preston said. He grabbed the ball from Gene and tossed it at the rim. Swish!

"And she was talking about you?"

"I didn't realize it at first and thought I'd blown my chances with her. But as we talked, it became more and more obvious we were talking about each other. We went through a long list of things we could do together and set up some ground rules about dating," Preston said.

"So, what are the rules?"

"Take it slow and easy, first. But we agreed we wouldn't be secretive about dating. We wouldn't make any display of it in the office, but if we saw someone we knew while we were out, we wouldn't try to hide that we were with each other. It makes a lot of sense."

"That's incredible! What did your family say?"

"God, Gene! I haven't told them yet!"

"Wait. What about this not being secretive?"

"It's not about keeping a secret, but trying to manage my mother. If I told her I was dating Erin, Mother would want to invite her over for dinner and immediately show her the wedding step. She'd assume we were getting married tomorrow."

"That does sound like your mother."

"G-Pop would draft a prenup before we saw each other this afternoon."

"You're seeing each other this afternoon?" Gene asked.

"Just going for a walk along the river to look at the leaves."

"Hmm. Right."

"I know she has a standing Sunday evening get-together with her former boss," Preston said. "It's the same thing as me coming to play basketball and have Sunday dinner with my family."

"I've got to tell you, pal, I'm really happy for you. You know she's been vetted and approved. We wouldn't have nominated her to run the company otherwise. I don't think even Jerico will have a background check run. Your mother did that before she was first hired."

"Just be cool, okay?" Preston said. "Remember, I said our first rule was to take it slow and easy. Don't go getting us married before we decide if we like each other."

"Yeah. I'll do my part. Sometime, though, we'll need to double date so we all get to know each other better. Agreed?"

"Agreed."

"GUESS WHO I ran into in town this week!" Jacqueline said at the Sunday dinner table. "Jordan Malone. I know you liked her in high school. The first thing out of her mouth was to ask how you were doing. She's still just as sweet as she was when you were kids. It's sad that life dealt her a bad hand. You know she married Ron Taft and he planned a career in the military. He was killed in Afghanistan or Iran or somewhere in the desert and left her with two little ones. So sad. She's just moved back to town so the children are closer to their grandparents. I suggested that you should get together next weekend and she said she'd love to."

"No," Preston said.

"Preston, you liked Jordan. And she was never mean or rude to you."

"No, Mother. You'll have to call and explain to her that I can't see her next weekend."

"Why ever not?"

Preston took a deep breath. This was exactly what he was afraid of, but there was nothing he could do about it now.

"I'm seeing someone."

There was silence at the table. Lawrence and Jacqueline sat open-mouthed. Gina grinned.

"That's wonderful news, Preston. I know your mother and grand-father are thrilled. They are just too surprised to speak," Gina said.

"Yes. That's right. Who?" demanded Jacqueline.

"Just don't make a big deal about it, okay?"

"About what?" Lawrence asked.

"We just decided it would be okay to see each other last night. Kind of in the middle of the night."

"You slept with her before you decided it was okay to see each other?" Jacqueline asked. She was more than a little dumbfounded.

"Mother, we aren't sleeping together. In fact, we want to take it slow and easy so we can see how things work out. There's no rush. We just want to see each other."

"Who?" Lawrence asked.

"Ms. Scott," Preston said.

This time Gina spit tea out her nose. Jacqueline made an audible gasp and Lawrence started to laugh.

"What is the problem?" Preston asked. "I know you two like her and she's been vetted six ways till Sunday. You should have no objec-tions to my seeing her socially."

"None at all," Lawrence said. "Absolutely none at all."

"What about all your protesting about dating an employee?" Jacqueline said. "I'd given up on her as a possibility."

"We had a little encounter after the shareholders' meeting Friday. It got us both thinking and we ended up both going bowling at one this morning. We didn't intend to meet, but once we were both there we got to talking. We set up some ground rules that would enable us to date. And one of them is that I shouldn't be late to pick her up. We're going for a walk this afternoon. Please excuse me from cleanup today. I'll make it up next time."

With that, Preston pushed away from the table and left his flab-bergasted family sitting in silence.

"I DON'T LIKE this! I don't like it at all!" Jacqueline said as she stared at her father and his girlfriend.

"And why is that, dear daughter? Are you shocked that Preston managed to do for himself what you've been frustrated in for so long?" Lawrence asked. "She's perfect for him."

"Too perfect! I should have seen it from the start. A perfect assistant in the office. Dutifully taking care of the menial tasks. Resetting his Rubik's Cubes. Able to make a presentation on the spur of the moment. A perfect candidate for CEO. There must be something wrong with her. She's competent, beautiful, creative, smart. What does she see in Preston? Is she just after the business after all?"

"My how the leopard has changed her spots," Gina chuckled.

"You stay out of this. Whatever she takes is something you won't have access to," Jacqueline barked.

"I already have all I want, Jackie," she answered. "What is it that you want? If he'd taken your hints to date Erin when you made them, would that have made it better?"

"He did it without me!" Jacqueline sobbed. "Oh, I'm a stupid mother. I only ever wanted him to be happy, but I always thought I'd have to provide that happiness for him—even if it was in the form of another woman. My baby is all grown up!"

"He didn't stutter or stumble once when he was telling us about her," Lawrence said. "We might be seeing a whole new Preston emerging."

"WE HELD HANDS," Erin said to Dolores. "That can't be considered too much for what has to be really our first date, can it?"

She sat with her friend Sunday evening, having rushed there after her date with Jerry to walk by the river. When they were together or she was talking about her date, they were still Jerry and Maizie. It was what had enabled them to communicate so easily early Sunday morning.

"I think after nearly a year, you know each other well enough to hold hands on a first official date," Dolores laughed. "I'm so happy for you!"

"I am, too. I think. What if this is a big mistake and I'm messing up my whole career at JeriCorp. Or his. What if his mother and grandfather don't like me? His family is so close. And I don't have any!"

"You've had family you were close to," Dolores soothed her younger friend. "I know you still think of them."

"Yes, and I think they would have been so disappointed in my first choice for a husband," Erin sighed. "Back then, I was still trying to replace them. Do you think I'm trying to replace my family with Jerry? Or that I'm trying to make up for the mess of my first marriage? I never intended to get married again, but I can't stop thinking of the possibility when I'm with Jerry."

"Well, you agreed to take it slow and easy, right?"

"Yes. In fact, that was his first suggestion. It was so sweet, Dolores. He knew I bowled with the ladies' league, so he decided to go out in the middle of the night to practice bowling so he could ask me out for something I liked to do."

"That's a keeper, in my book. You know how many guys I hear about who wanted to treat the girl to an elaborate meal at a fancy restaurant? It always ends the same. He figures if he spends a lot of money on her, she'll be obligated to pay him back with her body. The girls on the breakfast shift are most susceptible. Most of their customers are singles."

"He captured me on the lunch shift," Erin said. "As soon as he walked through the door, I just wanted to take care of him."

"And you still are, aren't you?"

"Sort of. I've got Cheryl trained to put away the laundry and wipe things down. I still make coffee in the morning. But I have to start working as soon as I get in. I can't do the domestic housework every day. He often offers to cook breakfast for me, but I make a point to eat something substantial before I come to work. We have coffee together while we plan out our day."

"I can't give you any sage advice. You'll just have to take it easy and see where it all leads. Trust your heart."

"If I did that, I'd have moved in with him Friday. I think I should listen to my heart, but trust my head."

ERIN HAD MORE fun on their dates than she'd had since high school—or college at least. Back then, she didn't feel obligated to put out for whoever was taking her out. She realized how that had changed with her later college years and through her twenties. Every date then had felt like the expectation was to sleep together—at least by the third date, if not the first.

When she kissed Jerry after they went for a walk, out to dinner, to a concert, or to a museum, she could definitely feel the pressure building for more. She kept asking herself why she hadn't just gone upstairs to his bedroom and called for him to join her. But she was enjoying the building pressure of dating so much, she didn't want it to end. And the kisses were becoming more intense with each date. He'd brushed against her breast during their kiss the week before Thanksgiving. She'd gone to bed with that feeling tingling through her body and reliving his touch as she touched herself.

"I HAVE AN official invitation for you," Mr. Carver said in the office Monday morning.

"Official?"

"Yes. I couldn't keep Mother from issuing it. I was going to invite you out on Thanksgiving, but Mother believes we've been seeing each other long enough that you should join the family for Thanksgiving dinner," Carver said.

"Oh my. That *is* an official invitation, isn't it? You have to tell me what you want me to do. Is it too much, too soon for me to join a family celebration? I thought I could make a simple Thanksgiving dinner for the two of us if you'd prefer that," Miss Scott said.

"Do you remember meeting Ellen Barrett and her husband last week when we went to the basketball game at the high school? I really had no idea her son was playing."

"I remember. I thought we did quite well. When she asked if we were seeing each other, we just said 'Yes.' We didn't try to explain anything. And she accepted that without further questions."

"I'm sure it has gone through the office. She's close friends with Shannon Duval and once Shannon knows something, the office knows."

"Yes, but it was our first real test of being public about being a couple. We passed."

"Well, I think we can pass the family test, too," he answered. "Mother's invitation aside, Erin Scott, it would be a privilege if you consented to join me with my family at our holiday gathering Thursday."

"Preston Carver, it would be my pleasure to join you."

SHE'D SAID IT so convincingly, but Thursday morning, she was a nervous wreck. She'd seen both Jacqueline and Lawrence at Board meetings and once or twice in the office since she started dating Preston, but going to their home—basically throwing the relationship in their faces—was a new level of intimacy.

Do they think I'm sleeping with him? What has he told them?

She dressed three times, trying to make sure she had the right balance of holiday festive and family informal. She finally chose a casual skirt and blouse, deciding that was as good as it was going to get. She'd offered to simply drive to Jerico House herself, but Preston said he was driving from the penthouse and would like to pick her up.

She'd grown rather fond of his older Continental, and had driven it to business meetings in St. Louis on a couple of occasions. She would just as soon ride in the truck that Preston and his grandfather shared. The three of them had driven down to Cloudhaven to review progress the first of November. It was good. It was also good to be sandwiched in the front seat between Preston and Lawrence. They'd held pinky fingers on the trip, much to Lawrence's amusement.

Preston was a bit of a traditionalist and came to her apartment door rather than texting his arrival to her and waiting for her to come down. It was almost as if he expected to be interrogated by a parent or big brother. Erin thought perhaps she should have Dolores over to meet him when he came up one day. That might shake him up too much, though.

She held his hand on the way to the car and he opened the door for her. The male influence in his life had skipped a generation between

Lawrence and Preston. She felt he was constantly mirroring his grand-father's formality in dealing with other people. Perhaps he had found that was an easier way for him to interact with others. She found it a delightful difference between him and most men of their generation.

She waited for him to come around the car and open her door before she got out and took his hand, as they walked up the steps to the massive doors. The last time Erin had been here had been to get the family's proxies so she could save Preston's job. Or take it. She found the entrance of the old mansion just as imposing as she had on that first visit.

"Welcome!" Jacqueline said when they entered the house. Lawrence and Gina were just a few steps behind her. "Happy Thanksgiving!"

"Thank you! Happy Thanksgiving to you, Mrs. Carver." Erin handed Jacqueline a bottle of wine.

"None of that, Erin. This isn't the office. I'm guessing you call Preston something other than Mr. Carver when you are on a date. You must call me Jackie."

"Thank you, Jackie."

Lawrence stepped up and gave her a bear hug.

"And I'm Lawrence. This is my special friend Gina Gabriola."

"Thank you, Lawrence. I seem to recall you have a fondness for Wild Turkey. I hope you'll share this." She handed him a bottle of the bourbon and greeted Gina. "I'm Erin. It's nice to meet you, Gina."

Preston stepped past his grandfather and swept another woman up in a hug to spin her around.

"And this is the wonder woman who is responsible for the survival of this old monstrosity, Matilda," Preston said, setting the house-keeper cook down in front of Erin.

"I've heard so much about you, Matilda," Erin said. "It seems the Jerico family would cease to be if it weren't for you."

"I'd like to say you're exaggerating, but you're probably right," Matilda said. "Mr. Lawrence, why don't you open that bottle you are cradling so protectively and pour cocktails for everyone. The bird just came out of the oven and needs to rest a bit before a carver gets to it." She looked meaningfully at Preston.

Lawrence poured Wild Turkey on the rocks for everyone and they toasted the holiday and each other. Preston did carve the turkey into professional-looking slices of both light and dark meat. They all exclaimed over how tasty the food was. It was a sign of the family's acceptance of all people that Matilda joined them at the table as part of the family.

The food and the company were excellent. Of course, Erin was asked questions she'd already answered for Preston about her home life and departed parents, but it was all a part of getting to know each other outside the office and business. She found herself enjoying the company and the holiday.

PRESTON, OF COURSE, walked her to her door rather than just dropping her off at the curb. She kept hold of his hand as she opened the door and pulled him inside. She made tea and they sat in her living room together to sip the hot beverage. It was not long, though, before they lost interest in the tea in favor of each other. It was the first time they'd truly made out. Their hands stayed above the waist, but as their lips joined, the passion heated up.

"We could easily get carried away," she gasped. "A part of me is more than willing."

"I don't want a part of you," he said. "I want all of you. So, I think I should head home now before we do get carried away."

They both moved reluctantly to the door where they kissed again and narrowly avoided returning to the sofa.

"I'm not running away," he said. "I just want to know we're both ready."

"I won't run away from you, Jerry," she said. "Goodnight, love."

Chapter Twenty-Seven

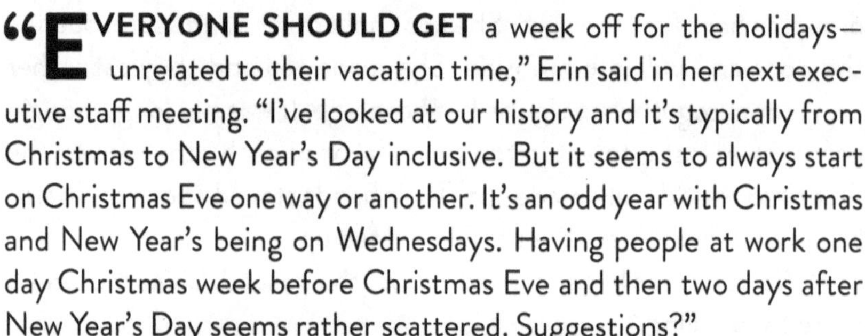

"**E**VERYONE SHOULD GET** a week off for the holidays—
unrelated to their vacation time," Erin said in her next executive staff meeting. "I've looked at our history and it's typically from
Christmas to New Year's Day inclusive. But it seems to always start
on Christmas Eve one way or another. It's an odd year with Christmas
and New Year's being on Wednesdays. Having people at work one
day Christmas week before Christmas Eve and then two days after
New Year's Day seems rather scattered. Suggestions?"

"Official policy is a half day Christmas Eve plus Christmas
Day, and a half day New Year's Eve plus New Year's Day," Dirksen
responded.

"Are we satisfied it's the right pattern? How many people are
going to use up sick days the day after Christmas?" Erin asked.

"Sick days and personal days have to be used before the end of
the year, don't they?" Duval asked. "It seems like we're just giving
people the opportunity to cash them in."

"Don't like it," Carver said. "Two weeks off."

"That is a strain on the company finances," Masters said. "We've
always managed a week off at the end of the year, but I don't think we
can stand the pressure of giving everyone two weeks off. Especially
after the layoffs last year. Employees would be wondering if we were
shutting down over the break."

"I can see that as an interpretation. We'd have to message it pretty carefully. But I agree that we can't afford to just shut down the company for two weeks," Erin said. "Even though I'd like to be in that position. We still have commitments we have to live by and remember our contractors wouldn't be paid for that time. Miss Anders, let's suppose there were three options. Which would you prefer? One, the entire week of Christmas off plus an early out on New Year's Eve and New Year's Day. Two, an early out on Christmas Eve with Christmas Day through New Year's Day off. Three, early out on Christmas Eve with Christmas Day off and the entire week of New Year's Day off. What would appeal to you most?"

"Oh, wow! Uh... I'd probably opt for Christmas week off. I'd be able to visit my parents if I left on the weekend. That's a total of nine days in a row with weekends on either end. Plus, the New Year holiday. The Christmas to New Year's option only includes one weekend. I don't see many people opting for the New Year's week option. Christmas is a much bigger holiday for most people," Miss Anders answered.

"I lean that way myself," Erin said, "but I don't want to make a unilateral decision. I'd like us all to agree on the right choice."

"I have to say that I agree with your assistant regarding the unlikely acceptance of option three," Duval said. "The other two, though, could be a toss up."

"Personal choice?" Carver asked. "Each employee could choose their preference."

It was good to hear Preston engaging with the other execs in this discussion. He kept his answers short and simple, but he was definitely engaged.

"Could we make that work?" Erin asked, turning specifically to her legal counsel, Ms. Dirksen.

"As long as people declared their preference in advance so their managers can adjust the workload, I think it's possible," Dirksen answered.

"I think we'll have most people choose the Christmas week option," Duval said. "But I'd expect a lot of them to tack on two personal days or sick days New Year's week. We'd need to be prepared for that. Does that bring us back to the equivalent of two weeks off that Preston suggested?"

"I don't think so," Masters said. "Sick days and personal days are carried as a company liability. Unlike just giving two weeks off, if a person takes sick or personal days, it erases a debt. It's actually a positive."

"That brings us back to just keeping with the standard holidays and letting those who want to use up their off time cash it in," Duval said.

"Except those of us who haven't been here long enough to accrue time off would be stuck in an empty office," Miss Anders said. She looked around at the people staring at her for her uninvited input. "Sorry."

"You're right," Erin said. "It also pulls the rug from under the idea that the company is doing something nice for people for the holiday. I think I'm tending toward option one as well. Anyone else?"

After a minute or two, with a couple more comments, all the executives agreed on the Christmas week off option. With limited additional business, the meeting was adjourned and the execs left the penthouse.

"Did you get everything you need to type up the notes?" Erin asked Miss Anders.

"Yes, Ma'am. I'm sorry for bursting out when I wasn't invited to," said the assistant.

"It was a good point. I'm not going to reprimand you for that. We'll do some work together on when it's appropriate and when it isn't. I don't think you have much to learn."

"Thank you, Ms. Scott."

Erin returned to her desk and reviewed the other reports that had come in over the long weekend. Preston had gone back to his desk.

"We could have given everyone two weeks," Preston growled.

"Masters had a good argument against that," Erin said. "My personal preference would have been the same, but I think this way will work better. Do you have plans for the holiday?"

"Um... No. Family celebration on Christmas. Go out to a wild party on New Year's Eve," he snorted. Erin looked surprised.

"A wild party? Wow! Who'd have thought it?"

"To me, that amounts to lining up all the cubes in a row and seeing how long it takes me to solve all of them while having a drink of G-Pop's Wild Turkey after each solution. The trick would be to see how many I could solve before I passed out."

"That... Actually, that sounds painful," Erin laughed.

"Do you have plans?"

"Even fewer than you have."

"We could..." Preston cut himself off when Erin glanced toward Miss Anders at the other end of the office. "...um... discuss it later."

"Good idea," Erin said.

After Thanksgiving evening, and the dinner they'd shared on Saturday that almost ended up in bed, Erin knew the time was approaching when they would spend the night together, either at her apartment or his. She wouldn't be sneaky about it, but she rather thought that having the entire week of Christmas off would be a lovely opportunity. She tried not to think about how her plans the previous Christmas had been thwarted.

IT ALMOST BECAME irrelevant the next week.

"That's not the way it's done!" Preston declared.

"It's not your responsibility any longer," Erin said.

"The recommended year-end bonuses and stock options always come before the Board of Directors. The recommendation from Finance is just a recommendation until the Board votes on it."

"That's not what the bylaws say," Erin responded. "It was your privilege as CEO to bring the recommendation to the Board to act on it, but the bylaws clearly state it is the CEO's decision regarding allocating executive bonuses except his own. The only one that has to be brought before the board is the CEO's bonus, and that was set in the employment agreement."

"That's too much authority to be in the hands of the CEO. It needs to come before the Board."

"Are you, as Chairman, ordering me to forgo my authority according to the bylaws and take this to the Board of Directors? For what? Their rubber stamp? Exactly what in the table of bonuses do you object to?"

"It's not the amounts. It's the process. It's supposed to... It's always been done..."

"Mr. Carver, do you intend to fire me or would you like my resignation?"

"Wh... What? N... N... No! That's not... I just... I'm..."

Preston began to hyperventilate and was near to passing out. He turned away from Erin and headed for the stairs to his bedroom.

"Need... to sleep," he said as he stumbled up the stairs.

Erin watched him go with her mouth open. When she first started, Jacqueline had warned her that when Preston felt overwhelmed, he retreated to his bed for a while. She'd only seen it happen once. That was the day he'd come back from the diner having found out Maizie no longer worked there.

Erin had spent hours over the past week locked up with Ellen Barrett in Human Resources and Leroy Masters in Finance negotiating the table for year-end bonuses and stock options throughout the company. Part of that had come down to the executive bonuses. Her major impact had been to reduce the executive bonuses by half—including her contractual bonus—so that more could be distributed to the employees. She thought she'd done a particularly good job. For the past several years, executive income and bonuses had been excessive, in her opinion. The previous year, executives had all received bonuses, but employees had not. She was not going to let that happen on her watch.

I mucked that up royally.

The past day or so, since her relationship with Jerry had heated up, they seemed to have more conflicts. He'd been in the office steadily since Thanksgiving and was paying more attention to how she was doing her job. She had snapped once before, suggesting that he should be on the job site. Of course, he knew more about what was happening on the job site than anyone, but saying he should be on the site made it sound like she didn't want him in the office, which made her wonder if that was what she really meant.

Suggesting he could fire her or she could resign was a little over the top for the size of the issue. Why was she being so snappish? And it wasn't only with Mr. Carver. Mr. Duval had challenged her decision to cut back the bonuses, too. She was pretty sure that Duval had complained to Preston and that had sparked the confrontation this afternoon. There was really nothing wrong with bringing the decision to the Board, except that she didn't want to be challenged on it. That wasn't a good reason. If she was right about the bonuses and options, she should be able to convince the Board.

She didn't want Mr. Carver to fire her and she didn't want to resign over this. What's more, it was apparent that the confrontation would damage her personal relationship.

Am I trying to run away?

She needed to pull up her big girl panties and face the facts about her relationship with Jerry. She was scared. She didn't believe he would ever treat her like her husband had, but she'd shown that she had poor judgment where that was concerned. She'd made a bad bet on her first marriage, blindly following him and abandoning her career choices. She couldn't do that with Jerry. This job was important to her. She was good at it. She wasn't willing to sacrifice it to be with Jerry. The question was, could she sacrifice Jerry to keep her job?

When five o'clock came around and Miss Anders cleaned things up, , Erin stayed at her desk. One thing was certain: She wasn't leaving the office without a resolution today. If Mr. Carver couldn't deal with it today, she'd sit at her desk all night until he could.

PRESTON DIDN'T COME downstairs until almost six o'clock. Erin was still at her desk. She looked up and he turned to go back upstairs.

"Jerry, please don't go. I really need you right now."

"You need me?" he snorted. "What for?"

"Because you are you and I've not been fair with you this afternoon. I'm not used to avoiding conflict. I always just wade right in, resolve it, and move on. I knew that would upset you and I should have chosen a different tack."

"You were right. You have the right to make the decision without the Board's approval."

"Maybe so, but there is nothing wrong with getting the Board to approve it. I was being overly protective of my status. And the thing is, I know better. You've always supported my decisions. I need to recognize there's a problem when you don't."

"Last year, I saw the company lay off thirty people for the first time since I've been here. Seeing the cuts you were making reminded me of that. I'm sorry," Jerry said.

"In a way, I'm trying to make up for it. No one got bonuses last year except the executives. That didn't make sense to me. I know how concerned you are about your people. How did it happen?"

"I left it up to the Board. They passed the bonuses resolution and I didn't really even read it. I couldn't believe you were taking action to correct my messes," Preston said.

"I can't do it without you," she answered. "I'll take the decision to the Board, but I need to know you agree with the stance. I need your vote. Mr. Hathaway and the new board members look to you for the spirit of the company and how they should vote. If you are behind me, then I know it will pass. Is the bonus structure I put together satisfactory with you?"

"We should cut the executive bonuses completely. I suppose that would really start a war, though. I'm satisfied. I'll support you, whether you take it to the Board or not."

"I will. Our meeting is next Wednesday and I'll put it on the agenda."

"Maizie… This is probably the wrong time to say this, but I love you. I've been in love with you for a long time now."

"It's probably too early to make such declarations, but I love you, too. Let's plan to do something special during our week off over Christmas. I'd like that."

They kissed. Before it got too intense, Erin slipped out of his embrace and grabbed her coat.

"I'll see you in the morning," she said.

PRESTON ALMOST TURNED around to run back upstairs when he saw Ms. Scott was still there, but she stopped him by calling him

Jerry. It was almost like a code word that got them out of office mode and into dating mode, except it didn't quite go that far.

It was such a silly fight. He recalled an incident when he was maybe eight years old that he'd been playing on his bicycle with a croquet mallet and ball, pretending he was playing polo. The incident involved a girl about the same age he was who wanted to play and borrow his mallet. He'd created a god-awful fuss about needing the mallet for his big match in the morning and ended up being sent to bed for his rudeness.

Of course, there had been no big match the next day. In fact, Preston couldn't remember having ever played that game again. He couldn't remember ever seeing the croquet mallet again. But he did remember going to bed when he lost control. That was one of the more childish behaviors he carried into his adult life. It was a wonder that Maizie had waited for him.

The thing was, he agreed with her regarding reducing executive bonuses. When he'd realized executives got bonuses when all the other employees went without and thirty had been laid off, he was furious. He wanted to reprimand them, but his voice—Royce Duval—had been the driver of the bonuses in the first place. So, Erin was acting on his behalf in the way he wished he had acted. Why was he so upset that she wasn't taking the decision to the Board?

He'd apologized. She'd apologized. They kissed and made up. He wanted to live in that kiss and to move their relationship up a notch. If he could find the words. If he could avoid making a hash of things again. She was much too valuable to him to lose. Either as CEO or as his partner. He was hoping she would be his partner for life. She was the first woman he'd ever considered as a life partner—a wife. He had to find a way to address the possibility with her. He had to make his mouth work without panicking.

THERE WAS SOME heated discussion of the bonuses at the board meeting. Lawrence and Jacqueline had been alerted to the issue and decided it would be fun to watch, so the three officers who had spearheaded the coup attempt earlier in the year were resigned as far as the vote was concerned. They were all surprised though when Preston spoke up at the meeting. He had a carefully prepared statement that he read.

"I have had a lengthy chat with Ms. Teresa Lincoln of Allard Holding. Ms. Lincoln, thank you for your advice and for your participation on our Board." In reality, the 'chat' had been several email messages. Erin was surprised to find that Preston had contacted her. "I believe our policy regarding executive bonuses, increases, and stock options should be revised. I am looking to the model used at Allard for an example. Ms. Lincoln, would you mind giving us a brief description of the model we discussed?"

"Certainly, Mr. Carver," Erin's former boss said over her video link from Philadelphia, the national headquarters of Allard. She'd been at the shareholders' meeting which elected the new Board and attended the first Board meeting thereafter in person. Her usual attendance, however, was remote. "We have a very simple model. It is our opinion that no executive ever contributes more than his or her employees. The difference in responsibility is reflected in base salary. But at Allard, no executive receives a higher percentage bonus or stock option than the average across the non-executive employees. If we determine, for example, that the bonus level for the year is two percent, it is two percent across all levels in the company. Of course, we have some flexibility built in to recognize extraordinary performance and substandard performance, but that is no greater for executives than for any other employee. Mr. Carver?"

"Thank you, Ms. Lincoln. I have asked that this be brought before the Board at this meeting so we can prepare to address it. It is my intent that we adopt a similar policy and have it approved in our bylaws at the next annual shareholders' meeting," Preston said.

"That's a pretty radical shift," Ms. Dirksen said.

"I believe Mr. Carver has opened the door for discussion, but that since this has come as a surprise to the Board at this meeting, the discussion should be tabled until our next meeting. At that time, we will all have a draft of the proposed bylaw changes that we can refer to so we are responding to the same thing," Erin said. "Is there other business to be brought before the Board? If not, Mr. Carver."

"This meeting of the Board of Directors of JeriCorp Architecture and Development is hereby adjourned. Happy holidays to you all," Preston read from his prompt card.

The meeting was adjourned.

Chapter Twenty-Eight

"YOU WERE TERRIFIC," Erin said when she and Preston got back to their office. "I had no idea you'd spoken to Teresa. It's a great plan."

"I didn't feel like I'd given you enough support for the work you were doing," Preston said. "I want to become a better partner."

"You don't want to, like, have your old job back? Seems like you could do it now, much more effectively."

"God, no! I've improved enough to be able to read my prepared statements aloud. But I haven't improved as an executive officer. You were right that I've been hanging around the office too much. I should be back out at Cloudhaven keeping that project on track. I should be making trips up to St. Louis to check on the Allard project. I should be doing the things a Chief Architect does. Most of all, I should be having faith in my Chief Executive. You are what our company has needed for seven years—ever since I took over as Chairman of the Board."

"Don't short-sell yourself, Mr. Carver. You've done a lot to create a corporate culture that is employee-positive. And you have clearly established the vision. I like working with you."

"Um… Would you like to start the holiday season with me Saturday? I'd love to put aside the business and cook a nice meal for Jerry and his girlfriend."

"Mmm. Jerry's girlfriend thinks that would be a great idea. She'll see him at five for a little goodnight kiss."

"Yes. He's looking forward to that."

IT APPEARED THAT the Chief Architect/Chairman of the Board and the Chief Executive had mended their fences. Now Erin could think about her relationship with her boyfriend. And the more she thought about it, the more pleased she was. She began to look forward to Christmas as she'd thought she never would again.

The last two days before the holiday vacation were busy, though. Preston had discussed the bonus policy with Ms. Lincoln, but he hadn't actually written the policy or amendment to the bylaws. That needed to be taken care of so the board members could review it and discuss it at the January meeting.

They worked on it and went out to Jerico House to review the draft with Lawrence and Jacqueline. After a few more revisions they sent the draft off to the members of the board. They gave a little gift to their assistant and told her to have a good time visiting her family, then found themselves alone in the penthouse.

LAWRENCE AND JACQUELINE had invited the couple back to Jerico House for dinner, which cooled their potential ardor for the night.

"What are your plans for the holiday week?" Jacqueline asked.

"I don't really have family to visit. I might find a way to see a friend from Cleveland. My bowling team is planning a little party the day after Christmas. It's our usual bowling night, but there's no league play that night, of course," Erin said. "Aside from that, I'll probably watch sappy Christmas movies and eat peppermint fudge."

"Are you going to make peppermint fudge?" Preston asked excitedly.

"Oh, it's one of my specialties," Erin laughed.

"I'd love to learn that one. I've never been successful making candies," Preston said.

"Then I invite you to my kitchen for a change."

"And as we are inviting people, we will officially invite Erin to share Christmas with us," Lawrence said. "Please join us."

"Oh, thank you! Of course, I'd love to."

Matilda called everyone to the table for a very homey meal of chicken alfredo on pasta. The atmosphere was relaxed as everyone settled down for the vacation. The stresses of the office melted away.

ERIN HAD DRIVEN to Jerico House and returned Preston to the office. She declined the invitation to join him and said she'd see him Saturday afternoon. She drove home with her heart racing.

Her whole body was tingling with anticipation. She could have joined him. All she had to do was accept his invitation to come up for a nightcap. With the kissing and petting in the car, though, she knew they wouldn't be drinking if she went up to the penthouse.

Yes. She'd made her decision. As a famous basketball player had once said, it wasn't a question of if, only of when. Erin had decided.

JERRY WAS CHOPPING vegetables for his special stew when she arrived Saturday afternoon and she quickly joined as his sous chef.

Of course, she didn't get her hands on a vegetable or a knife before they'd kissed. It was definitely a kiss with intent. He sautéed the onions and garlic, then added the meat. After adding broth, he put in the potatoes, carrots, and other vegetables. The kitchen was filled with the delicious aroma.

Between each step, the couple found themselves locked in an embrace that became more passionate with each step.

"Jerry, how time-sensitive is dinner?" Erin gasped after an intense kiss when everything had been added to the kettle.

"Dinner?" he asked as if only just considering the subject. "Oh, this one isn't time-sensitive at all. I can reduce the heat to simmer and let it cook for a couple of hours. Why?"

"Please do that."

He reduced the heat, made sure the kettle wouldn't either stick or boil over, and turned back to her.

"Now, Jerry, my love, take me to bed."

"To... Upstairs... My bed... You want... I mean..."

"Yes. I want. I'm ready."

He might have needed it spelled out for him, but once he got the point, he moved into action. He swept her up in his arms and carried her up the stairs as she continued to kiss his face and his lips. They fell to the bed, continuing to kiss and pet, pulling at each other's clothes until both were naked.

"You're so beautiful," he whispered as he continued to pet her breasts and move down to her butt. "I can't believe we're finally going to do this."

"I can't believe we waited this long," she answered.

Once they were committed, they slowed down and simply explored each other's body. Erin was lost in his touch and he feasted on her as if he was starving. No part of her went unkissed.

Soon, he was positioned to consummate their love when he suddenly rolled to the side and reached into his side table drawer. He pulled out a condom.

"Oh, God! Thank you. I was going to say that. Thank you for remembering."

"I've... um... never had sex without a condom. Not that I've had sex that often with one either."

"If we ever get to the point where we decide to have children, you can throw them away and never use them again. Until then, though, let's stay safe."

"The very thought of children with you makes me so excited I'm shaking."

"Let me help."

She took the condom and rolled it onto his erection, then threw a leg over him and perched above.

"Is it okay this way?"

"Wow! Yeah. It's really okay."

She slowly lowered herself onto him, joining them for the first time.

"I never even considered falling in love with you," she said. "I don't know how it happened."

"I fell in love with you while you were still waiting tables in the diner. I want to be with you."

"Sharing an office hasn't spoiled it for you?"

"You have to be kidding. I've been going crazy with desire. This. This is everything I want."

They moved together and Erin thought how much more satisfying this was than anything in her short marriage. This. This was also what she wanted.

"I MEAN... REALLY... Just wow!" Preston managed as they cuddled together.

"I have to agree," Erin sighed. "Just wow!"

"I don't know what to say. I've never felt this way. Is it normal? Is this what it feels like to really be in love?"

"My experience has left me a long way short of this. I know sex affects the way we feel in the moment. I suppose we should wait to see if we feel the same tomorrow."

"Will you stay, Erin? Don't go away tonight."

"I think I probably have a change of clothes and my night-time necessities in the car. I don't see a reason to go back to my apartment."

"Did you plan this?"

"I don't think this could have really been planned. But I was open to it. Jerry, we've been getting closer and closer to this moment for weeks. Ever since the annual meeting when we kissed. When I kissed you. I was so brash."

"You couldn't have done anything in that moment that I wanted more. Maizie... Erin, all my life I've thought love and... and anything that comes after that... was just a fantasy. I couldn't love because I was unlovable. Who wants to be with someone who is so tied up in anxiety all the time. Is it... Is it really possible?"

"You are not unlovable, Jerry... Preston. We might have different ways of expressing our anxiety, but everyone gets anxious over something. I've been tongue-tied. Even since I was hired as CEO—I mean, that very night—I went home and cried myself to sleep because I didn't know if I could do this and I was ashamed of having taken your job. I was so afraid it would mean that we could never have a future. I refused to let myself even consider it."

"I insisted that I could never be involved with you because you were my employee and that was just too much of a cliché. Would I ever be able to believe you wanted me because of me instead of because of your job?"

"Do you think all the women you dated or met were just after your money?"

"I always thought I was just a guy, maybe with some social problems. I even asked a girl out when I was a senior in high school and she accepted. It was great. I fell madly in love with her and she became my first lover. But then she tried to convince me that she was pregnant with our child. It wasn't possible. We'd never made love without a condom. It turned out that she was pregnant, but by another guy in our class. She wanted to force me into marrying her so she and her child would have a rich life with everything she wanted. Including her other lover. I was devastated. I thought I was in love with her and she was just in love with my money. From that point on, I just assumed everyone I met was."

"I'm not. Even when I was a waitress trying to make a mortgage payment and pay back the loan on my 401k, I never thought about a hero coming to save me and bathe me in riches. I just knew making a living was something I had to do so I could get on with my life. I needed to get a job and earn my way. I'm not after your money, Jerry."

"I'm confident of that. You have a much higher earning potential than I have. What I got mostly from inheritance, you will earn. But I'm not after your money either. It didn't even enter the equation when I fell in love."

"What equation is that?"

"Um... Intelligent plus fun plus pretty plus competent, multiplied by a great personality and really nice person equals love. How'd I do on that?"

"I think I could use the same equation," she laughed.

"I suppose we should eat. We hardly even interrupted the timing of dinner," Jerry said.

"Who says we're done?"

ERIN DIDN'T GO home Saturday night, but went with Jerry on Sunday to dinner at Jerico House. Jacqueline was speechless.

"Hmm. Got together early this morning, didn't you?" Lawrence said.

"Lawrence, don't probe the obvious. Can't you see they're in love?" Gina asked.

"Are you... Did you... Have you...?"

"Mother, I'm the one who can't finish a sentence. Did I inherit all my social anxiety from you?" Preston teased.

"You are! You did! Oh, my!" Jacqueline exclaimed.

"Erin and I are a couple," Preston said. "I think I'm old enough to have my lover spend the night with me. And join me at Sunday dinner with the family," Preston laughed.

"Yes. Yes, you are," Lawrence said. "You are also old enough to keep us informed if we need to be making plans for the future. Jackie, that means no prying. Preston and Erin will tell us anything we need to know. I've never heard you speak of being a couple, Preston. That's welcome news. Erin, welcome. You are welcome at our table."

"Thank you, Lawrence. Um... We're still a little overwhelmed, so being out with the family is... uh... kind of... overwhelming. I guess I said that."

Preston looked at her in wonder and both started giggling like teenagers. It was a new experience for Preston to be calm and have a girlfriend who was anxious.

It took a while for things to settle down. Matilda, of course, was immediately accepting of the news and gave them both a hug, then served a pot roast for Sunday dinner. It took Jacqueline most of the meal before she was back to her usual talkative self.

ERIN HAD HER weekly glass of wine with Dolores Sunday after-noon, then stopped at her apartment to pack a bag with more than a single change of clothes. Then she went back to the penthouse where she stayed with her lover for the rest of the Christmas vacation. They joined the family for Christmas brunch at Jerico House and then took the pickup south to Cloudhaven.

The weather was crisp and clear with an inch of fresh snow on the ground. Driving down the access road into the development was a different experience than it had been the first time she was here. All the grading and excavating of the streets was complete. The sewer, water, power, and fiber optic lines were all trenched in so there would be no overhead wires in the community. The lodge was framed and weathertight so the crews could continue to work through the winter finishing the inside.

Running on a tangent away from the lodge, the cabin townho-mes had been started. One was weathertight for interior winter con-struction. On the other side of the street, six portable buildings had been moved in so workers could stay during the week. Erin checked her cell phone and discovered a strong signal available.

"I told you once a long time ago that I wanted to take you to the cabin and show you the things that inspired me to create Cloudhaven. It's a little cold to go out on the lake, but we can at least take a walk around the estate."

"You have an estate out here?" she laughed.

"Well, Duval and his partners weren't really the only holdouts," Preston laughed. He pointed ahead. Just off the road was a house all decorated for the holidays. Lights twinkled along the roofline and outlined the trees. "I held onto my little piece of property out here on the edge of the community. It didn't really register like their 160 acres. My estate is only five acres."

He pulled up to the house which was a bit bigger than Erin had imagined. It had been added onto a couple of times and the cabin was the same style as the new structures Preston had designed for Cloudhaven.

"This is beautiful, Preston."

"Come in and take a look around."

They went inside and kicked the snow off their shoes before removing them and putting on slippers, found in abundance in the mudroom. Then they toured the rustic interior.

"I can imagine many relaxing days here," Erin said. "I have to admit, though, that I can't imagine living in this long term. It's just a little too primitive. I hope that isn't heartbreaking to you."

"Oh, no. I agree," Preston said. "What do you think about this, though?"

Preston lifted a cloth off a table in the middle of the living room, reminiscent of the work table in their office. What he unveiled was a model of a beautiful home, stylistically in keeping with the resort and townhomes, but like them, complete with all the modern conveniences.

"How delightful!"

"I have the foundation staked out just up the hill from here. Would you like it as a wedding gift?"

"It's... wedding? What do you mean?"

Jerry sank to one knee.

"Erin Scott, will you marry me?"

"Jerry! It's... You... We just... I'm..."

It was so sudden and out of the blue that she found herself hyperventilating and growing woozy. Jerry jumped to his feet and caught her as she fainted.

When she awoke a moment later, they were sitting on a sofa and she was held in his arms.

"I'm s-s-s-sorry," she said. "I don't know what happened to me."

"Happens to me all the time," he laughed. "I didn't mean to shock you so much you fainted."

"It's... so sudden. Jerry, we just became lovers. I don't know..."

"I guess I let myself get ahead of things. I don't even have a ring here or anything. Um... Just forget I mentioned it, okay?"

"Are you kidding? I will never forget it. And even if I'm not quite ready yet, I'm not saying no. Jerry, I do love you."

"I love you, Erin. I love the way we work together. I love the way you've always been a step ahead of anything I needed. I love cooking with you. I love... talking to you."

"I love making love to you, Jerry. Do you have a bed in this little cabin?"

"YOU DID IT? You asked her to marry you?" Gene exclaimed as they paused their Sunday morning basketball game. It was really just shooting around because it was too cold and slippery for anything else, the weekend after Christmas.

"Yeah. I did it."

"Congratulations. I think. Did she say yes?"

"She didn't say no."

"Uh… is that okay?"

"It was dumb of me to ask so soon after… we became lovers. She's been staying with me all week."

"I knew the right woman for you was out there someplace," Gene laughed. He took another shot, but it was obvious they were finished playing. "Congratulations. You needed a woman who could take control. She's sure shown she can do that."

"Yeah, but she's not like that. Not with me. Except in the office."

"What do you mean?"

"The company couldn't have a better chief exec. She doesn't mince words. She's direct and tells people what she expects. Then she backs off and lets them do their—our—jobs. Even Duval has grown to respect her. She just doesn't take any bullshit from him."

"God knows we waded through enough of that over the past few years."

"Yeah. My bad."

"No. I think we all knew what was happening from the start. It seemed like the best solution we had, though."

"Yeah. But Erin… She isn't like that when we're together. She doesn't order me around or rush me to say things. She's as orderly as I am. I mean, the first thing she does when she comes into the office is still to grab disinfectant wipes and wipe down all the surfaces. She's about got Miss Anders in the same mode. I don't think a germ could live anywhere in… um… our bedroom."

"Our?"

"Well, she's stayed with me all this week. She's patient and quiet. And she's fun to cook with. We made a great cassoulet yesterday."

"She stayed last night and you left her this morning to come and play basketball? Are you crazy?"

"You and I agreed to play today. Of course I came here."

"Dude, you could have called and cancelled. I'd have understood."

"We have lives. She was ready to go home this morning to get herself ready for the coming week back at work. She has a Sunday afternoon visit with her friend to drink wine and gossip. Oh. Don't tell Mother or G-Pop about this. They know we've become lovers, but they don't know I popped the question. Prematurely ejaculated the question, I'm afraid."

"I hate to tell you this, but you and she might be the only ones in Jerico City who are surprised by this."

"Erin was so surprised, she hyperventilated and passed out," Preston said.

"Oh, that's a match made in heaven!"

Chapter Twenty-Nine

NOTHING IS AS easy as it seems it should be. A couple in love with a marriage proposal on the table should progress smoothly to a wedding. But it was a rocky road of love.

Erin was unwilling to consider the proposal until she'd been divorced a full year. That would be early in February.

"Not to discount your excitement and the potential, but it seems even a year is rushing things a bit," Dolores said as they sat with their wine on Sunday afternoon. "I'm a big believer in the idea that when it's right, it's right. But an entire company is going to speculate about the CEO of the company and its Owner/Chairman getting married, and it won't be pretty. Divorce an employee, who then gets fired, and then go to work as personal assistant for the head of the company, before being miraculously promoted to CEO of the company, and finally turning around to marry the owner… Honey, you have a big public relations nightmare ahead of you."

"In one way or another, it's exactly what Jerry and I have been afraid of ever since we first started dating. And we've been very circumspect about our relationship inside the company. Dolores, I've spent every night of the past week in his apartment. But the company has been essentially closed down during that period. Tomorrow, everyone is back to work—at least for a day and a half before New Year's. Last year they were greeted with the news that five percent of the full time employees had been laid off. This year they get met by an announcement about the owner and CEO getting married? And Miss Anders will be at her desk first thing tomorrow morning. Am I just going to walk down the stairs from his bedroom with him while she rushes upstairs to make sure everything is neat and clean?"

"If she's as astute as you say she is, she probably assumes you are lovers already," Dolores said. "But living together in what is really her office seems a little like throwing it in her face."

"I'd like to live with him for a while and make sure we really fit and can tolerate each other, but I don't think he'd be happy joining me in my apartment. It's so small by comparison. My kitchen is nothing as elaborate as his. My bed isn't even as big. He's six-two. He needs a large bed."

ERIN PROVED HER hypothesis when she invited Jerry to spend the night at her place. He was happy to be invited into her home to spend the night. Making love was as wonderful and intense as it had been all week in his apartment. But the bed was uncomfortably crowded to sleep in and he woke up in the morning stiff and sore from sleeping in a new position.

"We really can't spend the night together in the office during the week," Erin said. "It isn't because I don't want to sleep with you."

"No. It would be embarrassing to walk downstairs in the morning with Miss Anders watching us. I don't think she signed up for that. I could spend a few more nights in your apartment, but the bed is a little small for two people."

"We could come back here on the weekend," Erin suggested.

They stepped off the elevator together and that was almost as embarrassing as walking down the stairs. Miss Anders looked at them in surprise and then blushed scarlet.

"We went out for an early breakfast," Erin hastily said. "Give me a minute to make coffee and we can get started on the day's schedule."

"Yes, Ms. Scott. Mr. Carver. I've reset the puzzles on this level. I'll go upstairs while you get settled," Miss Anders said.

Mr. Carver's laundry had been delivered already and Miss Anders took the laundry bag to his bedroom to put things away. Erin came running out of the kitchen in time to hear a gasp from Miss Anders upstairs.

"Ohh!" Erin moaned as Preston came to see what was wrong. "I dropped my undies in the laundry chute all last week. I forgot we sent them out together."

"Oh, dear. Well, I enjoyed discovering what kind of lingerie you wore. Perhaps she will, too," Preston said. They were both blushing over a cup of coffee when Miss Anders returned from the bedroom suite.

"I hope you don't mind, Mr. Carver, but I rearranged your drawers to make room for... um..." she paused and blushed again, suddenly unsure if the underwear she'd just put away was Erin's. "...the new things in your laundry. I'll change them later if you wish."

"Thank you, Miss Anders," Carver said. "I-I-I'm sure it's... f-f-fi.. okay."

"How does our calendar look for this week?" Erin asked brightly. "I hope your holiday break was all you wanted it to be."

"Yes, ma'am. The schedule is light. Many employees are taking an extra day or two of personal time and won't be back until Thursday. Some elected to take vacation time and not return this week at all. You are due to visit to St. Louis for an inspection. Mrs. Duval indicated that she and Mr. Duval would drive separately as they planned to spend New Year's Eve in St. Louis."

"I see. Mr. Carver, would you like to accompany me on the site visit? I know the crew always likes to see you when you stop in," Erin said.

"I don't think anything significant will be happening at Cloudhaven this week," he said. "A trip to St. Louis might be just what we need."

They packed up Preston's car and left in time to reach St. Louis for lunch.

THEY AVOIDED THE issue of staying at each other's apartment by simply staying in St. Louis for the full week. It was New Year's and they chose to celebrate there, and then to spend another couple of days to celebrate each other.

"We agreed to keep our relationship out of the office," Erin said. "As long as our office is in your apartment, we really can't have our relationship there. Poor Miss Anders blushed crimson when she found my underwear mixed in with your laundry. I was definitely not ready for that."

"I want to be with you," Preston answered. "If you'll have me with you. Your apartment isn't really big enough for two, though."

"At least my bed isn't," she laughed.

"My alternative locations are either too remote at Cloudhaven, or too near to G-Pop and Mother."

"Talk about embarrassing! Just coming down the stairs from your room with them waiting would be a lot more than I could take right now."

"What should we do? I mean, do you want to be with me? Live with me?"

"Yes, love. I'm having a little difficulty with the idea of getting married again—especially so soon after my last failure—but it doesn't mean I don't want to live with you," Erin said. She kissed him again and since they really hadn't gotten out of bed New Year's Day, the kiss almost ended with them making love again. She was pretty sure it would soon. "We could... I know this sounds like a big move... It *is* a big move... We could find an apartment together and furnish it the way we want. You know, as a kind of compromise?"

"Well, it's not like we couldn't afford it, is it?" he said. "I mean, you've got a CEO salary now."

"Don't think I'll let you out of carrying your share," she giggled. "We're pretty equal on this, Mr. Chief Architect."

"There are some nice riverside apartments just up the river from us. Our company didn't build them, but I did check them out. They're good. We could see if anything is available."

"It will take us a little time to get things squared away. I still have two months left on my lease. We'd have someplace to stay while we get the new apartment prepared. No matter how uncomfortable the bed is. We could get that replaced."

"And we could still use the penthouse on weekends. I only make an elaborate meal on Saturdays," Preston said. The next kiss was nearly the one that joined them together.

"I could live with that."

"We'd still need to join G-Pop and Mother for Sunday dinner, at least part of the time. Is that too embarrassing?"

"They'd know we were living together. I could survive their scrutiny, even if I did arrive looking freshly... um... satisfied."

"I'd like to satisfy you right now."

"Yes. Please do."

"SO, WE PLAN to get an apartment separate from the company and Jerico House so we can be together," Preston said. "I rushed a marriage proposal, but Erin isn't ready for that."

"I haven't said no," Erin clarified.

"I'm so glad we're marking this milestone in family history," Lawrence said. "We don't plan nuptials either, but Gina has consented to shack up with me for the foreseeable future."

"When he dragged out that prenuptial agreement, I suggested we keep things informal," Gina said. "I have all I need and if Lawrence accepts my baggage, I'll haul it over here."

"We all have remnants of the past hanging over us," Erin said. "I'm glad Jerry overlooks mine."

"Jerry?" Jacqueline said. "I haven't heard you use that name since your college days."

"Maizie and I met long before you hired her, Mother. Gene had suggested I make a weekly trip out to eat lunch—in order to practice meeting people. After my first week experimenting, I didn't go anywhere Maizie wasn't waiting tables."

"You'd met and didn't recognize each other in the office?" Gina asked.

"Seeing Erin in a suit and glasses with her hair down as opposed to her waitress uniform with its little cap was an effective disguise. I don't think we said a dozen sentences to each other for the first week she worked for me. And the next week, I discovered who she was."

"I'd only ever seen Jerry in dark glasses, a mask, and a hoodie sweatshirt," Erin said. "Some of the waitresses speculated he was homeless, but I knew he was too generous for that. Still, seeing him in a suit and tie in the office was so different I didn't recognize him. I just knew I liked him."

"You mentioned sponsoring a cube competition this spring. What inspired that?" Jacqueline said.

"Something we both enjoy," Preston said.

"We still have to get the proposal approved by the national organization. And then if the company sponsors it, the board will need to approve it, too. Like everything, there are so many steps to take, to get to where we'd like to be," Erin said. She looked meaningfully at Preston and he acknowledged she was talking about their relationship as much as the competition or company.

"There is one other matter we should come together on, Preston. Gina and I are getting along quite well. You and Erin have found each other. It seems there is one other solo person at this table and we should consider fixing up some blind dates for your mother. She's been so focused on finding you a mate that she's ignored her own needs."

"Dad!" Jacqueline shouted. "Don't you dare."

"Payback's a bitch, Mother," Preston laughed.

ERIN AND PRESTON were in their new apartment several months before there was a significant change. He'd about forgotten about asking Erin to marry him. They were happy living together, even when they had disagreements. For example, he objected to her going to St. Louis with Duval for the opening of the new Allard building that fall.

"Royce Duval and I are far past the point of him having any thoughts about despoiling me. He wouldn't risk his job and there is nothing he has that I don't have more of with you," Erin said.

"Was it a choice? Did you need to decide if you would hook up with Duval or with me?"

"Jerry! How could you even imagine that? Duval has never held the slightest interest for me. You know that. I grant that I was naïve to believe he only wanted to show me the development site the first time I rode to Cloudhaven with him, but I set him straight immediately."

"I'm still uncomfortable about the trip to St. Louis."

Preston was so upset about the planned trip to St. Louis for the grand opening of the new Allard Building that it made Erin pause to consider what might really be on his mind. They both had the utmost faith in each other. It couldn't be a threat that Duval would seduce her.

"Sit with me, Jerry," she said, leading him to the sofa overlooking the rooftop patio that evening after work. "Dear, tell me what is really bothering you. What are you worried about?"

"I... She... I don't want her..."

"Want her? Who her? You don't think Miss Anders is a threat, do you?"

"When you went to Cloudhaven with Duval, Shannon showed up here, trying to... I don't know what she was trying to do. She ruined my lunch and said you were off with her husband and she was available to me. I don't want her to come in here again."

"That certainly won't happen. She's been the financial controller for the project. She'll be in St. Louis with her husband for the opening," Erin said. "Besides, aren't you coming to St. Louis with me?"

"What?"

"Cloudhaven can do without you for a few days, can't it? You are the Chief Architect who designed the Allard Building. I just assumed you'd be there with me."

"Go with you? You'd take me? In public?"

"Have we been shy about being together in public? Of course I want you there!"

"But this is business, not personal."

"I see. And you think I haven't told Dee Bonner that you and I live together? Do you think that Teresa Lincoln and the other members of the Board don't know we're lovers? I have no difficulty at all in letting the world know I am engaged to the Chief Architect of JeriCorp. If anyone wants to make something of it, let them. I will defend our relationship if I must, but I won't deny it."

"Um… Uh… Engaged?" Jerry stumbled.

"I guess I just said yes."

Jerry broke out into a wide grin.

"I love you, Erin Scott!"

"And I love you, Preston Carver."

"Wait! I have a ring! It's upstairs!"

He raced up the stairs and opened a secret drawer in his bureau. Then raced back downstairs with the ring.

"I want to place this ring on your finger as a sign of my love and promise of our future," he panted.

"Jerry! It's beautiful! When and how did you manage to get this?"

"Um… Last December. I went to Memphis on a weekend trip so no one would know me or who it might be for."

"It fits perfectly."

"I'm lucky."

"But that's before we even started, um… making love with each other."

"I already knew, but I couldn't say anything because I didn't know if you'd accept."

"There was never a doubt in my mind that I'd accept. I just needed to get my head and heart on the same page."

NINE MONTHS LATER, in June, Erin stood on the wedding step of the Staircase of Dragon Jerico to marry Preston.

The fourth step of the dragon staircase was considered the wedding step. It was where Isolde LeClerc and Drake Jerico stood to recite their vows. Isolde considered herself true to Drake—after they were married. Being pregnant with Joseph Carver's child when they said their vows was conveniently forgotten by her.

It had been two and a half years since Erin's divorce from Bruce was final and she decided that was long enough. She'd lived with Preston for a year and a half of that and people had come to accept the Chairman and the CEO as a couple.

On the wedding day, Erin invited everyone she could think of to witness the wedding. In the hall of the Staircase of Dragon Jerico, there were chairs only for Lawrence, Gina, Jacqueline, and Matilda. Lawrence walked her down the stairs to his grandson before taking his seat. Dolores was Erin's matron of honor. Gene Hathaway was Preston's best man. The rest of the guests stood in the hall, looking up at the grand stairway.

Of course, her bowling team and the other waitresses from the diner she kept in touch with were there. Her personal assistant, Cheryl Anders, had helped plan the event with Jacqueline. The executives of JeriCorp and their spouses, the other board members, and Dee Bonner of Allard had happily accepted the invitation. Dee and Erin often got together, now that they lived only two hours apart.

The minister, an old friend of the Jerico family, stood below the couple as he administered the vows.

"I promise to love you through good times and bad, to stand beside you through lean years and years of plenty, to establish our family and rear our children to love and respect their parents and their siblings. I promise to keep myself unto you and faithfully keep these vows."

The minister, being a minister, turned to the gathered witnesses and gave a short sermon about the meaning of marriage and the tradition of Jerico weddings on this staircase. Then he gave his blessing and pronounced them husband and wife. The couple lost themselves in a kiss on the staircase until the minister cleared his throat and tapped them on the shoulder. Then he introduced them to the witnesses.

The reception was catered in the dining room and living room. Matilda couldn't keep herself from being busy with the caterers. After the crowded stairway hall, the other rooms in the house seemed spacious, but people still congregated in the hall, just to examine the dragon more closely.

"Congratulations, Preston and Erin," Duval said in greeting. Shannon was firmly attached to his arm. "Lovely service. We hope you have a long and fruitful life together."

"I just love weddings," Shannon said. "It makes me remember why I married this guy. You know, Erin, since you started at JeriCorp, Royce and I have grown closer, too. You're a good influence."

"Thank you, Shannon. I hope you have years of happiness ahead of you, too."

Shannon beamed at Royce and they moved away to partake of the luncheon buffet.

"You two give us all hope," Gene said when he wrapped the two in a hug. "Now that you're settled down, I can finally focus on finding my own happily ever after, you know?"

"Don't tell me you've been waiting for Preston!" Erin said.

"It just happened to work out that way. I had a lot to concentrate on in turning the business around from where I found it. I think I can spend some quality personal time now," Gene said.

"Don't forget Sunday morning basketball now that the snow is gone and the weather is decent," Preston said.

"I'm betting you'll find better things to do on Sunday morning than get sweaty outside. But I'll be around—unless *I* find something better to do."

IT WAS THE seventh generation wedding on the Staircase of Dragon Jerico. The first wedding had been between Isolde and Drake when Isolde knew she was likely already pregnant with Joseph Carver's child. Drake had no idea why his son and namesake was dark-haired and brown-eyed when both he and Isolde were blue-eyed blondes. It never occurred to him that Drake Junior was not his son.

When Isolde's second son, Arlen, was born, the difference in the two boys was remarkable. Isolde doted on her second son, feeling guilt over the tryst that resulted in her firstborn. Perhaps Drake had some underlying discomfort when he looked at his two sons. He and Drake Jr. made life so hard on Arlen, that the boy resolved to leave home when he was just fifteen.

Isolde gathered up all the money she could find and packed it with a good rifle and a set of carpentry tools in the buckboard wagon. She helped Arlen hitch the gray mare to the wagon, kissed her son goodbye, and never saw him again.

Drake swore his second son robbed him and took Drake Junior's inheritance, but Isolde pleaded with him not to attempt to find Arlen.

He got what he wanted, after all: one son to inherit the house, the business, and Drake's position in Jerico City.

Arlen went back east and managed to make a living as a carpenter. He married and had children. Somewhere along the line, a census taker altered the spelling of his last name to be like the Bible: Jericho.

On a Sunday in June, standing on the Staircase of Dragon Jerico, Arlen's three times great-granddaughter Erin Jericho Scott married his brother's three times great grandson, Preston Jerico Carver. Just over a year later, Jerico Scott Carver was born, becoming his own sixth cousin.

Erin and Preston, with their children, lived part of the year in the house he built for her in Cloudhaven, and part of the year at Jerico House. Eventually, Jerico Scott Carver became an architect and took over as chairman of JeriCorp from his father and as CEO from his mother.

The End